No Distance *Too Far*

Books by

Lauraine Snelling

*Golden Filly Collection One**

*Golden Filly Collection Two**

Secret Refuge (3 in 1)

DAKOTA TREASURES

Ruby • *Pearl*

Opal • *Amethyst*

DAUGHTERS OF BLESSING

A Promise for Ellie • *Sophie's Dilemma*

A Touch of Grace • *Rebecca's Reward*

HOME TO BLESSING

A Measure of Mercy

No Distance Too Far

RED RIVER OF THE NORTH

An Untamed Land

A New Day Rising

A Land to Call Home

The Reaper's Song

Tender Mercies

Blessing in Disguise

RETURN TO RED RIVER

A Dream to Follow • *Believing the Dream*

More Than a Dream

* 5 books in each volume

HOME TO BLESSING • *Book Two*

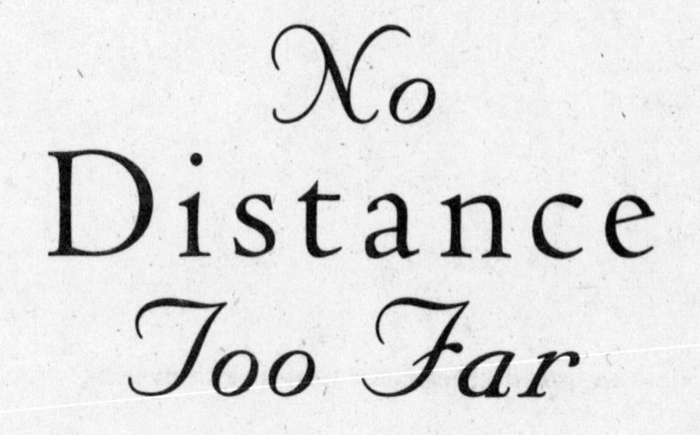

LAURAINE
SNELLING

MINNEAPOLIS, MINNESOTA

No Distance Too Far

Cover design by Dan Pitts

Scripture quotations are from the King James Version of the Bible.

Published by Bethany House Publishers
11400 Hampshire Avenue South
Bloomington, Minnesota 55438

Bethany House Publishers is a division of
Baker Publishing Group, Grand Rapids, Michigan.

Printed in the United States of America

Library of Congress Cataloging-in-Publication Data

Snelling, Lauraine.
No distance too far / Lauraine Snelling.
p. cm. — (Home to blessing ; 2)
ISBN 978-0-7642-0753-2 (alk. paper) — ISBN 978-0-7642-0610-8 (pbk.) — ISBN 978-0-7642-0754-9 (large-print pbk.) 1. Women physicians—Fiction. 2. Indian reservations—Fiction. I. Title.
PS3569.N39N6 2010
813'.54—dc22

2009050211

No Distance Too Far is dedicated to
our new other half of the family, the Hiltons from Ohio.
They made the Norsk Høstfest at Minot a delight for all of us.
I now have more grandchildren . . . ah, delight. If you can't get
them naturally, you adopt them.
Isn't God amazing in the way He provides for us?

LAURAINE SNELLING is an award-winning author of over 60 books, fiction and nonfiction for adults and young adults. Her books have sold over two million copies. Besides writing books and articles, she teaches at writers' conferences across the country. She and her husband, Wayne, have two grown sons, a bassett named Chewy, and a cockatiel watch bird named Bidley. They make their home in California.

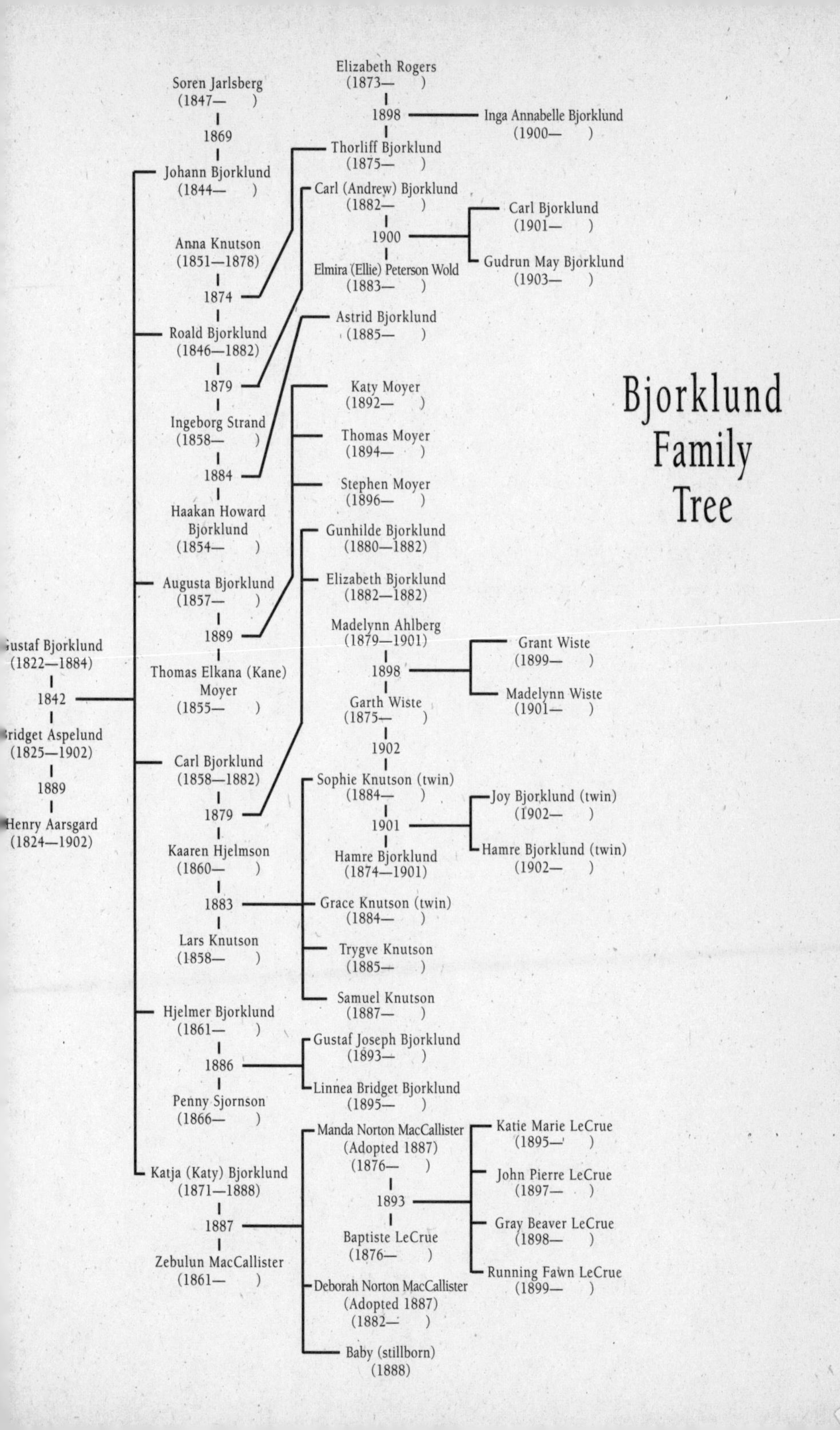
Bjorklund Family Tree
Gustaf Bjorklund (1822—1884)
1842
Bridget Aspelund (1825—1902)
1889
Henry Aarsgard (1824—1902)
Soren Jarlsberg (1847—)
1869
Johann Bjorklund (1844—)
Anna Knutson (1851—1878)
1874
Roald Bjorklund (1846—1882)
1879
Ingeborg Strand (1858—)
1884
Haakan Howard Bjorklund (1854—)
Augusta Bjorklund (1857—)
1889
Thomas Elkana (Kane) Moyer (1855—)
Carl Bjorklund (1858—1882)
1879
Kaaren Hjelmson (1860—)
1883
Lars Knutson (1858—)
Hjelmer Bjorklund (1861—)
1886
Penny Sjornson (1866—)
Katja (Katy) Bjorklund (1871—1888)
1887
Zebulun MacCallister (1861—)
Elizabeth Rogers (1873—)
1898
Thorliff Bjorklund (1875—)
Carl (Andrew) Bjorklund (1882—)
1900
Elmira (Ellie) Peterson Wold (1883—)
Astrid Bjorklund (1885—)
Katy Moyer (1892—)
Thomas Moyer (1894—)
Stephen Moyer (1896—)
Gunhilde Bjorklund (1880—1882)
Elizabeth Bjorklund (1882—1882)
Madelynn Ahlberg (1879—1901)
1898
Garth Wiste (1875—)
1902
Sophie Knutson (twin) (1884—)
1901
Hamre Bjorklund (1874—1901)
Grace Knutson (twin) (1884—)
Trygve Knutson (1885—)
Samuel Knutson (1887—)
Gustaf Joseph Bjorklund (1893—)
Linnea Bridget Bjorklund (1895—)
Manda Norton MacCallister (Adopted 1887) (1876—)
1893
Baptiste LeCrue (1876—)
Deborah Norton MacCallister (Adopted 1887) (1882—)
Baby (stillborn) (1888)
Inga Annabelle Bjorklund (1900—)
Carl Bjorklund (1901—)
Gudrun May Bjorklund (1903—)
Grant Wiste (1899—)
Madelynn Wiste (1901—)
Joy Bjorklund (twin) (1902—)
Hamre Bjorklund (twin) (1902—)
Katie Marie LeCrue (1895—)
John Pierre LeCrue (1897—)
Gray Beaver LeCrue (1898—)
Running Fawn LeCrue (1899—)

1

MARCH 1904
ATHENS, GEORGIA

The dream was a lie. She was in Georgia, not Blessing.

Staring out the window did nothing to calm the butterflies rampaging in her middle. Astrid tried swallowing—once, twice—no matter, they continued to spiral and cavort. She laid a hand on her diaphragm and closed her eyes. *Please, Lord, fill me with your calm and peace.*

A throat being cleared behind her caught her attention. She turned, swallowed again, and smiled. At least she hoped she smiled.

"Dean Highsmith will see you now." The young man needed to loosen his collar. He appeared to be near to strangling.

"Thank you."

"Come this way." He motioned her to accompany him, opened

a heavy carved door, and escorted her in. "Dr. Bjorklund to see you, sir."

Stiff, regal, he might have been a herald to a king. Were they always this formal? Astrid gave the book-lined room a quick glance, her attention snapping back to a huge map of the continent of Africa on one wall. She skipped over that and focused on the silver-haired gentleman behind a handsome desk of some dark wood she did not recognize. He stood and came around the end of the desk, a hand held out in greeting.

"Welcome, Dr. Bjorklund. I am exceedingly glad and grateful you decided to join us." He shook her hand, his washed-blue eyes staring directly into hers, as if seeking her soul. "Please, be seated and tell me about your journey." He motioned her to a leather winged chair in front of a cheery fire. "Marlin, please bring us tea . . ." He paused. "Unless you would prefer coffee?" When Astrid shook her head, he finished, "And make sure Cook sends up some of her pecan cookies. They might be a special treat for this northerner we have with us."

"Thank you, sir." Astrid sat, grateful for both the happy snap of the fire and the heat. The guest room where she'd stayed the previous night had not been heated, and while the South was known for its warmth, today, with a damp wind blowing, it felt more like Chicago. It had been raining yesterday and earlier this morning, not exactly a welcome she'd have associated with the South. All the things she'd read about this part of the country included sunshine, heat, and humidity.

Dean Highsmith, gold glasses perched on the end of a rather aquiline nose, sat down in the chair opposite her, nodding and smiling. "I received your application with enthusiasm. Rev. Schuman is an old friend of mine, and he has been raving about you." He paused for a moment. "I must say, you look amazingly young for a person of your accomplishments."

"I understand that, and yes, my youth has caused some to doubt my ability."

"I wonder why that is, that we do not expect a lovely young woman to be involved in the medical field. Stereotypes are sometimes difficult to overcome." He propped his elbows on the arms of the chair and steepled his fingers. "Be that as it may, tell me about yourself. What brings you here and where do you dream of going?"

I dream of going back to Blessing, she thought but knew that was not what he wanted to hear. "All of the story or a brief synopsis?"

A knock came at the door, and Marlin peeked in. "Cook will be sending up a tray as soon as it is ready."

"Thank you." Highsmith turned back to Astrid. "All of it."

All of it. Where to start? "I grew up in a very small town in North Dakota, the daughter of Norwegian immigrants who homesteaded there. My mother is a gifted healer. She took care of all those that she could and developed quite a pharmacopeia of herbs and natural medicines, gaining her knowledge from the native people, her mother's training, and a dependence on God to guide and continue her efforts."

"She sounds like an admirable woman."

"She is. Because I was interested in what she was doing, I sometimes accompanied her on calls, helped her forage and preserve her simples, as she called them, and learned by observation. My brother married a physician, and when he brought Dr. Elizabeth to Blessing, my mother stepped back so that people would go to a more formally or scientifically trained doctor and accept her into the community." Astrid felt as though she were telling someone else's story, as clinical as this was sounding.

"Through all this, I decided to become a nurse in order to assist Dr. Elizabeth with her practice. She began training me while I was still in high school. It was all such a natural thing. I have always been fascinated by God's creation of the human body. How intricately and wonderfully made we are. While my goal was to go to Grand Forks to study nursing, Dr. Elizabeth's goal was to train me so that I could go for further instruction at the hospital she trained at in Chicago, but as a doctor, not a nurse.

"After I graduated from the school in Blessing, a catastrophe of hoof-and-mouth disease wiped out all the cloven-footed animals, including the dairy herds that provided milk for my mother's cheese house. I decided we couldn't afford for me to leave for school right then, so I spent the next year in rigorous training with Dr. Elizabeth. She is a firm taskmaster, and we both loved all the textbook learning she put me through. As I said, I am in awe of the human body and loved every moment of the time spent learning and practicing. There is nothing more thrilling than helping a baby into this world." Her voice caught on that line.

He smiled. "I've not had that privilege, but I can believe that with you." Another knock sounded, and this time a white-aproned young woman brought in a tray with a silver tea service and plates of tarts and cookies.

"Set it there." Highsmith pointed to the low table in front and between the chairs. "And please pour."

Once they were served, the young woman left with a smile toward Astrid, and Dean Highsmith nodded. "Please continue."

Holding her saucer with cup on her knee, she did as he asked. "Dr. Elizabeth finally convinced me that I was ready for more training. We didn't do many surgeries in Blessing, so she made arrangements with Dr. Morganstein in Chicago that I be allowed to take the six-month surgical rotation if I could pass all the examinations a student at her school would have taken. One of the prime reasons for my going there, as far as I was concerned, was the opportunity to work on a cadaver so that I could learn more about the human body. I did pass the examinations, and I have now finished that training. I was planning to return to Blessing to assist in Dr. Elizabeth's practice there and hopefully become part of the new hospital that is being planned."

"Most commendable. Which is why you are so young in years. But evidently not so young in maturity. You appear to be very strong and capable."

"Thank you." She sipped her tea and took a bite of one of the nut cookies. If he had any idea how frightened she'd been, he'd not have thought that. While she had handled the trip to Georgia well, the thought of trains and ships and who knew what else to get her to Africa sent her entire insides into full revolt. Malaria alone was enough to keep her from going. After all, she had seen the long-term effects of that disease in Gerald Valders in Blessing.

"But what happened to bring you here?"

"Your friend, Rev. Schuman, was invited to speak in our church one Sunday. When he said the fields were ripe unto harvest in Africa and they desperately needed missionaries, especially medical missionaries, he looked right at me, as if I were the only person in the room. I feared . . . er . . . felt like God was speaking right at me. Dean Highsmith, going to Africa had never occurred to me until that point, and I have struggled with that idea ever since. Was God calling me to be a missionary or not? I have written back and forth with Rev. Schuman, who has been so encouraging—"

"No, if I know Ted, and I do, he has been rather overwhelming in his certainty that you are going to Africa to serve there." His broad smile made her smile back.

"Well, yes, but if this isn't God calling, what is it?" She studied her teacup before looking at him again. The peace within the room lay like a benevolent benediction. "So instead of going home to Blessing, I took the step to come here. Mor, my mother, always says God leads step by step, not mile by mile. That He never lights the whole path but only one step at a time. I want to be obedient, so I'm taking the next step." She wondered if she should add that her whole being was rebelling against it.

"And here you are." He held out the cookie plate to her. "Help yourself. These are one of Cook's many specialties." He took a cookie himself and crossed one leg over the other. "It is interesting to me that you have requested a two-year term of service. I hope you understand that when we train missionaries, we plan for them to serve as long as they are able—a lifetime. That is the kind of dedication God calls us to."

"But you see, I already have a calling to return to Blessing and work there. Is there some reason that I cannot be accepted for a two-year program? The person I spoke with on the telephone said that was a possibility." *Because if I can't, then we have wasted both your time and mine, as well as a train ticket.* Her heart leaped at the thought of going home, of being relieved from this confusion and uncertainty.

"Have you considered going as a nurse?"

His question caught her by surprise. She shook her head. "Why would I be willing to do that when I am a certified medical doctor?"

"And you are also nothing if not blunt and forthright." The corner of his mouth deepened as if he meant to smile.

She wasn't sure if that was a compliment or an accusation. She took another cookie from the offered plate and finished her tea, pondering if there should be an answer to his comment. She knew she had a tendency to bluntness; it seemed the fastest way to deal with questions. After all, why beat around the bush? She lifted her gaze to find him studying her.

"Is that a bad thing?" she asked.

"My mother used to say you can catch more flies with honey than with vinegar."

"That is, if you were in need of catching flies."

His hoot of laughter surprised her. Her brash comment surprised her even more. Her mother would be shocked. It seemed Chicago had changed her in more ways than just surgical knowledge.

"Life in Africa is not easy, but growing up on a farm in North Dakota, you did not grow up taking it easy either, I presume."

"No. We were taught to work hard. And now that I have been away from home, I understand that we grew up with very little in the way of niceties. But both my mother and my father are honorable, God-fearing people who try to live their faith in the serving of others. Some in Blessing consider us wealthy, but wealth is relative. No one has much." Thoughts of Mrs. Josephson's foundation and Dr. Morganstein, who were prepared to give thousands of dollars to build a new hospital, slipped through her mind. But like the widow's mite, her family gave what they had—and made sure no one went hungry.

"I see." He tapped his index fingers against his chin, studying her all the while. "All I can do is submit your name and application to our mission board to see if they will approve a two-year enlistment. In the meantime I have here a list of classes you will be required to take. If all goes well, you would be leaving for Africa in early July. We allow our students to return home for a short period of time before embarking if they have any affairs that need to be put in order. You will receive a list of suggested clothing and supplies for you to assemble to take along. As a medical missionary, the more supplies you can accumulate, the better. Our missionaries are always in need of the most basic of medical aids and equipment."

"I see." But she didn't. How could a doctor care for the people if there were no medicines, surgical instruments, and dressings?

Dean Highsmith started to say something and stopped.

Astrid caught a look in his eyes of . . . she wasn't sure what. Concern? Confusion?

"Do you have any questions?"

"Not at the moment, but I'm sure things will come up."

"I must tell you that you will be the only unmarried female in the school at this time. There are a number of single men, along with four or five couples who are accepting the call together. There's only one other doctor going through our program right now, and his wife is a nurse. Some of our teachers are missionaries on furlough or those who have returned from the field. They will surely be able to answer any questions you may have."

"One question. Will I be sent to the same area as Rev. Schuman? He said they are in need of a doctor there."

"Dr. Bjorklund, you have to understand something. There is a need for medical people all over Africa. The term *Dark Continent* is actually an apt description. There is little education, there's a terrible lack of transportation, and the sanitary conditions are beyond belief. But"—he held up one finger—"when the light of Jesus shines there, it glows so brightly that it cannot be extinguished."

Astrid resolved right then to talk to those who had been there.

"Mrs. Abercrombie will be here to show you to your room. We have placed you on the main floor, with the married couples. Tomorrow you will be interviewing with various staff members, and the following day you'll join the classes. Meals are served in the dining room. I have asked Dr. and Mrs. Gansberg to be your hosts for the first few days."

"Thank you." Astrid looked over her shoulder when she heard the door open.

"Good. You are just in time." He stood, signaling the end of the meeting. "Mrs. Abercrombie, meet Dr. Bjorklund. And don't let her apparent youth fool you."

"Thank you, sir, for the tea. And you are right; your cook makes delicious pecan cookies."

"I will tell her you said so."

"I am glad to meet you, Dr. Bjorklund. Your trunk has already been moved from the guest room and delivered to your new room, along with the books and supplies we provide for your studies. I thought I'd show you around our campus so you have a better idea of life here." Mrs. Abercrombie, who reminded Astrid of her grandmother, Bridget, with her white hair caught up in a bun high on the back of her head and wisps flying every direction, wore a warm smile that made Astrid feel at home immediately.

Since she'd come in after supper the night before and been shown straight to her guest room, she'd not seen any of the campus. Mrs. Abercrombie patted her arm. "Have you been in the South before?"

"No. This is my first time. I've lived in North Dakota all my life."

"Up there where it is so cold that people can freeze to death in their houses?"

"Yes, I am sure that has happened, but usually not if there is wood or coal for a fire. Sometimes people even burn straw or hay twists if they are desperate."

"Well, keeping warm is not a difficulty where you are going." Mrs. Abercrombie smiled up at her. "The building we are in was the first to be built here back in the late 1700s, when the college was established for educating the young sons of planters. Cardin didn't begin sending missionaries to other parts of the world until 1890, so while our college has already celebrated our centennial anniversary, our program for missions isn't really that old."

By the time they had toured the campus, Mrs. Abercrombie informed her there would be a tea the next afternoon for her to meet the other mission candidates in the program. She leaned closer. "Several of them are single and very handsome. With your striking blue eyes and warm smile . . ." She stopped and rolled her eyes. "My husband always says I see romance everywhere." Her chuckle made Astrid smile. "You are now free until suppertime. I'd suggest you unpack and get settled in, because you have a tight schedule ahead."

"Thank you. And thank you for the tour. What a lovely campus, and the flowers, well, my mor would be absolutely thrilled to see all these lovely flower beds and bushes. The magnolia trees—I'd read about them but to see them growing like this . . . This most certainly is a different world than home."

"I'm glad you enjoyed yourself. If you have any other questions, please feel free to ask one of us." Mrs. Abercrombie turned to leave. "You can find your way to the dining room, can you not?"

"If I get lost, I'm sure someone will show me the way. Thank you again."

Astrid watched her hostess smile and float away. How did she walk like that, so gracefully? Maydell would be green with envy. Astrid slipped into her room and, after closing the door, leaned against it to survey her new home. The walls were painted a lovely yellow and framed with white woodwork. Lace curtains graced the window, and French doors opened onto a peaceful courtyard. While the day was much like the cold and damp of Chicago, here a tiny breeze kissed the tree leaves. There was no such thing as a breeze on that northern lake; there was only wind or no wind.

She had a desk, bed, and chest of drawers, and a closet with shelves and sliding doors. A yellow rug brightened an aged hardwood floor, and a yellow print cushion softened the desk chair. The glass door showed a wicker chair and table that invited her to sit in the shade and enjoy the courtyard—when it warmed up, that is.

Within an hour she'd emptied her trunk, hung her clothes, and found homes for all that could be folded. Her books lined the shelves above the desk, and her writing kit now lived in the central desk drawer. She pulled her trunk out into the hall, where someone was supposed to pick it up for storage. It was not hard to believe that this had been someone's home at one time, before it was donated to the school.

She sat down at the desk and dashed off a letter to her mother.

Dear Mor and Far,

I have arrived safely and already had my incoming interview with Dean Highsmith, dean of the missionary school here at Cardin College. He is a pleasant gentleman and easy to talk with. He was not pleased when I said again that I am signing up for two years and no more. While they do accept some people for two years, they prefer a much longer commitment. He said that the missionary board may not accept my application for that reason and also because I am young and single. If they turn me down, then I shall know that I have done my best and, as always, the outcome is in God's hands.

I cannot tell you how close I came to changing trains and heading west. I wish that I were more certain that what I am doing is God's will. One step at a time. Right now the staff thinks I have a tight schedule, but they have no idea what my life was like in Chicago. This will seem like a vacation. I do hope I can find something medical to do to keep my hands in tune.

I've enclosed my address. Please give it to everyone who wants it, as I would so love news from home. Here I will have time to answer them. I will write to Elizabeth immediately. I'm afraid she might be furious with me, but I hope not.

Love from your daughter,
Astrid

As she read it over, she thought through the day's conversations. Even though she had been homesick and overwhelmed in Chicago, she'd still had the sense that she belonged there, if only for a time. But here she felt nothing fit. Where was that peace Mor and Pastor Solberg said came when in God's will? How long did one need to wait for it?

So sleepy she could hardly finish addressing the envelope, she unpinned the coil of wheaten hair at the base of her skull and lay down on the bed for a nap. When she woke it was dark outside and her clock said ten o'clock. Ignoring the growling of her stomach, she undressed and crawled back in bed. Would she be in trouble for missing supper? What were the rules here?

2

We missed you at supper last night."

"I'm sorry. I fell asleep and didn't wake up until long past suppertime." Astrid set her tray down on the table next to the gentleman who had spoken to her.

"You must have needed the sleep. You came directly here from medical school?"

"I did." She held out her hand. "I am Dr. Astrid Bjorklund."

"And I am Dr. Heinrich Gansberg, and this is my wife, Irene. I hear you are our newest medical prospect."

"I am glad to meet you. Please accept my apologies for last night." She sat down and let out a breath she didn't realize she'd been holding. People would be friendly. She would be welcomed. She wasn't sure why she'd feared she wouldn't be, but irrational fears seemed to be her lot lately. "Where are you from?"

"Pennsylvania. Reading, to be exact."

She poured milk over her oatmeal. "You had . . . er . . . have a medical practice there?"

"I did, until we felt the call to come here."

Astrid turned slightly on her chair. "Would you mind if I asked you some questions?"

"Not at all. Ask away." Deep commas on either side of his mouth obviously came from smiling a lot.

"Forgive me for being blunt—that seems to be a trait of mine—but I'm still not sure if this is where I am supposed to be. What made you decide to come here?"

"Well, our children are grown. In fact, our oldest son is taking over my practice. Years ago I dreamed of becoming a missionary. After I went to medical school, Irene and I were married, and I was invited to become part of an established practice in the rather midsize town of Reading. We went there, and there we've been ever since."

Astrid began eating while she listened.

"Until the doctor began having dreams of the mission field again," Mrs. Gansberg added, her smile gentle on the man beside her. "And they wouldn't leave him alone. Then a missionary came to our church."

"And still I hesitated."

"So God sent a little child." Mrs. Gansberg wiped her mouth with her napkin and laid it back in her lap.

"A child?" Astrid put her spoon down to give her full attention.

"A little negro boy was brought to our town by a local minister and needed a home." The doctor smiled at his wife. With matching silver hair and blue eyes, they might have been sister and brother rather than husband and wife.

"We had a spare bedroom, and the child needed medical care, so he came to stay with us." Mrs. Gansberg took up the telling again, the two going back and forth as if they'd rehearsed their speech.

"Adam had a large growth on the side of his neck, a goiter. After extensive prayer and research, my colleague and I removed it."

"I've never prayed so hard in my life. We all did. He was such a darling little boy."

Was. Did the child not live? Astrid could hardly keep from jumping in to ask questions.

"The surgery was successful. He has a scar on his neck, but that will fade with time."

"He was from the Zulu tribe in South Africa, and as he learned English, he said to us, one too many times, 'You must go.' "

The two exchanged a look so filled with love that all Astrid could think of was her mother and father.

Mrs. Gansberg laid a hand on her husband's arm. "So we are going."

"I wrote to the school here, told them our story, and asked if they had need of a doctor."

"That was six months ago, and here we are."

"Did I understand someone to say that you are a nurse?" Astrid looked to Mrs. Gansberg.

"Not by schooling but by assisting me and teaching classes in hygiene and family care to the miners' families up in the hills. Cholera nearly wiped the town out one year. After that we got the mining company to provide clean water and take care of the wastes. I hope to do the same in Africa." Dr. Gansberg nodded, emphasizing his point.

"So many diseases can be prevented," his wife added.

Astrid leaned forward. Such a fascinating couple. "How long have you been here?"

"Three months. You will learn about the diseases endemic to the area where you will be assigned and learn what you, as a doctor, can do. As you already know from your work in Chicago, some diseases can be cured, but for others the best we can do is to ease some of the symptoms. We will be returning home to gather supplies and then will leave from New York."

"God is so good to give us this privilege." Mrs. Gansberg refilled her husband's coffee cup from the carafe on the table.

"How can you bear to leave your home and family?" Astrid spread jam on her toast. *They are so certain, it just glows from them. Lord, you know I don't feel that way or think that way. What is wrong with me?*

"Don't you worry, Dr. Bjorklund." Dr. Gansberg patted her arm. "God has a special job for you to do, and He will make it all clear."

"Thank you." She sighed. "I hope so." As they left the table, she glanced up to see a young man staring at her from a nearby table.

"Are you really a doctor?" he asked.

His emphasis on *really* straightened her spine instantly. She kept her voice mild. "Yes, I am."

"You're obviously not a member of the clergy, however."

"No. Are you?"

"Yes. Recently ordained. I will be teaching at our training facility for natives in Africa."

"Well, Reverend . . ." She waited for him to fill in the blank.

"Highsmith. The dean here is my uncle."

"Have you been to Africa before?"

"No, but I have always planned to go there. I am the third generation in our family to fulfill this calling." He spoke as if he dared anyone to challenge him.

Like Dean Highsmith's young assistant, this man needed to take some of the starch out of his collar, Astrid thought, but kept her face as neutral as possible.

"I am surprised they are allowing a young unmarried female like you to participate in our program." The way he said it made sure she knew how he felt.

"I believe the need for medical doctors is paramount." She could hear the stiffness in her own response. How could this young Highsmith be so different from his uncle, who despite having some misgivings about her, was open to whatever the Lord intended?

"I'm sure male doctors are preferable."

"Perhaps, but sometimes you have to take what you can get. I've always believed God has a use for all of us, male and female. Isn't there a verse about all being equal in the eyes of God?"

"That is not an exact quote." If possible his voice grew more stiff.

"No, but close enough. Excuse me, I have to get to my first interview." She picked up her tray and left, mentally shaking her head. So much for flies and honey. How many classes would she be required to take with him? she wondered. Somehow she didn't see a friendship building there, even though God had surprised her with Red Hawk's friendship. But Red Hawk had never questioned her right to be a doctor. Just her opportunity to take advanced classes. She smiled, then winced as she remembered his disappointment that she was going to Africa when so many of his people needed medical help. *Lord, please help me to be understanding.* She added another line. *And understood would be nice.*

The tea that afternoon where new students were introduced was both pleasant and not so pleasant. The man and woman who were hosting the gathering had returned from Africa due to medical reasons. The man, Rev. Clement, had finally regained his health after nearly dying from malaria. While he was polite, he left her feeling less than welcome.

As she met the others, she realized she was right in the middle of dissenting camps. Should she be allowed to go or should she not? She heard a comment from a male person behind her about her being too young and female. Why would God tell her to come here if she couldn't go? Or had God told her? Back to that same old question.

She kept her company smile in place and a lock on her tongue. Now was not the time to ask the questions boiling beneath the surface. She wanted to spend time with Rev. Clement and his wife, to ask more about their life in Africa, but the tea was not the place. Rev. Clement taught the class on daily life in the bush, which she was looking forward to, after having heard him describe the area where they worked. *Primitive* was the word that came to mind. Having lived on open plains, she had a difficult time picturing jungle so dense one needed a huge knife called a machete to hack one's way through. And witch doctors sounded similar to the medicine men of the Indians, only more evil. Did demons really exist? Another question she wanted to ask him.

HER BIBLE CLASS the next day focused on the New Testament. "To share the love of Christ is our primary reason to live. And our primary reason to go to the rest of the world as Jesus commanded us is to tell the Good News to those who have never heard." Rev. Thompkins smiled at those in his classroom. "Read and memorize Jesus' Great Commission at the end of Matthew, for that will be the focus of our studies. Tonight I would like you to read Matthew again and ask God to show you something new in your reading. Be ready to share that tomorrow." He handed them a list of questions. "These are guides for your studies."

When he dismissed the class, Astrid headed for her room to divest herself of one petticoat before settling in the wicker chair in the shade on the veranda. By suppertime she had finished reading the book of Matthew and made some notes. She remembered how she had read through the entire Bible as one of her assignments when she was in high school. But this time she did as her new teacher said and looked for new meanings. She had a list of questions to take to class the next day.

At supper she sat next to the Gansbergs again.

"How was your day?" Dr. Gansberg asked.

"I read the book of Matthew all the way through, all at once. I don't think I've ever done it just like that before."

"And what did you learn?"

"That I have more questions. When I was in confirmation, our pastor always teased me about having so many questions."

"Did he give you any answers?"

"Sometimes. Sometimes he told me to look for the answers, and sometimes he said that I should make my list to ask God when I get to heaven."

Dr. Gansberg chuckled. "He sounds like a very wise man."

"He is. But he was not able to answer my most recent question."

"May I ask what that is, if it is not too personal?"

"Well, I was wondering if God is really calling me to become a missionary and go to Africa. I still don't have the answer." She turned to look at both of her new friends. "You seem so sure. I don't have that certainty."

"But you are here." Mrs. Gansberg's smile warmed Astrid all over.

"I am trying to be obedient. I took the step I thought I should."

"Good for you."

"But when will I know?"

The doctor turned to his wife, who replied, "When the time is right, you will know for sure. Our God is a God of wisdom and purpose. He never leaves His people without surety."

"Well said, my dear. I knew you would answer better than I." He leaned closer to Astrid. "My wife has always listened and obeyed God's Word. I don't know how she puts up with the likes of me."

"Would you pray for me?" The words were out of her mouth

before Astrid had time to think. She'd never asked anyone other than her mother and Pastor Solberg to do that. And they didn't even need to be asked.

"We most certainly will." Mrs. Gansberg reached for Astrid's hand.

I didn't mean now. Astrid glanced around, as if they were doing something illegal. But at the warm clasp, she sighed and let herself go.

"Father in heaven, we know that you love Astrid in ways far beyond our understanding, that you have a definite plan for her life, and that you are revealing your plan step by step. Let her rest in you and in the knowledge of your love so that she can be blessed here in this school. Let her know she is being blessed to be a blessing, be it in Africa or wherever you choose. Thank you for the privilege of bringing her into our lives. In Jesus' name, amen."

She squeezed Astrid's hand and patted her cheek with the other.

Astrid realized the doctor had placed his hand on her shoulder. "I feel like I've been hugged. The best hug ever."

Mrs. Gansberg's smile put a twinkle in her eyes. "God is like that, the best hugger ever."

"I wish you could meet my mother and father—in Norwegian we say *Mor* and *Far*. They're like the two of you. Love just flows out of them."

"Ah, Dr. Bjorklund, you have the gift of words, that is for sure. Thank you."

They strolled together into the chapel for evening devotions. Astrid looked around. Such a diverse group. And here were two of God's servants, like Matthew said. *Just think,* she reminded herself, *if you hadn't come here, you would never have met them.* One good reason to have come. She had a feeling there would be more, but when and how she had no idea. She already knew she could do without young Rev. Highsmith. *Judge not, that ye be not judged,* one of the verses from Matthew floated through her mind. *Oh, jumping grasshoppers.*

I can't even make it through one day without failing. Lord, I'm sorry. Thank you for your mercy and forgiveness. Could she make it through to bedtime, or was that the whole point of what Jesus had said in the Sermon on the Mount?

THE DISCUSSIONS THE next day in Rev. Clement's class were different from any she'd had before. When she asked her question about recognizing demons, the teacher told several stories from his time in Africa about casting out demons in the name of Jesus.

"When you meet the true evil of demons, you will know it. But know that when a demon looks at you, he sees the angels of God and Jesus himself circled behind you. It terrifies him, so he leaves."

Astrid tried to swallow, but her throat was so dry that she coughed instead. This man would not lie. She could see something in his face, such certainty in his voice.

"You need to be all prayed up for such times as that. You need to know God's Word so you can throw it right out there. God will protect us through His Word and His spirit."

He closed the class with prayer just as he had the day before. "Lord, keep us in your Word, for your Word is truth. Teach us to pray and to live your Word. Amen."

Those in the class left silently. Astrid knew for sure it would take her a long time to let all this soak in. She'd just met a man who had participated in true miracles. What other surprises did God have in store for her?

THREE DAYS LATER she received a large envelope with the return address of the hospital in Chicago. What could they be sending her?

Hoping for a note from Dr. Morganstein, she opened the envelope to find two letters from Mr. Landsverk, postmarked from Blessing clear back in December and January. Her hand shook a little as she held them. He had written to her after all. And she had convinced herself that not hearing from him was another confirmation she needed to follow this path. Even so, she struggled with the emotions that his coming back into her life stirred. But she realized she didn't really know him, and the earlier letters had only made their distance more obvious. Still, the picture of Joshua that flitted through her mind made her smile. Dark curly hair, tall like her brothers, laughing dark eyes, and a smile that set her pulse to pounding. A fine-looking man, as Sophie had said more than once. A note from the hospital said the letters had just arrived and were mailed again immediately. Where could they have been all this time?

3

Blessing, North Dakota

Gamma?"

"What is it, Inga?" Ingeborg raised her voice to be heard in the parlor. "You'll have to come here. I have my hands in the cookie dough."

Inga, dragging her Christmas doll by one arm, came to lean against her grandmother's skirt.

"What is it, little one?"

"When will Emmy be home from school?"

Ingeborg glanced up at the clock. "In about an hour. When the big hand is on twelve and the little hand is on four." Emmy was a little Indian girl they had discovered in their haymow at the beginning of winter. She'd never said a word, but they knew she was not deaf.

"I want her to come home now." Inga held up the back of her hand. "Kitty scratched me."

Ingeborg glanced down to see a red line on the little hand. "She did at that. Did you hold her too hard?"

"No. I dropped her."

"I see." Ingeborg kept a tight grip on her lips to prevent a smile from escaping. What a scamp.

"She ran behind the stove," Inga said as she pointed.

"Why did you drop her?"

"It was an accident."

"Would a cookie make your hand feel better?"

Inga nodded soberly and looked up at her grandmother. "And milk, please."

"You go get the jug, and I'll get the cookies. I might have to have one with you."

"And milk?"

"I think I'll have coffee."

"I'll have coffee too." Inga pulled open the icebox door and took out the small jug Ingeborg kept there for just this purpose. She brought it to the table and pulled out a chair. "Is Carl still sick?"

"I think so." Ingeborg set two coffee cups on the well-worn oak table and arranged the sourdough cookies on a plate. One pan was still in the oven, another ready to put in. She poured one cup full of coffee and the other about a quarter full. After returning the pot to the stove, she filled the one cup with milk and set it in front of Inga, who was kneeling on her chair, her elbows propped on the table.

"Thank you." She grinned at Ingeborg, her Bjorklund blue eyes, so like her father's, twinkling. "I like coffee with you."

Ingeborg tweaked the little nose. "And I like mine with you." She passed the plate. "Circle or square?"

"Square." Inga took the appropriate cookie. "There are three circles and now only two squares." She broke her cookie in half. "And now I have two triangles."

"How did you get so smart?"

"You made me." She took a bite of one. "And Pa."

Ingeborg knew Thorliff played games with Inga, who would be four in two months, helping her learn numbers and the alphabet, shapes and colors. He'd print out simple sentences and have her sound out the words.

"I been teaching Emmy." Inga dunked her cookie in her cup. A tan drip appeared on the white pinafore she wore over her wool dress.

"What have you been teaching her?"

"How to count. She holds up her fingers." Inga showed how they did it. "How come she doesn't say words?"

"I wish I knew. Oh, the cookies." Ingeborg jumped up and, using her apron folded over for a potholder, opened the oven door. She grabbed the thicker potholders from off the warming shelf of the stove and pulled out the pan of cookies. Browner than Haakan liked them, not that he wouldn't eat them this way, but while she liked them crisp, he liked his thick and soft. She set the pan on the table, slid the other pan in, and closed the door. After lifting the cookies off the pan and setting them on wooden racks, she put more wood in the stove and settled the lids back in place. "More coffee, ma'am?"

Inga giggled. "I not ma'am. I am Inga."

"Well, would Inga like more coffee?"

"Yes, please, ma'am."

"Uff da. You are too smart for your britches."

"I don't wear britches. I am a girl." Her tone carried a hint of reproach. Then after a moment, she said, "How come boys wear britches and girls wear skirts?"

"That's a very good question. Maybe because skirts are prettier and girls like to be pretty." *Even though britches are a far sight easier to garden and work in.* After all these years she still remembered wearing britches when she was out plowing and seeding the land after Roald had died that terrible winter. She'd do it again in a minute if so many people wouldn't be offended. Haakan first and foremost.

"Would you make me some britches, Gamma?"

Ingeborg made a face. "I don't think so. Your pa wouldn't like that. Nor your ma either."

"But when I ride my pony, pants would be better."

Out of the mouths of babes. "Well, since you don't have a pony yet, I guess we don't have to worry about britches."

"Pa said maybe in the summer."

I do hope he remembers, because his little daughter isn't going to let him off the hook. "We'll see."

"When Ma says 'We'll see,' it means no."

Ingeborg barely hid a chuckle as she got up to answer the telephone. "Hello." She still got a thrill out of hearing a voice come out of the earpiece.

Thorliff, her elder son, responded. "Hello, Mor. Just wanted to tell you that I'll be out to pick up Inga in half an hour or so."

"So soon? We were just having coffee."

"And she's filling your ear with all kinds of news, I'll bet."

"That she is."

"Is it Pa?" the little girl asked, looking eagerly at her grandmother.

Ingeborg nodded. "Oh, would you stop by Garrisons' and pick me up some cocoa? I was going to make chocolate pudding for supper, and we're out of cocoa."

"Of course. Anything else?"

"No, thank you." She set the earpiece back on the black prongs. To think that just like that she'd have cocoa. Ah, these modern conveniences. "You want to beat the eggs for pudding?"

Inga drained the last of her coffee and set the cup down. "Yes."

"Wipe off your mustache." Ingeborg shook her head. "Not with your sleeve, silly."

As she set out the ingredients, she thought about the quilting meeting they would have next week. She knew there would be more discussion about gathering things for the Indian reservation in South Dakota that Astrid had asked them to help with. She was hoping Astrid would be home for this meeting. She could answer the questions likely to come up better than Ingeborg could. Any day now Astrid would be getting off the train. Surely she would telephone when she was ready to leave Chicago.

She set the bowl in front of Inga. "Have you cracked an egg before?"

"When one fell on the floor."

"Well, this one has to go into the bowl." She tapped an egg on the edge, separated it with both hands, and let the egg drop into the bowl. "Now I'll help you do it." She stood behind Inga, who was kneeling on another chair, and with her hands over the little ones, they picked up an egg and tapped it on the edge of the bowl. The egg dropped in, along with half the shell.

"Oops."

"That's all right. We can use this half of the shell to dip out the bits and pieces." Ingeborg did that as she talked. "See? That's why you have to hang on to both sides of the shell."

"Baby chickens come from eggs."

"Yes, they do."

"How come there is no baby chicken in this one?"

"Because we gather the eggs every day, and the hen doesn't have a chance to sit on the eggs to make chicks grow."

"But in summer we will have chicks again?"

"We sure will. Now let's crack another egg. Crack it easy."

The first tap did nothing. So Inga cracked it harder.

"Quick, get all the egg in the bowl."

This time the little girl held up both sides of the shell and then looked down into the bowl. "No shells."

"Very good." Ingeborg handed the slotted wooden spoon to her granddaughter. "Now you can beat them." She let Inga beat away while she measured and poured sugar, flour, and milk into a pan. Setting that on the stove way back to heat slowly, she checked on the eggs. Holding Inga's hand, she said, "This way," and using a circular motion, whipped the eggs.

Hearing boots on the porch, Inga wriggled down and ran to the door. "Pa?"

"I'm here."

"I hope you brought the mail too," Ingeborg called.

Thorliff pushed open the door and scooped his daughter up in his arms.

"You're cold!" she said, hugging him.

"I know. What do you expect? It's winter out there." He set her down and laid a package on the table. "Your cocoa, your mail, and I think maybe there is something in there for good little girls."

"I was good, huh, Gamma?" Inga looked toward Ingeborg. At her grandmother's nod, she turned to her father. "And Emmy will be home when the big hand is on twelve and the little hand is on four, and that is almost here." She darted across the room. "We started the pudding. I helped crack eggs, and I beated them."

"And none on the floor?"

"Nope. In the bowl." She peeked inside the brown bag. "Peppermint sticks!"

"There's a letter from Astrid." Thorliff shucked his coat and hung it, along with his scarf and hat on the coat-tree.

"Good. You need some coffee to warm you up?"

"As if I'd ever turn down coffee." He snitched a cookie. "You burnt them."

"I did not. They are nicely browned and a bit on the crisp side.

That's all. You don't have to eat them, you know." She poured his coffee, filled her own cup, and fixed Inga's before taking the letter to the table. Slitting the envelope, she pulled out the single sheet of paper.

> February 29, 1904
> Dear Mor,
> The adventure continues, but this is a hard letter to write. I would have written days ago, but I just made the decision. I am going—I'm actually on the train right now—to Athens, Georgia, to a missionary school at Cardin College. I have talked with them on the telephone, and they assured me they have a two-year program that I could sign up for. I don't think I would have even considered it could they not let me go for a short time. I cannot contemplate spending my life as a missionary, no matter how desperate the need. Does that show a lack of faith or trust? I don't know. I am just trying to do what is right.

Ingeborg dropped her hands to her lap. "Oh no." Tears stung her nose and made her blink.

"What?" Thorliff stared at her. "She's going to missionary school."

She nodded. "She's not even coming home first."

"Well, that's a wise thing to do." Sarcasm crackled his voice.

Ingeborg wiped her eyes and picked up the letter, reading aloud from the beginning.

> "I have had a terrible struggle with this decision, as you well know. Finally it hung on what you say so often about God guiding us step by step. I am taking this step with my teeth gritted, but you know that I want to be obedient to what God is calling me to do."

"Elizabeth is going to be terribly disappointed." Thorliff rubbed the side of his nose.

Ingeborg nodded and returned to reading aloud.

"I know this is not easy for any of us, but I figure two years is what I would have been going away to school for or on an internship, which Elizabeth has suggested I might do. Well, perhaps my internship is going to be in Africa. If only the entire thing did not terrify me so much. But I can do this one step at a time, and I ask that you pray for me, Mor, more than you ever have before. I am writing to Elizabeth too and to Pastor Solberg.

"Dr. Morganstein will be in contact soon regarding the new hospital. She and members of her board are planning a trip west as soon as spring comes. They do not want to brave the North Dakota winter.

"I will send you my new address as soon as I know it. Please don't be angry with me, and if you say I must come home, you know that I will. I love you and want so badly to see all your dear faces and be home again.

"Your loving daughter,
"Dr. Astrid Bjorklund

"P.S. I do love signing my name this way. I now have a paper to prove me legal. A."

This time Ingeborg used her apron to wipe away the tears.

"Gamma, why are you crying?" Inga leaned against her grandmother's knee.

"She's crying because your Tante Astrid is going to another school before she comes home. This is a sad letter for her—and for us."

The jingle of a harness caught Inga's attention. "Emmy is home." She ran to the door, tears forgotten.

Thorliff reached across the table and clasped his mother's hand. "I am so sorry."

Ingeborg sniffed and tried to smile. "We shouldn't be sorry that our girl is doing what she feels the Lord is calling her to do."

"Maybe not. But this is a shock, no matter how much we know she's been struggling with it." He shook his head slowly. "I guess I really didn't think she would go."

"I wish she had telephoned first."

"I think she couldn't, because it might have made her change her mind."

"I think you are right." Ingeborg looked back at the beginning of the letter to the date. "February 29 she wrote this. She is already at the school." She heaved a sigh, wiped her eyes again. Speaking softly, she continued, "But is this the right decision given the conflict she is in? Give us your peace. Dear God, please protect my daughter. To Africa. Oh, Lord, so far away."

4

"To Africa?" Joshua Landsverk stared at Thorliff. "What do you mean she is going to Africa?"

"Astrid wrote that she was on her way south to missionary school and then will spend two years as a medical missionary in Africa. She believes God is calling her to do this."

"Why didn't she write to me, let me know?" Joshua stared up at the steeple on the Blessing Lutheran Church. The church service had been such an uplifting time, but now this.

"She said she made the decision to take one step at a time. And this seemed the next right step."

"Two years." At the moment two years yawned like an impossible canyon with no bridges in sight. *Go get her. Go tell her how you feel.*

Two voices shouting in his head nearly drowned out what Thorliff said next. "Pardon me?"

"I said Elizabeth is terribly disappointed too. She was counting on Astrid's help here."

"It was that pastor who visited. If only he hadn't come here." Joshua's fists clenched in his black wool jacket pockets.

"That's what I said too, until Mor reminded me that if God were indeed calling Astrid to this mission, He would have found another way to let her know about it."

"But what if this isn't God calling her? What if she is making a mistake?"

"Then we need to be praying that God will make it clear to her, again my mother talking."

"I thought she was excited about building the hospital here."

"Me too." Thorliff raised a hand to acknowledge he heard someone call his name. "I need to go, but why don't you come out to the house for dinner today?"

"I have to give Johnny his guitar lesson first."

"Good. Then we'll see you as soon as you're finished." He strode off, leaving Joshua with a plethora of unanswered questions.

Nothing was going the way he'd thought it would after dreaming of Astrid for so long. The dream and the reality seemed to move further apart. Was it supposed to be this hard? Maybe this was God's way of making sure any relationship would be based on truth and not false perceptions. And he thought the trip to see his family had been hard enough.

"Mr. Landsverk, are you ready?"

He looked down to see Johnny Solberg, guitar in hand, shifting from one foot to the other. How easy it would be to say no, but he nodded instead. "Let's go inside. You been practicing?"

"Every day. Well, almost every day." The boy held up his left hand. "See my calluses?"

"Good for you. That will make holding down the strings much easier." Together they mounted the steps to the church and went inside. The smell of smoke from the extinguished candles still hung on the air. Their booted feet sounded loud on the wooden floor. "You been working on tuning your guitar?"

"I have, but when I think it is right, Ma says I'm off key. How come she can hear it better than me?" Johnny sat down on one of the chairs in the front row and held his guitar on his lap. He plucked the low E string, tilting his head to listen better.

"We'll tune it to the piano, like I do mine." Joshua struck the key, and Johnny thumbed his string. Hit the key, thumb the string, hit the key, thumb the string. "Are they the same?"

"Seems so to me."

"This is something we'll keep working on. Let me tune it for you today." Joshua took the guitar, adjusted the pegs, and plucked each string, turning pegs as needed and then stroking across all the strings. He handed the guitar back. "There you go. You were really close." He picked up his own guitar, checked the tuning, adjusted one peg, and then strummed all six strings. "Okay, let's start with 'She'll be Coming 'Round the Mountain.' Do you have that memorized by now?"

"Pretty much." The two played through the tune once, then again with Joshua picking up the beat.

"Okay, now you play the straight chords like that again, and I'm going to pick the melody. Ready? If you miss one, just keep on going. Don't stop and start again. Guitar players miss chords all the time." Joshua tapped out one, two, three, and away they went. When they finished on the last chord together, Johnny's smile rivaled the sun beaming in through the side windows.

"You did that real well. See? All your practicing is paying off. Let's try 'Red Red Robin.' "

"I need the music for that."

They played through five or six review songs before Joshua said,

"Okay, time for something new." He pulled a sheet of paper with the words to a familiar song and the chords printed under the words. "You need to learn to play by ear too, so we'll sing this one. Here are two new chords. C major and C augmented." He showed him the fingering and played them a few times, fingers moving back and forth on the strings against the neck of the guitar.

Johnny got one but kept missing on the other. "I know this is a harder one. You have to reach with that little finger and then make sure you push it tight against the strings." He helped place Johnny's fingers at the correct frets. "Now pick them up and do it again—and again—and again. There you go. Good job. Now you know the other chords, so we'll play it through slow, and I'll call the chords." They played slowly, pausing long enough for Johnny to get his fingers in place with each change before continuing.

"If you don't look out, you're going to chew a hole in your lip." One side of Joshua's mouth was turned upward.

"But I want to get it right."

"What? Chewing your lip? You got that down pat."

Johnny grinned at him. "No, the chords." He tongued his lower lip.

"Raw, huh?"

"Sorta."

By the end of the lesson, Johnny had a list of exercises to play through and two more tunes with chords. He folded his papers and stuffed them into his coat pocket. "Thank you. When you are building your house, I could help you. Sorta pay you back, you know." He studied his boot and then looked at Joshua out of the corner of his eye.

"I will really appreciate that. I know what a good worker you are." The grin Johnny sent him was all the reward Joshua needed. They walked out together, guitars slung on their backs with their straps. Johnny made sure the door was closed behind them.

"See you next week," Joshua said with a wave. He headed down the plowed road, snowbanks on each side, to the Bjorklunds. His step would have been lighter had he been able to look forward to seeing Astrid there.

The family was about ready to sit down to eat when he knocked on the door and obeyed the "Come on in" call. He hung his coat on the tree with the others and made sure all the snow was off his boots before he left the rug. Propping his guitar against the corner of the wall, Joshua crossed to the chair left for him.

"We about figured you forgot," Thorliff said.

"No, but we got to playing and kind of lost track of time. Johnny's going to be a right good guitar player."

"According to him, it sounds like you are a right good teacher," Dr. Elizabeth said, leaning around her husband. "Will he be ready to play with us pretty soon?" Besides being a physician, Elizabeth was an excellent piano player, now joined by Joshua on the guitar in church on Sunday mornings.

"At the rate he's going, he will be. His ma says he's practicing all the time. She has to drag him away for his chores and lessons. He'd take it to school, but his pa won't let him."

"Let's say grace before the food gets cold," Haakan said from the end of the table. As they all bowed their heads, he paused. Then with a sigh began, "Heavenly Father, we thank you this day for the food you have provided for us and for those hands that have prepared it. Thank you that we can be gathered together, a family, both ours and yours. I ask your special blessing today and every day upon our Astrid. Lord God, if she is indeed obeying your call to the mission field, we ask that you give her strength and courage, that you give us accepting hearts so we can support her. We all want to be your obedient servants, but so often we are just not sure how. What we do know is that you cover and surround us with your mighty love and with the assurance that you have a plan for each of us, which is always for our good. In Jesus' precious name, amen."

Joshua felt his throat closing. Haakan talked to God like they were the best of friends. He knew God in a deeper way than he'd heard before. *Lord, I want that closeness with you. I want that sureness. Show me. Teach me.* He passed the bowl of potatoes with those thoughts still in his mind and settling into his heart. As the food went around the table, the conversations picked up.

He thought to the table that had been at his father's house. In spite of his visit, which had brought a return of communication, he could no longer call it home. Silence reigned there but for the clink of utensils on the dishes. His mother had served them and waited to eat until they all left the table. If there was anything left. His father gave the instructions for the day's work, and they left to do his bidding. Joshua looked up with a sense someone had said something to him.

"Pardon me. I guess I was woolgathering."

"Gamma, what wool is he talking about?" Inga sat between her mother and father.

"It's just a figure of speech."

"What's a—"

Her father tapped her shoulder. "Later. Right now you eat and listen."

"I was saying that you did a fine job on the work on our house." Hjelmer Bjorklund looked to his wife, Penny, who nodded and smiled.

"Thank you. I never realized how much I enjoyed building things until we started on the windmills. Your house was a real learning time for me. I had good teachers too. That Toby is a fine carpenter."

"That he is."

"And we were able to move in before Christmas, just like Hjelmer promised," Penny said, nudging her husband with an elbow.

"Took us a while to finish it, though."

Hjelmer leaned forward to look down the table at Joshua. "She hasn't been able to add anything to the to-be-finished list for three whole days."

Joshua chuckled along with the rest of them. *The List* had become a thing of dread in the last couple of weeks. Penny had a knack for finding things not quite finished, like a missing screw in a stair tread or a window that wasn't caulked sufficiently. It took them some time to figure out a problem with the plumbing, but they did.

"Sophie talked to me about some remodel work on the boarding-house. That should keep us going through the middle of April. Then as soon as we can pour the concrete, we can start on your house, Joshua. That and a couple of small houses I'd like to build for sale."

"And mine?" Freda, a cousin of Ingeborg's who recently moved to Blessing from Norway, asked as she poured more coffee.

"Oh, that's right. Well, looks like we have plenty of work."

"You better hurry on all that, because we have a hospital that needs to be built too." Elizabeth glanced at Ingeborg. "By the way, Dr. Morganstein wondered if you would be willing to show and discuss more of your simples when the group from Chicago comes to visit."

"You know, Mor," Thorliff said, "you ought to write all that up, and we could publish a small home-companion-type book so people could use what they have on hand to help themselves."

Ingeborg stared at her son. "Why, I . . . I wouldn't know where to begin."

"Begin with A. Alphabetized is always the best. That cough syrup you make works better than anything else."

"You know . . ." Hjelmer nodded slowly, as if waiting for his thoughts to catch up.

"Now we're in trouble." Andrew, Ingeborg's younger son, raised his eyebrows, rolled his eyes, and looked at Haakan.

His wife, Ellie, poked him in the side. "You be polite."

Eyes narrowed now, Hjelmer tapped a finger on the table. "What if you were to make up some of your simples, package them, and sell them at Penny's store?"

"We'll sell the booklet to go along with them. Although we need a better title than *Simples*." Thorliff nodded as he thought. "*Remedies. Ingeborg's Remedies*." He continued. "I could print the labels like I do for the cheese house. This could even become a mail-order business."

"One of the things I dream of for our hospital is a pharmacy," Elizabeth said. "I guess I have a lot of dreams."

"We could sell the remedies there also."

"I s'pose you want to take a wagon out and sell like the traveling medicine men," Haakan said with a grin at his wife. "Though their stuff is mostly alcohol."

"Uff da," Ingeborg muttered. "The ideas you come up with."

"Ah, but you see, Mor, your receipts work. We could make another wagon like the one we're doing for the windmill construction, and—"

"Thorliff, don't tease your mor." Haakan was having a hard time keeping from laughing, so Ingeborg pushed back her chair and stood. "The polite children in this family and those who are kind to others will now have pie for dessert. The rest of you can continue your harebrained schemes in the parlor. Uff da! The things you come up with."

For a moment Joshua thought she was truly upset, but when she glanced at him, he caught the glint in her eyes.

Inga leaned over from her father's lap and whispered in her carry-across-the-pasture voice, "You can have pie. You are comp'ny."

Thorliff burst out laughing first, and the others followed.

While the women rose to clear the table and set out the pie, the men watched as Haakan fetched his pipe from the shelf behind the stove and proceeded to clean it, fill it, tamp it, light it, and lean back in contentment.

"Smoke rings, Grampa?" Inga insisted, standing next to him. Carl and a little dark-haired girl someone called Emmy, along with Hjelmer's children, stood in a half circle around them.

Haakan blew one smoke ring, then another. The children laughed and clapped.

Who did the new little girl belong to? Joshua wondered. She'd not been there the last time he'd been invited. With that dark hair and brown skin, she looked like an Indian. Why would they have an Indian in their home? Why would anyone want one of those thieving animals in their house? Why, if Pa were there, he'd—

Joshua forced his attention away from the girl and back to the conversations flowing around him. What a family. How could Astrid bear to leave this? If only he could have talked with her before she made her decision. Would she listen to what he had to say?

THAT NIGHT BACK in his room at the boardinghouse, he lay on his bed, hands locked behind his head, and thought back to his trip to Iowa. He'd gone with such high hopes, but perhaps now that he'd had time to think about it, he'd only done it because of what Pastor Solberg had been hammering them about. Forgiveness. He had needed to forgive them and ask for their forgiveness. He'd come to realize that not accepting it or giving it was, as Pastor Solberg said, destroying him.

All during the train ride, he'd stewed about how to do this. What to say, what not to say. He'd not let them know he was coming, just showed up at his sister's door. She was so shocked, she nearly collapsed.

Her arms around his neck felt almost like their mother's. Even their voices would be hard to tell apart.

"Why didn't you warn me?" Avis asked.

"I wanted to surprise you."

"Well, that you did. Are you moving back here?" She hung his coat on the peg, along with his hat and scarf. "Come over here by the fire and get yourself warmed up. Did you walk from town?"

"Got a ride with old Buck. Made him promise he wouldn't blab all over the county."

"Sit, and I'll get the coffee."

"Where's Albert and the children?"

"Gone to town. You know it's almost Christmas." She refilled the firebox on the kitchen stove. "Surprises and all that."

"I didn't bring anything." He felt about three inches high. Didn't even think of it. *What kind of uncle are you?*

"Before they get back, I have to say something. Come, sit here a moment." He patted the chair beside him.

She sat down, never taking her eyes from his face. "You aren't dying, are you?"

"Well, not that I know of. I need to ask your forgiveness."

"For what?"

"For leaving in such a huff and not keeping in contact. You're the only sister I have, and I . . . I needed to tell you this."

"Oh, Joshua, little brother, of course I forgive you. I don't blame you one bit for leaving. Pa gets worse by the day. I don't know how Frank puts up with him. 'Course, they are a lot alike. I always tried to do all I could to help Ma, but she was stubborn as all get-out." Her voice dropped to almost a whisper. "She taught me a lot about loving someone not very lovable."

"Our mother—" His voice cracked. "I think of her every time I take out my guitar. Always thanking her for insisting I learn to play it. I play for church now and whenever there is a dance anywhere around. I'm even teaching our preacher's oldest son."

"You go to church, then?"

"I do. The people in Blessing make strangers feel welcome from the moment you step off the train. Not that I was completely a stranger. The Bjorklunds turned that half section they bought from me into clean and beautiful wheat fields."

"You're farming again?"

"Nope." He shook his head. "I drill wells and build windmills. This winter I worked on the inside of a big house. Become a fair carpenter. Bought me a lot in town, and my house will go up come spring." He took her hand. "Why don't you and Albert leave this part of the country and come on out to Blessing?"

Avis stared deep into his eyes. She nodded slowly. "We might just do that, but don't go holding your breath." She got up to pour his coffee. "You will stay here with us through Christmas, won't you?"

"Most likely, since it is only two days away." He covered her hand with his. "But tomorrow I'm going to see Pa and Frank. You planning on spending Christmas back at the house?" He almost said *home* but then changed his mind. It wasn't home to him any longer, if it ever had been.

The next day he'd borrowed a horse and rode over to the place where he grew up. He stopped at the end of the lane and stared ahead at the two-story house, the big red barn, and the outbuildings. There was the machine shed he'd helped build, a shed-roofed addition to the barn. He rode on up, knowing it was near noon and most likely everyone would be at the house for dinner. A dog he didn't recognize announced his arrival.

He dismounted, tied the horse to the gatepost, and overcoming every sense he had that said run, mounted the steps to the back porch and knocked on the door. Nothing out of place. Even the woodchips swept up. Nothing had changed here.

"Well, I'll be . . ." Frank stepped back. "Come on in. What a sight for sore eyes." He raised his voice. "Pa, Joshua's come home."

The welcome caught Joshua by surprise. "Hello, Frank." He shook his brother's proffered hand.

"Susan, set another plate. Here, let me take your coat."

Joshua stared around the kitchen. Nothing had changed. Except for the man limping through the door to the parlor. His dark hair had gone nearly white, lines were cut in his face, and his jowls sagged. Who was this old man, and where had his father gone?

"Where is Aaron?"

"He's over helping a friend for a few days. We got rid of the cattle and hogs, so winter is kind of slack now." He pointed to the chair. "Sit, sit."

"I see." Joshua sat in the same chair he'd always sat in. Susan set the serving bowls and meat platter on the table, and they each helped themselves. Except for his father. Frank dished up his plate, as he did his own.

What was going on here? He stared at his brother, willing him to make some kind of comment, but the meal was finished in silence, just like all the meals he'd eaten at this table all of his life. Some of the characters had changed, but the meal was still the same.

When Susan refilled his coffee cup, he said, "Thank you." The words dropped like pebbles in a still pond, but the ripples hit the shore, and still nothing happened. Other than she shot him a look accompanied by a small smile.

"Thank you for a good dinner," he said when they finished.

"You are welcome." The words seemed to be dragged from a deep well.

"I need to go see to my horse." Joshua moved toward the door.

"You are coming back in, are you not?" Frank asked.

"Yes. Can I put him in the barn?"

"Yes. We still have horses. I left them in today because of the cold."

The huge barn seemed empty, with spiderwebs on the milking stanchions, the floors swept clean. He led his horse into a vacant stall, removed the saddle and bridle, and snapped the halter, attached to a tied lead rope, on the horse's head. Tossing the animal some hay, he returned to the house. It didn't seem that cold to him, but then, he was used to North Dakota now, not Iowa.

He paused on the porch. *Lord, what am I to do?* The verses about seeking the man who has done you wrong floated to the front of his mind. "Well, I am doing that, so I might as well be about it." He scrubbed his boots free of snow on the brush by the door and stepped back inside.

He sniffed appreciatively. "Something smells good."

"I'm making a spice cake. You will stay for supper, won't you?"

"I . . . I don't know. I need to talk with Frank and Pa, and we'll see how that goes." He paused a moment. "Can Pa hear?"

"Yes, he just can't speak. Was struck down by apoplexy a month or so after your mother died. God rest her soul."

"And Pa?"

"He's fading away day by day. He would just sit in that chair from dawn to dusk if Frank didn't take care of him. No will to live. Seems like the part of his brain that willed him to work died."

"So I can talk to him?"

"Yes. He may respond, or he may not. You saw him at the table. He feeds himself if the food is put before him. He sat out on the porch before it got too cold. I think the shock of finding your mother dead on the floor might have started this, but I don't know. Doctors don't know."

"Why did no one write to me?"

"Frank said he was done with writing bad news."

"I see." He didn't but couldn't figure what else to say. He walked into the parlor, where his father sat in a rocking chair, an afghan over his legs, staring outside. Frank sat in another chair reading a farm magazine.

"I have something I need to talk to you about, if you wouldn't mind," he said to Frank. "Pa too."

Frank put the magazine down on the table beside the chair. "I'll come over there."

Joshua swallowed, feeling his heart pick up speed. Frank set a chair down and went for another. When the three of them sat, Joshua leaned forward, elbows propped on his knees, hands loosely clasped in front of him. He hoped his heart wasn't going to jump right out of his chest. "I come to ask for your forgiveness."

His father's eyes widened slightly.

Frank stared at him, shock blinking his eyes. "For what?"

"For the way I left here so angry and never wrote, never came back. Rage and hate are terrible sins. So will you please forgive me?" He stuttered on the last words. He looked to his father, who was slowly nodding. A tear leaked out of one eye and ran down his cheek.

He looked to Frank. He was shaking his head. "I never realized . . ." He stared at his brother. "Of course I forgive you. That's what brothers do. Can you forgive me?"

Joshua nodded. "I did some time ago. That's why I was able to come."

Frank reached for Joshua's hand on one side and his father's on the other. "I wish Aaron was here. He'll be glad to know you came."

Joshua reached for his father's hand and held it. The last time he remembered holding his father's hand was when he was a young boy.

Joshua sat up on his bed at the boardinghouse and turned both his hands over to look at the palms. He'd held his father's hand and felt nothing but love. How could that be? He would never understand, but returning to Blessing had not been easy. The only question remaining was why had he waited so long. If he was wrong about Astrid, was this God's way of showing him it was time to return to Iowa for keeps?

5

Why did she feel this sense of dread?

"What's bothering you?" Haakan asked his wife, his voice gentle in the predawn darkness.

"The quilters meeting today."

"You don't have to go, you know." As they lay on their backs, he took her hand, holding it between them, his thumb rubbing the back of hers.

"I didn't mean to wake you."

"I know. So what is the problem at quilters?"

"The request from Astrid that we send a wagonload of supplies to the Rosebud Indian Reservation. The discussion was heating up last month, so we tabled it for people to pray about. I told you about that."

"So why worry? Perhaps God will have sent a spirit of unity like you prayed for."

"I did ask for that, didn't I?" Was that a heavenly chuckle she heard or the wind?

"What else is bothering you?"

She rolled onto her side and laid her cheek on his shoulder. "I want Astrid to come home, not go to Africa. I know that is a selfish prayer, but I just can't seem to let it go. You'd think I'd trust God's will in this, but so far I can't. I just want her to come back here."

"I imagine when God asked Abraham to lay his son on the altar, he most likely felt the same way. After all, it was his only son. And he even thought God was asking him to kill his son. That's what they did with sacrifices. You know the story. And step by step Abraham went ahead."

"But what if I never see her alive again?" She heard him inhale deeply. "I left Norway, and I never saw my mother again. Astrid will go to Africa, and we'll never see her again."

"Then we'll see her in heaven."

Ingeborg fought the tears but gave up and soaked the shoulder of her husband's long underwear. "That's not enough," she sobbed.

"Hush. It will be all right." His voice shook as he tried to comfort her.

Ingeborg felt the covers lift behind her back and a small body crawl into the bed. Emmy snuggled up behind her, and a little hand patted her shoulder.

"Gamma, no cry." The patting continued. "Pease, no cry."

Ingeborg's tears stopped. She raised her head. "Emmy can talk!"

Haakan's soft chuckle floated through the darkness. "I knew one day she would."

Ingeborg rolled over and gathered the little girl into her arms, feeling Haakan's strong arm surrounding them. "All right, Emmy, Gamma no cry. Gamma kiss you instead." And she did. All the while, her thank-yous danced heavenward. *Emmy can talk. Thank you, Father. Emmy can talk.*

"COME, FREDA," INGEBORG said to her cousin later that morning. "Come to the quilting with me. You need to get out and be with our neighbors more."

"No, thank you. You go. Me and Emmy are going to the cheese house. I need to wax a couple of wheels, and I'm experimenting with something."

"What?"

"I'll let you know how it turns out."

Sometimes I wonder whose cheese house it is, Ingeborg thought as she gathered her sewing things. "Will you help me carry the machine out to the buggy?"

"Sure. I have the stack of squares I stitched together. Didn't get the long strips sewn together, though. Should make a top right quick."

"I just don't understand why you won't come." Ingeborg picked up one end of the treadle sewing machine cabinet and walked backward when her cousin took the other.

"Ingeborg, I'm just not cut out for meetings and such." When she got a bit upset her strong Norwegian accent grew even heavier. Something like the sewing machine they carried. Usually Haakan and Andrew carried it out, but she'd forgotten to ask them. When they got to the steps, Haakan hollered at them to wait.

With a guilty sigh Ingeborg did just that. Much as she hated to admit it, hauling the machine to the sleigh in the winter wasn't something she'd wanted to do.

"Why didn't you ask?" Haakan said.

"I forgot."

"So did I." He and Freda settled it into the back seat of the sleigh. "There now. Anything else?"

"That basket on the table and the soup kettle. I need to tie the lid down on that."

"You picking up Kaaren?"

"Ja, and Anna." This was the first time for Anna. She'd been almost as stubborn as her mother-in-law.

"Then you can all three sit in front."

Back in the house she tied a dish towel from the handles and over the top of the deep kettle and stepped back for Haakan to pick it up. "And you could pray I keep my mouth shut today."

Haakan winked at her. "Now why would I want to do that?"

Ingeborg bent down to kiss Emmy. "Bye. You be good for Tante Freda."

Emmy nodded, clutching her doll to her chest, her cough still not all gone.

I should have let her go to school today. Ingeborg thought again of taking her along, but Inga had a cold and was staying home with Thelma. Andrew and Ellie's two little ones both had runny noses, and Emmy didn't know the other children. Now that she had spoken— not that she'd said anything else today—at least there was hope they'd learn more about her. Interesting how she'd picked up the language from Inga. No one else called her Gamma. Or maybe she already learned English from someone else. Hmm.

When she reached the front of the Knutsons' house, Ingeborg hallooed from the sleigh, and the two women came out. The way the snow was melting, they'd soon be back to wheels. Spring couldn't come soon enough for her.

Kaaren nestled her soup kettle on the floor and set her baskets on the back seat, as Ingeborg had.

"Are you sure there is room for me?" Anna asked.

"We can squeeze into the front." Ingeborg sniffed. "You can smell spring in the air."

"If I don't get going on the spring cleaning, we won't be done by Easter." Kaaren waited for Anna to get in first, then climbed in and tucked the blanket around them. "We don't really need this today, warm as it is."

"Freda and I started on the upstairs yesterday. Scrubbing walls has never been one of my favorite things to do, but everything clean again feels so good."

"Well, into the lion's den," Ingeborg muttered for Kaaren's ears only when they arrived at the church and started to unload the sleigh. They set their pots of soup on the stove, and Ingeborg held open the door for Anna and Kaaren to bring in the sewing machine. As often as the sewing machines were hauled in and out, they should have bought one for the church.

"Oh, I forgot to tell you the news. Emmy can talk."

"What did she say?"

"She said, 'Gamma, don't cry. Pease don't cry.' "

"And the reason for the tears?"

"Not important, but isn't that grand?"

"It is." Kaaren studied her. "If it makes you cry, it's important. Now, what brought it on?"

"Astrid. The thought of never seeing her again."

"Isn't that kind of borrowing trouble? If she goes, it will only be for two years. That's what her letter said."

"I know. But you know how easy it is to not make sense in the middle of the night." Together they returned to the church and set their sewing baskets on the tables that were already set up. Hildegunn took seriously her responsibility to prepare for the day. This was the first year she'd not been president in a long time, so she'd taken over the quilting preparations.

"Good morning, everybody," Sophie trilled as she burst through the doorway. "Guess what?"

They all turned to look. "What?"

"Remember Mr. Jeffers?"

"Who could forget him? That scum."

"No, no. The *real* Mr. Jeffers, the young man who came looking for his father." She set her basket on the table. "He checked into the boardinghouse after yesterday's train. He's over talking with Thorliff today. I'm so curious, I'm about to burst."

"Leave it to Sophie," Ingeborg said sotto voce.

"Did you ask him anything?"

"How could I? I didn't know he was there until I checked the register this morning." She unbuttoned her coat and laid it on the collection. "There's a fascinating story in there somewhere. I just know there is. Where are the things we are collecting for the reservation?"

Silence hit the room like a lead blanket.

She looked around. "What? What did I do now?"

"We have not made that decision yet." Hildegunn Valders straightened her shoulders, causing her considerable bosom to expand.

"Sorry." Sophie rolled her eyes. "I forgot there was dissension about this. We all know it is the right thing to do, so let's just go ahead with it."

Mary Martha tapped her coffee cup for attention. "Let's get seated, shall we, ladies, so we can get started with our meeting."

Sophie stopped by her mother. "Gracious, you'd have thought I let a skunk loose in here the way the noses went up."

"Hush." Kaaren never had been able to keep ahead of Sophie, but her half-hidden grin said how much she didn't care this time.

Ingeborg kept her face straight but knew it was perilous. At least Sophie was taking the onus off her. And Sophie couldn't care less what Hildegunn thought. Maybe that was the best way to deal with a stubborn woman who wanted to rule the group and always felt she knew best.

"Is Ellie coming today?" Sophie asked Ingeborg as they sat down.

"No, she didn't want to bring the children. Carl is ill again." Earlier in the winter he'd had a bout with croup, and they weren't taking a chance on it happening again.

"I'm glad Helga comes to our house to watch the children. I'd hate to bundle them all up to come. I tried to talk Maydell into coming, but she says she dislikes sewing about as much as cleaning the slop pail."

"Sophie!"

"Well, that's what she said." Sophie shrugged. "And Rebecca spends every morning helping Benny catch up so he can go to school."

"Ladies."

They turned to face forward.

"Let us open by standing and singing 'Onward Christian Soldiers,' " Mary Martha said. "I'm sorry, but Elizabeth telephoned to say she could not come due to a waiting room full of sick people."

"All she has to do is hang out the *Closed* sign."

Mary Martha started the first line, and they all joined in. She led them in prayer after that, and then everyone sat.

"We'll start with announcements. The fourth Saturday of this month we will be cleaning the church to be ready for Easter. The more people who show up, the sooner we'll get finished. We are starting at nine o'clock, and dinner will be potluck. Bring cleaning supplies." She looked up from her paper. "Does anyone have anything to add to that?"

"Bring ladders too so we can clean the gutters and dust the ceiling and rafters," Hildegunn added.

"Good. Thank you."

"We have here a thank-you note from Maydell. 'Dear church

women, thank you for the lovely wedding gift. The quilt you made looks so pretty on our bed. Thank you too for the presents for the housewarming. You all make such pretty towels and linens and things. And we really needed a new broom. Sincerely, Mr. and Mrs. Gus Baard.' "

"Time we get going on another one. You never know when these young folks are going to take a shine to one another."

"Seems a shame more of our young women don't come to quilting."

Ingeborg knew it was Hildegunn speaking, but she didn't turn around. *Ignore her,* she commanded herself. *Let someone else stick up for those not here.* When no one did, Mary Martha continued.

"We'll move on to old business, then. Our first topic is the wagon of supplies for the Rosebud Reservation in South Dakota. We've had some discussion in the past, but today we will be bringing this to a vote. I was hoping we could all agree, but since that doesn't seem possible, we will vote, and like all other votes in our great country, the majority will rule. I pray that those not happy with the decision will gracefully accept the will of the group." She glanced around. "Is there any more discussion?"

Mrs. Magron raised her hand. "Yes, I have a question. If we help this new Indian reservation, how will we have enough to help those we usually provide assistance for?"

"That is a good question, and one I know concerns us all."

Sophie raised her hand. "I asked Thorliff if he could talk with the Indian agent up north and see what their needs are."

"And what did he find out?"

"The agent said the government has been providing according to their agreement this year. Since the new agent took over, the supplies have been getting through, so the people are not starving to death like they were before. He said they need more school supplies and will need more seeds for planting gardens and fields come spring. He has convinced more of the families to take up farming practices to help feed themselves."

"That is wonderful."

"Did he say anything about sickness?" Ingeborg asked.

Sophie shook her head. "No, he didn't."

"Thank you for following through on that. Anything else?" She glanced around the room. "Then I will call for a raising of hands. How many agree that we should assist the reservation that Astrid asked donations for?" She nodded and counted. "And against?" She nodded and counted again. "The majority rules. We will be collecting provisions for the Rosebud Indian Reservation. Who would like to be in charge of writing to them to see what supplies are needed most desperately?"

Kaaren raised her hand. "I will."

Ingeborg breathed a sigh of relief. Now she didn't have to. Her volunteering would have roiled the waters for sure. A *humph* from behind her made another woman's position quite clear.

"Is there any other business we need to address today?" Mary Martha waited a moment. "Good, then we can begin our quilting."

Ingeborg raised her hand. "I want to thank you all for helping make Emmy's quilt. She loves it. That and her doll go with her everywhere."

"Ellie made her the doll, right?"

"She did. Perhaps dolls for little girls would be a good thing to make for the wagon."

"Do Indian children play with dolls?"

"Isn't that the way every culture passes on how to care for their children?"

"I don't know. Just asking."

"Well, if anyone feels like making rag dolls, go right ahead. You know, I was thinking. What if we asked the schoolchildren if they would like to be involved in this project?"

Silence fell while they considered the new idea.

"Okay, let's take our places, and we can talk about such things among ourselves," Ingeborg said. "Kaaren, are you planning on reading to us today?"

"If you want."

"Ja, we want," Mrs. Geddick said.

Ingeborg felt like someone was staring daggers into her back. She didn't bother to turn around. This time Hildegunn could not blame her. Other than for the fact her daughter was the one who sent the request.

As the work got underway, she chose the first shift on the sewing machine. This way she would not get badgered into an argument. *Uff da,* she scolded herself. *You are not feeling very Christian, and here there wasn't even an argument. What had happened to change the hard feelings from last month?*

She turned around when a chair scraped back. Hildegunn stood and fetched a box from the side of the room. "I have to say that I don't approve our being coerced into helping those Indians so far away when there are those closer to home that need help too, but here are two quilts that I finished at home so we can start filling the barrels." She laid them across two chairs. "My Benny helped me choose the colors."

Coerced. The word made her want to jump up and scream in Hildegunn's face. *But she brought two quilts. This makes no sense whatsoever.*

Kaaren leaned over her shoulder. "Prayer in action, dear sister. We just saw a miracle happen."

"But isn't there something about giving with a joyful spirit?" she whispered back.

"True, but praise in everything tops that, I think, at least in this case."

And to think I wasted good sleeping hours stewing about this meeting.

Father in heaven, I stand, or rather sit, in awe. My Benny, *she'd said. Was that part of the transformation?* Whatever it was, God had done it. A miracle indeed. Now if He would work another and bring Astrid home.

6

Dear Mr. Landsverk,

I owe you the most abject of apologies. Today in the mail I received a large envelope from the hospital in Chicago. It contained two letters you had written to me that somehow had gone astray in the mailing process. I felt hurt that you had not lived up to your word to write to me, and therefore I did not write to you either. It wasn't your fault, and I should not have jumped to conclusions.

Joshua felt like jumping himself. He had finally heard from Astrid. He continued reading.

So please accept my plea for forgiveness and forgive me.

Another act of forgiveness. Was this a lesson he had to keep learning over and over? His first rush of feeling was to continue being angry. But now that he was reading the letter for the second time, all he could find was gratitude—and indeed forgiveness. He reinforced the knowledge by repeating one of the verses he'd learned. " 'Forgive, and ye shall be forgiven.' " He said it once more for good measure. Maybe this was something he would have to repeat for the rest of his life. Maybe that wasn't such a bad idea. He stared at the letter, the ink blurring on the page. So much had happened. How would he get it all sorted out?

> I am at a college in Athens, Georgia, enrolled in their four-month missionary school. I have applied for a two-year term of service, and we shall see if that is approved.

Was it being Christian to pray that she not be approved? He grimaced. Good thing God could see the whole picture and would do the best for everyone. Where had he heard that? Most likely from Pastor Solberg. And to think he almost didn't get off in Blessing when he returned from Iowa but had planned to continue on west until the train tracks ran out. Except he kept remembering Astrid.

> I didn't make the final decision until the day before I was to leave Chicago, and I still struggle with the question of whether I did the right thing. I know it caught all of my family by surprise. It did me too. I will have time at home before I leave for Africa, if I am chosen to go, so we can talk then.

That was his glimmer of hope. He counted off the months. March, April, May, June. She'd be home the end of June. If only he could have his house done by then. But as soon as they were able, he and Trygve would be heading south to dig wells and install windmills. No matter where he was, he'd be back to Blessing when Astrid was home. He had to be if he was to know God's will for them. He read the second letter.

Dear Mr. Landsverk,

So I have to apologize again and commend you for your courage in returning to Iowa to speak with your father. Forgiving one another seems to be a difficulty for all of us at one time or another. Perhaps that is why Jesus told so many stories about it. I should have read both letters before I replied, but I was so compelled to write immediately that I didn't, and then someone knocked on my door, as it was time for another appointment.

I have now met all my instructors and all the people in the missionary program. This promises to be an interesting four months. Actually three months and three weeks now. And yes, I am counting the weeks until I get on the train to head west. I miss my family and Blessing so very much.

Mr. Landsverk, are we good enough friends that I can write to you my heart and struggles?

Sincerely,
Dr. Astrid Bjorklund

Joshua sighed and stared at the perfect penmanship. Did she do everything so perfectly? Maybe if he wrote more often, she would write more often, and they would indeed get to know each other better. He shook his head. Writing letters, putting ideas and thoughts on paper, was not easy for him. If only he had done so for his mother, that would have pleased her so much. The thought manacled his throat. He could never ask her to forgive him. It was too late. What if he'd not gone to Iowa? It might have been too late there too. He heaved a sigh that made him shake. Gratitude for the one and sorrow for the other. The light and the dark of it. Was all of life to be like that?

Hearing the bell tinkle for supper, he folded the letter and laid both envelopes on the bedside table. Now he knew what he was going to do that evening. Work on that idea for the windmill self greaser and write to Astrid—or rather Dr. Bjorklund, in spite of the fact that she was Astrid to him and always had been. He hesitated at the thought.

If they were to have a future together, he needed to understand her as a doctor too. Putting those thoughts aside, he headed for supper.

The new man at the boardinghouse was standing in the arched entry to the dining room. Miss Christopherson had mentioned him last night, but he had eaten before Joshua came back.

"Hello. I'm Joshua Landsverk." He thrust out his hand.

"Daniel Jeffers."

"Do you have a table?"

He shrugged. "I didn't realize they were assigned."

"They aren't, but when one has been here for a time . . . well, we are all creatures of habit. You can join me if you'd like." *Joshua Landsverk, this is not like you. What is going on?*

"I'd be pleased. Conversation is always pleasant during a meal."

Joshua thought of all the years of silence at his father's table. And how much he enjoyed a meal at the Bjorklunds'. Again, light and dark. Once they were seated, he asked, "What brings you to Blessing?"

"It's a long story, convoluted, with no ending in sight."

"Really?"

"Did you know a man who bought the general store here, called himself Harlan Jeffers?"

"No. When I lived here before, Penny Bjorklund owned it, and when I returned, she had it back. I know there was some unpleasantness with the interim owner."

"The man purported to be Harlan Jeffers. Jeffers is my father's and, of course, our family's last name. My father disappeared on a trip west, so I came looking for him. I hoped and prayed the man I'd heard was here was my father. It wasn't. That man had somehow appropriated my father's name and took the money he had with him."

"So you caught him?"

"No. He was encouraged to leave here by the good folks of Blessing and was gone before I came to town."

Miss Christopherson stopped at their table. "Good evening,

gentlemen. I'm glad to see you have met. Supper tonight is baked chicken with mashed potatoes and gravy. How will that suit you?"

"Are there choices?" Mr. Jeffers asked.

"Yes. You take it, or I could look for some leftovers from dinner for you." She smiled.

"Chicken sounds fine. It smells wonderful."

"Mrs. Sam is the cook here, and this boardinghouse is known all up and down the railroad as the place to get a good meal." Joshua looked up at Miss Christopherson. "I'll have the chicken too."

She nodded and glanced back at Jeffers. "Mr. Landsverk usually has coffee. Is that all right with you?"

"Yes, of course."

When she moved on to the next table, Jeffers watched her. "They are fortunate to have such a good staff here." He turned back to Joshua. "Do you want to hear more?"

"I do."

"When I learned of the havoc the imposter Jeffers had wreaked here in Blessing, I was more determined than ever to clear my father's name. And to find him, or at least a trace of him. So I took the train back East, stopping in every town the train stopped at and asking the same questions. Did a man named Harlan Jeffers stop here during the fall of last year? I'd go to the saloons, the sheriff's office, the banks, any public place. When I left, I always made sure everyone had my address just in case."

Miss Christopherson set their plates before them, and Lily Mae filled their coffee cups. "Anything else, gentlemen?"

"Thank you. This looks delicious," Mr. Jeffers said.

Joshua was intrigued. What a story this was. "Did you ever find a trace?"

Mr. Jeffers shook his head. "I went back home for the winter and to set my father's affairs in order, assuming that since he had never contacted us, he was dead. He would never willingly treat my mother like that—not let us know where he was, I mean—let alone his business associates."

"What did your father do?"

"He worked for a farming machinery company and invented things on the side. He'd received some encouragement on improvements to a seeder and was checking on a list of possible partners."

"And he just disappeared?" Joshua cut his chicken and took a bite. "Was he sick at all?"

"No, at least not that we knew of. He was forty-seven years old. They say I look just like him. He had just been paid for a good sale and said he would be heading for home after another two stops."

"From where?"

"He didn't say. And I didn't think to ask. Two years ago the telephone was such a new device that I always marveled I could even be talking that many miles apart."

"So you've talked with the people he saw last?"

"Yes, in Alexandria and Fargo. After that I'm not sure if he headed north or continued west. When I heard of a man in Blessing with the name of Jeffers, I came on up here. And now I am back."

"Why did you come back?"

"I liked the people here. They made me feel welcome, and I . . ." He paused. "I feel like I owe them something. Crazy, I know. But that phony Jeffers tarnished my family's name here. My mother has gone to live with my sister and her husband, and I don't want to live in that big old house alone. So on one hand I'm searching for information on my father, and I guess on the other . . . well, I liked it here. 'Bout time I settled down, as my mother reminds me. Besides, Thorliff and Haakan Bjorklund purchased a set of my father's blueprints. I need to know if they were able to make a prototype of the seeder and how well it worked, if they did."

"Now that part I do understand." Interesting that no one had mentioned that. He shrugged inwardly. *Must have happened when I was gone from here.*

"What about you?"

Joshua told him his story, another tale of someone coming back to Blessing. "This is becoming a real boom town with all the building going on."

Miss Christopherson approached the table. "Would you care for more supper, or are you ready for your dessert now?"

Joshua smiled at her. "It's apple pie, right?"

"Yes, sir, dried-apple pie." She smiled back. "Your favorite."

"Pie for me."

"Me too. The meal was delicious," Mr. Jeffers said.

She took their plates and returned to the kitchen.

"I'm thinking I can move the business to Blessing that my father and I were putting together," Jeffers said. "The railroad is right here, lots of farms, and North Dakota farmers are real progressive thinkers." He propped his elbows on the table. "So what is it you do, Mr. Landsverk?"

"I dig wells and erect windmills over them. Or just put up the windmill if the well is dug deep enough. Hjelmer Bjorklund goes out and gets the orders, and then our crew comes along and does the job. I bought a lot here in town and plan to put up a Sears and Roebuck house come spring."

"There's a lot of new houses and new businesses here since my first visit."

"There's talk of building a hospital. People here all work together. It's an amazing thing. A good thing."

"I'll be talking with Thorliff Bjorklund in the morning. He said he might run an article about my father in his newspaper and perhaps can search for information this way."

"Like a missing person story." Joshua inhaled the fragrance from the warm apple pie set before him and took a bite. "Thank you, Miss Christopherson. Delicious."

"I'll tell Mrs. Sam."

Jeffers took a bite. "Tell her thank-you from me too."

They finished their pie and coffee, talking about things in general, and then headed out the arched doorway. Joshua bade him good-night and returned to his room. This was a great story to write to Astrid about. A mystery in their own backyard. Although she probably knew about the first part, but not what happened when Daniel Jeffers left.

Joshua stacked the drawings he'd been working on for the windmill. He was about ready to take some of the iron pieces and see about constructing a full-sized one to make sure it worked. He and Mr. Sam had been discussing how to build it for weeks and now was the time to do it.

Sitting down with a fresh sheet of paper, he started writing again, this time with a pen.

> Dear Dr. Bjorklund,
>
> I had the most amazing conversation over supper tonight. Remember a man by the name of Jeffers who came to town looking for his father because he'd heard the man who bought Penny's store was named Jeffers?

He continued writing the story until the end, filling two sheets of paper.

> Isn't this an interesting mystery? I think we should make up a Wanted poster of Harlan Jeffers and put it up in towns all around. Be nice if we had a photograph of him.

He laid his pen down and stretched his arms above his head. He'd not done this much writing at one time since he graduated from school. Farmers didn't need to write a lot, especially if they were the hands and feet and not the brains of the outfit. He stared out the window. Moonlight was casting shadows on the snow, which was melting fairly quickly.

He'd checked his lot, but the ground was still frozen with ten, twelve inches of snow and drifts. He'd not measured down in the cellar. There would be standing water down there pretty soon.

Returning to his letter, he continued.

> Thank you for writing to me, and you are forgiven. I was thinking that maybe in your letter back to me, you could tell me about something that you like. I'll tell you one. We had Mrs. Sam's dried-apple pie for supper. That woman makes the best pies anywhere. My mother baked good pies too, especially her rhubarb cream pie, the first every spring.

He started to tell her about his trip back home and then decided not to. He needed to think on it some more first.

> I hope you are enjoying your classes and the warmer weather. The snow looks to be melting here, but Hjelmer reminded me that many blizzards have hit during March so not to get my hopes up.
>
> Your friend,
> Joshua Landsverk

THE NEXT MORNING after breakfast, he walked over to Hjelmer's house, and the crew took his sleigh out to Lars's machine shed, where they were building the house on wheels for the well-drilling crew. A door at either end of the mobile house allowed for ventilation for the hot summer months, and shelves and cupboards lined one end, along with a small stove that vented through the slightly pitched roof. On one long side were two long narrow doors on hinges that lifted up, screens on the inside. Brackets and braces lined the outer walls for carrying long pipes and the blades. Now they were building the boxes to attach underneath for the tools.

Hooks for hammocks were drilled into the two-by-fours for strength. Most of the lumber would be hauled in one wagon or shipped directly, depending on the location.

"I think we should call our company Blessing Well Drillers and Windmills," Hjelmer said, standing back to study their handiwork. "We'll paint that right on the side."

"Pretty long for a name," Haakan answered. "What about Blessing Wells or Blessing Drillers? When someone asks you can always explain."

"True. Maybe we should just say Bjorklund Enterprises." Hjelmer stroked his chin and repeated the name.

"Sounds pretty highfalutin." Haakan sighted down one of the boards to see how straight it was.

"Highfalutin means what?" Trygve asked the question Joshua was thinking.

"A fancy term for *fancy*."

"Oh."

"Did you know Jeffers is back in town?" Joshua asked the group.

"Not the imposter?" Haakan frowned.

"No, the real Jeffers' son who was here looking for his father. He's thinking of moving to Blessing. Bringing his business here."

"Has he found out anything about his father?"

"No. But not for lack of trying. Sure makes you wonder."

"Well, all I got to say is that imposter better never stick his nose back in Blessing." Hjelmer set to sawing the end off one of the boards. "He wouldn't have a nose for long."

"But what if he killed the real Jeffers to get his money?" Trygve asked as he slid his hammer into the loop on his tool belt and carried the board over to the side of the rig. "Things like that do happen, you know."

"And his identity?"

Haakan shook his head. "There is probably some reasonable explanation."

"Well, maybe we'll never know."

"I hope young Jeffers finds out what happened to his pa. Not knowing is an awful way to live," Joshua said as he braced the board against the others and drove the first nail in. All those months he'd not known about his family. That was something he had to forgive himself for, not an easy task.

"Thorliff will find out, you watch." Trygve slammed a nail home. "I heard the dinner bell. Ilse was making beef potpie."

As the men headed for the house, Joshua kept thinking back to the conversation the night before. Was this what making friends felt like? He'd not had much time for friends since grammar school. Could friends be part of this new life of his? He glanced around at the men he was walking with. Or were they already?

7

Athens, Georgia

What else struck you anew in the book of Matthew?" Rev. Thompkins asked as he looked out over his class, eyebrows raised.

Astrid thought hard about the question. She'd reread Matthew again to see what else stood out.

Dr. Gansberg raised his hand. "I guess I keep going back to the Sermon on the Mount. If we had no other Scripture, all that one needs to live the God kind of life is right there. People say they can't understand the Bible, but Jesus laid God's plan out very clearly, it seems to me."

"You are right, Dr. Gansberg. I'd like to suggest you take the reading one step further and memorize those chapters." He looked around to include the entire class. "When we memorize the Word, the

Holy Spirit can bring it back to our minds when we most need it. We can indeed feed on it as we are commanded over and over, especially in the Psalms. God's Word is food for our souls and spirits, but more than that, the answers are there for us to live by."

Astrid thought back to all the verses Pastor Solberg had required them to memorize, how they had groaned and secretly complained. Someone had grumbled out loud once, and they all had to memorize Psalm 139. No one made that mistake again.

"Something I have learned through the years is that the more Scripture I memorize, the more easily I learn other things. My mind is clearer, and I reason better," Rev. Thompkins said, looking right at her.

She leaned back in her chair.

He smiled. "Try it; don't take my word for it."

He might as well have said, "I dare you."

"You heard right. Memorize the entire Sermon on the Mount, and that's just the beginning."

He pulled some folded papers out of his pocket. "This is what I do. I write the verses I want to memorize on papers to fit into my pocket, so when I have a few moments, I can pull them out and go over them. I break a chapter down into several sections and work on one at a time. I am always pleased when I realize how much I have accomplished, and rather painlessly as well. I was amazed at first when a teacher taught me this procedure."

"At least men have pockets," Astrid commented before she caught the thought and stomped on it.

The class chuckled. Mrs. Gansberg leaned forward. "By tomorrow you will have a pocket that can go with you everywhere, my dear."

When she turned to thank her benefactress, she caught a rolling of eyes and an exasperated look from one of the younger men, who often sat with young Highsmith. He'd remarked a few days ago about single women in the mission field being a liability because they'd need to have men around to protect them.

Her thought then and now was that when that young man was injured or caught one of the deadly diseases, he might be really grateful to have a doctor near, even if she was female.

God, I don't want to have get-even thoughts like that. You said to take every thought captive unto Christ. How do I do that? They sneak up on me and get away before I have time to grab them.

"Anyone else, what did you notice?"

Astrid raised her hand, and at his nod, she said, "Many people were healed just by touching Jesus' clothes. Often they didn't ask or thank Him. Sometimes He didn't even say anything. But the verses say many were healed."

"Interesting, isn't it?"

"Do you believe miracles like that go on today?" There. She'd voiced one of the things that bothered her. Was she alone in wondering this?

"What does the Bible say about time and God?"

"That time means nothing to Him."

Someone else added, "That He is the same yesterday, today, and forever."

"Another place says that God never changes."

"If that is true, what does it mean?" Rev. Thompkins locked eyes with her, but instead of intimidating her, she felt he really cared that she understand.

"That if He cared for them before He will care for them now?"

"You are correct."

"But then why don't we see it?" *Many times I did all I could and prayed and others prayed, and still the patient died.*

"All right, everyone open your Bibles to Matthew 17:19. What does Jesus say to His disciples when they asked Him why they couldn't heal people or drive out demons?"

"The Scripture says because of their unbelief."

"And how much faith did they need to cast the mountain into the sea?"

"The size of a mustard seed."

"How big is a mustard seed?"

"Very small."

He looked around the class. "I tell you that as God grows your faith, you too will see miracles. But you must have eyes that see and ears that hear." He bowed his head. "Lord God, increase our faith that we may see you in action. Amen." He smiled around the room. "I'll see you tomorrow."

"Would you like to join us for a glass of iced tea?" Dr. Gansberg asked as they left the classroom. "We feel in need of a restorative."

"As do I." Astrid pretended to mop her forehead. "I sure hope his promise of thinking more clearly because I am memorizing Scripture is valid and true. I can tell I need to know my Bible far better than I do."

"You think that might be one of the reasons why we are here?" Dr. Gansberg asked.

His wife patted his arm. "Let's get fortified before the discussion takes off again."

When they sat at a table, one of the students working there brought them glasses of sweet tea, as they called it. Astrid drank more than a sip, relishing the cold slipping down her throat.

"You asked a question today that has bothered me ever since I started studying medicine," Dr. Gansberg said. "Thank you for having the courage to ask."

"About the miracles?"

He nodded. "I have seen people live, and I have seen people die, but no one has lived because he touched the hem of my coat. Never have I been able to say, 'Take up your bed and walk. Your faith has made you well.' Nor have I ever heard the blind rejoicing because now they could see." He drew rings with his glass on the tabletop.

Is there more that we don't know or see? Of course there is. Dear God, how do we do the healing you said we should?

She could hear Rev. Thompkins as if he were seated right there at the table with them. "You will find the answers to any question in the Word of God."

"Thank you for the tea break. I need to go start memorizing." Astrid pushed back her chair. "Thank you, both of you."

Back in her room she picked up her Bible, a tablet, and a pencil, adjourned to her shady nook, and turned to Matthew, chapter five. She read the chapter through, broke it down into sections, and started in. She read both silently and aloud, over and over again. She wrote out the blessing verses she had started with and then closed her eyes to see if she could brand the words on the backs of her eyelids. *Blessed are the merciful: for they shall obtain mercy* caught in her throat because of all she had grown up with in Blessing and all the healing God did through so many doctors and nurses. She paused to pray a word of thanksgiving, and time disappeared.

When the bell from the brick tower above the chapel building chimed for supper, she tucked the paper into the waistband of her skirt. Pocket or no pocket, she was going to class tomorrow with a good part of that chapter in her mind.

Along with a beginning list of questions to which she wanted answers.

THAT NIGHT SHE took a deep breath and started a letter to Elizabeth, deciding to add more each day.

> Dear Elizabeth and Thorliff, and Inga too,
>
> I know you were terribly disappointed when I came here instead of back to Blessing. I hope that by now you have forgiven

me and that you are both praying with me that I learn what God's will is in all this. I keep reminding myself that two years will go by very quickly, and yes, I'm not really planning on anything until I know if I am approved or not.

My favorite class is being taught by a returned missionary, Rev. Thompkins. His love for God just flows out of him, like it does from Pastor Solberg. He has challenged us to memorize the entire Sermon on the Mount and complete books of the Bible. It is a good thing that I memorize quickly. I think all my medical training helped with that.

This campus is a lovely place, and I am so grateful for warm weather. I know Mor would be enthralled with all the blooming flowers and trees and bushes. Everything blossoms, and so many have wonderful fragrances.

My big concern is finding something to do that uses what I have been trained for. A class on tropical diseases starts next week. Is it awful to say I am looking forward to that? More tomorrow. Back to memorizing.

She looked at the letter. Maybe she should send this part first so that Elizabeth would hear her apology. *No, I'll wait one more day.*

How strange it was not to be helping her mother with spring cleaning. Every year she had helped her mother scrub walls and floors, beat rugs, wash curtains and bedding, and wash the windows—if there wasn't still frost on them. Funny . . . well, not funny but peculiar, for she never had cared much for all that cleaning. Of course it looked lovely when finished, but then the house wasn't that dirty before they began. The Saturday before Palm Sunday everyone would be at the church, cleaning and polishing every inch. The thought made her more homesick than ever. What kind of weather were they having in Blessing? Why had no one written to her? Was everyone mad at her for not coming home?

THEY HAD NO classes from Wednesday of Holy Week on. Many of the students who lived nearby had gone home for the entire week. Dean Highsmith had invited the remaining missionary students to join him and his wife for dinner after church on Easter Sunday.

Astrid stared at her reflection in the mirror. She had no new bonnet or hat for Easter, nor a new spring or summer dress. Other years she and her mother had sewn new gowns for Easter. She'd thought to sew a new dress for Inga too. Had Mor done that? She just wasn't getting enough news from home.

On her way to the service, a thought struck. *I can pick up a telephone and call Mor. Surely everyone will be at their house.* The decision lent wings to her feet. Suddenly the need to hear her mother's voice consumed her like flames devouring split wood. She silenced her thoughts as she entered the church.

The pastor raised his voice when the organ silenced. "He is risen!"

"He is risen, indeed," responded the congregation. They turned the pages in their hymnals to the opening hymn. After the last hallelujah as the Easter story was read, Astrid felt as though she were one of the women running to the tomb. She could feel the shock of seeing the magnificent angel, the joy that Christ had indeed done what He'd said He would do—rise again, overcome death. Walk and talk with His disciples. Christ the Lord is risen today. Hallelujah!

"This is the first time in my life that I am not at the church I grew up in for Easter," she confided to the Gansbergs as they left the church. "We don't have a fancy organ like this one or carved pews and carpet on the floor, but there is much love and rejoicing that we can celebrate together." She paused for a moment. "I did love hearing the organ, however. I think heaven is going to sound like Easter Sunday all of the time."

Mrs. Gansberg put an arm around her shoulders and hugged her. "Astrid, you say the best things."

Astrid blinked back a quick onslaught of eye moisture. How she wanted to hug her mother. Far too. "I'm going to telephone my family after dinner. It will surely shock them, but I thought it would be a good idea."

"Your mother must miss you dreadfully."

But she would never complain. "My mother is my hero. No one could have a better mother than I have."

DEAN HIGHSMITH AND his wife were gracious dinner hosts, but Astrid couldn't help thinking of home, where everyone would be gathered together after the Easter service, enjoying Mor's cooking. A pang of homesickness hit her hard. She startled back to the conversation around her when she realized the dean's nephew was speaking to her.

"I still do not understand why a young female as yourself would want to go to Africa." He stared at her with raised eyebrows.

Astrid swallowed and made herself relax. "I think I have explained that this was not my idea but a calling from God. I am just praying that I heard Him correctly." How she managed to smile at the pompous young man was beyond her. She kept a smile in place. "Maybe some things are not for us to understand but to seek and trust." She glanced up to see Dean Highsmith covering his mouth with his napkin. Did he think this amusing?

Glancing at the nephew, she knew he didn't. Actually she wondered how he could swallow his food, his collar was so tight.

"There is something I don't understand."

He nodded, as if granting her permission to speak.

"Why does my being here bother you so much?" There, she had put what had been bothering her right out in the open.

His neck and shoulders stiffened. "I—I see it as a waste of resources."

"A waste?" She tipped her chin down and slightly to the side.

"Yes. You are taking the place of a man to do this job."

"I see. And how many trained male doctors have applied since I did?"

His eyes flashed. "That is beside the point."

"All right, children, this has gone far enough. I declare a moratorium on any further discussion. We will wait and see what God reveals to us, for we know and trust that He will do exactly that. As the Scripture says, 'Be ready to answer when you are questioned.' " He raised a hand toward his sputtering nephew. "I know that was not a direct quote, but that was the meaning of the verse." He laid his folded napkin beside his plate. "Let us adjourn to the veranda, where the dessert will be served." He pushed back his chair and smiled at the others.

On their way out, Astrid asked Dean Highsmith where there was a telephone she could use. He showed her to his study. "Use mine."

"How will I pay you?"

"Let this be my gift to you."

"But—" As he raised his hand, she nodded. "Thank you. You are most generous."

When she heard Gerald Valders' voice asking what number was wanted, she nearly burst. He didn't need a number. He needed a name. "Ingeborg Bjorklund, please."

There was a pause. "Astrid, is that you?"

"It is indeed. Happy Easter, Gerald. Or should I call you Mr. Valders now that you are a papa?"

"Oh, our Benny. What a gift you have given us. I will tell him I talked with his Doc Bjorklund, and he'll shout and clap. Let me ring your house." His chuckle tickled her ear.

"Hello."

A boulder stopped in the middle of Astrid's throat. She couldn't force a word past it.

"Hello?"

"Mor, I—"

"Astrid. Oh, thank you, God. Haakan, it is Astrid calling us. Happy Easter!"

Astrid could hear shouting and laughing. Tears nearly blinded her. "Happy Easter, Mor!" *Oh, Lord Jesus, I want to go home.*

"Where are you?"

"I am at Dean Highsmith's house. He invited all of us who stayed on campus to have dinner with him and his wife. I just had to hear your voice. I miss you all so much."

She could hear her mother sniffling. "I sent you a letter this week with all the news, but I forgot to ask you to send me some of my summer dresses. It is too warm here for wool skirts and long-sleeved waists."

"Ja, I will."

"Everyone is all right there?"

"Elizabeth is not feeling well. She's looking pale and tired all the time."

"Have you given her a going over?"

"She keeps putting me off. Says she just needs more rest. I've been helping her some at the surgery."

"Spring coming will do us all a lot of good. You've had more snow?"

"Ja, and freezing at night. But the sun is getting warmer. I am glad you are where it is warm and the sun shines."

"Thank you, Mor. I need to be going. I wish you could come and see the flowers. I sniff a different one for you every day. I love you."

"And I love you. Learn all you can."

Astrid hung up the receiver and wiped her eyes. What a marvelous invention to bring such joy across the many miles between home and Georgia. *What could be wrong with Elizabeth? She was in great health when I left Blessing in August.* Tired all the time, pale? So many things could start with those symptoms. She needed more information.

8

Blessing, North Dakota

"You didn't tell her that I nearly fainted at the piano on Easter, did you?"

"No, Elizabeth, I didn't. But she asked me some questions, and now I am asking you some questions. And I expect honest answers."

Elizabeth rolled her eyes. "When have I not been honest with you?"

"I'm not sure, but I think you know what is wrong."

"I've missed my second monthly."

"I suspected that."

"I was being so careful." Elizabeth lay back against the pillows on the bed. "I should be through the worst of it in another month or so."

"Are you keeping food down?"

"Not much. I force myself to eat small amounts and lie down afterward. Sometimes that helps, and sometimes it doesn't."

"You need to be drinking warm water, not coffee. We could flavor it with a little honey and ginger."

"All right." Elizabeth grabbed her hand. "You know I'll do whatever I have to do to carry this baby."

"I know, and right now I'm saying bed rest for a few days at least. Sitting in the sunshine might help. Let me think of some things in my simples that will calm your stomach. Have you told Thorliff?"

Elizabeth sighed. "No, because he will only worry. We've been so careful since we lost the last one."

"Well, it does take two." Ingeborg grasped Elizabeth's wrist and counted her pulse. "Does Thelma know?"

"I'm sure she has figured it out. I think Thorliff is afraid to mention it, or he deludes himself into thinking it's something else. Like I have." She lowered her gaze, shaking her head. "Can we keep this news from spreading throughout Blessing, at least for right now?"

"I don't know why not. But remember we have some mighty astute women who will most likely figure it out." Ingeborg laid the back of her hand against Elizabeth's cheek.

"I'm not running a fever."

"I didn't think you were, but I learned long ago not to take anything for granted."

"You are wise. Sorry I snapped at you."

"Do you find yourself unusually touchy?"

"Oh my, yes. That should have been an indication." She thumped her fist on the covers of the bed. "This is taking a big chance."

Ingeborg watched her daughter-in-law and wished she could take away some of the pain and fear. "God must want this baby to come into the world, and He figures you and Thorliff are the best parents for little him or her."

Elizabeth leaned back against the pillows, eyes closed. "I keep reminding myself that with God nothing is impossible. Even a healthy baby and a strong mother." Silence stretched for a bit. When she spoke, her voice was soft and sounded far away. "Isn't it ironic that I, the one who loves to help babies into this world, should have so much trouble having my own?"

"How well I know. After Astrid . . ." Ingeborg sat down on the edge of the bed, her mind praying while her medical eyes studied her patient. How to get her daughter-in-law to just rest and let the worries go? Sometimes knowing too much was a cross to bear instead of an aid. She decided the question didn't really need an answer. After all, she had none. Except that long years ago she'd learned that life was not fair and not always understandable. The only thing one could absolutely count on was God himself, and for some unknown reason He seemed to feel farther away when one needed Him the most.

Going by feelings rather than faith was the culprit. God said He was the same yesterday, today, and forever. So if that was true, and she absolutely believed God's Word was true, then there was no possible way that He would leave one of His children to suffer alone. His love was too great for that. She understood that was where faith came in, and faith had to grow and be strengthened just like muscles did.

"I can tell you are thinking." Elizabeth's smile lacked her usual sparkle.

"Of course. I'm thinking on how much God loves us and lives up to His Word, which says He will never leave nor forsake us. No matter what."

"So what is He telling you to do with all this?" She rested her hand on her abdomen.

"Same as He always does. To hold His hand and keep on walking with Him."

"You said I had to stay in bed."

Ingeborg smiled her gentle, loving smile. "As long as you keep a sense of humor, you'll be all right."

"Pa, Gamma is here" came a voice from the hallway. "You didn't tell me."

"Guess who." Elizabeth raised her eyebrows.

"In here, little one. My lap is waiting for you," Ingeborg called.

Inga burst through the door that Thorliff had opened and, darting across the room, threw herself against Ingeborg's knees. "Did you see Scooter? He's this big now." She held her hand waist high on herself.

"Is he really?"

"Some of us have a slight tendency to exaggerate." Thorliff leaned against the doorjamb as if hesitant to enter. Arms crossed, he glanced from his wife to his mother.

"I wonder where she got it." Innocence was not always easy to portray, but Ingeborg made him chuckle.

"Innocent until proven guilty." He shot questioning looks his wife's way. "Would it be better if a certain someone went out to Grandma's to play with Emmy?"

Inga glanced over her shoulder at her father. "Gamma is here, so Emmy can come here to play with me."

Ingeborg stifled a chuckle. Inga had far too much reasoning power for a child approaching her fourth birthday. Maybe that was because she was around adults so much, but still, she was beyond her years.

"Let's let it be for today."

"All right, but I need to get over to the office," Thorliff said. "She can come with me or—"

"She can stay here." Ingeborg hugged Inga and whispered in her ear. "You'll be good and quiet and help mamma feel better, won't you?"

Inga nodded and turned to her mother. "Doctors don't get sick."

"What makes you think that?" Elizabeth asked.

" 'Cause how can you take care of sick people if you are sick?" She stated it in a way that said, How could anyone think differently?

"That's a good question. I think Grandma is going to go check on my patients, and you can sit in here with a puzzle, go play in the kitchen with Thelma, or go with Pa to the office. I am going to take a nap."

"Thelma is scrubbing the floor. She told me to leave." Inga switched her attention to her father. "Can I draw on big pieces of paper?"

He nodded. "I have to be writing, so you can write too."

"And Scooter can come?"

"Let's go get him." He looked from his mother to his wife. "I'll be back later."

Inga gave her grandmother a kiss, another to her mother, and trotted out the door with her father.

"I'm not sure if that was a threat or a promise." Elizabeth sighed. "Can you please bring me a basin in case I need it?"

"I will and I'll also bring some warm honey and ginger water to be sipped. Then I'll check the waiting room."

As Ingeborg saw Elizabeth's patients, she kept repeating herself. "Dr. Elizabeth needs some extra rest. You'll have to make do with me today." But in spite of that, the morning flew by as if blown by the north wind.

She had the pleasure of telling Dorothy that it did indeed appear she might be with child again. Her Adam was now about ten or eleven months old. They'd be very close in age, but too late to worry about that now. She suggested ginger tea for nausea.

After checking on the tenderness on Benny's right stump, she and Rebecca tried some new ways of padding.

"So you are using your crutches all the time?" Ingeborg asked.

"Not at home. I scoot there." His cheeky grin made her laugh.

At home. He knew he had a home now. "You've been here how long now?"

"I came just after Christmas. Does the snow stay here all year around?"

Ingeborg shook her head. "No, but as the snow melts, the mud gets outrageous. You try walking outside with your crutches, and the ends of your wooden legs will sink in to your knees."

He looked to Rebecca.

"I tried to tell you," she said, "but once it dries out, you'll be able to use the wagon too."

"Have you thought about a wheelchair?" Ingeborg asked.

"Gerald has been looking for one, but they are so cumbersome. We were talking with Mr. Landsverk, and he's thinking of a way to make lighter wheels."

"Wonderful." Ingeborg patted Benny's shoulder. "How's school going?"

His grin faded. "I'm way behind."

"I have no doubt you'll catch up. We'll make sure you get extra help." Ingeborg looked to Rebecca. "Next time I come to town, I'll bring some wool that's not been carded yet. We'll try that for padding."

"Thank you. Come on, Benny. Let's get you back to school. Pretty soon we won't be able to pull the sled at all."

Ingeborg went back and checked on Elizabeth. She was sound asleep, the worry lines on her face smoothed out with rest. *Lord, bring healing and strength here. A healthy baby and a healthy mother—that's what we ask for. And thank you for your answers in advance.*

When Thorliff came home for dinner, she put the *Closed* sign on the door and joined him and Inga in the kitchen.

"Gamma, I colored all morning. Pa drew me cows and horses and houses, and I colored and colored. I made trees too. Scooter messed on the floor, and Pa got mad at him."

Thorliff shook his head. "It's a good thing I didn't say what I was thinking, or you'd have heard about that too." He turned to his daughter. "And who was it that was supposed to take the dog outside to do his business?"

Inga stared at the floor. "Me."

"And why didn't you?"

"I forgot."

"Did Scooter ask to go out?"

She shrugged, her lower lip a shelf. "I din't hear him."

Thelma set a plate of buttered bread on the table. "He always asks to go out, but you have to get there right away. He does well for one so young."

"This kitchen always smells good," Ingeborg commented.

"Thelma baked cookies."

"How is Elizabeth?" Thorliff asked.

"Sleeping. The more we can get her to sleep, the better. She also needs to eat as much as she can, even if it's only little bits at a time."

"Is it what I'm thinking?"

Ingeborg nodded, noting the pain in her son's eyes. "Let's not go feeling guilty but pray instead."

"But—"

"We are dealing with what is, not lugging guilt from yesterday or imagining the things that could, but rarely do, happen tomorrow. If you worry, she will worry, and then—"

"I will worry." Inga looked at her grandmother. "What is worry?"

Ingeborg and Thorliff both tried to stifle their laughter and failed.

Inga laughed along with them. Thelma served them steaming beef potpie, the crust a golden brown and the insides full of chunks of beef and root vegetables.

"I usually put cabbage in, but we ran out of it long ago." Thelma refused to sit down with them, rather serving first and eating later, a habit they couldn't get her to change.

INGEBORG HUNG OUT the *Closed* sign again after the last patient left at three o'clock. She checked on Elizabeth, who had been awake, eaten, drunk some of the warm honey-flavored water, and then dozed off again, now with Inga beside her on the bed, her book lying beside her. She left a message with Thelma that she would be back in the morning and headed for the post office before going home.

"I didn't hear the sleigh bells," Mrs. Valders commented when Ingeborg walked in.

"No, I was over at Elizabeth's, and I'm just going home." She leaned over to open their box and withdrew two letters, one from Astrid and one from Augusta. "What a delight."

"I thought you'd appreciate that."

"That little grandson of yours is an absolute joy," Ingeborg told Mrs. Valders. "We were working with a new way to pad his prosthesis."

"Benny is the best thing to come to Blessing in a long while. Though Toby and Gerald's arrival was the best of all. But Benny, he has so much love in that little body of his that he can't give it away fast enough."

"Why, Hildegunn, what a lovely thing to say." Ingeborg checked Andrew's and Kaaren's boxes, pulling out more mail. "This is a bountiful mail day for all of us."

"I know. I was going to call you to say you had mail, but you came in before I could. Have you given any thought to starting home mail service here?"

"Mail service?"

"With a box for each family at the lanes and a rider to deliver it. They are doing it in other places."

"Hmm. You mean something like the way we pick up cream cans?"

"That's right. And Mr. Valders says there will be a big push to sign more people up for the telephone this spring."

"Someone has to set the poles and string the wire. I imagine these men of ours will come up with a good way to do that too. Thank you." She waved the envelopes and headed out the door, grateful that Hildegunn didn't ask what she'd been doing all day.

As she started toward home, Ingeborg wished she had thought to bring the skis. She'd not been skiing this winter and wasn't sure why. Walking cross-country didn't work. She kept sinking into the snow, its crust melting so it wouldn't hold her. Going around by the road took extra time, but she wasn't in a hurry. The sun was shining, patches of earth were showing, and the Chinook breeze kissed her cheeks with spring's promises. She felt like raising her arms and twirling, just as she knew Inga would do with the least bit of prompting. She leaned over and gathered snow into a ball, lobbing it at a leaning fence post, her aim true. Not bad for a grandmother. A crow scolded her from a nearby cottonwood tree.

Spring had indeed arrived. Now if they could keep the river from flooding, all would be well. As if they had anything to say about it. *Lord, that too is in your province. Let the melt and the runoff balance out so the river keeps running to Winnipeg and stays within its boundaries.*

Within its boundaries. Astrid belonged to Blessing, not to Africa. Ingeborg was sure of it. And then a glimmer of hope rose up. Could Elizabeth's pregnancy be God's answer to Astrid?

9

Athens, Georgia

Restless was the only word she could think of to describe how she felt.

"So how many verses did you memorize last night?" Dr. Heinrich Gansberg asked.

"Two chapters of James."

He shook his head. "How do you do it?"

"Well, I had memorized some of the verses as a child, and I just filled in around them. Besides, I had all evening." *And I'm not used to having so much leisure time.* She thought a moment and then asked a question, one of many that had been bothering her. "Don't you miss practicing medicine? I mean . . ." She twisted her mouth back and forth and then chewed on her bottom lip. "It's been almost two months since I finished school, and I've not had anyone to treat."

"And this bothers you?" the older man asked with a smile. "I'm looking at this more like a vacation, a chance to rest up before I get to Africa and never again have more than a minute to memorize and study my Bible."

Astrid nodded slowly and blinked a couple of times. Her eyes felt sand laden, even though she'd been getting plenty of sleep. Perhaps it was the nightly nightmares that kept her from feeling rested. If she was lost in a blizzard one more time . . .

"What's really troubling you, Astrid?" Mrs. Gansberg asked. "Have you thought on the verses where Jesus says to rest in Him? To let Him carry the heavy load?"

Heaving a sigh, Astrid shook her head. "No, I haven't. I've been cramming as much Bible knowledge into my head as I can. It's like all the time I spent in the operating room and caring for patients in the wards is now used to pack my brain with Bible passages. I can't think that that is a wrong thing."

"No, not wrong. But there is a difference between good and best."

"What do you mean?"

"Look at it this way. Good is memorizing Scripture. Good is doing your lessons to the best of your ability. But best is spending time with Jesus. Talking with Him, listening to Him, praising Him."

Astrid gave a gentle little snort, more ladylike than how she felt. "Are you saying there needs to be some balance in my life? I don't think my self understands that concept."

"Many people don't." Her smile reminded Astrid of her tante Kaaren's smile, gentle and with the kind of love that made one feel bigger than they had before.

"Including me," the doctor interjected. "I've heard those comments more than once through our years together." The doctor sent his wife a look of love and gratitude that made Astrid feel like a special friend. While their professions brought them together, the time they'd spent talking grew a friendship the likes of which she'd not known before. Even more so because the Gansbergs were so much older and had already lived a good portion of their lives. Yet they treated Astrid as one of their equals.

"Thank you, both. You have become so dear to me in such a short time." She pushed back her chair and stood up. "I'll bring us some more iced tea. You want lemon cookies too?" she called over her shoulder as she walked across the courtyard, their favorite place to sit and visit. Stopping, she turned to wait for an answer.

"He always wants cookies. You know that." There was another of those smiles, so very similar to the smiles between her mor and far. Someday, Lord, I want those kinds of smiles between me and the husband you have in mind. A picture of flashing dark eyes above a brilliant smile skipped through her mind. She needed to write to Joshua again. Was he the one? Or was there someone else? Someone she hadn't met yet? While she'd not dwelt on these thoughts, they reappeared every once in a while. He did make her heart pick up speed, but— There it was again, the little three letter word that carried such a load. Besides, would he be willing to wait for her if she went to Africa? But if he didn't, then that would be God's decision, wouldn't it? She sighed.

"Thank you." She picked up the pitcher and the plate of cookies the cook's assistant handed her across the counter.

"Y'all have a good day now." The soft southern way of speaking fell gently on her ears. *"Have a good day."* As if one could fail to have a good day in a place of such beauty and serenity. No wonder missionaries liked to come back here for some respite. She strolled past the bed of vibrant peonies that hung droopy heads over the bamboo frame that kept them from being flattened by the rain. She had seen one floating in a clear glass bowl full of water and tipped upside down in a shallow bowl, which held it like it was in a vacuum. Like the water jar she used to set for the baby chicks, it bubbled out as the chicks drank from the saucer. Were the hens setting already? Had that nasty one made it through the winter without ending up in the stewpot? The back of her hands wore scars from being pecked by that hen. But she was such a good mother, managing to hatch and raise ten or twelve chicks with every setting. With her thoughts turned homeward, Astrid set the plate on the table and refilled the empty glasses.

Dr. Gansberg held up his full glass. "When I look at this, I am reminded about the lecture on water in Africa. How scarce clean water is, how we will need to boil the water we drink and cook with." He sipped from his glass, his eyes closed in bliss. "No one makes iced tea like the women in the South."

"That's one of the things that concerns me," Mrs. Gansberg said, her voice soft in the rustle of the magnolia trees overhead. "I know God says to fear not, but I have to be very careful not to do that. We went through a cholera epidemic after the spring floods one year, and I don't want to do such a thing again."

Astrid thought to the lecture they'd heard that morning from a returning missionary regarding the fearsome health situation in Africa. He'd spoken about the huge black mamba snakes that were quick to inflict their often fatal bite. Was that why she was having so many nightmares? The people there took for granted their having to keep vigilance against vipers, wild animals, and insects.

"And yet, in spite of all that," the teacher had said, "the Christians in Africa are the most joyous people you will ever meet. They truly understand that God delivers them from evil, that He provides for their needs, and that He is right there to answer when they call." He'd looked around at each of those listening. "And that, gentlemen and ladies, is why I keep going back to Africa."

A shiver had run up her back. Would she feel the same way after her two years? If she was allowed two years. And when did her thoughts turn from "have to go" to "be allowed to go"? This was one of those things that needed some thinking time.

THAT NIGHT IN her room with the door to the veranda open and grateful for a screen door that foiled the nightly insects, she took out the journal she jotted in occasionally and wrote her question: *Have to go or be allowed to go?* She wrote the date. *April 21, 1904.*

> Today I realized that I have had a change in my attitude toward serving in Africa. All along I've been not wanting to go there, but only to return to Blessing. Now I realize that going there to serve those far less fortunate than us is a privilege, and if this is God's will, I will go joyfully.

She studied that last word—*joyfully.* Did she really feel that, or was it just a nice or good thing to say? There was a difference between going and going joyfully. *Lord God, when did I turn into such a thinker?* She smiled at that one. Maybe that was one of the reasons she was here—to learn to think, to ponder, to memorize God's Word and let it sink deep into her most secret places, as the psalmist said. Feed on the Word.

She sighed and closed her journal, picking up her Bible instead. Tonight she wanted to finish memorizing James. So turning to James chapter one, she closed her eyes and repeated it from memory, then on to chapter two, only stumbling in two places and sneaking a peek to correct herself. She read through the first half, remembering when Pastor Solberg talked about the tongue and the evil it could do. The part about the bit on a horse in chapter three was very clear to her, after having worked with horses through the years. How many times had she wished she'd not said something? After she had the first part finished, she picked up her writing pad and pencil. She'd thought of sitting at the desk with an ink pen and well, but a pencil was so much easier.

Dear Mr. Landsverk,

Thank you for the letter I received last week. I am grateful you have forgiven me for being so short with you. Interesting, is it not, what missing mail can do to a friendship? You were so wise to go home to your family like that. What a shock it must have been to see your father in such a state. Sometimes sorrow does that to a spouse. The body experiences the sorrow, as does the mind and heart.

I am finding this a very peaceful interlude, for though I hear some of the others grumbling about all the work and study here, I can hardly keep from laughing. They ought to try medical school! I have been concerned that here I have no one to practice my medical skills on. My hands seem to itch for a stethoscope or scalpel, but if and when I go to Africa, I will dream of times of leisure like this.

I am memorizing whole books of the Bible. One of our professors, the one who teaches Bible, says that we will not always have the Scriptures available, so we must have the Word of God inside of us so that the Holy Spirit can bring it to mind when we need it. I think I remember Pastor Solberg saying much the same thing and assigning memory passages. Now I am grateful for all that too.

I cannot say I am missing the snow and cold of North Dakota. How Mor would love to see the flowers blooming here. As I learn more of Africa, I wonder why God has blessed our country so much more than that one. Someone said He is referred to as "the white man's God." How strange. Of course Dr. Red Hawk said the same thing. Is that how much of the world sees us?

I think I am becoming more of a questioner, if that is possible.

Your friend,
Dr. Astrid Bjorklund

She stared at the letter for a few moments. She already looked forward to hearing a reply and yet didn't have that anxious anticipation she knew Sophie had had over Hamre or even the soft anticipation Grace had had waiting for a letter from Jonathan. But Sophie's second marriage to Garth was calmer. Maybe all the medical training had taken some of the romance out of a possible relationship for her.

She addressed the envelope and picked up the ongoing letter to her mor and far.

> April 21 we sat under a whispering tree, drinking iced tea and nibbling on lemon cookies. Of course Dr. Gansberg does not nibble. In two bites the cookie is gone. His wife tries to remonstrate with him, but he gives her that special smile you give Far, and he reaches for another cookie.
>
> I have been in a wondering mood lately, just in case you haven't noticed. As I memorize Scripture, I have to think about it more. Perhaps that is one reason to memorize it, correct? I am in the book of James now, and goodness but James wrote a diatribe about the tongue. It can start a raging fire, and it makes me think of some of the hurtful things people have said through the years. How sad that we let ourselves do that when we could instead give someone words that are like golden apples or honey, as the psalmist says. I want to do the latter.
>
> How are Emmy and Inga getting along? Are they fast friends by now? I imagine Carl is feeling left out. I suppose by now he is twice the size of when I saw him.
>
> Thank you for telling me about Gus and Maydell's wedding. With Grace engaged to Jonathan, that just leaves Deborah and me who are still single. We will probably turn into old maids one of these days.
>
> How is little Benny doing? I so fell in love with him and almost wished I could adopt him myself. And what about Elizabeth? You didn't answer my questions yet. Is she feeling better?

I will address this letter tonight and send it off to you. Thank you for loving God and living His love for me.

Your loving daughter,
Astrid

With two letters ready to mail, she thought of writing a third—to Benny. If she printed carefully would he be able to read it now? She blinked and stretched. Then again, maybe tomorrow night. She'd gotten into the habit of turning her light out by ten o'clock. In spite of nightmares, she slept peacefully here, perhaps because she wasn't listening for a summons during the night. Which made the nightmares even more confusing. Should she have asked Mor to pray about them?

DEAN HIGHSMITH STOPPED her in the hall the next morning. "Dr. Bjorklund, the committee would like to conduct your interview tomorrow morning at ten."

Astrid took a deep breath, studying his face for any information. "Thank you. Do I need to bring anything?"

"Just yourself. I'll see you in the conference room then."

Astrid inhaled deeply. *All right, Father, how do I keep from stewing on this for the next twenty-four or twenty-six hours?*

A verse floated into her mind from the Sermon on the Mount. *Take therefore no thought for the morrow: for the morrow shall take thought for the things of itself.* She chuckled to herself. When this was all said and done, she'd have to tell Pastor Solberg about it. In the meantime she'd do what she needed to do and let God take care of tomorrow. *Please, Lord, help me keep from thinking on—no, stewing on—no, be honest and call it downright worrying, for that is what it is.*

10

Astrid took another deep breath. *Lord, I want to want what you choose, so please guide me through this process, and may the decision be yours, not mine.* With a fluttering heart she entered the conference room.

"Welcome, Dr. Bjorklund. It is good of you to come," said Dean Highsmith.

She was glad to see he would be leading the meeting. She remembered him to be fair-minded in her first interview with him. Schooling her features in a pleasant smile, she said, "Thank you." Was that the appropriate answer?

"Please be seated." He nodded to the only vacant chair remaining at the table.

Astrid took her seat, wishing her stomach would sit down with her and not go flitting about the ceiling like a moth after a lighted lamp. She nodded to those around the table as they were introduced. Rev. Thompkins, who taught the New Testament class, smiled at her as if it were just the two of them for a discussion. She breathed a sigh of relief, only a little sigh and as silent as possible so they wouldn't detect how tightly she was strung.

The man at the foot of the table with a neatly trimmed white beard shuffled the papers on the table in front of him. "Now, Dr. Bjorklund, we have some questions for you."

Astrid swallowed past the lump in her throat and nodded. What else could she do? Fear crept in, tapped on her shoulder, and leered, his dark eyes glittering.

"First of all, I do hope you have enjoyed your studies here, as I am sure they were quite different from those at medical school. We have never before had a young female come here directly after her medical schooling."

So I am the first. Is that good or bad? God, this is in your hands. She'd quit counting the times she'd told herself that since arising at dawn to sit out on her veranda and listen to the world come to life. She'd not heard meadowlarks calling, but other birds sang, and she'd wished she knew what they were. Oh, to be back out there.

Would dawn in Africa be like that? Another question she would ask the missionary on furlough who'd spoken to the group.

"I have. This has been a marvelous respite. The weather in either Illinois or North Dakota . . ." She shook her head, eliciting chuckles from those who knew what she meant. "Spring has barely started in either of those states yet."

"One thing we'd like to know, and I understand you wrote about this in your essays, what is it that made you decide to come here?"

"Do you mean here to this place or to the missionary school?"

"Both would be good."

"Rev. Schuman had a hand in both. He spoke at Blessing Lutheran

Church last summer, and when he said that medical missionaries were needed, I felt he was looking right at me. I have struggled with that thought ever since. Was . . . is God calling me into missionary service? I have not heard any direct answers, but I knew that I did not want to go to Africa. I am a homebody, and I thought He was calling me to be a doctor in our town of Blessing, to help found a hospital and outreach clinics, especially to those on the Indian reservations. I have attended six months of a surgical rotation at Alfred Morganstein Hospital for Women and Children in Chicago, and I passed all their tests to be a fully certified medical doctor. My mother has always said that God only guides us one step at a time. So without any more clarity than that, I asked for admittance here because Rev. Schuman said I should come here. And if God is calling me to Africa, he, I mean Rev. Schuman, would like me to come to work with him." She heard several small chuckles in spite of the thundering of her heart.

Nodding as he spoke, the man said, "I see. And what do you believe now?"

Astrid unclenched her fingers in her lap. "I came here saying, 'Lord, I do not want to go to Africa.' Then I realized I was saying, or rather pleading, 'Lord, do I have to go to Africa?' The other day I heard myself praying . . ." She paused, swallowed, and sniffed. She heard one of the women at the table sniff too. With a deep breath she continued. "Praying, 'Lord, if you will it, I will go to Africa.' And yesterday afternoon, I heard myself saying, 'Lord, if this is your will, I will joyfully go to Africa.' " She blinked several times and felt a tear meander down her cheek. The hush in the room made her hesitate to look at those around her.

"God be praised," someone further down the table said.

"Thank you, young lady. Now, I see here that you have asked for a two-year term of service."

"Yes, because I do know I am needed in Blessing too."

"You think God won't provide for the needs of your people there?" someone asked.

Astrid started to answer, paused, and thought a long moment. She blinked and barely shook her head. "I never thought of it that way."

Dean Highsmith coughed into his hand.

Surely he is covering up a chuckle. The thought made her want to smile at him.

"I'd like to add something here," the dean said, glancing around to get permission. Several nodded. "I have met with Dr. Bjorklund several times. She's been a guest in my home, and I must tell you that I have never met a more honest and forthright young woman in my life. I haven't seen her in action in a medical situation, but Dr. Morganstein sent a letter highly recommending her. I included that letter in the packet you have all read. Now, does anyone else have questions to ask Dr. Bjorklund?"

"How will you adjust to a different culture, one with such daily dangers?" A man on the right side of the table leaned forward as he spoke so he could see her better.

"Well, my mother taught me to shoot a rifle, and I am a pretty good shot. I grew up on a farm that began as a homestead on what was then the frontier. I have never had money to spend, so I am thrifty and can make do with very little. I am not afraid of hard work." She glanced around the table, catching smiles on a couple of faces and rolled eyes on others. "While I've not had to deal with vicious snakes and jungle animals, I trust that if God wants me to go there, He will provide. My mother reared her children with the knowledge that life is not easy. We must work hard, do our best, and leave the rest up to God. I guess I've been learning those lessons since childhood."

"How do your parents feel about their young daughter going to Africa?"

"The same as I do. If that is where God is calling me, then that is where I must go." She knew her mother suffered with the thought of her only daughter on the other side of the earth. While she'd never said so, her tears spoke for her.

"You have written that you have two brothers. What do they do?"

"They are both doing exactly what they dreamed of. Thorliff went to St. Olaf College in Northfield, Minnesota, and returned to Blessing to start a newspaper, the *Blessing Gazette*. He is married to Dr. Elizabeth Bjorklund, and they have a daughter. All my brother Andrew ever wanted to do was farm, and that is what he is doing. He is married with two children and has a home on the Bjorklund land. He and my father, along with my uncle and his boys, raise mostly wheat and feed for our dairy cows to support my mother's cheese house."

"You have an industrious family."

Astrid nodded. "I originally thought I was going to become a nurse to help my sister-in-law in her practice, but instead, she insisted that I train to be a doctor, and I'm glad she did."

"How does she feel about her trainee leaving for Africa?"

"She is terribly disappointed but agrees that a two-year term would be similar to my going on for further medical training." Astrid ordered her shoulders to go back down where they belonged. Why did she feel they'd been grilling her for hours?

She glanced up to catch a slight smile in the dean's eyes. She must be doing all right, then.

"Are there any further questions, comments?" he asked, glancing around the table.

One of the men who'd been leaning back in his chair, arms crossed over his chest, raised one finger.

"Yes, Rev. Arbuckle." While Astrid had nodded to him at the introductions, she'd not seen a smile anywhere near his face.

"I have to say that I believe we would be making a grave mistake in sending a young woman, not yet nineteen, alone with no husband"—he emphasized each point with a sharp nod and fierce glances at those around the table—"to Africa. Unless . . ." He paused and leaned forward. "Unless she is sent to work in an established hospital and not out in the bush. Rev. Schuman, as I understand, operates out of a small village and uses a bicycle to call on patients and to travel to other villages." He shook his head. "But even sending her to a city would be a mistake, I think." He turned to look directly at Astrid. "Go home, find a husband, and then the two of you see if this is something that appeals to both of you."

Astrid smiled politely while inside a banked fire threatened to combust. As if she'd come here on a whim. That she was dying to go to Africa, thinking it was a romantic adventure.

Dean Highsmith, eyes narrowed, stared at the other man. "Would you go against the will of the almighty God?" His soft words dropped into the silence, spreading out like ripples on a still pond.

"No, not at all." Arbuckle blinked and huffed a sigh. "I-I-I think God must make it very clear that this is what He wants. That's all."

"You think we are not all praying along these very lines?" Another pause. "Dr. Bjorklund herself has reiterated how this must truly be God calling her."

One of the other men leaned forward, meeting Arbuckle's eyes. "Jonas, when you see the burning bush, you come get us, all right?"

Slightly snide, Astrid thought but hoped the feather-light chuckles would ease the tension in the room.

Dean Highsmith laid his palms on the table. "Since I see no other questions, I declare this meeting to be adjourned. I thank you all for coming and also Dr. Bjorklund. We will be notifying you sometime in the next month of our decision. Meanwhile, I trust that no matter the outcome, you will feel that your classes here have been a valuable use of your time." He nodded to Astrid. "You are all invited to dinner in the cafeteria, and you won't even have to stand in line to serve yourself. One of our students will be your host."

As they all stood, the scraping of chairs on the waxed walnut floor was louder than the conversation. Astrid turned to leave the room, but Dean Highsmith stopped her with a touch on her shoulder. She looked up at him, hoping he wouldn't catch her awful need to go hide in a corner and cry out her frustration.

"Won't you please join Rev. Arbuckle and me for the meal?"

She stared at him, catching her words before they tumbled forth. *Why would I want to spend time with that man?* Somehow he seemed to hear her thoughts and she flushed.

"Trust me, it's important."

Trust me. God wasn't the only one saying that lately. Maybe she'd misheard the dean, he'd spoken so softly. God seemed to be trumpeting his request. Or was it orders? Here she'd been struggling so with this whole fear thing, and Rev. Jonas Arbuckle acted like he was the only one who'd given any thought to the dangers of Africa.

Astrid ordered her lips to smile and her head to nod while a voice inside kept shouting, *Run, run. Go home to Blessing, where you don't have to put up with one more man saying you are too young, you are not married, you can't possibly be a real doctor.* But she said aloud, "I'd be glad to." *Liar! You don't have to go that far. But be polite.* That had to be her mother's voice. Gracious and kind, two words that the Bible repeated over and over, and at times like this, two of the hardest to obey.

She almost asked to be excused and said she would meet them in the dining room later, but she realized she might not get herself out of her room if she returned there now. Instead, she walked between the two men to the cafeteria, trying to think of something to say.

Dean Highsmith pulled a chair out for her at one of the smaller tables set for four.

"Thank you." She sat and smiled up at him.

After the men seated themselves and they had all picked up their napkins, she glanced at Rev. Arbuckle. Brooding might be a way to describe him. His well-trimmed dark beard matched his equally dark hair, though tempered with bits of silver creeping in. Hard to guess his age since his face wore lines of anger. Laugh lines did not lighten his dark eyes as they did Dean Highsmith's. Talk about two men who looked so opposite. Although the dean's hair might have been dark in his youth, the silver of it added to the air of distinction that fit him and his position.

They gave their orders to the young man who waited on them, and then the dean turned to Astrid. "I know that Jonas's remarks in the meeting offended you, and I want to give him an opportunity to explain why he feels the way he does."

What could she say? He clearly didn't believe young women should be in the medical or missionary field. But her curiosity was aroused. Surely there was a story here. She nodded.

"First of all, Rev. Arbuckle has served many years on the mission field, leaving for Africa when he was not much older than you. He has been back in this country on leave, and we have asked him in the meantime to serve on our mission board."

"I see." She turned to the man, feeling scrutinized by eyes that seemed to burn right through her.

"I beg your pardon," he said in a low voice, "if I said anything that offended you."

Rolling her eyes seemed a telling answer, so she kept still and silent.

"Africa eats men and women alive. For some reason I have come through twenty years unscathed, but most are not so fortunate."

"Let's be honest here, Jonas, you are not unscathed." Highsmith turned to Astrid. "Jonas's wife died and is buried in Africa, along with his daughter and one son. Two of his sons were sent back to America, or they might not have survived either."

Astrid swallowed and blinked. She looked to Rev. Arbuckle again and saw eyes still filled with pain, not the anger she had originally surmised. "I am so sorry."

He nodded but brushed his hand as if to push an invisible cobweb away.

She wanted to ask him for particulars, but the hand made her wary. He obviously did not want to talk about his family.

"I was training young Africans to be ministers and teachers. That's what I am. A teacher. Or was."

"And will be again." Dean Highsmith spoke with all the assurance at his disposal.

"We shall see."

"In the meantime Jonas is helping our students prepare for missionary service in Africa. Today he will be lecturing about the living conditions, and tomorrow he is conducting a session on tropical diseases."

"Are you a doctor also?" Astrid asked, then smiled at the young man serving them. "Thank you."

Also noticing the server, Rev. Arbuckle said, "You realize that young man is probably your age or a bit older? He will finish college here and then attend Bible School for a year or more. And if he can pass the exams, he will be considered for the missionary field—if he still believes he has the call to do so." Adding with a sharp nod, "And no, I am not a doctor."

Astrid sighed to herself. Ah, back to her age. "I know that you feel I am too young, but I have more medical training than many men far older than I. Isn't it better that I am not married, so that I have the flexibility to go now without burdening a family?"

"Your husband would have to have the desire to go also."

"If I were a man, would you be saying the same things?"

"I believe nineteen is too young for a man also. The more life experiences one has, the more one can adjust to the culture there, to the climate, to the calling."

"Would you want one of your sons going there?" *Lord, please keep me from arguing with him.*

Rev. Arbuckle slowly shook his head. "The cost can be too great."

"Would you go back?"

Strangely, this time he nodded. "Africa has become home to me."

"Will you go back to teaching?"

Again he nodded. "Strange, is it not? Here I am doing my best to discourage you, and yet I am praying to return." He leaned forward. "But I am teaching young people, African young people, to do the serving and the ministering. I believe we should be training doctors and nurses, schoolteachers, and businessmen to go out and take care of their own people."

"I think Rev. Schuman disagrees with you."

"He says the people can't wait that long, that while we must train native people, we must also bring the gospel and medical help to them now." Arbuckle leaned back in his chair. "We are all called to different parts of the body."

Astrid stared at her plate, where the food had disappeared as they talked.

"We have banana cream pie for dessert," Dean Highsmith announced.

"More iced tea?" the server asked.

"Yes, and bring us three pieces of pie." Highsmith smiled at Astrid. "I know. I am just trying to keep you two here a while longer. For some reason God made me think the two of you would be good for each other."

"Dean Highsmith, ever a mediator."

"You do your calling; I'll answer for mine. Keep the discussion going. I believe there is more to be shared."

Astrid sucked in a breath. "My mother always said that it is not polite to ask personal questions."

That brushing of the hand again. "Ask away. Let us not stand on propriety."

"How old would your daughter be now?"

"Twenty years. She died at fifteen in a cholera epidemic. All three of them were gone almost overnight. We had shipped the two older boys back to the States for school. Perhaps that is what saved them."

"Everyone didn't die at that time."

"No, but white people had not the constitution for the climate that natives had, so the number of deaths was higher in the white families."

"Did you have it too?"

"A light case. Sometimes understanding God's will in situations like this is near to impossible."

"Perhaps understanding is not what is needed but acceptance and trust."

He stared at her. "Where have you gained such wisdom?"

She was sure he was thinking *at such a young age*, but he refrained from saying it. "I think I am quoting my mother. She has many pearls of wisdom that I find myself echoing now."

"I think I would like to meet your mother."

"Come to Blessing. You wouldn't be the first to seek her counsel. I am just beginning to realize how very fortunate I am."

The slice of pie appeared in front of her like magic. She'd been so engrossed in their discussion she'd not even noticed the server bring it.

Rev. Thompkins stopped at their table. "I'm sorry to interrupt, but Bible class is starting in just a few minutes."

"Thank you. I'll be right there." *And thank you for getting me out of this situation.* She once again let go of a breath she hadn't realized she'd been holding. How do you disagree with a man who has experienced and lost so much? And yet she still hoped she was following God's will. How she would like to have asked Dean Highsmith what he had hoped to accomplish by this discussion.

Both of the men rose when she did.

"Thank you for the time," Rev. Arbuckle said with a slight bow. He looked to the dean too. "But I still don't believe going to Africa would be the best thing for you."

Astrid shrugged. "Since I am not convinced of it either, I guess we'll just have to see what God decides. I will keep praying for clarity, and I hope you will too." She nodded to both of the gentlemen and made her way to the door. Out in the hall an attack of exhaustion made her sag against the wall for a moment. What had that been all about? Her mother would most likely have taken her to task for her forthright questions. But if she was indeed an adult now, doing adult things, surely discussing such deep matters was part of life. If it wasn't, it certainly should be. She sucked in a deep breath of energy and headed for her Bible class. An errant thought caught her by surprise. Did she really want to meet with Rev. Arbuckle again?

11

Blessing, North Dakota

"When the mud is dry, we will start building all the windmills I sold last fall." Hjelmer walked around their nearly finished wagon, nodding all the while. "You've done a good job here."

"Thank you." Joshua slammed shut the lid on one of the side boxes that were reinforced to carry heavy tools and supplies. "We just need to paint it."

"That isn't a necessity."

"I know, but it will protect the wood from the elements."

"Very true. Go see what colors Penny has in stock, and you can get on it."

Joshua noticed that Hjelmer didn't say *we*. He must have some other project in his thoughts. They'd been working together up until now. Should he say something or just let it go? Curiosity was usually a good thing, but sometimes it got in the way. "So how long do you think it will be before we head out?" He spent every minute he could working on his own house. Now that the water was nearly out of the earthen basement, he could think about pouring the concrete. Leaving it to cure while they traveled meant that when they got back, he could order his house from the Sears and Roebuck catalog. Thinking of the house automatically sent his thoughts careening to Astrid. Was he doing all this in vain, trying to get his house built so that he had a place to bring his bride? That is, if she agreed to marry him. Waiting had never been one of his strong suits.

He put his tools away and glanced at the sun. He could probably get the paint before dinner and be ready to paint that afternoon. That is, if Penny had any paint in colors that would be appropriate for a work wagon. None of those wild colors like he'd seen on a gypsy wagon years ago when the gypsies camped for a time near his father's farm. Now he wished he'd paid more attention to how their wagons were designed inside for living and working space. He and his younger brother had watched them dancing and laughing around a fire one night. Had his father known, he'd have tanned them both. Joshua couldn't see why everyone feared and hated them so.

"I'll be over at Thorliff's," Hjelmer said as he turned to go.

"Okay." He watched his boss walk down the street. Something was up indeed. Hjelmer had that faraway look on his face, a sure indication he was thinking hard on something new. Once he and Trygve headed out to dig wells and set windmills, there weren't too many men left in Blessing to draw on for general work. With Hjelmer most likely off selling, they needed another set of hands. Oh well, it was none of his business until Hjelmer chose to fill him in. He glanced out across the fields to where spring work should have started, but the fields were just too wet. The heavy machinery would compact the soil, which needed to be loose for the seeds to sprout.

Too wet, too dry. He was glad he wasn't farming any longer.

Striding down the street, he jumped up on the boardwalk, ignoring the two steps, and pushed open the door to the mercantile.

"Good morning, Mr. Landsverk," Penny called from the aisle off to his right. "Grand morning, is it not?"

"That it is." He tipped his flat-brimmed hat back so he could see better in the dimness after the brilliant sun outside.

"What can I be getting for you?"

"We're ready to paint the wagon, so I wondered what you have on hand. I think we'll need three or four gallons by the time I give it two good coats."

"Would whitewash do?"

"I was hoping for something more substantial." Glancing around the store, Joshua inhaled the rich aromas of leather and oil, metals and cloth, liniment and soaps. It still seemed strange to him that she no longer carried food and feed, although if he inhaled deeply enough, he was sure the fragrance of spices and the pickle barrel still lurked, as though they had permeated the wood.

"Over here." Penny led him to shelves along the back wall, where rakes, shovels, hoes, and tools like hammers and saws hung from pegs and racks. A spinner rack of garden seeds caught his eye. No sense thinking about a garden since he wouldn't be in town to take care of it. Did Astrid love working in the garden like his mother had, or did she do it because growing food to eat was a necessity? So many things about her he didn't know. Maybe that would be a good topic to bring up in his letter tonight. Coming up with things to write about took some doing. Saying "I miss you" over and over got a bit boring, even though he most assuredly did.

He jerked his thoughts back to answer Penny's question. "Ah, sorry. What did you say?"

"I asked if black would be all right. Someone ordered three gallons and then decided they didn't like it. I can give you a good deal on it."

"Black." He'd pictured dark blue or green, but this wasn't the time to be choosy. "Three gallons, eh?" He squinted his eyes, estimating if he could get by with that.

"I could have more in a week."

"All right. I'll at least start with that. Think we'll whitewash it on the inside, so give me a couple of gallons of that too." The bonging of the church bell announced that noon had arrived. "I'll take what I can now and pick up the rest after dinner."

"Good. I'll put it on Hjelmer's account, and it'll be sitting out on the porch when you get back. If you see Sophie, tell her that her ledgers came in."

"I will." He tipped his hat and grinned at her. "Good day."

"Oh, are you and Johnny playing for church on Sunday?"

"I believe so." One more thing to add to his to-do list—practice time with his young protégé. "Johnny sure is working hard at his guitar."

"I know. Pastor Solberg is so proud of him. I wish Dr. Elizabeth had time to teach Linnea to play the piano. She wants so badly to learn."

"I could show her some basic chords on the guitar, if you want." How had those words gotten out of his mouth? He didn't have time to take on one more thing. "Won't Jonathan be back fairly soon? College lets out in May. Maybe he could find the time."

"That's a good idea. And yes, basic chords would be wonderful. She's been picking out songs when she can get to the piano. We might get a real music group going here. You still playing at that Grange Hall in Grafton?"

"Not as often." He'd spent the winter doing everything he could to bring in extra money to pay off his lot and save up for the house. Owing someone money needled him. He picked up four of the cans by their wire handles and headed out the door. Where would he find paintbrushes? Mr. Sam would be the one to ask. He kept all their tools and supplies in good order. "See you later."

After he dropped his armloads off at the wagon, he whistled on his way to the boardinghouse. Life was much easier since they'd pulled the wagon into town from the machine shed out at Lars's. What could be better than a spring day like this one? Sun and breeze to dry the wet land. As he had at the store, he leaped the stairs to the front door to the boardinghouse. Someone had put up the screen doors while he worked this morning. He opened it to step right into the vestibule, since the oval-glassed doors were latched open.

A slight breeze tiptoed through the hallway, blowing away the last of the winter doldrums with a breath of spring. Mrs. Wiste wasn't behind the desk, so perhaps she had gone home for something. Sophie generally spent the morning over her bookwork behind the chest-high partition. Joshua pushed open the swinging half doors into the dining room, where bright sun from the long windows nearly blinded the eyes, reflecting off the white tablecloths.

"Good afternoon, Mr. Landsverk," Miss Christopherson called in greeting. "You sound mighty chipper."

He smiled as he took off his hat and hung it on the coat-tree by the door. Her greeting never failed to lift his spirits. "How so?"

"I heard you whistling down the street. What a pleasant sound." She set the basket of fresh rolls on his table. Not that it had his name on it, but it was where he always sat.

"Thank you." He inhaled with a grin. "Something sure smells mighty tasty. But then it always smells good in here." He pulled out his chair and sat down, glancing around the room as he did. "Not too many here for dinner today, eh?"

"No, the train is late, and that large family must be waiting over at the station. They checked out earlier. I'll bring your dinner right out."

"Thanks." Joshua snagged one of the rolls from the basket and held it to his nose for a moment. There was something about the smell of fresh-baked bread that always reminded him of home and his mother's kitchen. She had loved to bake bread. Her love of cooking was legendary, but she said there was something healing about baking bread, perhaps because the good Lord referred so often to the bread of life. Still warm. He took a bite before even buttering it.

A shriek at the same moment as a crashing of metal to floor jerked his attention to the kitchen. The "Oh no!" brought him to his feet and leaping for the doorway.

"What happened?" As the words left his mouth, he saw the pot sideways on the floor, a puddle spread out around Lily Mae, who was holding her hand and weeping, the front of her dress and apron soaked as well. "How bad is it?" He crossed the room in two strides. Mrs. Sam was ripping off the apron, holding the garments away from her daughter's body so she wouldn't burn further.

"You want me to go for Dr. Elizabeth?" he asked.

"No, no. Nothin' like dat." Mrs. Sam glanced at him over her shoulder. "We put her hand in ice water. Cools it off." She nodded toward the dining room. "You dinner be out in a minute."

Joshua watched the young weeping woman as her brother, Lemuel, picked up the kettle, set it on the table, and went for a mop. "You're sure?"

Miss Christopherson took his arm. "Thank you, but she'll be taken care of. Your dinner is getting cold." She picked up a plate with one hand and the coffeepot with the other and preceded him out the door.

Thorliff and Hjelmer entered the dining room as Joshua obediently sat down.

"Better bring on two more plates," Hjelmer said. They stopped beside Joshua's table. "You mind if we sit here? Got some discussing to do."

"No, not at all." He motioned for them to sit.

"What happened in the kitchen?" Thorliff asked.

"A pot of hot water slipped or something and burned Lily Mae's hand. Hopefully her clothes kept the rest of her from being burned. I wanted to go for Dr. Bjorklund, but Mrs. Sam said no in a way I didn't figure I should argue. They put her hand in ice water."

Miss Christopherson sailed through the door with two filled plates and set them in front of the men. "Coffee will be right out. Oh, you need more rolls." She quickly grabbed silver and napkins from a nearby table.

"How is Lily Mae?" Thorliff asked.

"She'll be all right. At least the kettle wasn't boiling yet. And thank God it was water and not grease." She headed back for the kitchen.

Thorliff looked relieved.

"Is Elizabeth feeling better today?" Hjelmer asked quietly.

Thorliff nodded. "Had her close early, though, to rest in case there are any emergencies Mor can't handle."

As the three men dug into the baked chicken and rice, Joshua kept his questions to himself.

"You got the paint?"

"Black. Three gallons. I'll see if I can make it go far enough." He buttered another roll and took a bite. "Mr. Sam is making sure the drilling machinery is all tuned up. We could leave day after tomorrow if it is dry enough."

"Most likely the supplies won't be here for another few days anyway." The two men exchanged a look, and Hjelmer nodded. "I think you could tell something's been in the works."

Joshua nodded and set his fork down to pick up his coffee cup. He watched Hjelmer over the edge of his cup, now cradled in both hands.

"You remember young Daniel Jeffers was here last month?" Hjelmer asked.

"Sure, he told me about his missing father."

"Well, back then we talked a bit about his father's invention and the possibility of going into a partnership with him producing the improved seed drill."

"Here in Blessing?"

Both men nodded.

"But where, and who would you get to work for you?" Joshua asked. "There aren't enough able-bodied men around here to do the work that already needs doing. We need another man on our crew, as it is."

"I know that. On top of it, we most likely will have a hospital to build come summer too."

"And I want to build a house. I know I'm not the only one."

Thorliff and Hjelmer both nodded. "Not a bad place to be in, wouldn't you say?"

"True, but—"

"We decided we need to delegate some of the responsibilities. So starting today, you will be in charge of the windmill and well drilling portion of the business. I'll show you how to do the ordering and keep some simple record books. You will have Trygve working for you, and I think Gilbert too. They don't really need him on the farm, and he is a good worker. Being single, he won't have to worry about leaving a family either."

"Trygve won't be going with the threshing crew or help with haying?"

"Nope. He now works for us full time. You'll need to keep track of their hours too, and Penny will issue paychecks first of the month and midmonth."

"Who's going to get out and sell the new accounts?"

"I'm thinking word of mouth will most likely do that for us. I have a stack of letters and some orders people have phoned in to me. Might be enough to take us through the summer. I'll give them all to you to follow up on."

Joshua leaned back in his chair, slightly shaking his head. He could hear his mother reminding him not to rock the chair back on the legs unless he wanted to fix the chair himself. He kept the feet on the ground. Why wasn't he more excited about this?

"You look some doubtful."

"You have to admit that's a healthy dose of news over dinner."

Miss Christopherson stopped at their table. "Can I get you seconds, gentlemen?"

All three nodded.

"We have dried-apple spice cake with caramel frosting for dessert."

"Maybe I'll skip that second plate, then." Hjelmer paused. "And maybe not." He turned slightly in his chair to look at Joshua full on. "We will double your wages for now and see how it all goes. I know it is a lot of responsibility, but you are more than capable of handling it all."

His heart skipped a beat at the compliment, but then he heard the old disdain of his father and hesitated again. "I'm not a salesman."

"But you know how to produce good service, and windmills will become more and more popular. We are at the edge of a boom. Let your work be your sales pitch. You can answer questions. That's what's important."

He glanced up to thank Miss Christopherson, then pushed his meat around with his fork. Double his wages and paid twice a month. He wouldn't need to pay for his room here while out with the crew, so that would be more money going into his savings and to pay off his lot. That would go a long way to paying off his debt. But he most likely wouldn't be here when Astrid returned. *If* she returned. But he could get his house sooner. And they still could write.

He looked from Hjelmer to Thorliff and back. "You're going to have to teach me how to keep the books."

Hjelmer slapped him on the shoulder, a grin creasing his face. "I knew we could count on you. I can guarantee you'll be pleased with this entire proposal." They shook hands, and Joshua inhaled, letting his breath out on a sigh.

"That's just the beginning," Thorliff said with a nod. "We're putting Toby Valders in charge of the building arm of the company, running the projects. We're going to add on to the old granary and set up shop in there for the manufacturing arm. Jeffers will be in charge of that. We're looking for someone with experience in steel manufacturing. I'm getting ready to send out advertisements to some of the regional newspapers, including those in Minneapolis and St. Paul."

With his dessert now before him, Joshua almost wished he'd not ordered it. But one bite put that idea to rest. He'd better enjoy the good food now, because once they were on the road, the cooking would be up to them if the farmers didn't invite them for meals. He sure hoped that either Trygve or Gilbert knew more about cooking than he did. Or at least one of them better be asking for some lessons over the next few days. He thought of one other difficulty. Gilbert spoke little English—he'd arrived from Norway less than a year ago—and Joshua spoke no Norwegian.

12

"I certainly hope the garden can be plowed, now that we've scattered the straw on it," Ingeborg commented after she ate her last bite of cake.

Ingeborg had spent the afternoons, after seeing patients at the surgery, pitching the straw and manure banking from around the house into the wheelbarrow and spreading it across the garden. With Emmy and Freda helping, the job had gone quickly. "I know you need every moment out on the fields that are dry enough to work, but the garden needs to get in too."

Andrew glanced to his pa, who blew a smoke ring into the air to make Emmy giggle. Maybe her delight in smoke rings came from something she'd learned about them from her years in the tribe.

"More," she pleaded.

Haakan shook his head. "Your grandma says we got to get out there and plow the garden. Means I can't spend all afternoon playing with smoke rings." He tweaked the little girl's braid of dark hair that had grown out quickly since they cut it off to get rid of the lice.

"What is plow?"

"A machine that the horses pull to turn over the soil." Andrew nodded at her puzzled look. "You can come ride the horses while we plow the garden."

"Horses." Her eyes sparkled. She nodded, hard enough to set her braids to bobbing. "I ride."

"You better help clear the table then, while we go harness up." Haakan stood and, walking to the stove, lifted a lid with the coil-handled lid lifter and tapped the remains from his pipe into the fire. After setting the pipe and tobacco container back on the shelf, he headed for the back door. "At least we don't have to wear winter jackets any longer." He settled his fedora on his head and followed Andrew out the door.

Emmy carried the empty plates over to the stove and set them in the dishpan waiting on the cooler part of the stove. "I wash?"

"No, I'll wash. You dry." Freda set the coffee cups in the soapy water and dug down for the dishcloth. "You brush the crumbs off the table into the scrap bucket. Those leftover bits of bread go in the same."

Emmy hurried through her tasks, keeping an ear cocked for the jingle of the harness that signaled the arrival of the horses.

One day Ingeborg had gone down to the barn for oats from the grain bin, and she turned around to find Emmy in the horse stalls, talking to the work horses and rubbing their noses. She loved the horses, singing to them in the language that Ingeborg hadn't heard since Metiz died. At least now she knew which tribe Emmy came from.

"Here they come," Ingeborg told her now. "You better put a sweater on."

The little girl grabbed a sweater off one of the low pegs that Haakan had put on the wall for the grandchildren and slipped out the door, her eyes sparkling in delight.

"Between her and Inga, what a pair," Freda said. "How come you didn't bring Inga back out with you?"

"She was over playing with Benny. Rebecca had asked if she could come since it is Saturday and no school."

"And how was Elizabeth today?"

"Restless, which means she is feeling better. At least I hope that is what it means. She got a letter from Dr. Morganstein asking when the men from the hospital board might come out on the train to talk with her and those of the community most interested in building the hospital. They don't understand how we work together as a co-op here in Blessing, that everyone who wants to can come to the meeting and have their say. Might be a bit of a surprise to them."

"When you consider that half the businesses in Blessing are owned and managed by women, well, that might be another shock for them."

"You know, I never think much about that." Ingeborg set the last of the clean dishes on the shelf. "Speaking of businesses, how are things in the cheese house? I've been so busy, I'm afraid I've let you do all the hard work."

"That's one of the reasons I left Norway, remember? To help you."

"Helping is one thing. Being forced to take over is quite another."

Freda *tsk*ed, muttered something, and shook her head. "Will dinner be here after church tomorrow?"

"No. Remember, we are having a church meeting, so everyone will be bringing food with them to church."

"How could I forget? You'd think that gathering things for the

Indian reservation like Astrid asked was of world importance. I just don't understand this. Haven't you been donating to a different reservation for years?"

"Yes. I don't understand it either. But maybe it's because we are asking for more than a barrel of castoffs and a couple of quilts."

"Andrew said you've sent a beef up there before."

"We just did what we thought God wanted us to do. And now He's asked through a different source, and I wonder if that is part of it."

"Meaning?"

"Meaning that Astrid wrote and asked for help because she has made friends with an Indian man who is in training at her hospital. That caused a bit of a hullabaloo. Then Emmy showed up here—another Indian, albeit a child. And what can anyone really say about a little one in need?"

"They can say plenty. I remember at home when a family of Sami came down from the north. With their dark hair and dark skin one would think they came from way south." While Freda tried hard to speak only English, every so often a Norwegian word slipped in. When she got excited, she spoke only Norwegian, which made Ingeborg laugh. "Their language was different; everything about them was different, so people refused to welcome them. They finally moved on from Valdres."

"Some of the women were not accepting of my friend Metiz, who helped us so much those first years, showing me what was edible in the wild and many natural medicines. She taught me how to tan rabbit skins for those wonderful mittens and vests she made. When we first came, she spent more time with her relatives further north, but in the last years she gave up traveling back and forth, and Haakan built her a cabin on the river, where she said her husband, a Frenchman, had owned land. Of course there was no record of title, so when we homesteaded the land, we just made room for her too. She and Agnes

Baard, besides Kaaren, were my best friends." Ingeborg let her mind wander back and then heaved a sigh. "But life goes on."

"I wish I could have come earlier."

"I gave up wishing to change the past a long time ago. Kaaren reminded me of that often after Roald died. She kept quoting Bible verses Paul wrote, about letting go of the past and the things that bind and pushing forward for the prize. Some of the time I wanted to shut her mouth for her." Ingeborg raised her eyebrows and smiled slightly, her head tipped a bit to the side. "Which would have been a shame, since I had fought so hard to keep her alive and not let her follow her husband and the two little girls who died that winter. Those were some terrible times. I would not wish them on anyone."

"Someday maybe you'll tell me the whole story."

"Someday maybe I will. I'm going out to check on the plowing." Ingeborg stopped on the top step and raised her face to the sun. Sun that felt warm again, not just a purveyor of light. *God, I thank you for the sunshine, for the growing grass and the drying ground. You have brought us through another winter, kept us well and safe.* She stepped down the stairs, thinking they needed to be painted again. The entire porch needed painting. Amazing how one noticed those things when the snow melted away and exposed the wood and the ground again.

Stooping down, she checked the canes of the rosebush to see if the sprouts were showing—not yet. Another week of warm weather and life would burst forth from the ground, the trees, and the bushes. She strolled around the house until she could see Andrew turning a corner, trying to plow as close to the fence as possible. No one liked hand-digging the corner pieces, where she usually planted the pumpkins and squash.

Emmy saw her and waved from the back of one of their oldest team. Haakan figured they were about due for retirement, but the sad way they acted when the other horses were harnessed and headed out to the fields reminded him to give them the easy jobs. They would turn over the potato patch and the corn patch too. He often used them to pull the wagons to town or the buggy on Sunday.

His concern for the animals made her love him even more. While Thorliff and Hjelmer talked about horses being a dying way of farming, Haakan didn't plan on selling his teams off.

She leaned on the rail fence, welcoming the invigorating fragrance of freshly turned earth. Andrew angled the team over to the fence so Ingeborg could give the horses each a piece of bread she'd stuck in her pocket. She laughed as their whiskery noses tickled her palm. How easy it was to laugh on a day like today. Sunshine and breeze, fields drying, the garden plowed. She knew Andrew would hook up the disc next and give the ground a couple of runovers with that, and— She glanced up at the sky. Nearing midafternoon. While she used to like to rake the garden smooth before planting, now with this late planting season, she needed to get the peas in immediately. Mark the rows, hoe a groove, and let Emmy drop the seeds into the ground.

"Thanks, Andrew."

"I'm not done yet."

"I know, so I'll thank you then too."

"Where are you going?"

"To get my planting box." Years earlier she had appropriated one of the two-foot-long toolboxes that had an iron bar from end to end for a handle. Tucked carefully in place were sticks with twine wound around them for markers, her trowel, jars with seeds saved from the year before, and a knife for cutting up the last of the potatoes she'd saved for seed. Every year she planted several hills of potatoes in the main garden, since the corn and potato patch would get worked up after he plowed for Kaaren and Ellie too. Somehow in the last few years, Andrew had taken over working up the garden plots for all of them. He would most likely go into town and do plots for Thorliff and Hjelmer too.

"Bye, Gamma," Emmy called from her throne on high.

Astrid needs to be here to help put the garden in. The thought made Ingeborg sniff. This was the first year she wouldn't be here to help at all. Last spring she'd managed to take a few hours away from the surgery to join her mother in one of their favorite things to do together.

"Lord, I am trying to leave her in your hands, I really am. Were you as lonely for your Son when He came down here to live as I am for my daughter?" She dug in her apron pocket for a handkerchief and blew her nose.

"You should be wearing a hat," Freda said, joining Ingeborg in the garden a few minutes later.

"I know. I always told Astrid that too, but today my head really needs to feel the sun to drive away the thoughts of winter." *And missing Astrid.* "Emmy and I will plant the peas if you help me mark the rows. I brought a bundle of stakes out, along with the rakes and hoes."

Freda put her hands on her hips and lifted her face to the sun. "You know one thing I am missing about a Norway spring?"

"The creeks and runoffs cascading down the mountains and through the fields. I missed that for years," Ingeborg said. "And the aspen trees leafing out, along with the oaks and maples. But I grew accustomed to this rich flat land and being able to see for miles. Sometimes I climb the windmill just to look out over the fields and farms. You can see forever."

"There's something else to be thankful for."

"What's that?"

"I don't see a single rock in this ground."

"Farther west you'll find rocks, but not here in the middle of the valley. I was amazed at that too. I would have built stone walls with them had we any. Haakan wasn't too enthusiastic about hauling in rocks for me to make a wall."

Freda chuckled with her.

Andrew made the last pass with the disc and stopped to lift Emmy down from the horse's back. "There you go. Mor will teach you how to plant."

"Not Mor. Gamma."

"She's almost as opinionated as Inga."

"She has a good teacher." Ingeborg took Emmy's hand. "Tell Andrew thank-you for the ride."

"Thank you."

"All right, little one, let's plant the peas." Ingeborg handed her a pint jar with dried peas. "I'll show you what to do."

THEY WOKE TO drizzle the next morning, after a downpour during the night.

"Great day for the meeting," Ingeborg grumbled from her place by the window. With the rising sun obscured by the clouds, what she'd really like to do was to crawl back in bed, sleep a while longer, and wake to sunshine.

"It might pass by then," Haakan said from beside the bed.

"The roads will be bad again."

"It didn't rain hard for very long. Most likely it's seeped in by now."

She could hear him getting dressed. Why was it that when she felt like a grumble, he always saw the brighter side? But was it the rain she was grumbling about or the upcoming meeting? Most likely some of each. She didn't hear his footsteps, but when his arms sneaked around her middle, she succumbed to the invitation to lean back against his strong chest.

"I think someone once said, 'All will be well,' " he whispered into her ear.

She clasped her hands over his. "Takk. I just don't like people arguing and getting angry. You know that."

"Maybe God will work another of His miracles, and everyone will agree and leave to enjoy dinner. Then if it is dry enough, we can play baseball. I was sure hoping to have that backstop up before now. You'd have thought with the late planting we would have found time to do that."

"Maybe if you weren't so busy helping Mr. Landsverk on his house . . ." She let her words trail off. One thing about Haakan, he always led the brigade to help those who needed it. She turned in his arms and kissed first his cheek, then his chin, and finally his lips. "I'll go get the coffee on."

"I think Freda already did that. Chokecherry jelly with sour cream on bread would be an easy breakfast and a real treat."

"You shall have your treat." She patted his cheek.

"LET US STAND for the benediction," Pastor Solberg said at the end of the service. "The Lord bless us and keep us. The Lord lift His countenance upon us. May He give us wisdom and joy for doing His will. And above all, may we know His love that covers every one of us and all that we do. Lord, we praise your name. Amen."

Hearing those words, Ingeborg hoped the congregation would say something very similar. She still thought the women's quilting group should have settled this, but as Haakan reminded her, they were being asked for a lot more than a barrel of clothing and bedding. So instead of filing out as they usually did, everyone sat down again.

Pastor Solberg stood before the congregation and smiled at everyone. "If there is anyone who does not want to stay for the meeting, you are now excused. This won't be a long meeting, so children, you can be patient a few minutes longer too." While a slight groan went up from the younger crowd, no one moved.

Ingeborg wished that Elizabeth could have come, but since she herself was the one who had put her daughter-in-law on bed rest, she could hardly be the one to complain. Thorliff and Inga sat on her other side, with Emmy between her and Haakan.

"Now, I know this request has brought some dissension to our family here, and if we are to live according to God's Word, we can't allow dissension to create problems for us. You know, dissension and his first cousin, bitterness, are like crabgrass. They love to get into a fertile and well-tilled field and send runners out to choke the corn or wheat or whatever is sown there. You all know how difficult it is to get rid of it once it has made a solid invasion. While I understand the need for help is great, my greater concern is the discord in our midst. So let us pray against that first. Let us search our hearts and confess unto our mighty God what has invaded our midst."

Ingeborg closed her eyes. Leave it to John Solberg to do something so unexpected. As the silence lengthened, she confessed her resentment of Hildegunn, who she felt was the instigator of the anti-Indian movement. She heard someone sniff and realized she was not the only one caught in this crabgrass.

After what seemed like an hour but had likely been only a few minutes, Pastor Solberg cleared his throat. "Heavenly Father, we praise you and thank you for this opportunity to grow closer as a family. We thank you that you invite us to come before you with our problems, and when we leave them with you, you will solve them and absolve us of our sins. We confess that we have sinned against you by thought, word, and deed. And against your Word and one another."

After a pause his voice changed. "I have good news for you. By the power of the almighty God, I grant to you loving forgiveness of the sins you have confessed these past few minutes. God has for us the unlimited grace to live forgiven lives, to walk in His ways, and to do His will here on earth. In the name of our Lord Jesus Christ, amen."

Ingeborg blew her nose and felt a small hand creep into the crook of her elbow. She looked down to see Emmy staring up at her, little worry lines binding her brows into one line. Ingeborg leaned closer and whispered, "It's all right. There are good tears too."

Emmy nodded and leaned the side of her face against Ingeborg's arm.

"Now, Mrs. Valders, I believe you have the letter sent by Dr. Bjorklund, in which she pleads for our help. Would you please read it aloud?"

A slight gasp stirred the quiet air.

Hildegunn stood and read the letter, only stumbling once.

> "I am writing this to all of you because I need your help. Well, not really me, but there are people in terrible need on the Rosebud Reservation in South Dakota. I know you've been sending quilts and clothing and food to the Indians northwest of Blessing, and I hope you don't quit doing that, but could you please find it in your hearts to do more? This winter has been terribly hard on people who are already weakened by lack of food, housing, and medical care. Please gather up what you can and have it shipped down there. I know God will bless you for being His hands to these people. As Jesus said, 'Inasmuch as ye have done it unto one of the least of these, ye have done it unto me.' "

"One of the daughters of Blessing sent this to us." Hildegunn spoke with emphasis on *daughters of Blessing*.

Ingeborg hoped her astonishment didn't show.

When Hildegunn finished and sat down again, Pastor Solberg stood. "I just want to remind us all of something Paul wrote in his letters. He said that when we choose to give, we should give freely and with a joyful heart. Now, the way I understand this, not everyone has to give to this need if they don't want to. So search your hearts. Secondly, I know some of us look on our Indian neighbors in a different way than perhaps God has instructed us to do. I would love to see all those feelings and opinions healed by the blood of Jesus so we can all walk forth in the glory of His love. The Bible says that Christ died for all." He let his gaze roam the room. "If anyone would like to talk privately with me regarding our neighbors, I would be more than happy to talk with you at another time. Yes, Thorliff, what is it?"

"I have here a letter from my wife that she asked me to read, since my mother won't let my wife out of bed." A healing chuckle rippled around the room.

"Go ahead."

> "Dear friends and family,
>
> "I'm sorry I cannot be there to speak from a medical point of view, so this will have to suffice. First of all, I have heard so many of you often say how blessed we are here in Blessing. Through the years I have seen your wonderful generosity to one another and to the strangers who have come to our town, some to stay and some to go on but always richer for having been here. Our neighbors to the south are starving, and that makes them prey to all sorts of diseases. I know we don't agree on everything, but if it were any of our own children dying of hunger or disease, the rest of us would put a stop to that immediately. I plead with you to consider these people as part of us without judging how different they might be from us and without recounting stories and excuses that close our hearts. Please, let us be God's hands to His hurting children.
>
> "In His service,
>
> "Dr. Elizabeth Bjorklund"

Thorliff sat down to some rustlings and muttered comments. Ingeborg glanced up to see Joshua Landsverk sitting with his arms clamped across his chest and a frown digging into his face. What had happened in his life to cause a reaction like this? He was not a happy man right now. One could surely see that.

"Any more comments?"

"Well, since food seems to be the first problem to be dealt with, I'd like to know how many families are on the reservation," Lars Knutson started. "I'd like to know what has happened to the food supplies promised by the government and what kind of man is running that reservation. Is he a good man or a crook?" He glanced around the room. "I know that letters would take far too long and are easily ignored. Now, the reservation northwest of us has improved since we took an interest in them. So perhaps we can help Rosebud in the same way."

"How will we get this information?" Mr. Valders asked.

"We could contact the young man at the hospital in Chicago."

"We could send a few men down to the reservation to look into the matter."

"Especially if those men were herding a few head of cattle and driving a wagon with beans and other staples in it."

Various men had offered these suggestions, making Ingeborg wish she had sat in the rear for a change so she could watch what was going on.

"But once that is gone, then what?" Hildegunn asked.

"That is a good question," Pastor Solberg said with a nod. "The needs are many. That's for sure."

Hjelmer stood up. "I would be willing to go if we can gather up the supplies and someone else would come along. We don't have cattle or hogs, but we do have beans and other supplies." He sat down, and Penny patted his arm. "Surely we can get down there faster by railroad."

Mr. Geddick stood. "I'll go with you. I can drive a wagon."

When the volunteering came to a halt, Pastor Solberg stood again.

"All I can say is thank you, praise God, and I know we are all hungry. Let's close with prayer. Haakan, would you pray for us, and then we'll sing the grace before we leave the room."

Haakan stood and turned to look around the room. "First I want to say how proud I am to be part of this family." He closed his eyes, and stillness eased its way back into the room. "Father in heaven, you know us all from the inside out. You know our hurts and our hearts. Thank you for all the heaped-on blessings you have sent to us so that we may send them on to others in need. Let this draw us closer together, Father, knowing that we don't have to agree on but two things, that we love you and want to serve you. In Jesus' name, amen."

Thank you, Lord, that I am married to this amazing man. Ingeborg stood with the rest of them, and they sang the grace.

"All right, while the ladies put the food out, I suggest the men join me out at the ball field. I have need of some suggestions there. I expect the children will help put things out too."

Ingeborg found herself walking out with Hildegunn. Without thinking she took Hildegunn's hand in hers and whispered, "Please forgive me?"

Hildegunn stiffened. She stopped and faced Ingeborg. "I . . . I must ask the same."

Ingeborg hugged the still stiff woman. "We don't have to agree. We just have to love each other."

"We do. Your Astrid gave us Benny, and now she is asking for help. How can I say no any longer?"

"You are a wonderful grandmother."

"Thank you. All the little ones are our gifts from God," she said. "No matter how they come."

All these years, Lord, I've seen only the irritable outside of her, and you've seen her heart. "Yes, they are, Hildegunn. Yes, they are." If only Astrid were here to see this. *Lord, how can I give joyously when it is my daughter you are asking for?*

13

At least he wasn't the only one who didn't donate something. Not that he had anything to offer. *Liar* said the little voice from inside that Joshua was trying to ignore. Yes, he had some money in the bank, but that was for paying off his loan at the bank. *You'd let children starve?* How could he shut that voice up? If that was indeed his conscience, he had a terribly persistent one. After all, they were Indians, and if they would work like he did, they'd most likely not be starving to death. *But who is giving them a chance to work?* the voice said. This war had been going on inside for the last two days.

He sendeth rain on the just and on the unjust. Where had he heard that lately? Most likely from Pastor Solberg. The man had an uncanny way of choosing Scriptures to illustrate his sermons that had a knack for kicking him right in the shins. Or perhaps more like a pitchfork to the behind.

It wasn't these children who stole your aunt.

He stared down into the basement of his future house, all dug out now with forms ready to pour concrete, all because his friends here in Blessing came and helped him—without his even asking. They just showed up. Haakan, Thorliff, Lars, Trygve, even Johnny Solberg, because he wanted to pay him back for his guitar lessons.

They just showed up. They saw a friend in need and came to help.

He could help someone else. That's what Haakan said one time when he asked if he could pay for the help. *"You just help someone else and they help someone else, and life goes on."*

Joshua wanted to pour at least one wall of concrete, but the team was ready to leave for Grafton in the morning, where they had the first well to dig and windmill to erect. The first of ten that were already spoken for. A month's work at least.

What would his pa say about donating to the Indian fund? That was easy. He'd say, "Let 'em starve." *But you don't want to be like your pa.* That voice again. He ambled down the dirt ramp that would one day be the outside stairs to his cellar. This hole in the ground was the promise that he would have a house of his own one day and in the not too distant future. He had a solid job, one he looked forward to doing. What could he give joyfully? A dollar? Easy. Two dollars? A bit of a stretch. Five? He swallowed. A week's wages.

He strode out of the cellar to be and headed for Pastor Solberg's house. Children shouldn't be starving to death no matter what the adults did. He remembered the look of awe on Emmy's face when he let her touch the strings of his guitar. Children like her?

"Come in, come in," Mrs. Solberg said when he knocked on their door. "Can you stay for a cup of coffee? Won't take long." She ushered him into the parlor. "Look who's here, John."

Pastor Solberg looked up from his desk, where he was writing. "Good to see you, Joshua." He reached out to shake his hand. "I hear you are all leaving in the morning."

"We are. Should be gone a month or less if all goes according to plan."

"Sit down, sit down. I'm about due for a break here anyway."

"I really can't stay. I just came to bring you something." He dug in his pocket and pulled out his money, handing Pastor Solberg a five-dollar bill. "For the reservation fund."

"Thank you, son. Do you want change?"

"No, sir. I thought that should help buy some beans and flour. And maybe . . ." He ducked his head. "Maybe there could be a bag of peppermint candy included?"

"I'll see that there is. They'll be leaving tomorrow, same as you. Got the railroad to donate the use of a boxcar, so things can get there more quickly."

"Good." Joshua clenched the brim of his hat.

"I'm surprised at this."

"Me too. But between you and that nagging voice inside, I decided to give in."

"I have a feeling there is a lot more story behind this than you are letting on."

Joshua nodded. "Someday I'll have to tell you."

"We'll miss you, especially on Sunday mornings. Everyone sings out more with you leading."

"My ma would like to hear that." Joshua backed toward the door. "I need to finish getting ready to leave. See you when we get back."

"Good night, then. And thanks for listening, both to me and that inner voice. God bless and keep you on this journey."

As Joshua walked back to the boardinghouse, he wasn't sure which journey Pastor Solberg had been referring to: digging wells or life in general. But both his step and his heart suddenly felt a lot lighter.

———

TRYGVE HAD THE teams harnessed and hitched to the two wagons by the time the sun rim peeked above the horizon. Joshua tossed a duffel bag into the black wagon with white letters proclaiming the business as Blessing Wells and Windmills.

Penny brought out a basket of food and handed it to Joshua. "This should help for today."

"Ma did the same," Trygve said. "We won't have to cook for a day or two."

"You have water along?"

"In the barrel."

"God go with you," Penny said with a smile. Joshua wondered that Hjelmer wasn't there to see them off too.

"Ma said the same." Trygve climbed up on the dray wagon while Joshua did the same with the other. Gilbert climbed up beside him, and they hupped the horses forward.

"Don't get stuck!" Penny called as she waved good-bye.

They'd spent the last two days making sure all their supplies were loaded and machinery was in good form. He had a list of supplies and materials long enough to last the run and a ledger to keep his records in. Hjelmer was particular about record keeping. The way he was growing the businesses, he had to be. He and Thorliff. As they drove down a road that a hundred years earlier the oxcarts had followed between Canada and the land that was now Minneapolis and St. Paul, he listened for the creaks of the wagon. One of the wheels already needed greasing, the meadowlarks were singing in the dawn, and the air was redolent with awakening earth. There was something to be said for spring in North Dakota after a winter that tested a man's mettle. Spring didn't tiptoe in here. It burst forth in a rush to remind both land and people they'd not been forgotten.

He shook his head at the way his thoughts were going. If Astrid were here, would she feel like he did? While he knew he didn't want to farm, he also knew he wanted to be near the land, not living in some city or even a big town. Far as he could figure, with this job he had the best of all worlds.

Following Hjelmer's instructions, they arrived at the farm south of Grafton as the sun was setting. Joshua stepped down from the wagon seat and, after stretching, headed for the farmhouse door. First thing was to make sure they were in the right place. By the time he mounted the steps, the door swung open and a man with a smile of welcome greeted him.

"I was beginning to think you weren't coming today. Name's Hiram Aarsgard." He stuck out his hand. "Have you had supper yet?"

"Good to meet you. I'm Joshua Landsverk, and no, we just kept coming so we would get here before dark."

"You can unharness your teams and let them loose in the small pasture by the barn, and when you're finished, you come on up here and the missus will have a meal on the table for you."

"Thank you, sir."

"Hiram."

"Yes, Hiram. Do you have a special place you'd like us to park our wagons?"

"Wherever you like. The dowser said we should have easy water over there where that post is hammered into the ground."

"How far down is the well you have now?"

"Me'n my sons dug that well down about ten feet. Never run dry, but I figured we'd keep that one, drill a new one, and put up the windmill. My missus is looking forward to water piped to the house, and I'm looking forward to the wind pumping water for the livestock. I saw that one over west of town that Bjorklund drilled last year. That windmill pumped out water for the garden even."

As they talked, the two men reached the wagons, and Hiram

showed Trygve and Gilbert where to park them. He extended his invitation to supper once again and wandered back to the house.

After supper Joshua sat at the fold-out table and made notes on the day's events before starting a letter to Astrid.

> Dear Astrid,
>
> We've just completed our first trip out with the new well-drilling wagon we built this winter. This farmer is so glad to see us, and his wife made sure we would not go to bed hungry. That saved us from cooking, not that we'd have needed to with the baskets of food sent with us from Mrs. Knutson and Penny.
>
> Even covered with dust our new wagon looks pretty striking. We painted it black because that's the paint Penny had available. I painted the trim in red. I know the dust will fade it all soon, but at least there is a good coat of paint to protect the wood.
>
> Gilbert has joined Trygve and me, so the three of us should be able to accomplish much more. With one man overseeing the well drilling, the other two can be building the windmill.
>
> Sunday was the church meeting regarding providing the help that you asked for. You will be proud of your people here. Pastor Solberg referred to them, or rather to us, as the family of Blessing. That man certainly is the shepherd of this flock, as he has so often said. When I think of the church I grew up in where brimstone flowed from beneath the altar, I cannot begin to compare the two. I wish my mother could have come to Blessing.

And my father, he thought. Perhaps he'd not have been so bitter if he'd heard preaching like Rev. Solberg's. The memory of the old man he'd not have recognized had he not known who he was rose up to choke him up every once in a while. He'd start a letter to them also.

He described the wagon and signed off with *More later. Your friend, Joshua.*

Trygve had already decided to take his bedroll outside and sleep under the wagon like they had to the last season, but Joshua opted for one of the hammocks strung between two hooks they had drilled into the two-by-four frame. Gilbert took the other hammock, and with the door and window open, a comfortable breeze blew through the wagon. Screens kept the insects at bay, other than a moth that got in to flutter around the kerosene lantern.

THE NEXT MORNING they started work as soon as the sun lightened the earth enough so they could see to harness the horse that would walk the circle to drill the pipe down into the ground. Since they were still in the Red River Valley, they didn't anticipate any rocks. After dinner they traded off the horses, and at about three o'clock they got a gusher.

"Will you look at that," Hiram said and shouted for his wife to come look.

Trygve wrestled the cap in place, and Gilbert and Joshua with a team dragged over the frame they'd been working on for the windmill. Three days later they released the tie-down on the tail, and the windmill turned to face the wind. While they'd been building the windmill, Hiram and one of his sons had been helping and running pipe to the cattle tank and to the house.

"You have to keep those gears greased," Joshua cautioned them. "And tie down that tail every time you go up there to work so you don't get knocked off the platform if the wind suddenly comes up."

Supper that night was more like a party as they celebrated the new rig.

"I love to hear it creaking," the missus said, "and the sound of the wind against the blades. Has its own song, don't it?"

"I hadn't thought that way, ma'am, but you are right. Once you get that hand pump in the sink, you can have water any time you want."

"You brought me your bill?" Hiram asked after supper.

Joshua handed him the totaled statement, including subtracting the deposit the man had made.

"This might be the best money I've ever spent," he said as he brought a metal box out of the bedroom and counted out the cash. "There you go, and don't you forget to stop in and talk with Henderson at the next farm over. He's kinda tight, but he sure needs one of these."

"You invite him over to see yours, and we'll leave you an address to contact Mr. Bjorklund to see when we can fit another one in. Right now we are doing a place about three miles from here. You know the Bensons?"

"Of course. They go to our same church. I'm the first one there to get a drilled well and a windmill. But I know for certain we won't be the last."

As he put the ledger away later, Joshua smiled. It sure would be nice if all the new jobs were this easy. And if all the women fed them as well as Mrs. Aarsgard, they'd never have to do their own cooking. Joshua leaned back in his chair and stretched his arms over his head, locking his hands. The last bit of anxiety over his new responsibilities dissolved before him. He liked this new job. Now if only Astrid would come home and forget about Africa.

14

Athens, Georgia

Astrid was sitting in the rear of the classroom today, hoping Rev. Thompkins would forget she was there and not ask her any questions. Her mind was whirling with all the possibilities for her future.

"As you all have prepared, you know we are studying Paul's letter to Timothy. You've all read it, I'm sure." At their nods he continued. "I thought this appropriate since so many of you are indeed young." He stopped and glanced at Dr. Gansberg and his wife. "Some are just young at heart but with a deep knowledge of the Word of God."

At least he did not say *you are indeed young men*, Astrid thought, still feeling disgruntled after the discussion with Rev. Arbuckle and his questions. While Paul had said that women should not pastor a church, he never mentioned being a doctor was not a good thing for those of the female persuasion. *If I ever teach, it will not be on spiritual matters but on medical matters,* she promised herself. But she knew that many medical men would still take affront at a young woman teaching them the latest in medical procedures and studies. No matter how qualified she was.

The thoughts did not make her happy.

"Dr. Bjorklund?"

She jerked her attention back to where it belonged, in the classroom, studying Timothy. What had he asked her? "I . . . I'm sorry. I guess my mind took off on its own. Would you please repeat your question?" She could feel embarrassment flaming her cheeks and up her neck.

"I asked what stood out to you in this letter."

Astrid made her mind return to last night's reading and the second time through early this morning. "I think Paul gave good advice for each of us, to do our best, to remember what we learned in our youth, to not feel . . ." She paused, squinting her eyes to remember what she had thought. "To not feel intimidated because we are young, that we have gifts to use for the body of Christ, and we must not shirk using them." She heaved a sigh of relief at his nodding.

"Very good."

"Someone else? What did you learn from the text?"

Dr. Gansberg raised his hand. "I think the advice is good for all ages, even though it's especially aimed at a young man. I feel I am being called to a new phase of my life, and I am very young in experience to this new calling." He smiled at his wife. "We were talking about that this morning."

"Anyone else?"

"I think Paul should not have told Timothy to drink a glass of red wine every day to aid his stomach." The young man shook his head. "Spirits never solved anything."

Astrid felt her eyes roll. Should she take him on or let him be? He always found something negative to say.

Rev. Thompkins looked to Dr. Gansberg. "Would you like to comment on that from a medical point of view, Dr. Gansberg?"

"How about history first?"

"That would be fine."

"First of all, you have to remember that wine was very important in those days. Much of the water was contaminated by animal and human waste leaking into the water sources. People could get very ill drinking the water. Wine is also an antiseptic and can calm a contrary stomach. It has a good many uses. Jesus thought it so important that at the wedding in Cana, He changed the water in the big casks to wine. It was so much better than the wine served at first that people commented on it. The Bible doesn't say to not drink wine. It says to not become drunk with it. As in everything, moderation."

Astrid watched her friend speaking so rationally and calmly. How could anyone dispute him without sounding like a petulant child? Even his gentle voice helped carry the lesson along. She caught a glance from Mrs. Gansberg, and it was all she could do not to wink. Instead, she raised an eyebrow, which brought a slight nod in return.

Astrid glanced across the room at the naysayer, observing his expanding girth. Jesus also never said not to eat the food around them, but He did mention gluttony. A comment like that would most likely be the kind that would make her mother shake her head and look sad, as if to say, "How could my daughter say such a cruel thing?" So Astrid said nothing. *You're letting your own hurt become an attack against others.* The internal voice gave her a jab.

Rev. Thompkins appeared to be having a difficult time with his throat. Maybe he should cover his eyes too, so the laughter did not leak out.

Someone else coughed discreetly and raised his hand. "I liked the way Paul told Timothy to remember what he'd learned at his mother's knee and went on to praise her and the grandmother too. My grandmother is the one who encouraged me the most. From the time I was little, she said that God had a special calling for me. I tried to run away from it for a while, but God would not let me go. So here I am, and though my grandmother has gone home to be with our Lord, I think she is watching over me and praying for me still."

Astrid caught the thought that tried to whip through her mind—the comment Rev. Arbuckle had made that she should get married and come back with her husband. Peter, the young man who had just spoken and whose name she was always forgetting, could become such a man, she was sure. He worked hard at his lessons, spoke wisely in class, and yet had a delightful sense of humor. He was pretty good-looking too. Not Nordic like the men in her family, he had wavy brown hair, which she'd call the brown of oak leaves as their color fades in the fall, and hazel eyes that crinkled at the corners. He had a deep voice, mid-baritone, that soared when they sang hymns, pulling the rest along with him. He had been polite to her from the beginning while not trying to force his ideas on her. Maybe if she didn't have Joshua Landsverk on her mind— She jerked, startled at the trail her mind was taking. *Astrid Bjorklund, whatever are you thinking? If Maydell were privy to your thoughts, she would burst her corset laughing.*

But what about Joshua? If she were truly bound to him, would her thoughts even consider another? She was certain no one could have pulled Jonathan from Grace's thoughts. Maybe this separation was a good test for both of them. Could it endure two years while she went to Africa? *If* she went? How many of the board agreed with Rev. Arbuckle's position?

She ordered her attention back to the discussion going on around her. Wouldn't Pastor Solberg like to be in the middle of this one? There she went again, off on a memory. What she needed was a good brisk walk to dispel all the thoughts of the ordeal of her interview with the mission board and then the dinner she'd been required to share with a man who really did not seem to like her at all. Was that what bothered her about him? That he didn't like her? She'd met other people who didn't like her. Red Hawk, for one, didn't like her at first. But given time and working together, they became friends. How could one person have two different callings? Surely God wasn't confused, so it must be her.

"Your lesson for tomorrow is to read Second Timothy and come prepared to discuss that too. I hope you are continuing in your memory work. Always remember, some of your greatest challenges may come when you do not have a Bible at hand. But if the Word is in your mind and heart, the Holy Spirit can bring it back to you at that moment in time when you need it the most." Rev. Thompkins paused, catching each one's attention deliberately. "Class dismissed." As everyone stood to leave, he beckoned to Astrid.

So much for my long walk. She made her way to his desk in the front of the room. "Yes, sir?"

"I thought perhaps you and I and the doctor and his wife could go to the dining room for a cup of coffee, or lemonade if you prefer."

Astrid nodded, studying his face and hands while he talked with Dr. Gansberg. Something was wrong, but she had no idea what. Was her teacher pale? His hands shaking? Sure it was warm, but he seemed both pale and ruddy. Silly. One cannot be both. The argument going on in her head nearly drowned out the conversation between the other three as they guided her with them to the dining room. Did Dr. Gansberg notice anything? She couldn't just out and out ask—could she? What she wouldn't give for her stethoscope right now. Or at least the chance to check his pulse. *Your imagination is taking over,* she remonstrated herself. *Or maybe you just miss practicing medicine.*

"So will that be coffee or tea or lemonade?" He beckoned the young man over from the serving table. "Can we have our drinks outside on the veranda?"

"Of course, Rev. Thompkins. I'll bring them right out. You want cookies to go with that?"

He nodded, thanked the student, and herded his three guests outside to a wrought-iron table with four chairs. Clusters of wisteria hung down from the trellis above, sweetening the air and luring the buzzing of honeybees.

Astrid breathed in lungsful of the fragrant air. She glanced up at the purple blossoms, some with bits of white like a throat, all small blossoms that grew in clumps, much like she pictured grapes growing. "Do you think we could grow something like this in North Dakota?"

Rev. Thompkins chuckled. "I don't know, but it grows well in parts of Africa too." He sat down and leaned back in his chair, all the time focusing on her. "So how do you feel your interview with the board went?"

Astrid stared at him, eyes wide. Nothing like jumping right in. She looked to Dr. Gansberg, as if he could help her. Back to the reverend. To be honest or polite, which was it?

"My mother would say that *fine* might fit here," she said.

"Fine?"

"And what would you say?" Mrs. Gansberg asked in a gentle voice.

In for a dime, in for a dollar. She had no idea where that old phrase came from, but it fit. "I get very tired of hearing that a young, unattached female would do better if she went home, found a man who wanted to be a missionary, and then came back. I didn't ask to come here!" Her heart tempo kicked up as did her voice tempo. "If you remember, going to Africa was not on my wish list. I did not just wake up one morning and think, oh my, I want to go to Africa, where they have fierce wild animals, mean venomous snakes, and natives who really don't like white people coming and telling them what to do."

"Not all feel that way," a soft voice said, breaking in to her diatribe.

"Well, maybe not, but the only one here who doesn't seem to feel that way is being pretty silent, and He's the one who started all this. If God's not worried about this, then why are all those around me so concerned?"

"Not all."

She heaved a sigh, a deep sigh that started in her toes and worked its way up, hopefully bringing along some of the baggage she'd been dragging around. Her eyes stung, and she sniffed. *I will not cry now!* She repeated the order and clamped her teeth. Anything to fight back the tears. This was not a crying matter. A man in these circumstances would not cry, so she would not either. "That's true. Not all." She sort of smiled at those around her.

"So what are you going to do about it?" Rev. Thompkins asked, leaning forward.

"You ask the hardest questions."

"*Simple* and *easy* do not mean the same, do they? But to get to the bottom of things, you must always ask questions, ponder them, and ask more questions. Do you think God is upset if you ask questions?"

Astrid thought about an answer. "Is asking questions doubting?"

"What did Jesus tell Thomas?"

"He held out His hands and said for Thomas to put his fingers in the scars and believe."

"Did He scold him? Mock him?"

"No." Astrid felt as though she needed to give more of an answer. She rubbed her lower lip between her teeth, eyes slightly squinted, all in the hope that an answer would come. The silence trembled on the edge of wisdom, as if far more than the teacher and the Gansbergs waited for the answer. Astrid sniffed and gave her teacher a steady look. "He loved him and was giving Thomas a chance to understand and to let his doubting go." She nodded, feeling a smile coming on.

"And Thomas fell on his knees and said, 'My Lord and my God.' " Tears burned the back of her eyes and throat. Was that what God was doing with her? Giving her a chance to let go of her doubts and fears and worship Him? Just worship and love Him, as He loved her?

"It's not about Africa, is it?" Blinking did not suffice, and a tear trickled down her face.

Her favorite teacher of all smiled much like she figured Jesus would smile. And waited.

"It's about my trusting Him, trusting He will lead me, no matter what those around me say?"

Mrs. Gansberg leaned over and hugged her, whispering in her ear, "You are blessed to learn this as young as you are. Hang on to it."

Astrid nodded and blew out a breath that let her cheeks stretch and relax. With that action, she felt her neck and shoulders let go too, the warmth traveling up her head and down through the rest of her body. Hugs could be heavenly. She shook her head slowly because of its heaviness. "How come I am so blessed?"

Rev. Thompkins gave her another of his Jesus smiles. "Because Jesus loves you. You are one of His chosen ones, and He has a very real and definite plan for your life."

"Plans for a hope and a future." She finished the verse almost unconsciously, the words rolling through her mind.

"Oh, there you are." Dean Highsmith strode through the door. "I just wanted to tell you that the board approved you for a two-year mission in east Africa, starting with working at the hospital in Mombasa and then moving to work with Rev. Schuman as you are able."

Astrid stared up at him. Her tongue stumbled around the words that she couldn't put in order. Her jaw dropped. "Really? You mean it?"

The dean smiled and nodded. "Yes, I mean it." He paused. "See? God triumphs. He brought you here for His purposes."

"Thank you." If she weren't sitting down already, she knew she'd have collapsed into the chair. She really was going to Africa. She sucked in a breath and blew it out. "When will I be leaving?"

"You will finish your studies here, so take advantage of every minute of your remaining time. Then you will have the choice to go home for two weeks or not. But you will be leaving by the first of July. The Lord surely has His hand upon you, my dear."

"Dean Highsmith?" His assistant paged him from the doorway, and he excused himself and left.

"Did a whirlwind just blow through here, or am I hearing things?" she asked her friends at the table.

"You heard right, and we can't be more happy for you." Dr. Gansberg patted her hand. "So then, we shall see you in Africa too. I will be serving at that same hospital for a couple of months to become acclimatized."

After the others had left, Astrid continued to sit out on the veranda, staring up into the clouds. Why did she feel as if she'd been run over by the westbound Great Northern train?

15

On the way back to her room to get ready for supper, Astrid stopped by the mailboxes and pulled out not one but two letters from her box. The one from her mor she slipped into her pocket; the other brought a smile as she studied Joshua's handwriting. Since he wrote so seldom, each letter was a treat. How would he handle the announcement she would send out tonight? Would he wait for two years? Did she love him enough to marry him? Did she love him at all? Was this really the man God had in mind for her? Ah, so many questions. She shook her head slowly and walked down the hall back to her room.

Once she was in a place where she could be alone, out on her veranda, she sat down in the wrought-iron chair, grateful for the magnolia-print cushion and the birds chattering in the trees above. Another sigh escaped, and she shook her head again. This must indeed be a sighing day, or perhaps week. She laid her letters on the table and, after staring at them for a bit, slit open the one from Joshua.

Dear Astrid,

Spring is beautiful, as always, on the prairie. The wild flowers are rampant, and the sun feels so good after the cold winter. I know that soon it will be so hot I will wish for fall, but today feels downright perfect.

We are back on the road again. Drilling the wells and building the windmills is going just as we'd planned. We set a well and windmill south of Grafton for a farmer named Hiram Aarsgard, and I know he is going to brag to all his neighbors. His wife was so grateful, she nearly cried when she realized that soon her pitcher pump would fill her sink with fresh, clear water.

I think we take water for granted in our country. Pastor Solberg gave me a letter he received from Rev. Schuman in Africa. Over there whole villages die of cholera from drinking bad water. Why they don't drill wells like we do, I'll never understand. Two men could push the bar that drives the bit into the ground if they don't have a mule. It isn't expensive or difficult.

Hjelmer and Mr. Geddick went off with the first shipment of goods to the Indian reservation that you asked us to take care of. They took the train as far as they could to speed up the trip. It is a good thing Samuel is there to help with the spring field work, along with Solem Brunderson. This way Gilbert and Trygve can work with me. They seem to like what we do as much as I.

My basement is ready for pouring the concrete. I was hoping to have that done before I left, but I just plain ran out of time. Why is it that once spring pops in, the pace picks up speed like a runaway horse team?

We had a sort of concert in church last Sunday. Johnny Solberg—I think I told you I've been giving him lessons on the guitar—and I played. Lars brought his fiddle too. Now, I know how much everyone loves the music at dances, but playing the hymns together brought tears to more than one pair of eyes. Johnny has a real true tenor voice and sings like angel. We kind of made up a song of our own and sang it then for the first time. I was so proud of him, I could have busted some buttons. I think Pastor Solberg probably did, and his wife used up two handkerchiefs.

Well, the rain has stopped, so we can do some setting up for drilling in the morning. May our Lord keep you safe.

Your friend,
Joshua Landsverk

Astrid stared at the page before folding it and slipping it back into the envelope. There was something different about this letter. She tapped the edge on her finger, hoping it would help her think it out. Maybe it was the sense that he seemed peacefully at home and part of the family in Blessing now. She laid the letter down and took up her mother's.

My dear daughter,

I cannot tell you how much I miss you, and if it weren't for little Emmy I might have gotten on that train and gone looking for you.

Astrid put the letter down and rubbed her temples with her fingertips. *Oh, Mor, if only you had done that, I would have been so thrilled to see you.* Astrid rolled her lips together. How would she bear being all that way from home, clear around the world? And now she knew that was exactly what was going to happen. Two years looked like a lifetime. Should she go home for a visit, or would that make leaving even more difficult?

She picked up the letter again.

We had an old Indian stop by the other day. Far says he thinks the man was here before, when Metiz was still alive. She interpreted for us then. Emmy knew him right away and ran to see him. I think he might be her grandfather, but I am not sure. Or an uncle. He thanked us for taking care of her. I was so afraid he was going to take her away, but he left her here. What a gift he had given us in this little girl. I know you will love her on sight. She was sad when he left but didn't try to go with him. I know there is a story there, and perhaps one day we will find it out. We invited him to come again.

Emmy is helping me plant the garden. She and Inga are great friends and a big help. Inga is here a lot of the time, which makes it easier for Elizabeth right now.

So what is wrong with Elizabeth? Astrid scanned quickly through the remainder of the letter but nothing else was mentioned about her. Should she call? While this wasn't an emergency . . . She tucked the thought away to mull over later. She read the rest of the Blessing news. Hjelmer should be back from the trip soon, and Mor was looking forward to his report.

I wanted to go along, but since there is illness on the reservation, I didn't want Emmy to be infected.

What have you heard regarding Africa? I am still in a quandary over your possibly going there. I have to keep reminding myself that God is everywhere and when He sends someone out to serve His kingdom, He will protect my only daughter. I think of Samuel's mother sometimes. She had to give her son up when he was small. How could she do that? Uff da. The girls are supposed to be asleep, but I hear giggling, so I will go check on them.

I hope you always know how much I love you and miss you. Come home soon.

Your mother,
Ingeborg

Astrid fought back the tears. Two years without seeing her family. What if her father had another attack and she wouldn't be there to help? What if he died? *Lord, I said I would go and I will, but right now I am having trouble with the joyful part. Please help me.* She heard the bell ringing for supper so knew there wasn't time to answer right then, but her evening would be given to letter writing.

"I hear congratulations are in order," Peter said as they stood in line waiting to be served supper.

"News sure gets around fast here. I didn't think anyone else even knew yet."

"Well, I think it is wonderful that you have been approved and so quickly too. I hope it goes that way for me."

"Why would there be any question? You have good marks; you fit the criteria. You believe you have the calling." *Not like me—too young and female.* The comments still rankled. How was she to get rid of them?

"I hope so, but my father said he thought I should wait until I have some pastoral experience here in the United States. He once dreamed of going to China as a missionary, but it never worked out."

Astrid picked up her tray and carried it to an empty table. Peter followed her, not picking up on her wish to be alone, and they carried on a conversation over the meal. When he made a comment that made her laugh, Astrid had a thought that caught her by surprise. *Why, he's flirting with me.* And lately she'd been admiring him. What was going on?

"What are you doing this evening?" he asked as they put their trays on the counter.

"Writing overdue letters," she answered. "Why?"

"I just thought you might like to go for a walk. For a change I have my homework caught up, and"—he grinned at her—"I'd like to get to know you better."

Astrid shook her head. "I really have to let my family know the news. Sorry." She almost said, "Another time perhaps," but then was glad she didn't. Why his sudden interest?

"I understand. See you tomorrow."

Astrid watched him walk off whistling, hands in his pockets. He became interested once he knew she'd been approved, she realized. Practical romance? She wasn't sure whether to laugh or be offended. With a sigh she slipped inside her room and, after turning on the gaslight on the wall, sat down to write her letters. Tonight they would be short.

Dear Joshua,

I enjoyed your letter that arrived today. I'm glad you are happy with what you are doing. I know having well water is a real joy. When I was really little, we had a shallow well. We pulled water up with a bucket, and then we had to strain it because it was often muddy. The deeper well with a pump got even better when Pa put up the windmill. It wasn't that long ago that the windmill took over.

I have been approved for a two-year medical missionary term and will be returning to Blessing for two weeks in mid-June. I hope you will be able to return to Blessing so that I get to see you before I leave. Sorry this is so short, but I have several other letters I have to write tonight too.

Your friend,
Astrid

She put his name on the envelope and addressed it to the boardinghouse, where he'd picked up his mail before. Would it get to him if he was still off drilling? She shrugged and set the envelope aside. Then paused. Why didn't it bother her that he might not get the letter or make it back to see her? Wasn't love supposed to deepen when apart and not become indifferent? She sighed again. One answer given and another still a mystery. This learning to trust God was sure an up-and-down adventure. On to the next.

After writing to her parents, Astrid wrote to Elizabeth next and then Dr. Morganstein.

Dear Dr. Morganstein,

Today I have received final approval for a two-year mission term to Africa. There has been discussion regarding my age, my gender, and my marital status. As you can guess, this has not been easy. I will go home for two weeks and then return to leave around the first of July. I will be assigned to a large hospital in east Africa for a while, no specific time, and then hopefully serve out in the bush, as they call the remote villages, with Rev. Schuman, the man who started all this.

I am wondering if you would be willing to send me, at this address, some medical equipment and supplies. Anything you could spare would be greatly appreciated. I have heard that the shortages of basic things like antiseptics and bandages are appalling. I want to make sure I have plenty of quinine for myself so that I do not succumb to malaria. Since I hope to be sent out to the bush, I will need surgical equipment too.

I hope this isn't too much to ask. Please forgive my boldness. Right now my mind is racing with all that I need to accomplish before I leave. Thank you in advance for any help you can give me. Oh, I was wondering too if you know of someone else I can contact with this request?

I remain in your debt,
Dr. Astrid Bjorklund

Astrid fell asleep thinking of mosquito netting and a long voyage by ship. What would she do during all that time at sea?

A RAIN CLOUD decided to sit right over their heads the next day, causing the students and faculty to hurry between buildings with their umbrellas held high. Water ran off the roofs and down the long heavy chains that directed it to run into the underground lines to carry it away. Astrid thought of the rain barrels at home that would be set to catch all this wealth of water. They always washed their hair with the fresh water in the rain barrels because it smelled so sweet and came squeaky clean.

Rev. Thompkins stood before his class, smiling and greeting them as they came through the door.

Astrid studied him, recognizing the same things she had the day before. He looked pale, shaky. How do you walk up to one of your teachers and ask, "Sir, how are you feeling? Are you sure you are all right?"

Instead, she stopped beside him and asked in a low voice, "Have you talked to your doctor lately?"

He whipped around and stared at her. "No. Why do you say that?"

Now he thinks I'm a fool. "Just some things I noticed. I . . . I think it might be a good idea."

"I see. I will take that under advisement. And now let's begin our class."

Astrid took her seat and glanced around. Dr. Gansberg and his wife weren't there. She shook her head. She'd like to have talked this over with the doctor to see if he noticed what she did. Maybe she was making this up, seeing goblins where there were none.

Halfway through the class Rev. Thompkins took a step forward, seemed to stumble, and then slumped to the floor.

Astrid was on her feet and at his side before any of the others shook off their shock and began to move. She loosened his necktie and checked his pulse. "Get a stretcher in here now."

Two of the men jumped to do what she said.

Rev. Thompkins was turning whiter, if that were possible. Astrid put her fingers on his carotid artery. Irregular. He was cold too. Was he bleeding internally? Heart? Stroke? *God, help me.* His circulation must have stopped somehow.

She began to massage the left side of his chest, and a little color crept into his face. But she could tell his body was in shock. She glanced around the room to see if there was anything she could use. "Bring me his coat from the coatrack," she ordered, "and any other coats or sweaters. Put a stack of books under his feet and legs."

A sweater was offered to her, and after rolling it and placing it behind his neck, she spread his coat over him, adding other jackets as the men shared theirs.

"I called the infirmary. They have a bed ready for him," Peter said at her shoulder.

"I think they will need to send an ambulance. But have someone search for Dr. Gansberg. And I need a stethoscope."

"Where can I get one?"

"Infirmary."

He charged out to do her bidding. The men returned with the stretcher and laid it on the floor.

Astrid stood. "Okay, you take his feet," she instructed, "and you take his shoulders. Lift him carefully on three and lay him on the stretcher." She counted, and they got him moved. She tucked his hands in at his sides. "Now let's have four people, one on each corner, and we'll carry him as quickly as possible to the infirmary."

They did so, meeting Dr. Gansberg coming down the hall. He turned, pulling a stethoscope out of his pocket as they continued. He put the ends in his ears and the chest piece inside the reverend's shirt.

"Stop for a moment," Astrid ordered. The bearers did.

"Let's go again," Dr. Gansberg said. "His heart is skipping beats."

Astrid held the doors open so they could enter, and the school nurse led the way toward a bed with the covers folded at the bottom.

"What happened?" Dr. Gansberg asked. Astrid told him, keeping her eye on Rev. Thompkins.

"I said they should call the ambulance."

"You are right. Did they?"

"The ambulance is coming down the street," one of the stretcher bearers said from the window. "Should we take him out to the door right now?"

"Yes."

With Rev. Thompkins tucked into the ambulance and Dr. Gansberg in with him, Astrid stepped back.

"No, you come too," the doctor said. "You were the first to see his symptoms."

"We're ready. Do you want to meet us at the hospital?" one of the ambulance men asked. "Or come now?"

Astrid climbed into the ambulance and took one of her teacher's hands in hers. *Lord God, you know what is going on. Thank you that we could be here for him and that you can heal him. Please, Lord, this man does so much for all of his students. Let us keep him here.*

THE NEXT MORNING Dean Highsmith entered the breakfast room. "I have an announcement," he said as the room quieted down. "Rev. Thompkins is stabilized and recovering due to the quick response of our own Dr. Bjorklund. Thank you for being observant and knowing what to do." He nodded to her and began clapping. The others joined in. Astrid wished she could stop the blush she could feel burning her face.

Thank you, Father, had been her offering all night, once she heard he was breathing better and his heart had resumed its normal beat.

After breakfast she went to the front desk, purchased stamps, and put her letters in the outgoing mail. She paused, trying again to understand all the implications of this decision. How would her family cope with the news? She thanked the woman at the desk and turned to go to her first class.

Dean Highsmith caught her going by his office. "Dr. Bjorklund, a telephone call just came for you. You can talk here in my office."

Her heart in her throat, Astrid picked up the dangling earpiece. "Hello."

"Astrid, this is Thorliff. You must come home immediately. Elizabeth might be losing this baby, and Mor said we desperately need you here. We have to save Elizabeth."

She composed herself enough to ask several questions about Elizabeth's condition.

"I'll catch the next train."

She hung up and turned to face the dean. "I have to go home right away. There is a family emergency with my sister-in-law, Dr. Elizabeth."

"I'll have Marlin call the train station and find out when the next train leaves." He turned to confer with his secretary.

While she lifted the phone, the dean took Astrid's hands in his. They were warm and strong. "Dr. Bjorklund, the words I spoke to you yesterday are the same today. God triumphs. He brought you here for His purposes. Wherever that leads."

16

BLESSING, NORTH DAKOTA

Ingeborg, you cannot keep up this pace."

She stared at her husband through eyes that felt as scratchy as a day-old mosquito bite. With a deep sigh she said, "What else am I to do? Tell everyone not to get sick, not to have any accidents, and above all, not to birth any more babies?" She'd just come home from being all night with one of the newer families south of town. While the baby had been slow to come, he'd entered the world with a healthy yell. Sometimes that was the way with first babies.

"They could have brought her to you at Thorliff's so you didn't have to travel so far."

She smiled up at him and leaned against his side, the chair she was sitting on creaking resentment at her movement. "And who was it that drove me out there and slept the night on their floor so he could drive me home after the grand arrival?"

"Well, at least I slept." Haakan stroked her hair with a callused hand. "I thought those days and nights of doctoring were over for you."

"They would be if Elizabeth hadn't gone and gotten pregnant again. For all she loves caring for others, her own body seems to betray her in this matter of having a baby." She looked up at Haakan again and whispered, "I am so afraid we are going to lose her. Then how will we manage with Astrid in Africa . . . and Thorliff . . ." She shook her head. "He will have a terrible time with this."

"Aren't you borrowing trouble? Like you say to never do?" He moved his fingers to rubbing her neck, digging deep with his thumbs in the tender spots.

"Ja, I guess I am, and I do know better. I thank God that He has a plan and that He is indeed in control."

"I hear a *but* in there."

She groaned with relief as his hands kept up their healing work. "But when I get so tired, those sick and frightening thoughts sneak in, and before I know it, they've taken up housekeeping."

"Right now you are going to your bed to sleep until you wake. I will take Freda to town to watch over Elizabeth, and we will post a sign that the surgery is closed for the day. Only if there is an emergency where life is being threatened will I let them call you."

"I should sleep at Elizabeth's."

"You will stay right here."

"Between Freda and Thelma, Elizabeth will stay in bed and sleep." *Please, Lord God, let it be so. I am so tired.* She followed Haakan to the bedroom and sank down on the edge of the bed.

He turned back the covers and knelt to unlace her shoes. He pulled them off carefully, rubbing her feet for a moment. When he looked up, she was half asleep but aware of his ministrations. He tipped her over on her side, lifted her legs, and tucked them under the sheet and light blanket. With each motion he touched her gently, his fingers lingering to soothe away the lines dug into her forehead. With the cover around her shoulders, he leaned over, kissed her forehead, and paused a moment with his hand on her shoulder.

When he left the room, he closed the door with a subtle snick.

Hours later, Ingeborg could no longer ignore the need to relieve herself, so she sat up and swung her feet to the floor. She'd slept so deeply that she hardly remembered crawling into bed. Haakan had been at work for sure. Grateful anew for the bathroom the men had installed over the winter, she washed her hands and face afterward and smoothed the flyaway strands of hair back with still-damp fingers. The house was quiet. Where was Emmy? Did Freda take her with her?

No one in the kitchen, but a pot was simmering on the back of the stove. Catching back a yawn, she stared out the screen door. No one on the porch. From the angle of the sun it was now late afternoon. Where was everyone?

Her big orange and white cat joined her at the door and chirped her request for the door to be opened. Ingeborg complied and followed her outside. The wondrous smell of growing spring wafted by on the breeze. A robin swooped with one of the bits of yarn she'd knotted loosely on a nail on a porch post and took it up in the cottonwood tree to add to her nest. The mister followed close behind, blue yarn in his beak.

Hearing a child laugh, she looked out across the field to see Ellie striding the path, Carl and Emmy running and laughing before her. That answered the question of where Emmy was. Ellie had fifteen-month-old baby May in a sling on her back and her sunbonnet shielding her face.

Emmy looked up as if drawn by an invisible string. Her "Gamma's up" echoed across the field, and she took off running, leaving two-and-a-half-year-old Carl behind to run as fast as he could. He could not keep up with the girls yet, much to his disgust.

"Gamma! Gamma! We baked cookies." Emmy was swinging a tin pail, which no doubt contained her treasures. When she got to Ingeborg, she threw her arms around her legs and hugged as if she'd been gone for days rather than hours. Looking upward, her brow wrinkled. "You sick?"

Ingeborg leaned down to return the hug. "Not sick, just tired."

"Bad tired, huh? Grampa said be quiet, very quiet. So we went to Carl's house."

"Where is Grampa now?"

The little girl shrugged and looked around as if he would pop out from behind the tree trunk. "Don't know. Freda gone to Inga's."

Ellie opened the gate, and Carl dashed through. "Gamma, you good now?"

"He thought you'd been sent to bed because you were naughty." Ellie slung the baby off her back and held her on her hip in the age-old way of mothers everywhere.

Ingeborg hugged Carl, who now had her other side in a hug grip and held out her hands for baby May. The little one gave her a toothy grin while wiggling to get down and walk too. Already she tried to keep up with Carl, much as he did with Inga and Emmy.

"Tired as I was, I must have been naughty somehow. But that baby who didn't want to come into the world after he'd started the trip finally gave up. It was a lusty boy, and he told us what he thought about all the indignities he'd been through."

"Was this that young family, Englebret . . . ? Ellie's brow wrinkled in trying to remember. "When I saw her in church, she was pooching out pretty far."

"Her name is Ida, his Oslo, and yes, you were close. Engebretson. They named the baby Rufus, after his grandpa."

"How long have they lived there now?"

"A couple of months. I'm going to mention him to Thorliff. He's looking for a job. They have only a small parcel, enough pasture for a cow or two and a small hayfield. He said he doesn't really want to raise wheat, not that they have room."

"Did you invite her to quilting?"

"I most certainly did. And if she feels well enough to come to church on Sunday, I invited them to join us for dinner too. He's hoping to talk his brother into moving here. Word is out that there are jobs to be had in Blessing."

Ellie smiled at her mother-in-law. "I'm sure you enjoyed birthing that baby."

"That I did. Been some time since I got to do that. I was more encourager than doctor. Interesting the things we can talk about in the dark hours of the night, in spite of her needing to scream once in a while." She glanced over to see Carl and Emmy sharing cookies out of the tin pail. "Don't you go spoiling your supper now, you two."

"As if anything would keep Carl from eating." Ellie reached for May and, settling her back on her hip, led the way into the house. "I have an idea you might have some strawberry syrup left. Doesn't a swizzle sound good right now?"

"If we were in town, I would take you and our three here, and we would go visit Rebecca's sweet shop. She's getting impatient for the strawberries to ripen for her sundaes and sodas." Ingeborg retrieved the strawberry syrup from the icebox. "You get the vinegar out while I chip off some ice."

"Ice cream?" Emmy and Carl snapped their attention at her as if drawn by a magnet.

"No. Swizzles."

"Oh." Emmy stuck out her lower lip. "I like ice cream best."

"Well, I do too, but there are no strong men here to crank the ice-cream maker, so we'll make do." In a few minutes they had mixed the ingredients and took their fizzing drinks out to the back porch, along with the tin pail of cookies and some more out of the cookie jar. Ellie sat in the rocking chair and snuggled a sleepy May against her chest.

"I should be home making supper."

"Why don't you and Andrew come here instead? There's a pot of ham and beans ready. I think Freda baked bread this morning, and I know I saw a pie on the counter in the pantry."

"She is such a hard worker. Reminds me of someone else I know." Ellie took a sip from her glass, held the cool against her cheek, and rested against the chair back. "How are your peas doing?"

"Haakan put up the trellis yesterday. I need to get out there and convince all those shoots to hang on to the string. Some of them can be so contrary. And yours?"

"Carl helped me put up the strings. You should have seen him bent over talking to the plants, telling them to hurry up and grow strong so he could eat the peas."

Ingeborg chuckled. "That must have been some sight. I remember the year that we had a violet growing out behind the barn. Thorliff came running to tell me, so Andrew and I wandered down there too. We tried to get Andrew to sniff the sweet smell, but all he did was blow on it. Thorliff thought that was the funniest thing. He started laughing, which set Andrew off. How could I not laugh along with them? Anyone seeing us would have thought we'd lost our minds."

"Andrew always said he was going to marry up with me. Where do you think he got that phrase?"

Ingeborg shook her head. "Heaven only knows." She sipped her drink. "I am so pleased that you thought of this. Guess I am just not ready for summer yet."

They let the twittering birds and children sing on the rising afternoon breeze. A cow bellered, answered by another one.

"The cows are ready for milking."

"I know. Goldy always announces the time. You'd think she carried a pocket watch."

"If you carried an udder as big as hers, you might want to get milked too."

"Point well taken. Did you leave Andrew a note?"

"Where else would I be with the horse and buggy there? Of course, I could have walked to town. I haven't visited with Sophie in forever. Other than at church."

"Andrew always comes by here on his way to the barn. You don't need anything from home do you?"

"You still have diapers?"

"Of course."

Ellie glanced down at the child sleeping on her lap. "She was fussy this afternoon and didn't want a nap, but look now."

"We can lay her on the bed if you want."

"Maybe later. Oh." She dug in her apron pocket and pulled out a letter. "Here. This came from Mor yesterday. It says she is coming to visit."

"All of them?"

"No, just her. Arne and Rachel aren't out of school yet, and Rachel can get the meals. I think Mor just wants to see her grandchildren. You'd think we lived on opposite sides of the state for the times we get on that train and go visit."

Ingeborg unfolded the letter and read it through quickly. "That's pretty much what she says, all right. Ah, Goodie, how wonderful it will be to see you." They became such good friends when she and the children came to live with them, those many years ago, after Goodie's husband died that terrible winter.

"You're right. We need to visit more often, and I still think we should convince Uncle Olaf that he could have his furniture making right here in Blessing. After all, so many of his pieces live here, why not the maker too?"

"He got flooded out one too many times."

"That's a terrible excuse."

The two women shared smiles, and Ingeborg passed the cookie plate so Ellie didn't have to move and wake the little one.

"I am so glad you came. We haven't had time like this for, well, it seems like years."

"What do you hear from Astrid?"

"Other than she is enjoying the missionary school and still not sure if they will approve her, not a lot." Ingeborg tipped her head back and set her rocker to creaking. "The thought of her being clear around the world in Africa . . ." She shook her head slowly. "No matter how much I pray for her and that situation, I have yet to find peace in it. I talked with Pastor about it, and I get the feeling he's in the same boat. Wouldn't you think that God would calm my mother heart?"

Ellie chewed on her bottom lip. "I'm glad Andrew has never wanted to be anywhere but here. I don't know what I'd do if I were you. What does Elizabeth say?"

"She doesn't talk about it." That was another thing that bothered Ingeborg. Elizabeth was counting on Astrid to come home and help her with the surgery and their dream of a traveling clinic and a real hospital. While two years would go by fast, the possibility of a change in plans had been a terrible disappointment. *Lord, I've prayed for them both. And I've prayed for me. You know all my prayers. Sometimes, in this situation, I wonder if you are really listening.*

"You sleeping, Gamma?" The little hand on her arm made her smile and open her eyes.

"Just thinking."

"You praying." Emmy nodded, her dark eyes intent.

"Ah, little one. You want to come on my lap?"

"Yes." She scrambled up, using the rocker of the chair as a step, and snuggled close.

Carl came to her other side. "Me too?"

With one in each arm, Ingeborg smiled at Ellie. "This morning I was so tired, Haakan ordered me to bed." Ellie arched an eyebrow, which made Ingeborg smile. "Yes, he did, and yes, I went. I had just woken when you all came across the field. I was trying to figure out where everyone was."

"Andrew and Lars are seeding the south section, and Solem and Haakan are disking the west. They were all at our house for dinner, which worked out perfect. After I got things cleaned up, Carl and I went out and worked in the garden. The potatoes are up, and since he helped plant those, he watches them carefully."

Carl nodded and looked up at Ingeborg. "My 'tatoes."

"We used to have a hoe with a sawed-off handle for the children. We need to check down in the tool shed and see if it is still there. It used to be hanging on the wall."

"I'll have Andrew check."

"Men coming," Emmy said.

"Which men?"

"Grampa and Andrew. Milk cows."

Ingeborg heard the telephone ringing, but before she counted the rings, Emmy said, "For us." She slid off Ingeborg's lap and headed into the house, Carl right after her. Ingeborg stood, stretched, and then followed them.

She lifted the earpiece from the base. "Hello."

"Mor, you better come. I think Elizabeth is getting worse." Thorliff's voice sounded tight with fear.

"I'll be right there."

"I'll come for you. I have the horse all harnessed."

I knew I should have gone in there, but here I am taking life easy when Elizabeth needs me. Ingeborg set the earpiece back and turned to see Ellie and Emmy starting to set the table.

"We'll take care of things here. You go on, and our prayers will go too."

"Takk. Mange takk." *Lord, help me know what to do for Elizabeth.* Ingeborg brought her black bag out of the pantry, mentally skipping through her simples to see what might bring down the swelling and what might give Elizabeth strength. Beef broth and a mild tea might help. All the while she muttered to herself until she looked up and caught Emmy staring at her.

"Inga come here?"

"Perhaps."

"Good." She patted Ingeborg's hand. "You make doctor better."

"I pray that is so." She glanced up to Ellie. "I'm going to call John and have him ask others to pray. I wish if there were new things that would help, I knew of them."

"Maybe Astrid has learned some new things. You could telephone her and ask."

"Interesting how I never think to use the telephone. I wonder how to get ahold of Dr. Morganstein. She would know, if anyone does."

"Elizabeth will know how to reach her."

"True." What did Thorliff mean by "getting worse"? Ingeborg fretted as she went out to meet her son. Would she have enough strength to sustain her until they could know what to do? *Lord, we need you.*

17

By the time they arrived, Elizabeth was asleep and Ingeborg couldn't see anything unusual, so she joined Thelma in the kitchen to finish making supper while Thorliff took Freda back home. Ingeborg checked on Elizabeth through the night but didn't notice any changes. The next morning she sat waiting for Elizabeth to wake.

"He worries more than a wet hen," Elizabeth muttered when she saw Ingeborg there.

"Only about you." Ingeborg felt Elizabeth's ankles and feet. There was some swelling but not any worse than the day before. "What made him think you were worse?"

"I got dizzy when I stood up and had to sit down real quick on the edge of the bed. He'd get dizzy too if he spent as much time in bed as I have." Lines furrowed her brow. "He says I fainted, but I was just dizzy."

"Of course he'd have to be pregnant to get the same feelings." The two smiled at each other. *Are the circles under her eyes darker, her skin more translucent, or am I, like Thorliff, imagining things?* Ingeborg held Elizabeth's wrist and counted her pulse. At least with this she could check records. She glanced at the paper she kept on the nightstand. About the same.

"I listened to the baby's heartbeat, and it is holding steady. Ingeborg, you know I know and understand what is going on. If I feel truly worse, I will tell you."

"Is that a promise?"

Elizabeth paused for a moment before she nodded. "I promise."

"Keep in mind that you might not always be objective. Your desire to take care of others is far stronger than your desire to take care of yourself." Ingeborg plumped the pillows so Elizabeth could sit up more comfortably.

"I am not an invalid."

"I know that, but you are a rather difficult patient."

"Doctors are supposed to be so. It's the law."

Ingeborg chuckled. "How much have you been up?"

"Only to the bathroom."

"What's wrong with the potty chair in here?"

"Inga thinks it the funniest thing ever."

"You didn't answer my question."

"I hate to make more work for Thelma and Freda." Elizabeth held up her hands, palms out. "All right. I promise that too. I will use the seat in here. I will drink plenty of water. I will stay in bed. Can Emmy come and play with Inga here in my room? I so love to watch them. Surely reading to them won't tax my strength."

"All right, if you promise to send them out when you start to feel tired."

Elizabeth rolled her eyes. "Maybe you'd better rephrase that. I feel bone weary all the time, but yes, I will send them off when I need to sleep." Hands flat on the sheet that covered her, she sighed. "Please forgive me for being cranky. I know you are all trying your best to help me keep this baby. I guess the good Lord is trying to teach me some patience."

"You want me to read to you?"

"Oh, please do. I've been reading the Psalms. The reminders to praise God are as necessary to me as breathing. You know all the times Kaaren reads at the quilting? That's my favorite part. I just wish I could go more often."

"The kind of sewing you do has lasting consequences." Ingeborg picked up the Bible lying beside the lamp and sat down in the rocker kept close beside the bed. "How about ninety-one to start with? 'He that dwelleth in the secret place of the most High shall abide under the shadow of the Almighty. . . .' "

A bit later, with Elizabeth sleeping peacefully, a light tap on the door brought Ingeborg to her feet. Thelma stuck her head in and whispered, "There's an emergency downstairs."

Ingeborg made her way down the stairs right behind the housekeeper. "What's happening?"

"Man bit by a raccoon that was foaming at the mouth. He's in the first treatment room. Their dog got bit too."

"Thank you. Is the sterile tray ready?"

"Ja, do you need help?"

"I'll call you if I do. Could you please telephone Freda and ask her to bring the girls in here? Elizabeth says them playing in her room helps her."

Thelma went off, shaking her head and muttering. But Ingeborg knew she would do as asked. If it took walking barefoot on coals to help Elizabeth, Thelma would be the first one to take her shoes and stockings off.

Ingeborg washed her hands in the sink in the hallway and entered the examining room. "God dag, sir. Dr. Bjorklund is indisposed, so I will be helping you today. I am Mrs. Bjorklund. Can you tell me what happened?"

"Can I speak Norwegian? My English is not so good."

"Of course."

With a grateful smile he told her of seeing the raccoon attack the dog, and in going to save the dog, getting bitten himself. When he realized the situation, he got his gun and shot the raccoon.

"You need to shoot your dog too, I'm sorry to say. Rabies is highly contagious."

"Other than stitch up this rip, what can you do for me?"

"It is already in your bloodstream, so when the symptoms strike—fever is the first indication—you come back, and we will do all we can to nurse you through it."

"Does everyone die from a rabies bite?"

"No, but I'll be honest with you, we have a hard battle ahead." Ingeborg cleansed the wound as she talked and got ready to put a few stitches in. "Do you need some help, or can you stand this?"

"I doubt it will hurt more than what you've been doing."

"Sorry. I should have warned you." Ingeborg sprinkled alcohol on the wound and proceeded to stitch the slashed skin closed. "I'm going to spread honey on the wound now, as it helps with both disinfecting and healing. Keep it bandaged, and I would suggest a sling for a few days to keep from banging it. Do you have a wife or someone to help you change the bandages?"

"Yes. My wife and our two children are at home."

"Where are you working?"

"For a farmer south of town. Owner told me to ride up here and get fixed up."

"I see. Well, return as soon as you feel the symptoms."

"Mrs. Bjorklund, I don't have money for all this."

"We don't deny medical care because someone has no money. We've all been there. You just come. Is there a telephone at the farm where you are?"

"No, ma'am. My cousin, who brought me here to help him, doesn't much like newfangled things."

Ingeborg showed him to the door, her heart heavy. *Lord, what can we do to help this young man?* If there was one rabid raccoon, there would be other rabid animals in that area. "Go with God."

"Ja, I will."

She watched as he swung aboard the workhorse using the fence as a mounting block, since he had no saddle, and one handed, with the wounded arm clutched to his chest. She'd forgotten to ask him how far away the farm was, but Thorliff or Haakan would surely know. How they kept track of all the families in the valley was beyond her.

"You leave that for me," Thelma ordered as soon as Ingeborg returned to the examining room. "I will clean up."

"I'll go check on Elizabeth, then. Is Freda bringing the girls in?"

"She said after dinner."

"Do you know where Thorliff is?"

"He prints the paper tonight."

"I think I'll go talk with him. Maybe he can put an article in regarding rabid animals south of here." Stepping out on the porch, she stopped to inhale the fresh air, and then followed the path over to Thorliff's office and the home of the *Blessing Gazette*.

Pushing open the door, the smell of ink smote her. Inga always called it stinky, but to Ingeborg it smelled of newspapers and hard work. Thorliff dreamed of having a more modern printer, but he kept investing his money in other projects. He wanted to put out a daily someday. Now he'd be satisfied to go to twice a week as soon as possible. But he needed an extra person to work for him to make that happen. Maybe they needed to see if there were any more relatives in Norway who wanted to come over, or maybe someone else from

Valdres, Norway. He'd said he was going to start running advertisements in regional newspapers stating that there were plenty of jobs to be had in the booming town of Blessing.

"Is she all right?" he asked, barely looking up from the layout he was still working on.

"Yes. You are not to worry."

"Right. That is so easy to say and hard to do. You didn't see her face. Just dizzy, my foot." He nodded toward the printer. "You want to come set type for me?"

"Remember how Astrid used to do that? She is so quick with her hands."

"And her mind," he said rather abruptly. "What brings you out here if Elizabeth is okay?"

Ingeborg hesitated. She knew her son well enough to know he was trying to avoid talking to her. Yet he had called her there to help Elizabeth. Maybe it was just getting to be too much for him. "I just treated a young man for a raccoon bite. His forearm was slashed rather severely."

Thorliff nodded and turned his head slightly. "And?"

"And the raccoon was rabid, foaming at the mouth. He shot the raccoon, and I told him to shoot his dog too, which had also been bitten. I thought maybe you could put a short article in the paper about rabid animals south of here and what people should do."

"Besides shoot them on sight?"

"I know. But some need to be reminded."

"I'll take care of that. I'll have to make room on this page. The others are all set."

"Thank you." She turned to leave but stopped when he started to say something else. At the door opening behind her, she turned to see who it was. "Why, Mr. Jeffers, how good to see you." Never would she have thought to say those words, because the imposter Harlan

Jeffers they first met had been a scoundrel who bought the general store from Penny and ran it into the ground.

The young man removed his fedora. His dark unruly hair still tumbled down on his forehead. "Good day to you too, Mrs. Bjorklund. I am glad to be back in Blessing and with a bit of news."

"You found your father's grave."

"How did you know?"

"My mother often knows things the rest of us don't. Sit down." Thorliff rose to shake his hand.

"I know you are busy. I'm going to go check into the boardinghouse, and then I'm going to talk with Hjelmer. Any chance we could bring Haakan into this discussion—and Lars?"

"If you wait until this evening. They are seeding and need to get it into the ground." Ingeborg nodded to both of the men. "I must get back to my post. I'd like to come to the meeting too, if that wouldn't be a bother."

"You know Far would invite you whether you asked or not. He always values your opinion."

"As do we all," Mr. Jeffers added.

"Well, my curiosity is certainly piqued," Ingeborg said with a smile. "You are welcome to come to our house. I'm sure Freda is baking pies today."

"Mor has been filling in for the doctor since my wife is under the weather."

"Where is your sister?"

"She is attending missionary school in Georgia, after doing a surgical rotation at a hospital in Chicago. Lots of exciting things going on here."

"Missionary school?"

Ingeborg stayed instead of leaving, interested to hear his reaction to Thorliff's words. She got the feeling he'd been looking forward to seeing Astrid. *Hmm.*

"She feels that God is calling her to go to Africa." Thorliff's voice tightened.

"Africa?" The shock on his face said more than the words.

"For a two-year term of service. At least she is hoping for the confirmation of that. Otherwise I'm not sure what she will do." Ingeborg felt like she was pouring oil on troubled waters.

"Other than come home where she belongs and is very much needed," Thorliff muttered.

Ingeborg studied her elder son. Was that resentment she was hearing or just frustration because right now his wife needed help? While he'd been pretty quiet when Astrid made her announcement, having the two doctors serving here and building a hospital had been Thorliff's plan as much as anyone's. When he wouldn't meet her gaze, she caught herself wondering what was going on. Thorliff had always been honest and forthright to a fault. Was he hiding something?

"I don't want to be far away from Elizabeth right now. Let's have the meeting here. Thelma can fix something for supper so we can eat and talk at the same time."

Something was out of kilter. She was sure of it. "I'll ask Haakan and Lars to leave the milking to the others and meet us here, then. What time?"

"As soon as possible. I'll get ahold of Hjelmer."

"What about the paper?"

"I'll print it tonight, same as always."

Ingeborg turned to Mr. Jeffers. "Is there a reason for us to hurry on this meeting or can it be scheduled for tomorrow night?"

"Tonight would be better for me. I need to get home and help my mother. I haven't told her the news yet, not something I want to do over the telephone."

"I see. Then tonight it will be." Ingeborg headed for the house before any more discussion. Inside, she called home and told Freda what was happening. "If you could tell the men as soon as they come up with the horses, that would be good. Are you bringing the girls in?"

"I just haven't had time. Inga said they could walk by themselves, but I didn't feel right letting them do that. As soon as these pies come out—"

"Bring two of the pies with you when you come. We'll serve those for dessert. Thelma will have her hands full as it is."

"How's Elizabeth?"

"Sleeping again. She is having a hard time staying in bed."

"I would too, but that must mean she is better. Oh, Pastor Solberg called. He asked for you to call him back."

"All right." Ingeborg hung up the telephone and walked slowly to the kitchen, pondering all that was going on. Why didn't John just call here if he knew where she was? She'd half expected him to show up this afternoon when she was praying for that young man. She paused and thought a bit. What was his name? *Oh, Lord, am I now losing my mind?* Still in the hallway, she stopped and leaned against the wall. Weariness rolled over her like a sudden storm. She ached in more places than she could count. *Am I catching something? If so, I need to stay away from Elizabeth.* But then who would take care of her? She stuck her head into the kitchen.

"Thelma, could you please bring a cup of coffee to the lying-in room?"

"Of course. Are you all right?"

"I'm not sure, but a bit of a lie-down and a cup of coffee will most likely set me to rights."

Thelma shook her head. "You are taking on too much."

Look who's talking. "Did Thorliff tell you there will be company for supper tonight?" At Thelma's nod, Ingeborg continued. "Freda is bringing in two pies along with the girls."

"Might be better to leave the girls out to your house one more day. You sleep here tonight, and we can switch off checking on Elizabeth."

"Get me up in a half hour or so, and I'll help you with supper."

Not sure if the grunt was a yes or a no, she entered the lying-in room, where most of the babies were born, and collapsed on the bed. Without Haakan to remove her shoes, she slept with them on. *Why am I so tired?* was her last thought before deep sleep claimed her.

"Ingeborg?" Haakan stroked her shoulder. "Supper is ready. Come now. You need to wake up if you want to be part of the meeting."

"Meeting? What meeting?" She rubbed her eyes and forced them open. "Did you say supper?" At his nod, she sat up and thumped her feet on the floor. "Uff da. I put my shoes up on the bed. Whatever was the matter with me?" Not expecting an answer, she smoothed tendrils of hair back to tuck up under the braids she wore woven around her head. "Thelma was supposed to come and get me."

"Freda is helping her."

"And who is taking care of the girls?"

"Ellie is, and Anna Brunderson has gone over to help her. We decided not to bring them today. You see, you must trust these younger women to do what needs to be done."

Ingeborg brushed at the spot on the nine patch on the diagonal quilt that she'd lain on. "I know better than this."

Haakan took her hands and pulled her up. "Come along now. You can fuss with that later."

"Is everyone here?"

"Ja." He paused and turned to look into her eyes. "You don't have to attend this, you know. I will tell you all that happens."

"I know. But something makes me think I should be there. But first I should go up and check on Elizabeth."

"You should come in and eat. When did you eat last?"

Since she couldn't come up with a good answer, she wisely kept her mouth closed. Was that why she had been so tired? Actually, now that she was awake, the achiness was gone, and she felt much better.

When they entered the dining room, she was pleased to see that Pastor Solberg was in attendance too. After he said grace and all the serving dishes were passed, Thorliff nodded to Mr. Jeffers to tell his story, and a strange one it was. He'd stopped at every little town and hamlet on the route between Alexandria and Blessing, and finally one day he found a place where someone had indeed buried a stranger. They'd found the body in a thicket by the road, and because of the rough clothing worn, they figured he was a vagrant and buried him.

"When I asked them if there were any gunshot or knife wounds, they said no. They thought the man died of natural causes, but they couldn't be certain. I had them dig the box up, and it was my father. He had a couple of scars, including missing the end of his right thumb, that made identifying him clear. I had them bury the box again. I can't see any reason to haul it back home, unless my mother insists, which I hope she doesn't." He cleared his throat. "So that answers part of the question. How the man who you all met here managed to steal my father's identity, I'll never know."

"Unless he came upon a dead body, changed clothes, and took on the new identity for himself. No one further west than Blessing would know who the other man was anyway." Thorliff rubbed the side of his nose with one finger.

Just the way his father did, Ingeborg thought, watching her son run the meeting without seeming to at all.

"Had he not been such a scoundrel, he might have gotten away with it." Pastor Solberg held his cup for Thelma to refill from the coffeepot.

"He did get away with it. He's not been caught again."

"Yet."

"True. That might be an answer we never get. But we do know

about the patent we all talked about for a new seeder. I've been giving it some thought, and . . ." Thorliff focused on Mr. Jeffers. "And like you suggested, I think we could build a production plant right here in Blessing. We could advertise in the larger papers for skilled machinists. The first stage would be constructing a building large enough to begin with. We could add more on later if need be."

"We will need more investment dollars." Lars held his hand over his cup to signal he'd had enough. Turning to Mr. Jeffers, he asked, "You have clear title to this patent?"

"I do, since my father and I were in business together. I already checked the legality of that. I would like to see this happen before someone else beats us to the production stage. Machinery is changing quickly these days, and while my father was quite a forward thinker, months have passed. I know this is an impossible question, but what kind of a timeline do you think we can plan on?"

Ingeborg stared at the schematic drawing on the table in front of them. It certainly would speed up the seeding process in the spring. If only they'd had the seeders in use this year. With the late spring and wet fields, grain that should be up several inches was just getting into the ground.

She turned at a tapping on her shoulder.

"Elizabeth is asking for you."

Ingeborg pushed her chair back and left the room as quietly as possible. She climbed the stairs, foreboding weighing on her like a sack of grain across her shoulders. She entered the bedroom to find Elizabeth with tears streaming down her face.

"I am spotting again." She dissolved into sobs in Ingeborg's arms.

Thorliff strode through the door. When they told him what was happening, he threw his head back and swallowed hard. "I telephoned for Astrid to come home. She said she would get on the first train going north."

Both Ingeborg and Elizabeth stared back at him in shock.

Ingeborg felt a huge weight slide off her shoulders as she turned back to Elizabeth. *Please, God, let this baby settle back in. Thank you that Astrid is coming home. Astrid is coming home! Oh, thank you, Lord. But what if she doesn't stay but returns to school?* The thought stopped her short. She sucked in a deep breath and slowly let it out. *I will praise your name, O Lord, for this time with my daughter. I will be grateful for every moment I have her near. Please, Lord, make me willing to be willing.*

18

If they could keep going like they had been, they'd be home a week early.

Joshua stared at the books, his eyes feeling like he'd just been through a sandstorm. Why couldn't he get to sleep? Most nights he was out before his head hit the pillow, but not tonight, so he'd gotten back up and sat at the table to catch up on the bookwork. They'd already completed eight of the ten wells and windmills they'd set out to do.

So far Hjelmer had not contacted them with more to do. The original agreement was that if they didn't hear differently, they should head back to Blessing on completion.

Surely he'd managed to sell enough more to keep his crew going. Why, they had three people that already said they wanted their wells dug. Neighbors of happy customers. He finished his page and pulled out a sheet of paper. Might as well write to Astrid. He tapped the end of his pencil against his chin. What could he say? It wasn't like anything exciting had happened.

Dear Astrid,

I hope you are enjoying your missionary school. The place sounds lovely the way you wrote about it. I have always heard there are a lot of blooming flowers and trees in the South. But you well know how beautiful spring is here in the Red River Valley. The wild flowers are just starting to bloom. We saw a patch of wild strawberries the other day, but there were no strawberries yet, the blooms just beginning.

I find that I am missing life in Blessing. I feel more at home there than I have any place in my life. Johnny is doing great on the guitar, and Linnea has a real ear for the piano. She picks out the tunes and already understands chords. She has taken some lessons from Dr. Bjorklund. I guess just enough to get her started. When we all play together, we are becoming a real group. When Jonathan gets here, we'll really sound good. I heard a rumor that someone is dreaming of an organ for the church. I dream of having a banjo someday.

As I told you in my last letter, I was hoping to have the concrete poured for my basement before I left, but I ran out of time. The thought of having a home of my own makes the days fly by, not that they need any help.

The three of us make a good team. Trygve has a good head on his shoulders for one so young. He works hard but also is always thinking ahead. We've been drawing up some ideas for improvements on windmills. Hjelmer is always on the lookout for new angles to explore, as you already know.

He stopped to think. Was Hjelmer so tied up in new things that he wasn't looking for more farmers who needed drilled wells and windmills? Moths bombarded the screen, trying to get into the light. A breeze squeezed through the screen to tickle his neck. He knew he should be getting to sleep and, with a yawn, realized he would probably drift off now. His mother had always said, *"Old man worry comes to chase away sleep."* Was he worried? He thought about that a bit. No, he didn't think he was worried. He did still have the loan to pay off, but his promotion helped. He liked doing this part of the business. Maybe that was his worry—having to give up what he at first hadn't wanted to do. He smiled. Life sure did twist and turn sometimes. He knew the truth now. He just needed to trust God. If there weren't more wells to dig, he would find something else to do. Jobs were plentiful in Blessing.

He returned to his letter.

> Guess I had better blow out the lamp and get some sleep. Sometimes I wish I could look ahead and see what the future holds, but then I am glad I can't. As Pastor Solberg said, "We know who holds the future." That is indeed a comforting thought.

His mind took off again. He daily hoped and prayed that Astrid would be part of his future—a close part. And as he drifted off, he wondered how he would feel if the answer was no. Could he still stay in Blessing? How much of Blessing was tied to his feelings for Astrid, or was it the reverse?

THANKS TO HIS late night, morning came mighty soon. Joshua woke to the sound of someone starting the fire in the cookstove. None of them minded a cold breakfast, but they all wanted hot coffee. He stretched and rolled himself out of the hammock, his feet hitting the wooden floor with a thud. After getting dressed, he gave the other hammock a push to wake the sleeper.

"Thought maybe you were going to sleep all day," Trygve said with a grin over his shoulder. "This getting our own breakfast is getting old. We need to find that next farm."

"I know. It can't be too far away. Since you have the fire hot, how about frying some eggs and bread?" The last farmer's wife had sent them off with a dozen eggs, a loaf of bread, and a jug of milk. When Joshua tried to pay for it, she fluttered her hands at him.

"The gift you gave me, I can never repay." She'd nodded over to the sink, where a hand pump now provided her water inside the house.

"The best thing you can do is tell all your friends."

"I will," she said with a nod. "I most certainly will."

After breakfast and a couple of hours on the road, they saw a sign that said their destination was one-half mile ahead.

"We should be set up by dinnertime," Joshua said, clucking to the team to pick up their speed.

Gilbert, who was riding with him this time, looked up from the spoon he was carving. "Not that you don't cook fine, but it don't measure up to the meals these places gave us."

"I know. We need to find a store and get some supplies too. Did you happen to bring a rifle along?"

"Nope. You?"

"Some fresh meat would taste mighty good."

"Trygve says he used to get lots of rabbits with snares."

"That's a downright good idea. Why don't you jump down and go back and tell him that."

"Yes, sir."

Joshua cringed inside at the *yes, sir.* Was he getting so old that young men could call him *sir*? He wasn't even thirty yet. He slowed the team, and Gilbert jumped down. Driving a team was always good thinking time, especially if he was alone. What would Astrid be doing now? She'd said she was memorizing a lot of Scripture. Driving the wagon would give him plenty of time for that, if only he had brought his Bible. Drawing his pencil stub and a piece of folded paper from his pocket, he jotted himself a barely legible note.

They turned into the lane leading to a farm that needed a good hand at fixing. The fence around the house had enough missing poles that a herd of beeves could go through at once. Boards covered a broken window in the house, and the steps would require careful maneuvering. A dog whose ribs were near poking through his hide came from under the porch and wagged his tail as if barking took more energy than he could summon. Off in the pasture a couple head of cattle stood listlessly in the shade of a barn that wouldn't provide a lot of protection in the winter.

Joshua had the strongest urge to turn around and head on up the road to the next farm on his list. Instead, he halted the horses and sat studying the house while Trygve pulled up beside him. They exchanged looks that matched in foreboding. This farm didn't seem ready to be a customer.

Joshua climbed down from his seat on the wagon and set his hat more firmly down on his head before heading to the house. For some reason, the thought of hallooing to announce their arrival didn't appeal. He bent down and petted the dog that joined him.

The front door had no screen, and when he knocked, no one answered. "Did they go off and leave you, fella?"

The dog sat and scratched his ear with a hind foot.

Joshua knocked again and, when no one came, peered into the window. A curtain covered just enough of the window that he couldn't see much beyond the rotting fabric. Surely they had the wrong place. The door was locked. He turned and looked over the land, heaving a sigh as he did so. The urge to go on took him to the edge of the porch, but something else pulled at him to go look in back.

He walked on around the single-story house and climbed the back stoop to rap on the door. No answer, but at least the handle turned on this one.

"You want me to come in with you?"

Joshua jumped at the sound of Trygve's voice from near behind him. "I guess. You s'pose they just went off and left everything?"

"The dog and the cattle even?"

"I know." Joshua pushed open the door and stepped into a pantry. Two more steps and he was in the kitchen, which smelled musty. A cold cast-iron stove stood against one wall, a table with four chairs took up the middle. "Anyone home?" he called. The house hunkered down, holding its secret close. Even the air felt heavy. A closed door most likely led to the bedroom. He opened the door, which creaked like it was nearly rusted closed.

"Oh, Lord." He breathed the words in the way that said both prayer and exclamation.

"How long you think they been there?" Both men stared at the two figures lying side by side in the bed, the quilt pulled up to their chins. The man lay on his side, the woman on her back.

Joshua closed his eyes and backed out of the room, shutting the door as he went. He headed for the back door, in a hurry to get the smell and sight banished from his mind. How long had they been dead? Weeks? Months? Had no one come by and checked on them? Had they been sick? How sick? Questions that had no answers.

"What do we do now?" Joshua asked and then took a deep breath of the fresh air.

"We feed the dog and check on the animals." Trygve sucked in a long breath also.

"And one of us rides to the nearest town and reports to the sheriff that these two people are dead in their bed." Joshua realized he was hoping Trygve would volunteer but knew he'd have to do it. "Let's unhitch the horses and see what we can do about the animals. I'm wondering where the local church is, rather than the sheriff." He pointed toward the barn. "Move the wagons over there."

Trygve climbed up on the lead wagon and led the way for Gilbert. As they unhitched, Joshua told Gilbert what they found.

"There's a grave under that big oak tree," Gilbert said, pointing his finger at a tree a hundred yards or so behind the house.

"I'll go take a look," Joshua said.

The questions continued to bombard him as he strode over. The mound of dirt was child size, and a small child at that. A cross made of two flat sticks held together by twine with the name Albion scratched on the crosspiece told the story. Had whatever took the child killed the parents also? Cholera from bad water? Typhoid fever? He headed back to the wagons.

Trygve stepped down from their wagon with a couple of leftover biscuits in his hand. He knelt down and held them out to the dog. "Here you go, boy. I'll get us some rabbits tonight, and you can have that too."

The dog wolfed the crumbled biscuits and, tail wagging, stared at Trygve.

"Give him one of those eggs mixed with a bit of milk. Too much might make him sick."

Gilbert walked back from checking the stock tank. "Dry as dry. What do you think they've been drinking?"

"Perhaps a creek or maybe mud puddles from that last rain. Use some of our water to prime that well and start pumping. Our horses need water also. But smell it and take a small lick first." He turned to Trygve. "Go ahead and set up camp. There's a woodpile alongside the house. I'll be back as soon as I can."

"I'll set a line of snares. Should be plenty of rabbits around here." He glanced back toward the house. "You don't suppose they starved to death?"

"With cattle in the field?" Joshua swung aboard the horse they used for riding most often. "I'll stop at the nearest neighbor too." He set the horse to an easy lope and headed back the way they had come. The last town was maybe five or six miles away.

About two miles back on the road, he turned off on a lane that led to a rather prosperous looking farm, although anything was prosperous compared to the one he'd left. A dog barked as he neared the house, and a woman came out on the porch to greet him. When he told her his story, she shook her head, murmuring reassurances.

"No wonder I've not seen her in so long. I told my husband I wanted to go over there, but the mister, he didn't take well to anyone coming by. You said the little boy died too? Oh, this is too sad."

"Is there a pastor or anyone around I can tell about this?"

"You go on into town"—she pointed back the way he'd come—"and tell Hanson at the general store. He is also part-time sheriff and the postmaster. He'll know what to do."

"Thank you, ma'am."

"How did you happen by there?"

"We had an agreement with him to drill a new well and erect a windmill. He paid his deposit last fall, but winter came before we could get over here."

"You drill wells and put up windmills?"

"Yes, ma'am."

"When you come back, you come by here and talk to my husband. He's out seeding now, but he'll be up to milk before supper. He's been talking about doing just that."

"I will do that." Joshua touched the rim of his hat with one finger and turned the horse around to lope back down the lane.

When he got to town, he slid off the horse and tied him to the hitching rail in front of the silver-sided building with a sign that said *General Store, James Hanson, Proprietor*. A cheery voice greeted him when he walked through the door.

"How can I help you, young fella?"

Joshua smiled back at a middle-aged man whose droopy eyes belied the smile that bracketed his rounded cheeks. He introduced himself and told his story again.

"And here I thought they just ran out on their bill. How sad. I shoulda gone out there, but . . ." He heaved a sigh and untied his apron. "Let me go get the missus to run things, and I'll get my son to hitch the team up to the wagon. I imagine we should bury them in the cemetery by the church."

"Could we bury them out there on their farm? The grave of their little boy is there."

Mr. Hanson nodded and held up one finger. "Wait here." He pushed through a hanging curtain, leaving Joshua to look around.

There he was where he could get supplies, and he had no money with him. He checked his pockets. One dollar bill and some change. He'd have to send one of the others back tomorrow. He eyed the rows of canned goods, picked up corn, green beans, and peaches and set them on the counter. The peaches would taste mighty good that night.

When Hanson pushed aside the curtain, he'd divested himself of his apron and added a hat. He eyed the cans on the counter. "That'll be forty cents. You need anything else?"

Joshua dug his change out and counted out the necessary amount. "Do you have a sack I can use? I'm riding bareback." With the sack slung over his shoulder, he followed Hanson out the door.

A team pulling a wagon came around the corner as they stepped off the wooden stairs. "You want to ride with us?" Hanson asked.

Joshua handed back the sack. "If you bring this, I'll get back more quickly on my horse." At their nod, he swung aboard his horse and galloped out of town, back the way he had come. On one hand he knew there was no rush. After all, these people had been dead for some time, but on the other, he had a feeling he needed to get back. Besides, he needed to go to that neighbor and see if he meant to do what his wife said. They could do the job immediately since they had several days before they were due at the next farm.

Back at the farm Gilbert had filled the stock tank. Trygve had rounded up some chickens gone wild, set his snares, and explored the barn. There were oats in the grain bin, a dead calf in the box stall, and some hay left in the haymow. He couldn't move without the dog following his every step.

"Did you look more in the house?" Joshua asked.

"Nope. Don't plan to. Do you suppose those folks own this property or the bank does?"

"No idea. But I do think this place was going downhill before they died. The sheriff is on his way out. I think he plans to take the bodies back into town in the wagon."

Trygve shook his head. "I wouldn't want that job."

"Me either. Maybe we should kill one of those chickens for supper."

"I don't think so, but I did find one of their nests. Will give us some more fresh eggs."

"Not sure we should eat anything here until we know what they died from." Joshua stared at the house, thinking again on the mystery therein. This place was a ways off the road, but still, how could no one have come by in . . . months perhaps?

When Hanson and his son drove up to the house, Joshua met them. "The back door isn't locked. The front is."

"What made you go looking?"

"Well, he hired us to drill him a well and put up a windmill. I was just trying to do my job."

Hanson handed him the tow sack. "We'll be about ours, then. I'll call you if I need more help."

Joshua nodded and headed toward their camp. He turned back and raised his voice. "If you do take them back to town, you might want to dig up the child's grave and take him too. Bury them all together." What did it matter to him? They'd be on the road again in the morning in some direction. What would happen to this place? With some work it could become a decent home for a young couple just starting out. Or for a single man. He climbed into the cook wagon and rattled the grates to shake the ashes down into the oblong metal box. That needed to be dumped too. And he wanted to get back to that neighbor.

He heard the jingling of harnesses and the clopping of trotting hooves. Peering out the screened door, he watched as a different wagon bypassed the house and came toward the barn. He went about laying a fire, lit a match, and watched the paper and shavings catch, sending a fine tendril of smoke straight upward. He added some small pieces, turned the damper wide open and, as the flames grew, added larger wood and set the lids back in place.

"Man here to see about drilling his well," Trygve announced from the doorway.

"Be right there. You want to get the rice started? Chop up the rest of that ham and throw it in." Joshua pointed to the cans on the table. "We'll have those too." He stepped outside. "Good day."

The man spoke from his seat on the wagon. "My wife said you came by. You want to come drill my well say, tomorrow, I'd be right pleased. Sorry, Calhoun's the name."

Joshua named the price, and they shook hands. "We'll be there soon after sunrise tomorrow."

He watched the man stop to talk to Hanson and then trot on out the lane. Now maybe he could get answers to some of his questions. If they had any.

19

Athens, Georgia

Please, God, don't let Elizabeth die. Please.

"We need to hurry, Dr. Bjorklund. The train is coming into the station." The driver looked at her over his shoulder.

"Thank you. Can I buy my ticket on the train?"

"I think so. But in case not, I'll let you out right at the station door. You go buy your ticket, and I'll get your bags to you."

Grateful for the man who'd been thinking further ahead than she had, she nodded and thanked him. Elizabeth was all she could think of. If only she had telephoned Dr. Morganstein requesting advice, perhaps she could have met with her in Chicago if she had much of a layover. Maybe she could still telephone from the train station.

She stepped down from the buggy as soon as it stopped, not waiting for the driver to assist her, and headed for the ticket window.

She could hear the screeching wheels of a train stopping on the other side of the building. Surely they'd make it wait long enough for her to get on.

"I need a one-way ticket to Chicago please."

"You'd best hurry, miss. This engineer will do anything to stay on time."

"Thank you." Astrid knew running was not ladylike, but she picked up her skirts with one hand, held her hat on with the other, and ran around the building. The conductor saw her coming and motioned her to slow down. All was well. Astrid fought to catch her breath. All these weeks of sitting around had certainly weakened her body even while the lessons had built up her mind and spirit. "Thank you." She let him guide her up the steps. "My bags aren't here yet."

"Yes they are, if that man flying around the corner is for you."

Astrid glanced over her shoulder. "Yes, that's my driver."

She'd just settled herself in her seat, the driver having stuffed her bags in the overhead shelf and wished her a good trip, when the conductor called, "All aboard." The driver jumped to the ground as the conductor swung aboard and the train began moving. *Thank you, Father,* circled through her mind, being chased by *In all things give thanks.*

Thoughts of Africa evaporated as her mind clacked *Save Elizabeth* along with the train wheels speeding north. Keeping her thoughts on praising God instead of worrying over her friend and mentor took severe concentration. At the least slip, fear snaked in and tied itself in knots around her heart. *Bring into captivity every thought.* Pastor Solberg had reminded them of that verse over and over. He said that was the only way to conquer fear and worry. He'd also said they had to prepare for the difficult times in advance. Like runners practice for a race, as the apostle Paul had said.

In an effort to conquer the fear, she started with the second verse in James. *My brethren, count it all joy when ye fall into divers temptations . . .* and continued to the end of the chapter and on to the next. She had memorized all of James and right now was grateful for that. As the miles passed, she moved into First John to be reminded how much God loves His children.

When the steward came through announcing the meal was ready in the dining car, she shook her head. The thought of eating made her stomach roil, let alone the actual doing. But she knew she needed strength, so she nibbled on an apple Mrs. Abercrombie had thoughtfully included in a small basket for her.

Reaching Chicago, she made her way to the ticket counter and purchased her ticket to Blessing, then crossed the black-and-white diamond marble floor to the telephones. Who would have believed there would be public telephones in a train station? Now just to figure out how to use one. She read the instructions, placed her nickel in the slot, and asked for the Alfred Morganstein Hospital for Women and Children. When a voice answered, she identified herself and asked to speak to Dr. Morganstein.

"Oh yes, Dr. Bjorklund, I'll get her. Where are you?"

"At the train station. I have a couple of hours until my train leaves for Blessing."

In a few moments Dr. Morganstein came on the line. "Astrid, dear girl, what is happening?"

"Thorliff telephoned me and said to come home because Elizabeth might be losing her baby, and all the doctoring needed is too much for my mother. The dean gave me permission to go home."

"Oh, I am so sorry to hear all this. What can I do for you?"

"Do you have any knowledge of what I can do for her?"

"This is an area we know so little about yet. Bed rest, eating beef, drinking milk with an egg mixed up in it, anything to get enough blood builders in her. She will get weak lying in bed, so make sure she moves her arms and legs while she is lying down. Deep breathing is also important. If she can get out in the sun, that can help make her stronger too. Perhaps Mr. Bjorklund can carry her outside. I know she wanted another child so badly, but I thought she understood how dangerous this was for her."

"She has lost two since Inga was born."

"There are some studies being done in New York. I will look into those and see if there is anything to help us. The main thing is to build up her strength and yet keep her down. Do you know how far along she is?"

"No. I wasn't even aware she was with child until this morning," Astrid answered with some degree of frustration. *How many other things have gone on in Blessing that I've not been told?* The thought clamped on her chest. *And how many other things will be happening while I am in Africa that I won't know anything about until a letter reaches me weeks, no, probably months, later?*

"Please insert another nickel," said the operator's voice, breaking into the conversation.

Astrid did as instructed, hearing the clinking of the coin as it fell into the slot.

"Sorry."

"That is all right. I will find out whatever I can. Now, about you. What has happened?"

"I have been accepted for a two-year mission term. The first part will be at a major hospital and the latter with Rev. Schuman in the bush, if the powers that be deem this possible. They are terribly concerned about my age, my gender, and my lack of a husband."

Dr. Morganstein chuckled softly. "It must be hard for them to accept you."

"They have struggled, but I have dug in my heels. God has done whatever needed doing, as I have been approved. But now this. The hardest part has been no medical work for me these months until the other day when Rev. Thompkins collapsed in class. They say I saved his life by getting him to the hospital so quickly."

"His heart?"

"Yes. But he is getting stronger again. I doubt they will let him return to Africa now. He is a wonderful teacher, knows his Bible so well. I feel privileged that I could be in his classes."

"Well, I'd like to chat longer, but the operator is going to ask you for more money. I will telephone you in Blessing if I can find out more. Keep me apprised, please."

"I will, and thank you." Astrid hung up the receiver and leaned her head against the walnut paneling. How did one go about studying and researching women and pregnancies? Why did some women have trouble carrying a baby to term and others sailed right through?

She sent a telegram to Thorliff, giving her arrival time, and then wandered over to the counter, where she bought a sandwich and cookies and then found a bench where she could sit and eat. When she checked the tiny clock she had pinned to her traveling suit, she still had an hour to wait. Only by repeating the Scriptures she'd committed to memory could she keep the worry and fear at bay. One didn't have to be in Africa to need strength to control one's thoughts.

When she boarded the train for St. Paul, she breathed a sigh of relief. At least now she was heading in the right direction—north and west toward Blessing.

Due to an emergency at one station, the train was delayed an hour, and no matter how hard he tried, the engineer could not make it up. The train from St. Paul to Fargo and then on to Grand Forks and Blessing had already departed by the time they arrived.

"So now what do I do?" she asked the ticket agent.

"Sorry, miss, but you have to wait for the next train, like everyone else."

"And when will that be? Can I send a telegram?"

"Tomorrow morning and no need to telegraph. All the stations along the way know." The agent fought to cover a yawn. "I'm sorry, but it is time to close this window."

"Where will I stay?"

"Most people sleep on the benches. You are relatively safe here. There are guards walking the premises all night long."

Astrid heaved a sigh. "Thank you." "For nothing," she wanted to say, but it wasn't the man's fault. At least she had a warm coat along so she wouldn't get cold. She finally found an empty bench near a family with three children, one of which was whimpering. She felt safe near them and knew she could sleep through about anything now, since her residency. *Lord, please keep Elizabeth safe. I have to keep reminding myself that you know all that is happening. While it is a surprise to me, it is not to you. And you have promised to keep me safe.* She mentally snorted. Here she was supposed to be going to the wilds of Africa, and she was worried about sleeping in a train station in a city. She glanced up to see one of the guards talking with the father of the family. The men nodded and talked a bit before the guard moved on.

The man walked over to where she sat and touched his hat. "I'm sorry to bother you, miss, but the guard suggested that you move a bit closer to us. There is safety in numbers."

"Thank you very much. I will do that."

"Here, let me help you." He picked up her two bags and set them under the long seat where the smaller of the children already lay sleeping. "If you take that end, we will look more like a family."

"Thank you." Astrid put out her hand. "I am Dr. Bjorklund and on my way home to Blessing, North Dakota."

"We are the Sommerseths, on our way to Grand Forks."

"Are you moving there or visiting?"

"Visiting to see if we do want to move there. Let me introduce my wife, Maureen."

"Did you really say Blessing?" the woman asked, her smile on the shy side.

"That is the name of the town where I have lived all of my life. We are northwest of Grand Forks. This train will continue on through the Red River Valley."

"And you did say doctor?" Mr. Sommerseth asked.

"Yes." Astrid thought about explaining, but a wave of weariness washed away the thought before it could take root.

"Is Blessing a big town?"

"No, but it really is growing. We are hoping to build a hospital there soon, and last I heard, there were not enough people there to fill all the jobs that need help."

"Really?" The husband and wife exchanged glances.

"Are you looking for work?"

"I am at that. My brother invited us to come out and look for work in Grand Forks."

"If you decide to take a look at Blessing, my brother Thorliff Bjorklund—he owns the local newspaper—is the one to talk to. Just tell him his sister talked with you. I'll tell him the same if you'd like."

Mr. Sommerseth nodded slowly. "I will keep this in mind."

Mrs. Sommerseth smiled at her again and hugged her daughter close. "I hope to see you again."

"That would be my pleasure." Astrid settled herself on the wooden seat and, leaning against one bag, brought her feet up on the seat and tucked her coat around her. Since her hat tilted at a strange angle, she removed the hatpins and set her hat on the bag under the bench. Closing her eyes, her ears seemed sharper. She could hear someone snoring an aisle or two over, a baby cried, and a mother shushed it. The guard's boots slapped the marble flooring, someone was humming, most likely to put a child to sleep. And her.

WHEN THE TRAIN left in the morning, they were all aboard and talking as if they'd been friends for months, rather than acquaintances due to missing a train. She said good-bye to the Sommerseths when they got off at their stop and leaned her head against the cool window. She had slept, but her body was reminding her that wooden benches were not the most accommodating to bones and muscles.

Thorliff greeted her when she stepped off the train. After a hug he took her bags and started off for the surgery. "Mor is with Elizabeth. Inga is out with Emmy at Ellie's. I cannot tell you how grateful I am that you came."

She tried to keep pace with him, but her travel skirt and boots slowed her down. "Thorliff, please."

He looked over his shoulder. "Oh, sorry."

As they passed the boardinghouse, Sophie came charging out the door and down the steps to throw her arms around Astrid. "I am so glad you are home. Now everything will be all right. I just know it will."

Astrid hugged her back and then pulled away. "We can talk later. I need to see Elizabeth right away."

"I know that. I'll come over before I head home. Tell her we are all praying for her and the baby."

"I will." Astrid took off after Thorliff again, this time picking up the front of her skirt so she could walk faster. "I talked with Dr. Morganstein, and perhaps some of her wisdom will help here."

"I hope so." He set her bags just inside the door. "Come on, she's upstairs."

"Why isn't she down here in the lying-in room?"

"She wants her own bed. Besides, it's quieter upstairs." He mounted the stairs as if the weight of the entire universe were pressing down on his shoulders.

And you, my brother, look like you've aged ten years. Is that silver I see around your face? Tears blurred her vision. "I need to wash my hands first."

"There is a basin inside." He opened the door carefully and stepped in when he saw Elizabeth was sleeping. Ingeborg crossed the room and drew her daughter into her motherly arms.

"Thank God you are here," she whispered.

"Oh, Mor, I . . ." Astrid hugged her answers. When she pulled back, she stripped off her gloves and removed her hat, then turned to the basin, letting the familiar action turn on the doctor in her. She soaped her hands, scrubbing them while she listened to her mother's whispered comments about the patient.

"Nothing we do seems to help." She shrugged, her eyes wearing the same sadness that Thorliff's did.

Astrid rinsed her hands before wiping them on a clean linen towel. She drew her stethoscope out of her black bag and crossed the room to stand by the side of the bed. *Oh, Elizabeth. God, help her. Give her your strength, for she looks to have none of her own. What is happening with her?* She lifted the bony hand and located the pulse on the inside of the wrist.

"Astrid, is it really you or am I dreaming?" Elizabeth's voice was as weak as her body appeared.

"I am here. I'm going to check you over now. Is there anything you'd like to tell me?"

"I want this baby to live." Her answer came fiercely.

"I know." *And I want you to live. Please, Lord, both of them, please.* Astrid set the stethoscope to listen to Elizabeth's heart and lungs, nodding as she did so. "Good," she said with a slight smile. But when she placed the stethoscope on the mound of baby, she had to move it several times to get a heartbeat. She could feel Elizabeth's eyes drilling into her.

Astrid heaved a sigh. "The baby's heartbeat is weak and erratic." She peered into Elizabeth's wide eyes. "Have you listened lately?"

"Two days ago. It was steady then."

Astrid turned to her mother.

"I found it that way this morning. Yesterday was slower than the day before."

Elizabeth clenched Thorliff's hand. "This baby will live."

Dear God, I hope so. I pray so. Astrid felt her mother's strength behind her. If only they could share their strength with the woman in the bed.

20

The next morning Astrid hugged Mor, then sat on the edge of the bed in the lying-in room while her mother got settled with a pillow behind her back. "Mor, what do you think is happening with Elizabeth's baby?"

Ingeborg yawned and shook her head. "It is not good."

"I know that. Today the heartbeat is weaker. But why, when we're doing everything we know how to do medically?"

"Ja." She reached out to take Astrid's hand in hers. "Babies die for all sorts of reasons. Something might be wrong with it, and so the baby dies in utero. While this is so sad, still it would be sadder if the baby lived with terrible things wrong with it. Sometimes the mother's body just can't carry the baby. Maybe someday we'll know answers to these things, but right now we can count on God knowing. The baby comes from Him and returns to Him."

"And breaks Elizabeth's heart in the process. And maybe her body too."

"I know. She's lost several, but they've not gone this far along."

"But why? Elizabeth is healthy. Thorliff is too. And she's taken good care of herself. Other than getting overtired, I'm sure. But still . . ."

"I wish I had the answers you want, but I don't."

"She's doing everything Dr. Morganstein said to do. We've all been praying—"

"So we have to leave this in God's hands."

But what if she and the baby slip through His fingers? Astrid crossed the room to stand at the open window, looking out but seeing nothing. Rev. Thompkins' voice came softly through her mind. *"The answers to all your questions are in the Scriptures. You have to search for them sometimes, but they are there." But Father in heaven, where do I look? I've not seen any verse that says do this or do that to make a baby live.* She rubbed her forehead, propped her hands on the windowsill, and inhaled the early morning fragrance. Even the meadowlarks were not up yet. She heard a chirping in the cottonwood tree that sheltered the house from the summer sun. The house finches were starting to wake. The sky had lightened, but the sun still waited to burst over the horizon and fling itself into the azure sky.

What is the sense of being a doctor or a missionary if I can't help people live?

You can help them heal; you can teach them things to help them live better; you can ease pain. The thoughts seeped through her mind like fingers of fog that hovered over the river. And like fog, she could not trap them or even slow them down.

"We must trust that whatever God's will is, be it that this baby live or die, He is God, and He is right." Ingeborg's voice slipped softly through the silence.

"But we don't have to like it." This was not a question.

"No, we don't. But we cannot play God either."

Astrid swallowed the tears that threatened every time she thought of the baby fighting for its life. Of Elizabeth wanting this baby so desperately. Of Thorliff, who tried to keep a stiff upper lip but whose haunted eyes said otherwise.

"I'm going back to check on her." Astrid left the lying-in room and climbed the stairs to the bedroom where the unseen fight continued. Moving as silently as possible, she entered the dim room where Elizabeth lay sleeping. Thorliff was already out of bed and down in the kitchen with his first cup of coffee.

Trying not to disturb the sleeping woman, Astrid laid her stethoscope against the lower quadrant of the mounded belly and listened. She moved the instrument before picking up the faint beat of the baby's heart. Listening carefully, she fought to decide if the beat was fainter than a few hours earlier or just the same. She forced back a sigh, fearing it would wake Elizabeth, a frown seeming permanent between her eyebrows. Her seal brown hair, streaked with red, lay in a coiled rope over one shoulder, the deep purple smears under her eyes setting off the prominent bones in her face.

How much weight had she lost? Astrid pondered, studying on what she might possibly do to help. *Get her outside in the sun.* Would carrying her down the stairs precipitate a crisis? They could put a chair in front of the window, so when it was wide open the sun could warm her for a while.

Making her way downstairs to the kitchen, she greeted Thelma and Thorliff and took eggs and cream from the icebox. What else could she add to make the drink richer with nourishing food? Vanilla and sugar—no, honey would be better. Strawberry jam might make it taste even better. Anything to tempt Elizabeth's taste buds. As she beat the concoction, she asked Thelma if they had any chicken broth.

"No, but I can get a chicken cooking pretty quick. There is beef broth in the icebox."

"I'll push this first." She dumped in the second egg. "Then the beef broth. And please make her some mint tea. That will help soothe her stomach."

"Any change?" Thorliff asked when she sat down at the table, full coffee cup in hand.

Astrid shook her head. "I don't think so, but every day brings her closer to term."

Thorliff stared out the window, slowly shaking his head. "I can't lose her, Astrid. I just can't." His voice broke on the words.

Staring at her brother's ravaged face, Astrid could feel the pain radiating from the man beside her. Her big brother, who could do anything and managed the newspaper, the building company, things at church, and the many people who came to him for help or advice, now looked as if even a needle prick might shatter him.

She laid a hand on his arm, thinking to say, "We're doing the best we can," but instead, she just held her hand steady and sent him all the strength she could muster, counting on more coming from the Father, who always hears His children, even when they don't think they are praying. *That's one of the things I learned at missionary school,* she realized, the Bible verse that had stymied her for so long—*the Spirit itself maketh intercession for us with groanings which cannot be uttered*—now a comfort. Praying always meant that God heard all thoughts as clearly as words, and the hopes behind the words, unutterable even, flew directly to His great heart. *God loves you and Elizabeth and this baby.* She hoped the love came through her hand, now stroking her brother's arm. When he turned to gaze at her, his blue eyes a turbulent sea, she stood and wrapped her arms around his shoulders, resting her cheek on the top of his head.

The telephone rang three shorts, so Astrid crossed the room and lifted the earpiece. "Good morning."

"Call for you, Astrid, from Dr. Morganstein in Chicago."

"Thank you, Gerald." After the slight pause and click she heard Dr. Morganstein.

"Is that you, Astrid?"

"Yes. Good morning."

"How's our girl?"

"About the same."

"If the baby dies, you will have to do a cesarean section." Dr. Morganstein sounded abrupt.

"Unless we can precipitate a natural delivery." Astrid quaked at the thought of a cesarean, especially since she hadn't performed any surgeries these past months.

"I agree, but you cannot let the fetus begin to decompose. Elizabeth's not strong enough to endure that."

"I'm not sure she's strong enough for any of the above." She kept her voice down, hoping that Thorliff, who was now talking with Thelma, would not hear.

"I agree, so we do the least invasive. I've been researching in all my journals to see if there is something that might help. I've spoken with a friend at Johns Hopkins too." She paused. "It is a criminal shame there is not more research being done on women who have problems bearing children. It is such a natural part of life, and yet the medical world is lax in pursuing information."

"I agree." Astrid watched Thorliff stand. He was moving as if in slow motion.

"Call me if there is any change."

"I will." Astrid hung up and blew out a breath. In an hour she needed to open the surgery. Ingeborg would take over monitoring Elizabeth.

"You're ready to eat now, and don't tell me you don't have time."

Thelma took her job of caring for those who took care of the sick very seriously. Her tone brooked no argument.

Astrid took a place at the table. The plate set before her looked heaped enough to feed three people. She glanced up, started to say something about that, changed her mind, and murmured, "Thank you."

They might rule the sickrooms, but Thelma held sway over her kitchen domain.

Astrid spread jam on her toast. "Thelma, please tell Mor I made a drink of cream, two eggs, honey, and strawberry jam and to make Elizabeth drink it. The beef soup can come later."

After wolfing down her breakfast, Astrid wiped her mouth with a napkin. "I need to wash and get ready for the patients. Thank you for the delicious breakfast, Thelma. You might call Freda and ask her to butcher a couple of chickens."

"I will."

Half an hour later, Astrid turned the sign on the door from *Closed* to *Open* and spotted Rebecca pulling Benny in the red wagon Toby had built for him.

Astrid ran out and caught Rebecca in a huge hug.

"We heard you got home yesterday," Rebecca said when they finally pulled apart.

"That's—"

"Hey, Doc Bjorklund, I came to see you."

Astrid felt her heart lift again at the sight of Benny's beaming face. He looked like an entirely different boy from the waif she'd known in the hospital. His face had rounded and his arms and shoulders muscled out, but the lock of blond hair that curled over his forehead had stayed the same. She bent down to give him a hug. "I'm so glad to see you."

"Ma said you comed home. I'm glad." He squeezed her neck and kissed her cheek.

Astrid kissed him back and took both his hands in hers. "Benny, you look wonderful. How do you like Blessing?" She watched while he swung his legs with the prostheses over the edge of the wagon and propped his crutches under his arms. Placing his feet squarely, he push-pulled himself to his feet, rocking a bit until he got his balance. She forced herself to let him do it all himself, sharing a look with Rebecca that said the same thing. "You are doing very well, young man. I am so proud of you, I could shout and cheer."

He gave her a cheeky grin. "I wouldn't mind."

Rebecca laughed, music like birdsong dancing on the breeze. "He is the most independent boy I know." Her look added, "And he's mine."

"So you just came to see me?"

Benny grinned at her. "Ma said you should look at the stumps. Hurts some."

"I will gladly do that. Come on in."

"Got to be quick. I am late for school."

"He is never late, and he never misses." Rebecca pulled the wagon out of the way as Benny managed the stairs, waving Astrid back when she reached to help him.

In the examining room Benny unstrapped his prostheses, laid them to the side, and unwrapped the padding they bandaged in place every morning. He held out his right leg. "See."

Astrid examined the stump and found it was reddened on one side and warm to the touch. Infection or just irritation? "How long has this been going on?"

He wrinkled his forehead and wriggled his mouth around. He shrugged. "Couple days."

Astrid checked with Rebecca, who nodded. "He's faithful about telling me if there is a problem."

"Let's use some salve on that. It's called black cohosh. If there is infection, that will draw it out. I want you to soak the stumps every night. Now let's look at the padding." She examined the now compacted wool fleece. "I think we need to reline these and add more wool to the wrappings. Time and use flatten the wool. Have you washed and fluffed it up?"

"Once or twice when it looked dirty."

"Fleece can be washed over and over. Just make sure the hide doesn't get hard and stiff." Astrid smeared some salve on both stumps and handed the wrappings back to Benny. "Let me see you wrap them."

Step by step Benny did as she had shown him in the hospital those months earlier, and then grinned up at her when finished. "I do good, huh?"

"You do very well. I know you hate to sit still, but soaking will be important. We can't let infection set in."

"I will do it." His voice carried conviction like a man three or four times his age.

Astrid saw them to the door and returned to the examining room to find that Thelma had it all in order again for the next patient.

THAT EVENING AFTER supper, Astrid walked over to the Solberg house and asked the pastor if he had a few minutes. After exchanging pleasantries and getting caught up on the news, the pastor asked how Elizabeth was doing.

"About the same. Thorliff is sitting with her now."

"I stopped by this afternoon, but you were with a patient."

"I know. How did we get along without a doctor around here all those years?"

"Your mother with her simples did most of the doctoring, and people dealt with more things on their own or ignored what they couldn't cure. Now, what is bothering you?"

"One of my teachers at the school said we can find answers to all our questions in the Scriptures."

Solberg nodded. "I agree."

"Then what about helping newborns? I have found nothing that refers to babies, other than the promise or threat that there would always be problems for women having babies."

"Threat, eh? Leave it to you, Astrid. But sometimes we have to look not for a specific verse but for examples. If God didn't care about women's health, why did Jesus heal the woman who'd been bleeding all those years, most likely due to having had children."

"True."

"What did Jesus say?"

" 'Who touched my clothes?' and—" she squinted to remember—" 'Thy faith hath made thee whole.' "

"So?"

"So then we can do the same, because He said, 'Greater works than these shall he do; because I go unto my Father.' "

"Exactly."

"Then why is Elizabeth still suffering? We have all prayed, and we've done the best we know to do, medically. She believes in healing, has helped so many, and yet here she is, so close to losing this baby and perhaps her own life."

John Solberg leaned back in his chair and closed his eyes. "I wish I knew."

"You have always said we must trust God, no matter what. My teachers at the school said the same thing, but trusting is hard when you watch people die in spite of all you've done and prayed for."

"That it is. So then we must think on death. Is it really such a terrible thing if the person believes in Jesus Christ and is going home to that heavenly place Jesus promised He would have ready? You know the verse. 'I go to prepare a place for you. And if I go and prepare a place for you, I will come again, and receive you unto myself; that where I am, there ye may be also.' " He looked to Astrid. "I know that death is part of life, but Christ stands waiting to take us into His heavenly home and the Father's arms."

Astrid waited, hearing sounds of children talking through the closed door to the study, one laughing. Sounds of life on this earth. The life she fought so hard to keep for her patients. "Do we just give up?"

"No." The word snapped through the silence. "There is a great divide between giving up and trusting God to do what is best. One is futility, and the other is faith."

Astrid nodded. That part she did understand, at least as much as she was able. She knew that verse was good comfort for the dying, for those who were waiting on heaven, but at this point she still struggled with her case. "So God is asking me to trust Him?"

"He is asking all of us to trust Him."

Astrid crossed to the window and stared out, seeing nothing. She sniffed back the tears that threatened again. They'd been lurking all day. "This is so hard." Her cry broke the dam, and the tears poured forth.

Pastor Solberg came and stood behind her, his hand on her shoulder. "Yes, it is. You cry it out. You yell at God if you need to, and you wait for the peace to come, for it surely will. He said so. 'Peace I leave with you, my peace I give unto you.' " He handed her his handkerchief. "He promises strength too for the journey and for comforting others. Your name, that baby's name, Elizabeth's name are all written on the palm of His hand."

Another voice filled her mind. *And, lo, I am with you always, even to the end of the world.* Astrid sniffed and blew her nose again. Trust. Not a big word but a life-changing idea.

21

What happened at that farm was really none of his business. Joshua reminded himself of that as they set the drill into the ground at the location Mr. Calhoun told them to, ten feet from the hand-dug well that had been serving him for ten years.

"We will most likely go deeper to get you cleaner water," Joshua reminded him. They'd discussed this the night before, but sometimes another mention was a good idea.

The man nodded. "So you said. That windmill will pay for itself before the summer is over. Have to find something else for our youngest son to do. It was his job to keep the stock tank full. But today I'll set three of the boys digging the ditch to run water to the house."

Joshua almost asked about school before he remembered it was Saturday. And school would be out for the summer fairly soon. Most likely the eldest was already helping out in the fields. "How many boys do you have?"

"Five. And three girls. Help for both the farm and the house."

With the bit set, the horse was snapped into place and began his walk in a small circle, drilling the bit into the earth. While he'd been involved in that, Trygve and Gilbert had laid out the lumber to build the windmill.

Joshua couldn't get the memory of the two bodies in the bed out of his mind. "What do you think will happen to the farm down the road?"

"Oh, someone will come along and buy it. I think when the little boy died, it took the life right out of them." He half shrugged. "Babies die all the time. You just got to get used to it." He studied on the drilling. "Shame you don't have an engine to do that."

"I know. We're working on it. You don't by any chance have a telephone, do you?" Joshua was still trying to decide whether or not to call Hjelmer. But then, Hjelmer had made him manager of the drill team, so maybe it was up to him to make the decisions.

"Clear out here?" Calhoun shook his head. "Cost too much." He spit a gob of tobacco juice down beside his foot.

"Folks went together in Blessing. We put in our own exchange and strung our wires on posts we sunk in. Mighty handy instrument."

"No fooling?"

"I heard other places have formed co-operatives too. You know if Mr. Rude owned his place free and clear? And how many acres he was farming?"

"Nope. The bank in Grafton carries the paper on it. You interested, you go on and talk to them. I think he had half a section."

"What about the cattle?" *Do I want to know all this?* he wondered.

"Guess I'll bring 'em on over here, make sure they get pasture and water. Most likely they'll go with the place."

Joshua oiled the gears that drove the bit into the ground and checked to make sure the drilling was continuing without mishap. He walked over to see how the construction on the windmill was going and dug his hammer out of the toolbox.

With the sun getting higher and hotter, he sent Gilbert over to pump them a bucket of water. After drinking, they soaked their bandannas and tied them around their necks again.

When the sun stood straight up, the missus rang a bell by the back door and hollered that when the men got in from the field, there was a bench by the house where they could wash up for dinner.

"Good thing," Trygve muttered. "I was afraid we were gonna have to eat the leftovers from breakfast."

"You don't want fried rabbit for dinner?"

"I should run a line tonight too. Maybe they'd like some."

"Surely their boys—" Joshua broke off his comment when the youngest boy, barefoot and one strap holding up his overalls, stopped a few feet from him. "How's the ditch digging going?"

The boy glanced down at his feet. "Shoes hurt."

"Barefoot is always best in the summer. But how can you dig without boots on?"

"Can't. Pa said to ask if you need help."

"Well, you can pick up the sawed-off bits of lumber and take 'em up to the house for your ma to burn in the kitchen stove. Makes good kindling."

The boy nodded and ran off to the barn, returning with a gunnysack. He picked up the ends and bits, stopping once to pull a sliver from his foot.

Winter feet. Joshua remembered those days of tender feet after a winter of boots and knit wool socks. Hands were the same. Took time to rebuild the calluses and heal up the blisters. He saw the men come in with the two teams and nodded to Gilbert to unhitch their horse and take him over for a drink before turning him out in the pasture

Mr. Calhoun had said they could use. They would put a different horse on for the afternoon shift.

"How many feet you gone down?" Calhoun asked after all the food had been passed.

"Twenty feet. We got water at ten but pushed on through. Like I said, you get cleaner water that way." Joshua took a bite of his chicken and dumplings and nodded to Mrs. Calhoun. "Very good, ma'am. Thank you."

"Beats our cooking," said Trygve, "but that's not much of a compliment."

"You work for one of those Bjorklunds?" Mr. Calhoun asked.

"We do. Hjelmer Bjorklund started drilling wells last year, and we went into windmills too. Every farm and house needs a windmill. No need to waste all that time and effort when the wind can do it for you without you even being there."

"And I will really have water to the house?" Mrs. Calhoun looked from her husband to Joshua.

"Soon as you have a hand pump in here to bring in the water."

"Mercy, but that is something wonderful."

One of the girls, with a shy smile, asked if the guests would like more chicken.

Trygve nodded and blessed her with a smile that made her cheeks flame pink.

"Thank you, Miss Calhoun."

Joshua rolled his lips together to keep from laughing. Trygve could no more leave off the charm than he could go without food. "Can you tell me anything more about the Rude place?"

"Well, part of it is shore on the lake. He called it Rude Lake after his pa. That's why those cows are still alive—they could drink out of the lake. The Rudes carried water from the lake to the house till a few years ago, when the neighbors got together to help him dig a well. He weren't much for socializing. Fair worker, but it seemed if something were gonna go wrong, it would happen to him. All the rest of us around here help each other out, but . . ." Calhoun let his words trail off.

Mrs. Calhoun clucked like a mother hen. "Worked his wife to death is what he did."

"Vinny."

She sniffed at the reprimand and gave her husband a look that made Joshua smile inside.

"You know that all the neighbors helped dig that well because the women got together and insisted, hoping it would make life easier on the missus."

Her comment reminded Joshua of the way the men of Blessing just showed up and helped him dig out the cellar for his house. They said that's what neighbors did. Looks like they tried that here too. So how had Hjelmer sold Rude on the benefits of a deeper well and a windmill?

"Would you like apple or custard pie for dessert?" Mrs. Calhoun motioned for her girls to begin clearing the table.

"That's a hard decision," Joshua said with a smile.

"Good. You take a piece of each, then." As she set about cutting and serving the pie, she nodded to Trygve and Gilbert. "You men the same?"

"You mind if I run some snares for rabbits tonight?" Trygve asked.

"You get rid of some of the rabbits around here, and I'll be in your debt. Young Frank goes out shooting every once in a while. Nothing much better than a mess of fried rabbit." She'd nodded at the youngest of the older three sons, none of whom had said a word after the introductions.

Thanking their hostess for the fine meal, the men returned to their jobs. Joshua hitched the next horse onto the drill arm and started him on around the well-trod circle. They had the stand for the windmill bolted together, ready to raise it in place when the drill hit water again. Over the winter they had worked out a new way to build the windmills, laying them out on the ground and then hoisting them into place with horse and manpower. They raised the windmill up by a pulley and bolted it onto the wooden platform. It cut off a day or more of the construction time.

Clean water came in as Calhoun and his boys were returning from the fields. Trygve capped the pipe, and after letting the horse out into the pasture, they all washed up for supper.

"You mean you got the water already?" Calhoun said, his eyes wide. "That's all it took?"

"Yes, sir. The water tables are pretty high here in the Red River Valley. You want to help us raise the frame in the morning, we'll have it done by nightfall."

THE NEXT MORNING Trygve handed Mrs. Calhoun six gutted rabbits when they were called for breakfast. "I need to do this at home more too. Mor always said we could live off the land here and never go hungry. My younger brother, Samuel, never took much to snaring rabbits. He'd rather go fishing."

"You folks live near the Red, then?"

"Yes, sir. Our land borders it." He turned to Mrs. Calhoun. "If you don't mind, I thought I'd take a couple pieces of that rabbit for the dog from the Rude farm. He followed us here. Poor thing's starving to death."

"There's plenty here. I'll cook 'em up, and you can also take some with you if you leave tomorrow."

"Where you heading next?" Calhoun asked as they passed the pancakes, ham, and eggs.

"Going south from here. That's our last for this trip, unless Hjelmer lets us know of more."

"Wonder how he found Rude, and I never heard nothing." Calhoun shook his head. "Don't make much sense."

"All those fields lying fallow don't make much sense either," one of the sons volunteered.

"Someone comes along, they can hay them later. If we had the money, I'd sure be in town seeing about adding that acreage onto ours."

"Shame it's not closer to Blessing, or my pa might be interested," Trygve added.

"So you folks really did get in your own phone lines?"

"We did. The people of Blessing have always worked together. They set up a community bank way back in the early days," Trygve told him. "Built a grain storage when they didn't like the charges from the railroad. A flour mill was the last big project, and that took care of shipping our wheat out to the Twin Cities. The less we have to depend on the railroad the better. They keep trying to suck the farmers dry."

Joshua listened to Trygve talking, amazed at his understanding of the political climate. The old saying that still waters run deep sure applied to this young man.

By ten o'clock they had the windmill frame standing, and the Calhoun men headed for the fields. Between the horses and the manpower, the windmill stood ready for the gear box and blades. The creaking song of the new windmill greeted the men when they returned their teams to the barn at the end of the day. The stock tank stood nearly full, and two of the girls were helping young Frank with the ditch digging.

Joshua showed the Calhouns how to maintain the windmill, reminding them again at the end that greasing the gears was most important. "Keep the brake ready for action too so you can shut it down in case of a high wind. Gets spinning too fast, and it might shear right off. Then you have a real problem."

Calhoun pointed to his oldest son. "Clarence, I put you in charge of the windmill."

"Yes, sir." Clarence studied the platform way above their heads, slowly shaking his head. "That's gonna take some doin' to get up on that itty bitty frame."

"Aw, you can do it," his younger brother said, clapping him on the shoulder. "You're not that far off the ground."

"Well, let's get eating, and these gentlemen can hit the sack so they get on the road again in the morning." Calhoun walked beside Joshua. "I take it you want all your money in one lump sum?"

"Yes, sir. That was our agreement. I have the bill for you right here." Joshua pulled a folded piece of paper from his shirt pocket.

THE FOLLOWING MORNING they hitched the teams and headed out for their last job. Two days later they were on their way home to Blessing, since they'd not heard any different from Hjelmer. The dog was already looking better, thanks to Trygve's feeding it twice a day. He'd not really stolen the dog, just not encouraged it to go home when it followed them down the road. It slept beside him under the wagon at night and sometimes rode along when invited.

"What you gonna call him?" Joshua asked.

"I thought to call him Rudy. What do you think?"

"Sounds fine to me. What's your mother going to say?"

"She'll say, 'He's your dog. You take care of him.' Then at the first storm she'll invite him into the house to lie by the fire."

Joshua chuckled. "I think you got you a good dog there."

"I think we got *us* a good dog. He's part of the drilling team now."

Joshua slapped the horses to pick up their feet. What if there was a letter from Astrid? At least he'd gotten his letters in the outgoing mail. They'd been gone from Blessing for just over three weeks, but it felt like a lifetime.

22

Ah, Astrid, my heart, you needn't understand it all. No one does but God himself.

Ingeborg realized she must have been praying in her sleep. She levered herself off the bed where she'd been resting in the lying-in room and crossed to the window to check on Blessing and at the same time inhale the heating morning air. *I must go home today, even for a little while.* The thought took root instead of fluttering out the window to mingle with the nesting sparrows. The morning trill of the meadowlarks fell softly on her ears and brought a smile to her mind and mouth.

Most likely Astrid was already seeing patients. Falling back to sleep had been a rarely taken treasure, and instead of allowing guilt to drab the morning colors, Ingeborg chose to let her heart sing praises. She'd learned long years ago that praises to her Father were the antidote to many ailments of the soul and emotions. They seemed to help the physical too. Closing her eyes, she let the birdsongs seep inside. A hammer rang on nails somewhere in town, someone building something. Laughter floated by, most likely from the boardinghouse. This house remained silent, because Inga was still at Ellie's. Thank God there was family nearby to take over child care and provide meals. Freda was indeed a godsend.

Ingeborg inhaled the warming air that tickled the sheer white curtains. May was nearly over. How time had picked up speed so much in the last years was another of those things beyond understanding. *Thank you, Father, that Astrid came home.* Amazing what a good night's sleep had done for her. If only they could provide rest like that for Elizabeth. That thought carried her out the door. She could hear women visiting in the waiting room. A door clicked shut somewhere else. Should she get herself a cup of coffee or go up to check on Elizabeth? She climbed the stairs, her hand using the smooth walnut banister rather than just trailing it.

Entering the bedroom, she found Elizabeth yawning and stretching her arms. "Good morning."

Elizabeth nodded. "Yes, I think it is."

"Have you eaten yet?"

"No. I was just thinking of ringing Thelma."

"Then have her bring up a tray for both of us." She studied the patient. "Your color is better this morning."

"Well, it is good something is." Elizabeth smoothed a hand over her growing mound. "I've not felt him move."

"You always refer to the baby as *he*."

"I know. Thorliff wants a son, and I want Inga to have a brother. Since I grew up an only child, I've always wanted her to have siblings."

Ingeborg sat down on the edge of the bed. "Let's give him a listen, then." She pulled her stethoscope from her apron pocket and set it against the lawn-covered skin. She moved it once, then again before finally picking up a faint beat. "Let's get a bit closer."

Elizabeth pulled up her gown to bare her belly, a frown deepening the lines on her forehead.

"Ah good. That's better." Better but not good. She moved the stethoscope to the other side. "And better still." Silently she counted the beats. What was happening in there?

"May I listen?"

Ingeborg handed her the earpieces, watching Elizabeth's face as she listened to her baby's struggle.

She handed the instrument back and shook her head slowly, as if caught in a thick mud. "Weaker."

"Ja, but still fighting. What would you tell a patient if you were the doctor on the case?"

"Bed rest, beef broth to build up the blood, and plenty of prayer. All the things we've been doing, and yet there is no improvement, only decline. I would probably say that the baby had only a slim chance and to call me immediately if anything changed. When the baby died, I would recommend a cesarean section to remove the dead fetus so the mother is not poisoned by the decay. If we could not trigger the body to go into labor, that is." A tear sneaked down her cheek and into her ear. "But since this is my baby and the last one I am probably ever going to have the chance to hold in my arms, I want to kick and scream. I know I've been alternately railing at God and pleading for this little one's life." She paused, staring toward the window. "I have to remind myself to be grateful for Inga."

A knock on the door and Thelma entered with a tray with plenty of food for two. "Thorliff and Mr. Jeffers are downstairs in the dining room. They asked you to join them, Ingeborg, when you have eaten, if you can." She set the tray on the small table they kept by the bed for that purpose. "Astrid has started office hours."

"Thank you, Thelma. Tell them I'll be down shortly." Ingeborg stood and, helping Elizabeth lean forward, stacked pillows behind her and helped her scoot upright. "Now, let's have grace and enjoy the food. Later, Thelma, let's move Elizabeth to the settee in front of the window, and I'll help you change the bed. Astrid and I were talking about carrying Elizabeth downstairs to the porch to soak in some sunshine."

Thelma nodded. "Good idea. Mr. Bjorklund can carry her down."

"Or you could let me out through the window with a pulley and sling." Elizabeth's raised eyebrows reminded them she was teasing. "Easier on Thorliff's back."

"His back should be fine. You'll be lighter than—" Ingeborg stopped, not wanting to remind Elizabeth how prominent her bones had become. A rather unattractive picture crossed Ingeborg's mind of a figure all bones and belly.

Thelma rolled her eyes and picked up the water pitcher. "You need to drink more."

"So I can relieve myself more and have to get up more and then get scolded for being out of bed."

Ingeborg let her smile show. Elizabeth was showing more signs this morning of strength in herself. Maybe their fears were ungrounded. Until one listened to the baby's heart.

A bell jangled downstairs. "That's Astrid." Thelma hustled out the door and down the stairs.

Ingeborg settled the tray table across Elizabeth's lap and poured one cup of coffee. "Astrid says you are to drink this first, and then in a little while I will bring beef broth."

"What is this?" Elizabeth sniffed but did as asked.

Another knock on the door and Thelma poked her head in again. "Remember the man with the raccoon bite?"

Ingeborg nodded.

"He's here. Astrid wants your opinion."

Ingeborg and Elizabeth exchanged sorrowful looks and sighs.

"I'll be right down."

"Tell Astrid I can taste honey, but I want to know what else is in this. Let's move me when you can get back up."

Down in the examining room the patient sat with head drooping and eyes closed. His wife sat in the other chair, her eyes never leaving his face.

"You have to do something!" Her voice cracked at the same time as tears overrode her strength of will.

"Has he been drooling long?" Ingeborg asked.

"Two, three days maybe."

"You must be careful in caring for him. We will give you morphine in an elixir to control the pain."

The woman's eyes darted from one doctor to the other. "He will get better?"

Ingeborg looked to Astrid, her expression giving her answer.

"I'm sorry, but now that it has reached this stage, rabies is always fatal. The most we can do is keep him comfortable."

"But . . ." The woman clamped her lips together and sucked in a deep breath. "You're sure?"

"Barring a miracle."

"I see." Tears trickled down her cheeks and she sniffed. "So I take him home and give him the medicine and watch him die."

Her husband groaned and swayed from side to side. He used the towel Astrid had given him to wipe his mouth. "Home."

"Yes."

Ingeborg helped him to his feet, and motioning the wife to take the other side, they supported him out to the wagon. The pallet in the back gave mute testimony as to how she had brought him in. After helping him crawl into the back of the wagon and watching him collapse on the quilts with a sigh, she checked his pulse. Racing.

Should they keep him there, where they could administer the drugs as needed?

Back on her feet, she puffed a breath and turned to his wife. "You have two options. Take him home or leave him here."

"To die either way?"

"Yes." What a terrible word to utter.

"Then I will take him home." The woman straightened her shoulders and clamped her bottom lip between her teeth. "The medicine?"

"I'll bring it right out." Ingeborg hurried back into the surgery, ignoring the beautiful morning, wishing only that she could provide a long lifetime of mornings for the man in the wagon. What dosage should she recommend? Would she want to be knocked out or be aware of those around if she were in this position? How could she ask such a thing? How much was a lethal dose? That thought made her hand shake as she mixed the potent medicine.

Taking the bottle back outside, she handed it to the woman now seated on the driver's bench. "Give him one tablespoon at a time whenever he gets restless. If you give him less, he will be more aware of those around him."

The two women stared into each other's eyes. The wife nodded. "Thank you." She backed the horses and drove away, Ingeborg watching as the dust rose under the horses' hooves. *Please, Lord, ease his suffering, and take him home soon.* She rolled her lips together and blinked repeatedly as she walked around the house and entered through the back door. She had to have time to compose herself before returning to the examining rooms.

Thelma handed her a cup of coffee and motioned her to be seated. "Miss Astrid is seeing the other patients now."

"Thank you." Sitting in the rocking chair with her head back, Ingeborg remembered Astrid writing from Chicago that there had been a discussion on vaccinations that had been developed. One was for rabies. But what about treatment for someone who had been bitten?

Did she want to vaccinate everyone in the region around the rabid animals? How far had the rabies traveled? And what brought it on?

She drained her coffee and headed back into the fray. Hearing the male voices from the dining room, she sighed. She was supposed to be in there for the meeting. She tapped on the closed door to an examining room. At the "Come in" she entered and whispered what she'd done in Astrid's ear.

"You go on," Astrid told her. "I'll take care of this. Go to Elizabeth when you're finished."

Leaving one room and opening the door to another was like stepping across a large divide. "Sorry to be so long," she said, "but we had a bit of an emergency."

"Glad you could come," Thorliff said, standing to pull out a chair for her next to Haakan. Daniel Jeffers and Hjelmer were both leaning forward, elbows on their knees.

"We've been discussing building the plant for manufacturing the seeder improvement right here in Blessing, as you know," Thorliff told her.

Haakan squeezed her hand gently. "I brought the wagon, in case you can come home for a bit today."

Ingeborg nodded and dug in her pocket for a piece of paper. "I have here a list of questions I thought about during the night." She unfolded the paper and laid it on the table. "I know you've discussed some of these already, but here they are." She read from her list. "Number one. Where will you find enough men around here to work in the plant?"

"We plan on running advertisements in regional newspapers and perhaps even in the national papers."

"Two. Where will you house them?"

"The boardinghouse to start with. We are buying land south of the flour mill so that we can extend the railroad siding and not have to put in a new one." Thorliff laid a sketch of a building on the table. "A simple building with a concrete floor, two story at one end to make office room. We'll make sure it is easy to add on to, for when we need to expand."

"I thought you were going to use the old grainery." Ingeborg looked from Thorliff to Jeffers.

"We think it best to use that for now so we can get started. But it just isn't big enough," Thorliff answered with a shrug.

"We've talked with Sophie about adding on to the boardinghouse, and while she is not overly excited about the prospect, she and Garth are discussing it." Hjelmer glanced around the table. "And we are talking about building a group of small houses across the tracks."

"Small houses?"

"One or two bedrooms, and a kitchen that includes sitting space . . . not sure whether a cellar or not. More the size of a large sod house." Hjelmer shoved several drawings her way.

Ingeborg studied the papers. "How will there be a well and outhouse, and a garden, on plots this small?"

"We are thinking of digging one well to take care of all of them, so each house would have running water."

"Inside bathrooms?"

The men shook their heads as one.

"Mor, most of the houses in Blessing don't have indoor plumbing yet."

"I know, but give us a couple of years, and that will change. You might want to wire them for electricity too."

Hjelmer grinned at Thorliff, an "I told you so" kind of look.

"The Women's Aide has been discussing this kind of thing, you know. Blessing is known for being progressive. If we are encouraging families to move here, we will need to provide schooling. And if the expansion goes on with Kaaren's school, we will need homes for families with deaf children also. These houses you are thinking of building are for single men who would most likely rather be at a boardinghouse. What about building another boardinghouse here if Sophie is not interested in adding on?"

Ingeborg glanced over at Daniel Jeffers, who met her gaze and smiled back.

"I feel like we are almost revamping Blessing with all these plans," he said.

"We are," Hjelmer said. "When you think that we are building a hospital, well . . . Thorliff received a letter from a dentist asking about office space, and there will be others. We must always be thinking ahead."

A knock on the door stopped the discussion.

"Come in," Thorliff answered.

Astrid stuck her head in. "Mor, sorry, but we need you." She smiled at her father and withdrew.

Ingeborg stood. "Thank you for inviting me." She left the room, her heart pounding. Was it Elizabeth?

23

Going home to Blessing. A tune picked up the words and danced through his mind. Joshua let the song grow, running it over and over until he was sure it felt right. Wishing he had paper and guitar, he flipped the reins over the backs of the team. "Pick up your feet, boys. We're almost home." The question that had been nibbling away at the back of his mind reared its not pretty head again. What if Astrid were on her way to Africa?

"You think Hjelmer has more work for us?" Gilbert called from the other wagon.

He nodded and tossed his answer back. "I'm sure of it. If not drilling wells, there will be something else." Confidence was not an issue here. Hjelmer always needed more help. Talk about an idea man. Between him and Thorliff, they could keep a crew of a hundred busy.

The biggest problem was not finding work but finding workers. He wished his brother would sell the farm and come join him here. Perhaps his brother-in-law too. What would it be like to have his family around? They could live in his house, once he got it up, while putting up their own. Astrid continued to float on the edges of his mind.

Please, Lord, let her be back in Blessing. He knew this prayer came under the heading of selfish, but how could he court her long distance? Neither of them was exemplary in letter writing. Her excuse was she spent every free moment memorizing Scripture. His? To be honest, he didn't much like writing letters, mostly because his were boring. *Yesterday we raised the last of ten windmills.* What an accomplishment. *Mr. Smith was well pleased, as were all the others. Other than the Rude couple.* The memory of seeing their bodies still bothered him, even though the sheriff had said the deaths were of natural causes, meaning some kind of sickness. Joshua shook his head. Too many things didn't add up.

He shook off the thoughts, rested his elbows on his knees, and let his mind float back to the tune that was still teasing him. Home to Blessing. Back to Blessing. He moved words around for both the opening line and the title. Home. Funny how Blessing had become home to him in such a short time.

Will Astrid be home in Blessing? Will she stay there if she is home? Or was she on her way to Africa? He'd gone to the grade school and looked on a world map to see which countries were in Africa. Somehow when he went to school, he'd not had a lot of interest in world geography.

Trygve, driving the other wagon, signaled a stop. Joshua did so, stepping down to get a drink of water from the barrel. The water was warm, but it was liquid and soothed the dust in his throat. He half filled a couple of buckets and watered his team and then handed the buckets off for the other. Any more water wouldn't be good for the animals. He soaked his kerchief from the spigot and wrapped it around his neck.

"Any biscuits left from breakfast?" Trygve asked, soaking his own bandanna.

Joshua nodded. "In the breadbox."

"Cheese?"

"Nope."

"Meat?"

He shook his head. Good thing they were nearing home. The larder needed restocking. "We shoulda kept those rabbits you snared."

Trygve shrugged. "Those folks needed them more than we did. Sometimes I wonder why more families don't teach their sons to run snare lines. There's always plenty of rabbits around."

"No reason girls couldn't do so." The family they'd just left had three girls. The oldest helped her mother in the house, but the next two helped their father in the fields because there were no sons. Yet. Perhaps the one under the mother's apron would break the cycle.

"You ought to go back and teach them how. That oldest girl had her eye on you."

Joshua enjoyed watching the red creep up Trygve's neck and collect on his cheekbones.

"Let's get rolling. I'm ready for some of my mother's home cooking." Trygve strolled back to the supply wagon and swung up into the driver's seat. He clucked the horses forward, making Gilbert scramble to get seated.

Joshua chuckled to himself. *One of these days, son, you'll find that special girl and then you'll be fun to watch.*

They saw the flour mill first, then the grain elevator. As the buildings grew into their entirety, the horses picked up their feet even faster. With home in sight they well knew the way and wanted to get there.

They parked the wagons behind the blacksmith shop and stripped off the harnesses. With the horses loosed in the pasture, the men retrieved their personal belongings from the chuck wagon and waved at Mr. Sam as they left for their homes. Joshua headed to the boardinghouse, the idea of a bath in hot water that didn't need to be hauled nor heated top in his mind. Besides, someone there would know if Astrid was in town or where she was.

"Welcome home," Gerald called from the steps of the bank building, which they'd come to call the new building that housed the bank, the post office, the barber, and the telephone exchange.

Joshua waved back. "Thanks. Good to be here." But he didn't slow down. Once he got a bath, he'd get a haircut. His mail, if he had any, would be at the boardinghouse. A letter from Astrid would be better than nothing. He took the steps two at a time and let the screen door slam behind him.

"Welcome home," Sophie called, sitting behind the desk in the foyer. "You have mail. We put it on your bed."

"Thanks." He stopped. "How you doing?"

"Getting bigger. One would think four children enough."

Joshua paused. She'd done it again. Forthright was a good word for Sophie, a trait that got her in trouble rather regularly. But he still hesitated discussing such personal things as having a baby.

Sophie leaned on the counter. "She's back."

Nonchalant would be appropriate here. Instead, he stumbled on the edge of the carpet. He didn't bother asking who or some other subterfuge. His voice squeaked instead. "Astrid, er, Dr. Bjorklund?"

Sophie rolled her eyes. "Who else would you be interested in? I'm not blind and dumb, you know."

"For good?"

"I don't know that, and I don't think she does at this point either. But she's staying at the surgery to be close to the other Dr. Bjorklund. If I'd known where to send mail for you, I would have done that."

"Thank you. I still have a room here, I take it?"

"Didn't have to use yours yet, but the way Hjelmer and Thorliff are planning, we might need to one of these days. They asked if I wanted to add on to the boardinghouse."

"And will you?"

She paused and wrinkled her mouth. "I just don't know. My husband thinks it a good idea, but I guess I need to think on it more. Besides the investment of money, I'd need to find more help, and you know what that is like here." She switched to a smile. "But enough about me and the boardinghouse. There's plenty of hot water, and if you want us to do your laundry, just toss the bag on the back porch. They're done for today but will be back at it early in the morning."

"Thank you. Not sure how long before we head out again, but surely we'll be here long enough for the laundry to get done. Thanks for the information." He turned and headed for the stairs.

In his room he dropped his belongings on the floor and reached for the letters on his bed. Three. Not a lot for being gone a little more than three weeks, but since two of them were from Astrid, he could feel a grin stretching his face. He pulled clean clothes from the drawers, grabbed his towel and shaving things, and strode to the bathroom down the hall, the door wide open saying no one was using it.

With the bathtub filling, he stripped and climbed in, his letters wrapped in a towel to keep them dry. He'd forgotten to lock the door. Out again and dripping to the door, he snapped the lock and returned to the claw-footed tub with a sloping back and deep sides. One could almost swim in it. He rolled another towel and lay back against the headrest he'd created. After drying his hands, he opened the earlier one from Astrid with a postmark of Athens, Georgia.

Dear Mr. Landsverk,

Thank you for writing. I feel almost guilty telling you I am writing from my table out on the veranda where the bushes are blooming, the birds are singing, and a little lizard is attempting to be brave and gobble up the crumbs I tossed him. He needs to hurry before the birds pick them all up. I am sure there is still snow on the ground in North Dakota, but I must say, I do not miss it a bit.

I understand your restlessness to be working on your house. Once I start something, I want to finish it as soon as possible, but a house would take a long time, relatively of course, no matter what season. I remember that is why Thorliff always tried to have the outside done in the fall so they could work on the insides all winter. Remember when you were working on Penny's house? She was sure it would never be done for Christmas, and yet all you workers managed to make it happen.

I am enjoying my studies here. The pace is so much slower than in Chicago that I feel guilty having so much leisure. Other students mutter about the amount of classwork, and it is all I can do to not verbally compare this with the hospital. Some of them already think I should not be here. As do some of the professors. One said that I should go home and find a husband who would want to accompany me to Africa.

Joshua stopped reading. She needed a husband to go to Africa? He chewed on the inside of his lower lip. But now she was home. Had she taken their advice and started looking at the young men at the school? Had she found one? On the other side, did he want to go to Africa? He caught himself shaking his head at that thought. But then, this was all new. He returned to reading.

I am memorizing amazing amounts of Scripture, more than I ever dreamed possible—or necessary. I never thought I might be in a place where a Bible might not be available. We are spoiled in our country, of that I am more assured all the time as I hear the stories of missionaries returning from other lands. I do hope you find the time to write again.

Your friend,
Dr. Astrid Bjorklund

He reread the line about memorizing Bible verses. Pastor Solberg had mentioned the value of that again the last Sunday before the crew left for drilling. Perhaps he'd better make it a practice to have his Bible along and do the same. He opened and read the second letter.

Dear Mr. Landsverk,

Why can't she call me Joshua? Does she even think of me as Joshua?

> I have amazing news. I have been accepted for a two-year term as a medical missionary to the British East Africa Protectorate. I was certain they were going to turn me down after the last meeting I had with the board that makes those decisions. I will be working at a hospital in Mombasa, the capital city, for the first while until someone decides that I can go work in the bush with Rev. Schuman. I am not sure if I am happy or not, but if this is God's calling for me, He will provide. I read a book that said "God will never call you to someplace He has not prepared for you." He will provide for all my needs. I have come to believe that implicitly.
>
> I hope to come home for a brief furlough before I leave the first part of July.
>
> Your friend,
> Dr. Astrid Bjorklund

Joshua felt the agony of a sucker punch to the midsection. She was going to Africa. This time at home would be a "brief furlough." He put the letter away and began scrubbing. He would spend every moment he could with her while she was here.

He paused, the washcloth dripping. If she would let him. Maybe she'd decided to leave him behind too.

24

Astrid sometimes felt the stethoscope should be affixed to her ears. After so many weeks of not practicing medicine, today she had barely taken a break. At least it had calmed enough for Ingeborg to go home for a few hours while Elizabeth slept under Thorliff's watch. Far better than the other day when she'd pulled her mother from the meeting because Elizabeth had spotted again.

"Can you cough for me?" she asked the small boy sitting on his mother's lap. He looked up at his mother, who coughed for an example, and shook his head.

She sighed. "He's been coughing for several days. I gave him honey melted in warm water, but that isn't helping. Please, Daniel, cough for the doctor so she can help you."

Daniel promptly vomited all over Astrid. Projectile vomiting at its best, or worst, as the case may be. Astrid smiled reassuringly, eternally grateful for the white apron that covered her clothing, neck to foot. The little boy whimpered and burst into coughs that sounded like they were wrenching out his innards.

Glancing up at the mother, Astrid received a nod of acknowledgment and set her stethoscope against the heaving back and then chest. She needn't have bothered. A croupy cough sounded like no other. "Let's get a tent set up, and I'll show you how so you can do it at home. Steam is the best antidote, and for his cough, I find that honey mixed with equal proportions of whiskey and warm water is the best expectorant around. We have some made up here along with steeped willow bark in the water, if you would like to purchase a bottle."

While she spoke, she rang for Thelma. She ignored the look Thelma gave her messed apron when she came in and set about turning towels into a tent to be used over steaming water. "I have something new in the pharmacopeia," she added. "It comes from California, a tree there called eucalyptus. Sprinkle the powder over the water, and it makes the steam more effective."

Thelma returned with a clean apron and a pot of steaming water that she set on the table. She indicated that Astrid needed to change and waited so she could take the messed apron out with her.

Astrid did as told and returned to her charges. "Now, this is easier done at home over the kitchen stove, but here is how to do it. Hold Daniel against your chest and drape a large towel or sheet over your head and the steaming kettle, trapping as much of the vapor as possible." She sprinkled the powder on the water, which immediately filled the room with the pungent aroma. Daniel shuddered with the coughing. Astrid fixed the towel over her head, took the boy in her arms, binding his arms with her own, and face out, leaned them both over the kettle. Still coughing, Daniel inhaled the steam, and after a few breaths, the coughing eased.

She rose up, handed the child to the mother, showing her again how to hold him, then motioned her to bend over the kettle and hung the towel over their heads. Stepping back, she tied her apron and listened for the wheezing to ease. Sure as the sun rising in the east, the child relaxed, the mother's crooning voice softened, and Astrid breathed a silent prayer of thanksgiving. She'd done a tracheotomy on a child in Chicago that was too far gone to respond to this simple treatment, but she would only do another in an extreme emergency.

"How often can I do this?" the mother asked.

"As often as needed. The relief gives his body time to fight the infection. When this happens again, the sooner you start the treatments, the better off he will be. Most children outgrow the croup as they get older."

"He's sound asleep."

"That's wonderful." Astrid lifted off the makeshift tent and folded it. "Do you have any questions?"

"How much are the two medicines you mentioned?"

Astrid named a figure and wrote her notes in the child's records. "If he gets worse and doesn't respond to the treatment, bring him in or telephone me."

"We don't have a telephone."

"I see." Astrid realized that she'd begun to take the availability of that instrument for granted. It had already saved several lives that she knew of due to the swiftness of medical response. "Send someone for me, then. He could choke and die if the mucous were trapped in his throat."

The mother nodded, her eyes shimmering with unshed tears. "Thank you, Dr. Bjorklund. You saved my Daniel's life."

"You are indeed welcome." Astrid ushered her out the door, the boy sleeping in his mother's arms. "Thelma will give you the things I suggested. She can take the payment also, either now or leave a note for later." Bidding them good-bye, she made her way back upstairs to check on her other patient. Since her mother had gone home after her last sitting, Astrid and Thelma were taking turns checking on Elizabeth, who had gone back to sleep after her breakfast and basin bath. Since there didn't seem to be any change, Astrid figured that was a good thing and returned to her office downstairs.

"Telephone for you," Thelma announced when she reached the main floor. "Sophie."

Astrid followed her into the kitchen and picked up the earpiece. "Hello."

"I won't keep you but thought you might want to know that Mr. Landsverk is back in town. The crew returned about an hour or so ago."

"I see." Was that her heart leaping or her stomach? Did it matter which?

"So?"

"So what do you want me to do?"

"I guess I want you to act a bit excited for a start." Her voice slipped from sweet to tart.

"Sophie, this is not the right time. I haven't even had a chance to talk with Far yet." Did she not realize how fragile Elizabeth was?

"You still need to take a break," Sophie snapped.

Astrid thought a moment. "What would you do?" If that wasn't an explosive question . . .

Sophie paused. "I'm thinking."

"I have patients waiting."

"I guess I would ask my friend to tell, er suggest, to him that she would be available for supper or perhaps sodas later in the afternoon. When do you close the surgery?"

"I have no appointments for after three o'clock, but I am watching Elizabeth too. I sent Mor home, and Thelma has a stack of laundry a mile high. Or several baskets anyway." She reminded herself to be accurate, not to exaggerate.

"Good. I shall suggest sodas if he asks."

Astrid twirled her apron sash. Did she dare leave for a few moments? She did wonder how their meeting would be. "Okay, Sophie, if Elizabeth is doing okay." *It's been forever since I saw him. What if he has changed? His mind, at least.*

"He was thrilled to hear that there were letters from you up in his room."

Her heart did another of those skippy beats she hadn't felt for a very long time.

"Sodas would be a fine way to get to know him a bit again." After all, she'd really met him at the soda shop, so this seemed most appropriate.

"I'll have him telephone you."

"If I'm with a patient, he can leave the message with Thelma." Astrid hung up the receiver. Her day had definitely taken a different turn. Should she change clothes? There wasn't time to take a bath. No. If a relationship were ever to grow between them, he needed to see her as she was. That was clear to her from the missionary school. Truth had to be the basis of all relationships.

She turned down the urge to look in a mirror, but smoothed errant strands of hair back into her snood and returned to the office—and her waiting patients. As she reached the door of the examining room, a thought hit her like a thick glass window. Why have sodas with Joshua, Mr. Landsverk, when she would most likely be leaving any day for the missionary school and on to Africa? She heaved a big sigh and, turning the doorknob, entered the room. Sometimes keeping too busy to think was a good thing.

At four o'clock she checked on Elizabeth, who was back to sleep after her dinner and some time sitting in the corner window settee. They had decided against carrying her downstairs because she seemed a bit weaker. Mor was back and had taken up her post in the rocking chair near the bed, knitting in her lap and prayers on her lips and mind. Astrid felt like she was fleeing a battlefield. Perhaps she should stay. Did she really want to see Joshua, or would it be better not to see him at all? She hesitated.

Ingeborg looked up. "Go for a walk and get some fresh air."

"I'll be at Rebecca's," she whispered. Mor nodded.

Astrid went downstairs, turned the *Closed* sign over, and walked to the Blessing Soda Shoppe.

Benny met her at the door on his flat cart that he pushed with his hands. "My Doc is here," he announced with a grin. Leaning closer he whispered, "A man is here to see you."

She patted his cheek and whispered back, "I know." She entered, feeling his gaze on her before her eyes adjusted from the bright sun outside and she dared look for him. He was waiting at the counter, where he'd been talking with Rebecca. Astrid stared.

He stared.

Was that trepidation in his eyes, or a shadow? A smile to match his growing one tugged at her lips, creasing her cheeks. She could feel it traveling from her face clear to her fingers and toes. Surely he was more handsome than she remembered—dark curly hair, broad forehead, square chin, and a smile that took her breath away.

"Welcome home."

His voice sent shivers up her spine. If she'd had any doubt that there was an attraction between them, it fled before the rampant stampede of emotions.

"I should say the same to you." *Brilliant.* What happened to her easy way of dealing with patients?

Eyes dueled with eyes, their faces swapping excitement.

"Would you like a soda?"

She nodded. Where had her words disappeared to?

"Rebecca apologized that the strawberries aren't ripe yet."

"Oh."

"I have chocolate, strawberry, or raspberry syrup canned last year, or butterscotch." Rebecca's eyes danced, and her grin told Astrid she knew what was going on.

Astrid looked back to Joshua, as if her gaze was drawn to him beyond her strength.

"You have to make a choice." Rebecca's voice, overlaid with a giggle, drew her back.

Good grief, what was the matter with her?

"I'm having strawberry," he told her.

How could such simple words sound like an aria? "Me too."

Joshua spoke to Rebecca without taking his eyes from Astrid. "That'll be two strawberry sodas."

"Thank you. I figured that out." Rebecca kept a knowing grin from taking over her face—barely.

Benny stopped his cart beside Astrid. "I'll have one too."

"Oh, you will, will you?" His mother leaned over the counter to smile down at him. "I thought you were going over to play with Grant."

"I am. But I would like to have a soda with My Doc." He grinned up at Astrid. "You want me to have one too, right?"

"Of course. Why don't you and I go outside and let Mr. Landsverk bring them out?" She caught a very brief pained look that hid behind his smile. He hadn't expected a chaperone. Neither had she. But Benny was special.

"Benny, you may join them for five minutes, and then I want you to take some cookies over to Sophie's house."

"All right."

Astrid felt a tug on her heartstrings. Caught between two male admirers. What a quandary. "Come on then, let's hurry so we can visit."

Sitting down at the table on the porch, she clasped her hands in her lap and leaned forward, closer to his eye level. "So, my friend, how is school going for you?"

He grinned his irrepressible grin that she still carried in her heart from the hospital in Chicago. "I am learning to read—from a book, not just the blackboard. Do you know that two plus three is five?" His eyes danced. "Pastor Solberg says I am catching up fast."

She started to say something, but he jumped in. "Do you know that people here in Blessing can talk with their hands? Sometimes teacher says, 'No talking and no fingers.' " He signed his name for her. "Do you know what that means?"

"Your signs mean *Benjamin Valders.*"

"I know. That's my new name. I got a mother and a papa and a new name. You fixed it for me." He dropped his voice. "I don't never want to go back to Chicago."

"You don't have to worry about that. Rebecca and Gerald adopted you for all of your life." She laid her hands along his jawbones. "Blessing is your home, Benny, for always."

He tilted his head toward her right hand. "Thank you, My Doc. You the best friend ever."

"That she is," said Joshua, setting two sodas on the table and handing Benny the third.

"How do you know?" she wanted to ask but took a swallow of the sweet fizzy drink instead. "The perfect drink for a hot afternoon. What a treat. Thank you, Mr. Landsverk."

Benny added his thanks. "I never had a soda before coming to my new home. Do they make sodas in Chicago?"

"Oh, I'm sure they do. How long until school is out?"

"Tomorrow's the last day. I'm sad that I can't go to school this summer."

Joshua chuckled. "You need to tell that to Pastor Solberg. I'm sure he doesn't hear such a thing very often."

"There are lots of things to do here in the summer, but you can keep on reading and learning sign language and your arithmetic."

"And if I'm home, maybe we can go fishing," Joshua said,

smiling down at the little boy. "I know some other boys who really like that."

"A fishing party?"

"I guess you could call it that. Someone told me that you really like to sing too." The boy nodded. "Next time we have guitar practice, you can come sing with us."

"Benny," called Rebecca.

"I'm going." He slurped the last of his soda and handed Astrid the glass. "You can come if you like."

"I think I'll stay here, thank you. Have fun." She watched him send his scooter down the incline someone had added to the porch and head up the smoothed path that ran up the street and down to Sophie's house.

"Looks like someone's been out on path duty," Joshua said. "Those weren't there last summer."

"I know." She turned her attention back to the man across the table. "I remember when Tante Kaaren learned sign language so she could help Grace. The rest of the town joined in and learned too. That's just the way the folks in Blessing do things, take care of one another."

"Well, they sure took this wanderer into the family. Did you hear about the party being planned for Saturday night? We'll have dancing at the school instead of at someone's barn. At least that's what I thought I heard."

"No, I hadn't. I've been so busy at the surgery that I've not been out to visit with anyone, not even my far. How do you know all this when you just got back today?"

"Think. Where do I live?"

Astrid grinned from behind her soda. "So Sophie still fills all her guests in on the news around town?"

"Well, maybe not all, but this one." He paused, his eyes holding her attention. "I'm glad you are back in Blessing."

"Me too. I'm not sure for how long, but I was grateful that they let me leave when Thorliff telephoned to say that I was needed here."

"Oh." He looked down, then at her again. "I was hoping you'd changed your mind about Africa."

Astrid felt herself stiffen, so she took another sip of her drink. "It's not my decision. It's God's. If that is where He wants me, I will go." *Please leave it at that. I've heard so much against.*

He leaned back in his chair. "Can I ask you a question?"

"I . . . I guess so, but I don't promise to answer." From the serious look on his face, it must have been important.

"How do you know that God is calling you to Africa?"

She breathed a sigh of relief. "That's been part of the problem. On one hand I feel He is asking me to go there, but on the other hand, I wonder if it is just me. And if it *is* just me, why would I dream up something like that? I have no need or desire to leave Blessing. I love it here. This is my home. I love my family, and all of Blessing feels like family to me." She clasped her hands on the wrought-iron table. "I have struggled and struggled with this. I want to live my life walking in God's plan for me, not my own plan." She paused and searched his face, seeking some kind of indication he understood what she was saying. He looked as puzzled as she felt.

"I knew that going to Chicago was in His plan. I felt certain . . . well, most of the time, and there was a measure of peace about the idea. When I got there, after I got over being homesick, I knew that was where I belonged. But the pull to Africa won't leave me alone." She heaved another sigh and stopped. "I wish I had a better answer."

"How do you feel when you are here?"

"Like I've come home. Home to Blessing." She studied a ragged cuticle on one finger. "But years ago Pastor Solberg said something that stuck with me. He said we can't always depend on our feelings. We need knowledge, and like one of my teachers at missionary school said, we can find answers to every question by searching the Scriptures."

"And what have you found?"

"Lots of verses about going to care for the lost, feeding His sheep, the harvest is ripe and the laborers are few. There are a lot more." An insatiable urge to chew the hangnail off clamped in her mind. "But nothing concrete about Africa. Perhaps I am searching wrong."

"And you cannot do those things right here?"

"I can and I am." The thought of Red Hawk's comment caught her attention. *"What if you thought of the reservation as your Africa?"* She looked into Joshua's face. "One thing I do know. My patients, the people who need me, always come first."

A silence fell between them, then stretched. She glanced up to see Mr. Landsverk watching her, his gaze warm on her face. What could she say?

"I think about you a lot," he whispered.

She nodded. She stared at her soda, the pink fizz at the bottom of the glass.

"I have a question for you."

She looked up again. He was leaning forward, his arms on the table, one hand not far from her own. Would it be proper to put her hand in his? The thought brought heat up to her ears. Of course it wouldn't. What was she thinking?

"I want to ask your father for permission to court you."

Her eyes widened. A smile tugged at the corners of her mouth. *Court me? Really?*

"Astrid!" Rebecca's shout brought her back with a jerk. "You're needed. It's Elizabeth."

"I'll walk you over." Joshua pushed back his chair. "Unless you want to run. We can do that too."

Astrid had already leaped down the two steps and began sprinting for the surgery.

25

Astrid burst through the door, panting to catch her breath.

"Upstairs." Thelma pointed toward the stairway.

Pulling herself up faster with a hand on the banister, Astrid could hear sobbing from Elizabeth's bedroom. She found Thorliff holding his weeping wife, tears dripping off his chin as well.

Astrid began to choke also, then taking a deep breath to control her mind and emotions, she ordered herself into doctor protocol. "What has happened?"

Thorliff looked up at her. "We cannot hear the baby's heart beating any longer."

"Let me try." She reached for the stethoscope and tapped the bell with a fingernail to make sure it was functioning before applying the end to Elizabeth's heaving belly. "Easy now. See if you can stop crying so I can listen better."

"He's dead. I know he is." Elizabeth fought for some modicum of control.

Astrid lifted the lawn nightgown and applied the scope directly to Elizabeth's skin, moving it slowly from place to place, angle to angle. She could hear stomach sounds, Elizabeth's heart, her lungs, but no small heartbeat. She covered the entire area again, her own heart growing heavier by the moment. *Little one, could you not have fought harder?* She blew her nose and wiped her eyes.

"I'm sorry, oh, Elizabeth, Thorliff, I am so sorry." She could hardly speak as her own tears lodged in her throat. *God, why? Why do you take these little ones? Why let them come here and then jerk them home again? This one didn't even get to take a breath.* The three held each other, crying until the tears dried up—at least for the moment.

Elizabeth was the first to speak. "I just don't understand."

A tap at the door and Ingeborg entered the room, her comforting arms enveloping them all. "No one ever understands the loss of a baby or a child."

"But I never even got to hold him."

"You will when he is born. That will help." Her silence brought a measure of peace, or was it the prayers she was offering on this altar of sorrow?

How will we get her body to think it is time for the baby to be born? Astrid wondered. Surely there were drugs or medications that could cause such an event, but she had no idea what they were. The few women she had helped with births at the hospital were well into labor. Common sense said the sooner the better. Unless Elizabeth knew the answer, but she wouldn't ask that question right now. Perhaps Mor would know what to do.

Why was it that the more she knew, the more she knew she didn't know?

What brought labor on? The water breaking sent the body into hard labor. She knew how to rupture those membranes. A sense of calm washed over her. Of course.

When Elizabeth fell asleep in Thorliff's arms, Astrid drew her mother out into the hall. "Have you had something like this happen in your years of caring for women?"

Ingeborg nodded. "Some have carried to full term and the baby has died either in the birthing or right after. Others lost babies earlier, and yes, I think one or two babies died about this long into the pregnancy."

"Did the women go into labor without assistance?"

"Yes. Usually the body knows far more than we do."

"How long do we wait?" At the hospital everything had swirled around her, and she just went where she was needed. Now she realized these were decisions she would need to make, especially in Africa.

"Twenty-four hours or so. And we pray. It will be easier on Elizabeth if her body takes care of this on its own."

"We could break her water." She remembered one late emergency delivery.

"Ja, but that will bring on hard labor without any preparation."

Astrid felt like a little girl wanting to curl up in her mother's lap and loving arms. "She tried so hard to have this baby."

"I know. And now we must assure her that it was nothing she did wrong that caused this. Somehow we have to trust that God knows best. And did what was best for everyone, especially that little baby. You know how often I've said that there was something wrong with a baby who died too soon."

"We'll know when we see the baby."

"Perhaps and perhaps not."

"How can you be so calm? This is one of your grandchildren." Astrid wished she could catch the words and stuff them back as soon as she said them. "I'm sorry, Mor, that was an unkind thing to say."

"Would ranting and raving do any good?"

"No. Not really. But sometimes you feel better afterward."

"Sometimes. But through the years I've seen feelings hurt more by getting angry. Kind and gentle words bring healing the most swiftly."

Astrid leaned against her mother's shoulder. "Do you think I will ever get to that point?"

Ingeborg patted her daughter's cheek. "You have learned much in these last years. Thinking kind and gentle thoughts is a prelude to speaking them."

They turned as Thorliff closed the door behind him. "She's sleeping soundly." His eyes wore dark shadows, all dressed for mourning.

"Far is building the box." Ingeborg took her son's hand. "He wanted to do this for you."

Thorliff blinked and shook his head. "She tried so hard. It's not fair. Other people have baby after baby, and we can't." He looked at his mother. "I know you wanted more children with my father, and you were denied until you married Haakan. Was there something wrong with my father's side of the family?"

Ingeborg heaved a sigh. "I don't think so. All these situations are different. Roald died before we could have more children. Besides, I bore only two children, and you have one. So there is a greater plan in progress than we know."

"So is it selfish to want another child?"

Astrid listened to them both saying much the same things the two sides of her mind argued, neither winning nor losing but rearing up again when she least expected it. *There are answers in the Scriptures,* she reminded herself, *but you have yet to find some of them. I know God loves us all, born and unborn. That never changes. I know He loves me, because He said so. Imperfect as I am, God loves me.* The good news took over, and her arguing voices were forced to stop or go into hiding.

Whichever, the peace they were all seeking tiptoed in and wrapped a feather-light shawl of love around her shoulders.

"I know God loves that baby, and He loves us. I know that. God will never change. He said so. Now we convince Elizabeth of that. Mor, please call Pastor Solberg."

A familiar voice came from the stairs. "She already did. I came as soon as I could get away." Pastor Solberg continued up the stairs. "I'm glad you know that, Dr. Bjorklund. That declaration will stand you in good stead for the rest of your life. Keep it in the front of your mind." He joined them. "I take it Elizabeth is sleeping?"

"Ja. I am going back in now so that she is not alone when she wakes." Thorliff gripped the pastor's hand. "Thank you for coming."

"Do you mind if I join you?"

"Not at all." Thorliff ushered Pastor Solberg ahead of him and closed the door.

LATER THAT EVENING, Ingeborg having gone home, Astrid went to the room she'd been sleeping in after telling Thorliff to call her if there were any changes. Weariness of the soul dragged on her shoulders and her knees as she mounted the stairs. She undressed and pulled her lawn nightdress over her head. Standing in front of the window, she inhaled the evening air, fresh and pure with a coolness that kissed her cheeks and throat. The western horizon still held a faint tinge of yellow while the sky deepened to velvet black toward the east.

She brushed and braided her hair in a loose night style, then sat against the pillows on the bed to read from a little book of devotions Rev. Thompkins had given her. She flipped to the section on love. The words that leaped out at her made her smile inside. *Love is patient and kind, not boastful or rude.* She closed her eyes and said them aloud. "Love is patient and kind." *Gentle* would fit here too. "Love *is*." She thought on that. *Is.* A small word to be sure but of great power. *Is.* Not *was* nor *will be*, even though it was both of those things, but *is.* "God is love. God *is.*" She tipped her head back and inhaled the peace flowing through the room on the breeze. *"Is."*

"Lord, please fill Elizabeth with these thoughts. Kind and gentle. Patient. She has tried to be patient these weeks, and now she will feel like it was all a waste. I know I would feel that way. But it wasn't a waste. Love *is.* She did this because she loves the baby. Father, heal her broken heart. All of our hearts." Anew she understood that when one member of the family weeps, all weep.

IF YOU MARRY HER, Joshua told himself, *this is the way it will be. Her patients come first. She warned you.* He'd taken this thought out all night and turned it over and around, trying to find something in it he could work with. She'd literally run back to the surgery, never saying "See you later" or anything. And things between them had been going so well.

That was what hurt the most. Maybe *hurt* wasn't the right word. Irritated? Maybe some better. All the times he'd thought about seeing her again, none of those dreams ended like this reality. They'd been enjoying their sodas, talking about real things, not the weather, and the telephone call ended it all. He should have raced her to the surgery and barred the door. Except this was Dr. Elizabeth who was in distress. Her own family.

Wonderful, now he was thinking evil thoughts on top of his unhappiness. He needed to put that away and think on what Hjelmer had said to him after asking him to come to the newspaper office. Would he be willing to head up one of the crews that would be putting up Mr. Jeffers' building to house the new company that would be manufacturing new seeders, or at least the new parts that would make the old ones much more practical?

That raised another question. Could these parts be modified to fit the old seeders or only the new ones? To be sure, there would be a better return on selling new ones, but why not both? He wondered if Jeffers had thought of that or thought on it and discarded it. He could ask all these questions at their meeting in the morning. Things sure were moving fast.

He levered himself off the bed and sat down at the table to write down all his questions and ideas. While the middle of the night was good for thinking, it was also good for forgetting good ideas. After he turned off the gas lamp, he stood at the window, gazing out at the dimly lit room at the surgery. The room where they took care of people who were sick. *Please, Lord, let that baby come before it kills Elizabeth.* His heart ached at the thought of the baby dying like that. Ever since he'd started dreaming about Astrid, he'd been thinking on children too. His children. He knew he could be a good father, better than the one he'd had. He flipped the sheet over himself and settled into the pillow. *Thank you, Father, for this new job, with even better pay. And I get to stay in Blessing, not be on the road for weeks on end.*

In the evenings he could finish the cellar and get the beams ready to build his house. Maybe by fall they would have it roughed in and could finish the interior. From the sound of things, Blessing was going to be a booming place. But probably without Astrid for another two years. Could he wait? His heart said yes, but then that nagging doubt crept in as to whether they really were right for each other. And circumstances weren't giving them a chance to find out. Was it circumstances or God's guidance? Joshua had to smile. When he'd first arrived in Blessing, that thought would have never crossed his mind. He sighed. Perhaps by being in town like this, he could get to see Astrid again. And things would go better.

INGA'S ROOSTER CROWING woke Astrid in the cool of the not yet risen morning. *If you had been there* . . . the sneaky voice stabbed at her. She shook her head. "No, I will not allow that. Love *is*. God is love. God is light." Humming a song from church, she flipped back the sheet and light blanket, grateful for indoor plumbing, although running barefoot through the dew-drenched grass would feel heavenly on her feet. She washed her face. A basin bath would have to suffice for today.

Once dressed, she made her bed and returned to her place before the window. "I will sing unto the Lord." She hummed a tune, simple and easy to remember, then set the words to it. "I will sing; I will sing; I will sing unto the Lord." She pushed herself upright. Perhaps Joshua, er, Mr. Landsverk would like to hear her song. And then she gasped. She had not even thought of him since she ran to Elizabeth. What did that mean? she wondered. How could she have such warm feelings when with him and then forget him altogether?

She peeked into Elizabeth's bedroom and saw her alone in the bed. Where had Thorliff gone? Quietly shutting the door, she made her way downstairs, following the aroma of coffee to the kitchen.

"He's out on the back porch," Thelma said, handing Astrid a steaming cup. "I'll bring breakfast out in a few minutes."

Astrid stopped before opening the screen door and studied her brother. His head was in his hands, elbows propped on his knees. Love *is*. How to say what she was learning to her older brother? After all, she was not the one to lose this baby. Being the doctor and an aunt were not the same as being the mother and the father. She opened the door and crossed to take one of the other rocking chairs. How many times had her mother sat in this chair, her prayers continual and always patient and kind? Sitting and sipping her coffee, she decided to imitate her mother. So without saying a word, she continued to hum her song silently, praising God for everything that came to mind and praying for all those who were grieving.

"Mange takk." Thorliff broke the silence.

"Velbekomme." She kept her eyes closed.

"She slept most of the night."

"Good. That will give her strength for this next step."

"Birthing the baby?"

"Ja, that is necessary."

"I figured as much." He looked up when Thelma set a filled plate on the low table in front of him. "Takk."

Astrid did the same, including a smile with her gratitude.

"I'll bring out the coffeepot." A bell chiming pulled her back into the kitchen.

Both Thorliff and Astrid stood and headed for the stairs. The bell was from the bedroom.

"Are you all right?" Thorliff asked as he burst through the door.

Elizabeth shook her head and held out her arms. "It has started."

Thorliff sat on the bed and held her close. "How bad?"

"Just cramps, but our baby—"

"I know. Let's just take it one minute at a time. You are the most important now."

"Astrid." Elizabeth held out her arms. "I am so grateful you are here."

The two clung together for a long moment before Astrid reminded her they'd better do a listening to see how things were progressing.

"You seem stronger," Astrid said after completing her evaluation.

"I want to pull the covers over my head and pretend this has never happened."

"I think I would too." Astrid dropped her stethoscope into her pocket. "How about a poached egg on toast?"

Elizabeth made a face. "I know I must."

"I'll bring up a tray." Thorliff left the room.

When he returned with a plate of food, Elizabeth ate and then fell back asleep, her brow frowning sometimes, relaxing other times.

"I'll stay with her," Ingeborg said after greeting her daughter. "You go take care of the other patients. When she wakes, we'll move her downstairs to the lying-in room. It is all set up. You don't have any babies due now, do you?"

"Not that I know of, so if you say not, that must be the way it is. How long has Elizabeth been away from the surgery?"

"More than a month on bed rest and needing more rest before that, so I've been helping out for more than two months."

"Why did no one let me know?"

"Elizabeth refused to. Demanded we all say nothing. I honored her wishes, but it was difficult."

"Until Thorliff took charge." Had Elizabeth been trying not to influence God's decision for Astrid? Her eyes filled with tears at Elizabeth's generous heart in the midst of her own difficulties.

"Right."

"Interesting timing in all this. I would have been coming home in mid-June anyway. They give students a two-week leave before the final preparations to ship out. I was afraid that if I came home, I would not be able to leave again."

"And will you?"

Astrid shook her head slightly, barely moving it from side to side. "I don't know. I just don't know."

"God will let you know."

"I'm counting on that." She kissed her mother's cheek. "Thank you for coming."

Since there were no appointments in the book, Astrid ignored her mixed feelings by refilling the bottles of medications they kept in a glass-fronted upper cabinet. Larger bottles of dried herbs were kept on the dark shelves below. In between she checked on Elizabeth and answered the telephone. Two people called for appointments for the next day. Then Elizabeth's stepmother called to ask how she was feeling, but Elizabeth did not want to talk with her right then, as the contractions were coming closer together now since she'd been moved to the lying-in room.

"She's busy right now; may I give her a message and have her telephone you later?" Astrid promised Elizabeth would call back the next day or so, since the family was going to a concert at St. Olaf College that evening.

Checking on Elizabeth, she nodded her approval. Thorliff sat with his back to the headboard of the bed, legs spread so that Elizabeth could sit between them, using her husband as a back support. He murmured encouragement in her ear whenever the contractions rolled over her. Weak as she was to start with, she was already panting after each onslaught.

"What am I? About a finger width?" she asked after Astrid checked her progress.

"Almost." Astrid took in a deep breath. "I'm going to rupture the membranes to hurry this along." She looked to Elizabeth, who nodded.

After the fluids rushed out, she changed the towels to lay down dry ones and said to Elizabeth and Thorliff, "I'm hoping to preserve your strength here, but you know the contractions will hit hard now."

"I know."

Lord, please make this work. Strong and healthy mothers wear out in labor, so help us here. While a baby that small should deliver easily, nothing about the pregnancy had gone peacefully.

26

As the windows darkened, Astrid lit a kerosene lamp and set it in the corner behind a screen. Elizabeth lay in Thorliff's arms, exhausted beyond thought, and still no baby. Motioning to her mother to come out in the hall, she leaned against the wall.

"We have to decide now. If we wait any longer, I don't think Elizabeth will make it through the surgery."

"I was afraid you were going to say that."

"You don't agree?"

"I've been pleading for God to lead us, but so far He is silent."

Astrid rubbed her temples and up into her hair. "How about we ask Elizabeth when she wakes up?"

"Ja, if she is coherent enough to answer." The two returned to the room just as Elizabeth woke again with a whimpering cry.

Astrid lifted the sheet to check on the baby, but no head was visible yet. But she could feel the head when she inserted her fingers. Could she bring it out with forceps? That would be better than surgery. She needn't worry about injuring the baby like she would if it were alive. "Mor, would you please get the forceps?"

When the contraction had passed, Astrid took Elizabeth's hand in hers. "Can you hear me?" At the nod she continued. "I can feel the baby's head about half a finger up in the birth canal. I am thinking to use the forceps. That way we don't have to do a cesarean. To do this, I will administer morphine enough to kill the pain but not knock you out. Then you can help when I tell you." Elizabeth nodded.

Astrid glanced at Thorliff, who'd turned as white as the sheets he sat on. "Can you handle that?"

He swallowed—and nodded. "Maybe you better administer a shot of whiskey to this participant."

"I can do that too. We have some here in the surgery cabinet."

Ingeborg approached the bed, holding a pan of antiseptic with the forceps submerged. "I asked Thelma to boil plenty of water and be here to help if needed."

As soon as they were set, Astrid checked Elizabeth one last time and shook her head. She'd not dilated any further. She gave Thorliff the shot of whiskey and administered the morphine to Elizabeth.

A knock at the door and Pastor Solberg stuck his head in. "I'm out here praying."

"Thank you." Astrid scrubbed her hands and laid a sterile sheet on the bed. "Elizabeth, can you hear me?"

Elizabeth nodded.

"Good. When I say push, you push with all you have. If we can do this in two or three contractions, it will be over." She carefully inserted the forceps. "Easy now. There's a contraction coming. I want you to roll with it and push at the crest." Elizabeth nodded, a frown melding her eyebrows, teeth clenched. "Relax as much as you can and breathe." Astrid watched the tightening body, praying that the forceps were in place. "Push, Elizabeth, push." At the same time she clenched the forceps and pulled. With a gush of blood and water, the dark little body slid out onto the sheet.

"Thank you, heavenly Father," Ingeborg whispered, stroking Elizabeth's hair.

Astrid cut the cord and wrapped the still body in a baby blanket, tears coursing down her face. She looked to Thorliff, who sat with his eyes closed, the tears leaking anyway. She laid the baby aside to massage Elizabeth's belly. With no infant cry, no squirming red body, no thrill of new life, they went about the business of tending to the mother. Finally the placenta was delivered

Tired beyond belief, they struggled on. Thorliff slid off the bed and nearly collapsed in the chair, still holding Elizabeth's flaccid hand. He looked to his mother. "Is she all right?"

"As much as can be. We'll give her some broth and enough pain medicine to keep her comfortable. Sleep now will be her best ally."

Working together, Astrid and Ingeborg stripped the bed and put down new linens. They bathed Elizabeth, slid a clean gown over her head, and settled her back down. When Thelma brought in the broth, Ingeborg spoon-fed her daughter-in-law, crooning encouragement all the while.

"I'll take the first watch," Thelma said. Astrid could see her eyes were red.

"If there is any change . . ."

"I know. I will come running for you."

Astrid nodded. "Mor, how about you take the second shift, and I'll do the third. Thorliff, you sleep as much as you can."

"I'll be up and down, I know. But don't worry about me." He looked toward his wife. "Just her." He stood and crossed the room to where the baby boy lay on the chest, wrapped in his blanket. "Should I take him out?" His voice cracked, and he swallowed hard.

"No. I think it will be important for Elizabeth to see him when she wakes. If she wants to hold him, that will help her heal too." Ingeborg rubbed her son's shoulder. "Something was not right with him from the very beginning."

"He needs a name."

"You and Elizabeth can name him in the morning." She pulled the chair closer to the bed. Setting the bell on the stand beside it, she motioned Thelma to sit down. "I'll bring you some coffee?"

"No thank you. I just had some."

Grateful that Pastor Solberg had gone home, Astrid and Thorliff filed upstairs, while Ingeborg took the room next door to Elizabeth's.

With only the sounds of the house settling for the night, Astrid breathed in a deep breath and held it before exhaling. Had she done the right thing, the best thing? Now to protect Elizabeth from infection, from bleeding, but she was so worn out, she had no strength to heal with. "Lord, she needs your strength. You have promised strength and wisdom to those who ask. Your strength shows when we are the most weak. We are asking—I am pleading—please don't let this be in vain. I know you said all things work together for good for those who love you, but I don't understand how that can be. I do know now that I don't need to understand but to wait on you in faith and trust."

She listed the things that she knew, that God was and always would be in charge of things. She knew that God loved them all with a fierce love that fought off the wiles of the evil one. She knew that little baby was now back in the arms of his Father. In the stillness, she heard Thorliff get up and go downstairs again. So he couldn't sleep either.

She dozed a bit but suddenly jerked awake, sitting straight up. What had she heard? Elizabeth? She rose and slipped her arms into the wrapper she kept on the bedpost. Padding down the stairs, she saw the light from under the door of the lying-in room. Her mother's door was half open but dark. Easing open the door to where Elizabeth lay, Astrid peeked inside. Thelma sat in her chair, slowly rocking, her needle flashing on what was probably a dress for Inga. Elizabeth was sleeping peacefully, her face pale, not flushed with fever.

Thelma looked up at her and nodded toward the chest where they'd laid the baby.

Astrid peeked through the space between door and frame. The baby was gone. She looked back to Thelma.

"The kitchen," Thelma mouthed.

Astrid nodded and made her way to the kitchen. She heard soft sobbing before she opened the door. Thorliff sat in the rocker in front of the window, his tears dripping down on the face of his dead son as he cuddled the little body close.

Astrid backed away and set her back against the walnut paneling. Using her full sleeve, she mopped her eyes and dug in her pocket for a handkerchief. Wiping her nose, she returned to the lying-in room to check Elizabeth's vitals. Assured that all was as well as could be expected, she heaved a sigh.

"Why don't you go on to bed, Thelma. I can't sleep anyway, so I might as well sit here. Has she wakened at all?"

Thelma shook her head. "She whimpered a few times but not enough to wake all the way."

"No excess bleeding?"

"No. I changed her a bit ago, but even that didn't wake her. When I spoon broth into her mouth, she swallows."

"Good. Thank you. Go get some rest. There are only two appointments scheduled for tomorrow, so barring emergencies, we should be pretty quiet."

"There's the party this weekend—Friday night or Saturday, whichever it is."

"Oh, that's right. Hard keeping track of things outside of here."

Astrid turned at a mumble from the bed. She watched Elizabeth frown and blink her eyes, but then she slid back into a sleep that appeared to be restful.

Astrid sat down in the chair when Thelma left the room and alternately spooned broth and rubbed Elizabeth's flabby abdomen. She could feel the minor contractions that always followed a birth. So far everything seemed normal. Warring between wanting to sing praises and wanting to wait and see, Astrid brought the book of First John to mind, glad she had memorized the first three chapters. She paused as verse five curled into her mind. *This then is the message which we have heard of him, and declare unto you, that God is light, and in him is no darkness at all.*

At first she repeated the verse in her mind but then remembered her mother always saying that sleeping or unconscious people could hear. So she began repeating it in a gentle voice that comforted her first and hopefully would also comfort Elizabeth. When her patient became restless, she spoke more firmly, returning to a softer voice when Elizabeth settled again. The restlessness appeared to coincide with the cramps. Some of Astrid's patients in Chicago had told her about these pains as the body struggled to return to life before pregnancy. Some said they were really bad, while others said one must just get through it.

Astrid added a couple of drops of morphine to the broth—enough, she hoped, to take the edge off the pain. From First John she went to First Corinthians thirteen, all about love. Her big delight: Love is . . .

Thorliff returned sometime later and laid the baby back up on the chest. "I'll be in the office. Call me when she wakes up."

Astrid nodded, keeping her thoughts to herself. How she longed to comfort her big brother, but everything she thought of sounded inane. Except for the Bible verses that kept coming to her mind.

Elizabeth stirred and opened her eyes when the rooster crowed. "It is over?"

"Ja, all is well."

Elizabeth turned to look out the window at the land coming alive after a night's sleep. "No, all is not well." She laid her hand on her belly. "Where's the baby?"

"On the chest. Thorliff asked me to call him as soon as you woke up."

"What is it?" Her voice came out in a whisper.

"A boy, like you thought."

"I want to see him."

"I know. That is why we kept him in here. Let me get Thorliff."

"No. Bring the baby first." She paused and heaved a sigh. "Please."

"I'll go call Thorliff," Ingeborg said from the doorway. "You stay here."

Astrid nodded. Right now, someone else taking charge was a big relief. She looked to Elizabeth, who stared at her, chin quivering, and a single tear slinking toward her ear. "Let me help you with some pillows first."

"No. The baby."

Astrid stood and crossed to the chest where the tiny body lay, lovingly wrapped in a baby blanket, most likely one of Inga's. She picked up the still form and carried him to his mother, laying him in her waiting arms.

"Have you really looked at him?" Elizabeth asked, staring down at the little face.

"No." *Yesterday I couldn't bear to, but now I can.*

"If I can see something wrong, I think it will be easier to bear."

Astrid sat on the edge of the bed and peeled back the blanket. Together they studied the baby, searching for any reason that he'd died.

She turned him over, and they both caught their breath. There was a hole in the spine, low in the back, just above the tiny pelvic bones.

Thorliff walked in, followed by his mother. "You found it."

"Ja, we just did."

"I saw it last night or early this morning, whatever it was. Something kept him from developing right. He could not have lived with that anyway."

Elizabeth nodded, tracing the tiny cheek with a gentle fingertip. "What are we naming him?"

"I thought Roald, after my father."

Elizabeth nodded. "That is good." Her chin and lips quivered. "When will you bury him?"

"Today. Far has the box all made."

"I won't be able to go, will I?"

"No, I think not. Now you must rest and get your strength back." He laid his palm along her cheek.

Astrid and Ingeborg left the room and the two they loved to grieve together. They waited in the hall, holding each other and letting the tears flow. "Was this why I had to come home, you think?" Astrid asked her mother.

"Ja. We needed you. And still do."

"I know." *But what about Africa? Haven't I made a commitment there too?*

27

"Can I play with all of you at the dance tomorrow night?" Johnny asked when he spotted Joshua sitting on the porch after lunch.

Joshua stared at his young protégé. Asking took a lot of courage. He should've offered to let him play, but he'd had so much else on his mind, he'd not thought of it. "Of course. The songs you know anyway."

"I've been practicing a lot. I asked Mr. Knutson which songs I needed to learn for the dance, and he said I should ask you if you think I am ready for this." Johnny pulled a piece of paper with a list written on it from his pocket. "I know most of these. You were gone a long time, you know."

Joshua scanned down the list. "Pretty complete. You have to keep up with the rest of us."

"I will. Thank you, sir."

Joshua grinned and tousled the boy's hair. "You're the one who has put in the work."

"When are you going to start on your house again?"

"I'll be starting in about fifteen, twenty minutes."

"I'll be there." Johnny leaped from the porch of the boarding-house and ran down the street, puffs of dirt from bare feet slapping the soil marking his way.

Joshua watched him go. Now if they could only find a bass player. While the gut bucket was sufficient for the beat, a bass fiddle would be really fine—and expensive. He'd played a while with a group that had a banjo too. He pushed himself to his feet and headed back upstairs to get his tools and leather gloves. While picking up his gear, he stopped to study the diagrams of the house he wanted to order. He could at least contact Sears and Roebuck and ask how long the waiting period would be before the house was shipped. Write a letter or telephone?

Why would they want to talk with him when he couldn't put in the order right now? But they could answer his questions, he reminded the common sense side of his mind. The one frequently in battle with giving up. Strolling down the stairs, the fragrance of dried-apple pie reminded him that a cup of coffee with dessert would be mighty tasty right now.

"Did you hear the news?" Sophie asked when his feet hit the main floor. "Dr. Elizabeth is on the mend."

"That's good to hear. The baby?"

"Died before it was born." She gave a sigh.

Oh, Lord, what will this do to Astrid? "How very sad."

"It is. They wanted this baby so badly. It was a boy but had a problem with his back, most likely why he died like that."

And here he'd been grumbling to himself that even though Astrid was in town, she sure didn't have time for him. "Maybe Astrid will be able to come to the party tomorrow night."

"I hope so. She needs to get out and have some fun. It's been a grueling trip home so far. A couple of square dances will help lighten the sorrow." She tapped a sheaf of papers on end and stacked them in one of the slots on her desk. Glancing up at Joshua, she grinned at him with raised eyebrows. "Astrid?"

"Um, Dr. Bjorklund." He heaved a sigh. "I need to be more circumspect, don't I?"

"Not with me, but there are others who think proper behavior is very important, especially between unmarried women and unmarried men."

Well he knew whom she was referring to. "You going to the dance?"

"I wouldn't miss it." She glanced down at her expanding middle. "Some think women carrying babies shouldn't be out dancing, but some of us are good at ignoring strictures that seem less than necessary." A sparkle lit her eyes. "Tante Ingeborg says exercise of any kind is good for the expectant mother. We have healthier babies that way, rather than staying out of sight and languishing on a settee in a shaded room." Referring to the mores of Victorian society well published in women's magazines made Sophie grin again. "I'm glad I live in Blessing and not in Chicago or Minneapolis."

Again Joshua felt a little overwhelmed by Sophie's candor. He decided to try a safer conversation. He wanted to ask where Miss Christopherson was but decided that could be misconstrued too. "Any idea when Jonathan will be back?"

"He's visiting his parents in New York City. Not sure when he and Grace will get here."

"Leaves us with no one on the piano now, with Dr. Bjorklund laid up."

"True. But we'll still have a grand time. We need to have dances and parties more often."

Joshua inwardly shook his head. Here she was a mother of twins, two stepchildren, and another on the way, and she was always ready to encourage community get-togethers. When he thought about it, he learned all the town news from Sophie. Between her and Mrs. Valders, secrets were nonexistent in Blessing, North Dakota. But with Sophie one never felt it was gossip, just passing on the news.

Sophie caught him lifting his head to trail the enticing smell coming from the kitchen. "If the pies were out of the oven, I'd get you a piece, but they are not."

He heaved an exaggerated sigh. "Guess I'll be on my way, then. Thanks." He slapped his gloves on her raised counter and moseyed on out the door. Down the street he could see Trygve and Gilbert loading the wagons to head out to drill more wells again early on Sunday morning. They had no intention of missing the dance. He whistled to catch their attention and waved. On one hand he wished he were going with them, but on the other, the anticipation of starting the new building picked up his feet and carried him over to his hole in the ground, as he called it.

The dirt floor was now dry from the snow melt, and he started clearing out dirt that caved in from the sides during the winter and spring freeze and thaw. As he tossed shovelfuls of dirt into the wheelbarrow, he let pictures of his house, his first home ever, float through his mind.

Johnny trotted down the ramp they'd built where the coal chute would be, grabbed the handles of the wheelbarrow, and pushed it up the grade to dump into one of the piles back a ways from the hole.

Hjelmer appeared next. "You got the boards to start your forms?"

"Nope. Didn't know I was going to have a chance to work on this."

"Okay. Johnny and I'll bring some over from the lumberyard."

"You need another hand?" Pastor Solberg asked as he joined him in the hole a few minutes later. "What with school out and the hay far from ready to cut, I need something to get me back in condition for haying."

"They're loading the wagon over at the lumberyard."

"You mind if I join them?"

"Not at all." Sure different from last fall, he thought. He'd been uncomfortable then when men volunteered. Now he just accepted gratefully. When the wagon arrived, they unloaded the lumber and stacked it off to one side.

"I'm sorry," Joshua said to Thorliff when he later joined them in the hole.

Thorliff nodded. "Some physical work will help. Elizabeth is sleeping and looking better."

"Glad to hear that."

Before dusk they had two walls framed in, ready for concrete. Thorliff had been pounding nails like he was trying to kill off his grief. No one had said another thing about the tragedy, but Joshua wasn't surprised. That's just the way men were.

He took his hat off and wiped his brow with the rolled-back sleeve on his right arm, staring all the while at what they'd accomplished.

"You bought the gravel and cement yet?" Solberg asked.

"No. I never dreamed I'd get this far in a month. Of course, until yesterday I thought I was heading out again to drill wells and put up windmills. I might actually get a house up this summer after all."

"Oh, we'll get your house up. Never fear." Solberg clapped him on the shoulder. "Maybe not finished, but up."

"We'll start grading that piece tomorrow at daylight," Hjelmer said after greeting them all and getting razzed for disappearing for a while. "I ordered a carload of gravel and sand. Should arrive in a couple of days."

Thorliff stared down into the hole. "Thanks, Joshua. I needed this kind of hard work today." He shook Pastor Solberg's hand. "Thanks, as always, for being here when we need you. Elizabeth asked if you could stop back by before you head on home."

Joshua got a lump in his throat just thinking about what they'd referred to. Burying a baby, and Dr. Bjorklund couldn't even be there.

Back in the boardinghouse cleaning up before he went down for a supper that had been kept for him, he thought back to those who'd helped him. Were they there for him or for Thorliff, or perhaps both? Why had it not been like that when he was growing up? He'd lived four miles from a small town, but he didn't remember people taking care of each other like they did here. Or was it that his father drove away those who would have been his friends? If that were the case, it must have been terribly hard on his mother. Maybe he'd ask his brothers and sister some more questions when he wrote, or if and when he could encourage them to come north to Blessing. On the way home, he had swung by the surgery, hoping to see Astrid, hoping she'd be sitting on the porch and he could at least say hello. But the porch had been empty, and he didn't want to knock on the door in case she was too busy. So he'd gone on to the boardinghouse. Perhaps tomorrow night she'd be at the dance.

"YOU GO ON home and get ready for the dance tonight," Ingeborg told her daughter the next afternoon. "I will stay with Elizabeth."

"But you love a party too."

"I know, but you've been gone, and this will be a good homecoming celebration."

Astrid stared at her mother. Was she ignoring the fact that she might still be going to Africa? "If only there was more we could do for Elizabeth."

"You're changing the subject." The tinkle of the bedside bell brought them both to the sickroom door.

"You decided to wake up." Astrid smiled down at her patient.

Elizabeth nodded. "It's over, isn't it?" Her hand shook as she brushed the tears from her eyes.

Both Astrid and Ingeborg sniffed along with her. "Ja, it is. They buried Roald yesterday. You have been sleeping after your ordeal. Thorliff is trying to protect you, you know."

"I know. Getting up to be there would not have been a good idea, but I wanted to. Why is it that good sense and what one feels do not always go hand in hand?"

"I wish I knew. But you are doing well. You know that."

"I do. And before you can remind me, I know that sleeping is a good thing, and my body will heal faster if I take it easy, and all this helps keep the bleeding under control."

Ingeborg and Astrid exchanged smiles. "Guess we're not needed here after all."

Ingeborg turned to Elizabeth. "I told this other doctor that she should go to the party tonight. I will stay with you."

"Actually, I think you should both go. Between Thelma and Thorliff, I have plenty of keepers. Perhaps tomorrow you could bring Inga home. I need to hear her laughing and singing and running up the steps."

Astrid laid the back of her hand against Elizabeth's forehead. "Still running a fever."

"I know, but not much, and it's not unexpected. Could I have something to drink other than broth? Like lemonade or iced tea?"

"Of course. I'll get it." Astrid stopped at the door, deliberately ignoring Elizabeth's cranky tone. "I'll bring one for all of us." *Do I go to the dance like Mor says or stay here?* Sometimes the answers to questions came down to a matter of guilt. If something happened to Elizabeth while she was gone, would the guilt make her so miserable she couldn't bear it? The thought of seeing Mr. Landsverk again made her pick up her pace. Things had just been getting interesting the other day when she was called for the emergency. Why had he not stopped by to see how things were going? Or was that asking too much, considering how little time they'd spent together?

She and Thelma fixed a tray, and she carried it back upstairs. Ingeborg was sitting in the rocker knitting, and Elizabeth lay sound asleep. Astrid set the tray on the low table near her mother and handed her a glass. "How long did she stay awake?"

"Maybe five minutes. The bleeding is normal, and her heart sounds normal, as does her breathing. Yes, she is running a slight fever, but I am so grateful it is not worse that I can't be concerned." She set the chair to rocking. "I find it interesting that we pray and pray for something, and then when God answers and it happens, we are almost too surprised to recognize it or to be thankful."

"We asked for healing for Elizabeth and lost the baby in the process." Astrid sipped her lemonade. "Could we not have one without the other?"

"Oh, I think so, but in the long run, one day looking back, we will see that this was God's most compassionate way to answer our prayers."

"But He could have healed the baby too."

"Ja, He could have. But He chose not to heal the little one here but take him home. Somewhere in the Old Testament it talks of how death may be saving the person from terrible things that would be happening later in life. I'll have to look up the place. Once I read that, I was not only comforted but able to face losing patients without as much sorrow."

"But what if Elizabeth is never able to have another baby?"

"Then she needs to be grateful for the one she has and trust that God knows best."

Astrid shook her head. "I pray that one day I will come to that trust and acceptance."

"I pray that for you too. Now, you go take a bath and get ready for the party. Take every moment and squeeze every bit of joy out of it."

"I wish Grace were here. I want to see her before I leave. *If* I leave."

"Ja, well, we've all been praying wisdom for you along that line too."

"You don't think I should go back to school and on to Africa?"

"I think you should do what God is calling you to do."

THAT EVENING ASTRID and Haakan took the buggy to the schoolhouse, and after Haakan tied the horse to the hitching rail, he helped his daughter out of the buggy. "You look lovely."

"Thank you. It's so long since I've been to a dance that I might have forgotten how."

He held his bent arm out to her, and she tucked her hand in the crook of it. "Seems strange without Mor here."

"Ja, and without Elizabeth on the piano. But the musicians will do well. There's lots of good food and drink, and people are ready to laugh and have a good time. There's Benny over there with the rest of the children."

"Don't you love his scooter? I couldn't believe it when our maintenance man at the hospital in Chicago showed it to me."

Haakan nodded. "He tries hard with the crutches, but this is easier. You did a good thing by bringing him here."

"Thanks to Rebecca and Gerald, who agreed to adopt him. I couldn't bear the thought of sending him to an orphanage or worse, back out on the streets. Chicago is not a good place to live, at least for the poorer people." She glanced up to where the musicians were tuning up to catch Joshua watching her. He sent a smile her way that kicked her heart up a notch.

"I see you've made one man very happy tonight."

Leave it to her observant father. She could feel the heat of a blush climbing her neck. Inga and Emmy ran over to greet her.

Astrid had only had a few moments with Emmy since she'd been home, but the little girl had already won her heart. It was easy to understand why her parents were so fond of her.

"How's Ma?" Inga asked.

"Sleeping but getting better."

"She sure sleeps a lot."

"True, but that is what she needs most."

"Are you going to dance with Mr. Landsverk?"

"Inga, what a thing to ask." Thorliff joined them, catching his daughter up in his arms. He looked at Astrid. "Elizabeth wanted Inga to have one parent here tonight."

"Well, Tante Ellie said Mr. Landsverk is sweet on Tante Astrid," Inga spouted, "and I asked what she meant, and she said—"

"That's enough," Thorliff said as he set her back down. "You and Emmy go play with the other children, and I'll come get you for a dance later on."

"Emmy too?"

"Of course." He watched as the two ran off. "They've become inseparable."

"It's good for both of them." Haakan nodded toward a greeting from Mrs. Valders.

When the dancing started, Samuel claimed the first dance and led Astrid into one of the forming squares.

"Did your mother tell you to do this?"

"Nope. I haven't seen you since you got home, so I decided dancing would be good."

"Thank you." She smiled as Trygve and his mother joined their set, along with Rebecca and Gerald and Penny and Hjelmer. The visiting stopped as Mr. Valders took his place near the musicians and called for their attention. The music started, and away they went, the women circling right and the men left. By the end of the dance, she was laughing and thoroughly enjoying herself.

"So are you home to stay?" Toby asked as he partnered her on the next dance. She didn't have to answer him, as the patterns whirled them apart. *I'll think about that tomorrow or Monday,* she told herself.

Thorliff approached her with the new man in tow. "Astrid, I don't think you've met Mr. Jeffers, have you?"

She shook her head and smiled at the man. "You are definitely not the Mr. Jeffers that I met, and I do know the story of what happened. He was an atrocious character."

"So I hear. The real Mr. Jeffers, my father, was a fine man, well loved by all who knew him. I hope one day we learn the entire story."

"For your sake, so do I. The uncertainty must have been terribly hard for your mother. And for you, of course." Astrid liked the man's smile. He sent a warm feeling right through her. He seemed so at ease and friendly. He would be a good addition to Blessing.

"It was and still is. I do believe I have talked Mother into coming to Blessing in the near future."

"Good. To visit?"

"No. I will be building a house here, and she is looking forward to a new life." He glanced at Thorliff. "It sounds like we'll all be starting a new life if our business goes the way we hope."

Thorliff nodded, and then acknowledged someone calling his name. "I'll be back in a minute."

"Have you met many of the people of Blessing?" Astrid asked.

"Only my business associates and those at the boardinghouse. I did meet your mother at our meetings. She is very proud of you.

I can understand why. It is a noble profession you have taken on. It must be very enriching."

Astrid found herself blushing. "Thank you. Why don't you come to church tomorrow and then join the Bjorklund family for dinner afterward? We'll make sure you meet lots of the people here." *Deborah. This might be the man for her. I'll have to ask Sophie what she thinks.*

"Thank you. I'd like that." He nodded and then added, "Could I have this dance?"

"I'd be delighted." Together they joined the others in a schottische, following the patterned dancers in the circle. Halfway through Astrid glanced over at the musicians to find Joshua watching her, his face sober. Would she get a chance to dance with him?

When the musicians took a break, Joshua approached her. "I'm glad to see you here," he said. "I was afraid you'd not make it."

"Mor made sure I came, and I'm glad I did. You all play so well together. What a delight."

"Thank you. I'm asking before anyone else can interrupt—may I have the next dance? It will be a waltz."

Astrid nodded as she smiled. "I think that can be worked out."

"Good. Come with me while I get something to drink." He took her hand and led her through the shifting and visiting crowd. So many people expressed their pleasure at her being home again that getting to the punch bowl used up most of the break time. He took a cup from Mrs. Geddick, who was pouring, and handed it to Astrid before taking one of his own.

He was studying her over the rim of his cup, and his smile set her neck to heating up again. What was there about him that caused such a visceral reaction? She carried the thought one further. And at the same time she'd not thought about him at all for days when she was in Chicago or Athens. Was there a difference between love and desire?

But that was nothing to how she felt when he took her in his arms and moved to the music. *Floating* was the only word she found to describe it. He turned them in a circle, one hand firm in the middle of her back and the other holding hers as if she were a precious ornament. When she looked into his eyes, she couldn't look away. Longing called to longing. Her heart quickened, and she dampened her lips with the tip of her tongue. As they turned, the music thrummed through her veins as if part of her blood.

"May I walk you home at the end of the night?" he asked when the music faded and stopped. "I mean, if you're going to spend the night in town again."

"I am, and yes, I'd like that."

"Good." He squeezed her hand that somehow had stayed clasped in his. When he left to rejoin the musicians, her hand felt lonely. Perhaps things would be different between them this time.

28

"Letter for you." Thorliff handed his wife the mail.

"From the Josephson Foundation." Elizabeth glanced over at Astrid, who had just brought dinner up.

"Well, open it." Astrid set the tray on the table next to the chair where Elizabeth was enjoying the fresh air and sunshine from the open window.

Elizabeth did as told and, after slitting the envelope, pulled out two sheets of paper. She unfolded them slowly, as if afraid of the contents.

Astrid bit down on her impatience. Elizabeth was recovering, but the pace at which she did normal tasks was indicative of her weakness. And Astrid didn't know what else to do for her. "Who, exactly, is it from, and what do they have to say?"

Thorliff, leaning against the doorjamb, cleared his throat.

Elizabeth sighed and laid the paper down on her lap and then handed it to Astrid. "You read it aloud, please."

Astrid took the letter and started.

" 'Dear Doctors Bjorklund.' " That made her smile. "They could have sent us each a letter."

"Easier this way." Thorliff crossed his arms, his impatience locked against his chest.

> "I am hoping to find you both well by now. I know you have been through great turmoil."

Astrid looked up. "Did anyone tell them about your losing the baby? I wrote a note to Dr. Morganstein but didn't think to contact anyone else there."

Thorliff shook his head, as did Elizabeth.

"Then they don't know the half of it." She continued.

> "In our last communication, we postponed anything further on the hospital in Blessing until the winter passed. We've waited even longer due to my aunt's increasing frailty. Now she insists on going forward and is pushing for this meeting to happen quickly. I know this project is near and dear to her heart, and she wants to be active in the planning. But due to her weakened strength, Dr. Morganstein will take her place for the meeting. She is anxious to see you both and volunteered to attend before we could even ask.
>
> "Would it be possible for us to schedule this meeting in two weeks? We would arrive on the train the night before and take rooms at your boardinghouse. If this will not be possible for you, I ask that you telephone me with an alternate plan. Or, as we hope, with your approval.
>
> "In the meantime I have included a list of the questions we

will be discussing so that you and your community can prepare for our visit. I believe that we will want one meeting with all those interested in Blessing. The rest of the time to be used in closed sessions, with you choosing those whom you think should be there.

"Thank you for your attention to this matter.

"I remain respectfully yours,

"Jason Josephson"

"Well, what do you think?" Astrid asked as she folded the paper. Her mind skipped ahead. How could she stay here two more weeks? Her leave was nearly up, and she needed to be preparing to return to the missionary school. She bit her lip. But Elizabeth . . .

Elizabeth tipped her head to rest on the back of the chair. "If I progress as I have been, I should be strong enough to attend the meetings."

"That's a big *if.*" Thorliff stared at the floor. "I'd say ask for three or four weeks."

Elizabeth looked to Astrid. "And what about you? Are you staying here or returning to your missionary plans?"

The tone of Elizabeth's voice revealed far more than her words. Astrid felt them stab in her heart. *Lord God, what am I to do? What are you asking me to do? I have to know.* She paused, chewing on her lower lip. *What can I say?* "I don't know."

"Do you have any idea when you will know?"

"It's not as if I've not been asking God and listening for all I am worth to His answer." Keeping the confusion from her voice—and mind—was getting harder and harder. She wanted to say firmly, "Don't ask. I will tell you when I know." But she didn't. "I am thinking I must write and ask for a continuance. You are not strong enough yet to take back the practice, and Mor is feeling the overwork."

"What if they say no?"

"I will deal with that if it happens. As Mor says, 'Today's troubles are sufficient for the day.' And I need to eat, get you settled, and reopen the surgery doors by one o'clock. Unless, of course, you have any further suggestions." There the bite crept in, in spite of her. She needed to remember how grateful she was that Elizabeth was still with them and not how frustrated they all were with her slow progress.

"The sooner we have the meeting, the better." Thorliff looked from his sister to his wife. "Am I understanding the gist of what you are saying?"

"I guess." Hesitation was not Astrid's normal way of doing things. Study it, get going, and get it done. "Would you like me to telephone them and say two weeks is fine?"

Thorliff and Elizabeth looked to each other and then both nodded.

Wishing she had kept her mouth shut, Astrid took the letter and made her way downstairs. Hoping that the line was busy, she picked up the receiver to a silent line.

"How may I help you?" Gerald's voice always sounded pleasant and steady.

"Good afternoon, Mr. Valders. I'd like to call Chicago." She gave him the number on the letter.

"Mr. Valders?" With a slight chuckle, he answered, "Yes, Dr. Bjorklund, I will get the party for you. Is there someone special you would like to talk with?"

Astrid heaved a sigh. "Yes. Mr. Jason Josephson. And tell whomever answers that this is in response to a letter he sent."

She waited while Gerald took care of the business and responded when Mr. Josephson said hello. "Hello, this is Dr. Astrid Bjorklund."

"Well, good to hear from you so quickly. How are things in Blessing?"

"Dr. Bjorklund is improving daily. We realized we'd not notified your aunt that Dr. Bjorklund's baby died."

"I'm so sorry. She has been concerned for her."

"Thank you. Tell her it was a boy but had a hole in his back. They call it spina bifida."

"That is so sad. Yes, she will want to know. I do hope you have good news for me regarding our meeting, though."

"We do. The two weeks will be fine. We'll make reservations for you all at the boardinghouse. I am assuming three of you will be coming?"

"Yes. You met Mr. Abramson and of course, Dr. Morganstein.

"You will let us know if there is anything else needed?"

"I will. I am looking forward to seeing you again. Give our regards to Dr. Bjorklund."

"I will. Thank you." After the good-byes Astrid hung up the earpiece and climbed back up the stairs to deliver the news. Thorliff was gone, but Elizabeth was just finishing her dinner.

Astrid glanced down at the more than half-full plate. "Well, it is set up, but now I have an order for you. Food, rest, and God's healing sunlight and summer breezes. You will eat more, move more, and follow your doctor's orders, or you will not be strong enough for the meetings."

"I can't eat any more."

"Then you will eat more often and drink the eggnog Thelma will bring you. I will talk with Mor and see if there are herbs that we can add to increase your appetite. We can add some molasses and honey . . ." Astrid switched into doctor mode, all the while watching Elizabeth, who had crossed her arms and stuck out her bottom lip like Inga in a pout.

"Is there anything you would like to say?"

"No!"

"Good, because I am going to help you back to bed right now, and when you wake, Thorliff will carry you downstairs so you can play with Inga on the back porch. I am going to open the surgery and telephone Mor to see what suggestions she has."

"You're ganging up on me."

"You're right." Astrid held out her arm to help Elizabeth stand. By the time they made it across the room to the bed, the patient was panting as though she'd been running blocks instead of walking ten feet. Astrid fluffed the pillows and drew the sheet up. "Use your bell if you need something."

"Where is Inga?"

"Playing over at Sophie's."

"Thank you." Elizabeth stared down at her clasped hands. "I'm sorry to be so cantankerous."

"I know."

Down in the surgery, Astrid turned the *Closed* sign around to *Open* and opened the door to let in the fresh air. Two women were sitting on the benches on the porch.

"Rebecca, how good to see you. Come in, both of you."

As they followed her in, Astrid motioned to the desk. "Please sign on the lines on that register."

"So what are you here for?" she asked Rebecca a few minutes later, in the privacy of the examining room.

"I think I am with child." Rebecca's face shone with joy.

"Oh, my dear friend, how wonderful. How long since you've had your monthlies?"

"I believe I have missed two months now. I wasn't paying attention at first, so I am not certain."

"Could it be three?"

"I don't think so. But between Benny and the soda shop I've been so busy. . . ." She raised and dropped her hands. "I haven't even told Gerald yet."

"Have your breasts been sore?" At her nod Astrid continued, "Nauseous in the morning?"

"Or the evening, whenever it decides to attack, but not a lot. That's why I wasn't sure."

"Have you found any thickening around your waist?"

"My skirts are tight."

"Looks like all the symptoms to me. I think you'd better tell Gerald that he's going to be a papa."

"He already is."

"You are right. I should have said *again*." She told Rebecca what to watch for and what to expect when with child and hugged her before she left. "Now, this is the fun part of being a doctor."

She heard Thorliff bringing Elizabeth down, then went and examined her other patient, this one for extreme weariness. She asked her standard questions but had no idea when finished what the problem might be. Prescribing a tonic she and Ingeborg had concocted, she told the woman to return in two weeks. "Make sure you get enough rest and eat extra meat and eggs."

"Thank you, Doctor. I will try." The woman's pale face told Astrid nothing more but that something was indeed wrong. She had learned so much in surgery at the hospital but again realized how little she knew regarding women's health.

"I telephoned my stepmother this afternoon while you were seeing patients," Elizabeth said at supper, picking at her food.

Astrid looked up from buttering a biscuit. "Good."

"I told her what happened, and once we both quit crying, she reminded me that my real mother lost several babies too. She died in childbirth, you know." She sniffed and heaved a sigh. "Do you suppose such things run in families?"

Astrid shook her head. "I have no idea, but that certainly would be a good question to send to someone researching women and pregnancies. You might ask Dr. Morganstein if she's heard anything like that. As you know, she keeps up on the latest information, not that there is a lot of it. Funny, or rather strange, that so many women die in childbirth and the medical world seems to ignore it." She stared out the window before returning with another question. "Why do you suppose that is?"

"Just remember, doctors scrubbing their hands before delivering a baby is still a relatively new procedure."

"So many things to learn." Astrid thanked Thelma for refilling her coffee cup. "Did I tell you Rebecca is in the family way?"

"No. How wonderful. So Benny will have a little brother or sister." Elizabeth leaned back in her chair. "Have I mentioned how much I like joining everyone for supper again? That bedroom is beginning to feel like a cave." She covered her mouth with her hand to hide the yawn.

"Be that as it may, let me help you back to your cave." Thorliff stood and pulled out her chair.

After finishing her supper, Astrid took her glass of apple juice out on the porch to enjoy the sunset. She sat down and put her feet up on the stool, letting the cool evening breeze relax her. Hammers were still pounding nails, and she could hear men talking not far from where she sat. Who was still working this late? Curiosity took over. She set her empty glass down on the low table and drifted down the stairs, following the sounds of labor and laughter.

"Hey, Astrid, you come to help?" Samuel asked.

"Help how?"

"We're getting Joshua's basement ready to pour the concrete. Come and see." He turned and headed down the slanted ramp. Astrid stopped at the top of it to see what was happening. Four or five men were nailing up walls and cutting boards, and Samuel was cleaning up the waste.

"Hey, Astrid, you come to help?" her far called, same as Samuel.

"I didn't plan on it." She caught Joshua's surprised look and smiled. There it was again, that feeling in her middle.

"Be careful you don't trip over something," he said, his voice adding to the curl of warmth.

"I'll stay up here and out of the way."

"Okay, boys, let's put this away and head on home." Hjelmer hung his saw on a nail on a beam. "Don't know about you, but I could eat half a steer."

"Besides, it's getting too dark to work." Solberg slapped Joshua on the shoulder. "See you tomorrow night."

Astrid greeted each of them as they drew even with her, Joshua being the last.

"May I walk you home?" he asked.

She nodded. "It's not far."

"Anything is better than nothing." He raised his voice. "Thanks, all of you."

They turned and walked across the lot. "I've wanted to show you my hole in the ground."

"Looks like you are close to ready for the house itself."

"Have to pour the concrete first. I'm buying a Sears and Roebuck house."

"Good for you." *Come on, think of something clever to say.* They reached the back steps to Thorliff's house. "Would you like something to drink?"

Joshua thought a moment. "I better not. Miss Christopherson holds supper for me, and it is already late."

"I see. Congratulations on your house."

"Thank you. I wish . . ." He heaved a sigh. "I better go. Perhaps I can see you tomorrow night?"

"Perhaps. Good night." She watched him walk whistling up the street. As Sophie would say, "There goes one fine-looking man." And enjoyable to talk with, as she'd learned the night after the dance and again now. Sitting in the porch swing had made her long for more.

THE NEXT MORNING, Astrid made another long-distance telephone call, this one to Dean Highsmith at the missionary school. After a few minutes of polite talk, she cleared her throat. "Dean Highsmith, I have a huge favor to ask."

"Yes."

"Would it be possible for me to extend this time at home for another three weeks? Dr. Bjorklund lost her baby, and I need to take care of things here until she is back on her feet. Also, we have a meeting with the foundation people from the Morganstein hospital in Chicago regarding building a hospital here in Blessing. It would help greatly if I could be here for that."

"So you think you would be back by the end of June?"

"Yes."

"That means you would be sailing with the group on July 6."

Astrid closed her eyes. *Lord is this your will? What am I to do?*

"All right, Dr. Bjorklund, but this is the final time. If you cannot make this date, we will consider our agreement with you closed."

"Yes, sir. Thank you, sir."

"We will be praying here, as I know you are there. Please extend our condolences to Dr. Bjorklund."

"I will. Thank you." Astrid hung up the telephone and leaned her head against the wall. Why did she feel like sobbing? Not just crying but heartrending sobs?

After catching up on her chart work, she saw two patients, and since there were no others, she turned the sign over and told

Thelma she would be back after a while. She needed a change of scenery.

THE NEXT TWO weeks passed in a blur, with Astrid running the surgery and Elizabeth gaining strength, but with none of the vigor they had hoped. While she could walk downstairs, she couldn't climb the stairs without assistance. Morning and afternoon naps taken on the porch were necessary, but what concerned Astrid the most was Elizabeth's lack of interest in their patients and the possible hospital. As she marked off each day on the calendar, her date to leave seemed to leap off the page. How could she possibly leave? How could she not? And Joshua had not once come by to see her for a walk or to go for a soda either. But then, she herself hadn't realized it for several days. She knew he was working long hours but still . . . Where was her mind and heart? What was God trying to tell her?

"What am I going to do, Mor?" she asked one afternoon when she and her mother were sitting on the porch watching Emmy and Inga playing in the puddles left from the rain that had passed over an hour or so earlier. The air smelled freshly washed, a fragrance like no other. The lilacs bent their blossom heads toward the ground, weighted by the water, yet wafting their fragrance with the abandon of the sun sending rays to every corner. The girls giggling, the birds chorusing their joy in the rain, and the cat purring in her lap sang of home and summer. Home here in Blessing, North Dakota, not some city or village on the dark continent of Africa.

Tears leaked from her eyes as drops fell from the eaves of the house, but the water from the roof flowed into the rain barrel, and her tears only made her cheeks wet.

"I hate to see you in such misery." Ingeborg took her daughter's hand across the small space between the two rockers.

"But I gave my word." A sniff accompanied the words.

"God will let you know."

"You keep saying that."

"I trust Him. That is all there is to it. I know He will take care of this for you."

"Gamma, Gamma," Inga called. "Come puddle with us."

Ingeborg started to say no, but instead leaned over and untied her shoes. "Take your shoes off. We are going to puddle."

Astrid brushed the tears away, shaking her head. "Puddling it is." The two hiked their skirts, drawing the back of the skirts between their legs and tucking them into the waistbands in front to keep them out of the way. Before long they were muddy to their knees, the girls muddied all over, and their laughter rose to tickle the happy leaves of the trees.

Just rejoice, she reminded herself. *You know you can trust Him. Just trust!*

29

Astrid and Thorliff met the visitors at the train late in the afternoon.

"Welcome to Blessing," Astrid said as their guests stepped down onto the platform. "This is my brother Thorliff, and he will see to your baggage." She introduced the three visitors and led them to the boardinghouse beyond the other end of the station.

"You are indeed out in the country," Dr. Morganstein commented, her arm locked through Astrid's. "Smell this air." She inhaled and then again. "This is marvelous." Her heels tapped on the wooden walk that had been constructed the year before.

Astrid hid a chuckle. The doctor certainly looked different in traveling clothes rather than her usual full body apron. And by the grip on her arm, the woman did not feel as confident in her walking as she used to. Astrid wondered how old her mentor really was, as age suddenly seemed to be catching up with her.

"I will get to see Benny while I'm here, won't I? And dear Elizabeth, besides at the meeting? How is she?"

"Yes to Benny, and we'll see that you have time to visit with Elizabeth too." They climbed the three steps to the boardinghouse, Mr. Josephson and Mr. Abramson talking with Thorliff all the way.

"Welcome to Blessing," Sophie said, greeting them at the door. "I am Sophie Wiste, Astrid's cousin."

After the introductions Sophie led them down the hall on the first floor and opened the second door. "I put you here, Dr. Morganstein, and the next two rooms are for you two gentlemen."

"Thank you for this. I won't have to climb those stairs. The ones at the hospital are getting to be more than I can handle, so we are putting elevators in this summer. That will make life easier on everyone."

Astrid thought of her races up the stairs when she was on call. "That will indeed help. And a good suggestion for our building here."

"If you would like, you could have supper served in your room. You also have your own necessary." Sophie showed her the bathroom, this being the only room in the building to have its own bathroom.

"Thank you. That will be most helpful. Can we also have a couple more chairs and a table to work at?"

"Yes. I will have them brought in."

"I will leave you now," Astrid said. "If you would like to visit Elizabeth tonight, Thorliff will come for you."

"I had thought to do that, but I will see her in the morning before our first meeting. Right now, I just want to sit down without the floor rocking and freshen up. What time will supper be served?"

"Whenever you like." Sophie nodded and backed toward the door. "If you need anything else, there is a bellpull by the bed. Breakfast starts in the dining room at six thirty for our work crew. For others, any time up until ten o'clock. Thank you for coming."

Sophie and Astrid left the room at the same time.

"Whew, am I glad that is over." Sophie pretended to wipe perspiration from her brow.

"Why is that?" Astrid asked, staring at her cousin. "You're not afraid of anybody."

"But this is *the* Dr. Morganstein. How many stories have I heard you and Elizabeth tell about her? How much of an influence could her goodwill be on this town? I felt like I was greeting royalty—all but the curtsy."

Astrid chuckled. "You were a gracious hostess." She skipped a beat but kept her hands from clapping. "Think what a difference it will make in Blessing if we have a hospital."

"I filled out all those questions, remember? I have as good an idea as anyone. This will bring more guests to the boardinghouse, both during construction time and when fully operational. Where else would people stay? I am thinking of offering a special rate for people who come because of the hospital."

"Leave it to Sophie, always the businesswoman. You'll be at the community meeting tomorrow night?"

"Of course. As will Garth and anyone else who has any dreams for Blessing. Between a manufacturing plant and a hospital—"

"Don't forget the people who want to help Kaaren with an addition to the deaf school."

"You are right." Sophie stopped at her desk. "This whole thing gives me chills."

"Why?"

"It's so much. There are going to be a lot of people moving here, first to help build and then to work in the buildings. And to think it all started with the farming and your mother's cheese house."

Astrid thought about that on the walk back to Thorliff's house.

If I go to Africa, I will miss all of this. The thought weighted her feet as she climbed the stairs to her room.

Wishing she could go home and talk with her mother and father again, Astrid spent the night in her room at Thorliff's house and woke along with the birds at dawn. She and Thorliff had gone through all the papers, answering the myriad questions the committee posed to those they knew wanted to be included in the decision. The town meeting was scheduled for that night. She dressed quickly and headed for the kitchen to help Thelma prepare the noon meal, at least as much as they could so early. When Elizabeth rang for breakfast, Astrid took the tray up.

"Here you go. Do you need help dressing too?"

"I do. And with my hair. I'm as nervous as I was when I first met the woman. Here she is in my town, and I couldn't even meet her train."

"Well, at least you get to come to the meetings." Astrid arranged the tray across Elizabeth's knees. "While you eat, I'll go change clothes so at least one of us is ready."

"Have you eaten?"

"Nope. That's why there's extra food on your tray. You didn't think I expected you to eat all of that?"

"I never know about you. Thorliff left for his office to work on the newspaper. Heavens, what if the edition went out late due to impending business?"

Astrid shook her head as she exited the room. If Dr. Morganstein asked about Elizabeth's mental attitude, how would she answer? Grumpy, critical, impatient with those around her, tending toward self-pity? Indicators that she still was not well? Then she reminded herself that grief and weakness sometimes did strange things to the patient.

By the time the guests started arriving for the morning meeting,

Elizabeth was seated at the dining room table in a comfortable chair with a footstool at the side.

"Don't get up, Doctor," Dr. Morganstein said when she entered the room. Taking the chair next to her former student, the elder doctor studied her. "I'm sorry things happened this way," she said softly, holding Elizabeth's hand. "Now you need to regain your strength. Are you being unruly, or are you a good patient?"

"Are you asking me or Astrid?" Elizabeth asked.

"I was afraid of that. Doctors are rarely good patients. But I am sure we are all in agreement that you need to regain your strength."

Elizabeth nodded. "I know that, and I want to do what is best, but losing Roald like that was far worse than I thought possible."

"You named the baby, then?" At her nod, Dr. Morganstein leaned closer and gave her a hug. "That was very wise."

"But now I might never have another chance." Tears brimmed, and Elizabeth ducked her head to hide her sorrow.

"That is true, and not trying again would be very wise. But you could adopt another child or more. Besides, with all the lives you will save with your medical gifts, your life will be full and a blessing to untold people."

Astrid watched the two, partially hearing what was being said but keeping the others visiting so the two could talk without interruption. When Thorliff stood to call the meeting together, she caught his eye and shook her head, nodding toward the two doctors.

"I thought perhaps you would like a tour of our surgery before we started the meeting. I know Astrid, er, Dr. Bjorklund, would be glad to show you around. In the meantime I will help bring in the coffee, and I think I smell cinnamon rolls."

The two men followed Astrid, asking questions and nodding approval at her information.

"You really do need an operating theater, don't you?" Mr. Abramson commented. "You have accomplished a great deal with minimum resources."

"Thank you." She showed them the pharmacopeia, where they compounded many of the medications they sold. "We combine many natural remedies with the more modern drugs, so we have the best of both worlds."

"You will need a department in the hospital for this and someone trained to compound."

"I thought we would look for someone when the hospital is nearing completion. Perhaps there will be an intern from Chicago who could be this person."

"Perhaps so. Dr. Morganstein has been talking of expanding the training for students who want to study medicines more than medical procedures."

At Thorliff's beckoning, Astrid steered them back to the dining room, where Thelma was pouring coffee and passing the cinnamon rolls. She glanced at Elizabeth to see how she was and received a firm nod. As soon as everyone was seated around the table and served, Thorliff called the meeting to order.

Astrid sat next to her mother, who took her hand under cover of the table and tapped "God is good" into her palm. Astrid nodded and glanced across the table to see Pastor Solberg next to Mr. Geddick. Lars and Kaaren sat at the foot of the table with Thorliff at the head. Mr. Valders sat next to Thorliff, already taking notes.

"Dr. Morganstein would like to say a few words at this point." Thorliff nodded to her and sat down.

She rose and smiled around the group. "First of all, thank you all for coming. I know you have many other things you could be doing this morning. I want you to know that proceeding with our plans is part of my dearest dream. My hospital in Chicago is, of course, first and most important to me. But it has outgrown its space. In order to expand, we need to move it, try to buy more land around where we are now, move a part of our services, or start a new hospital. We could do that in Chicago, but I believe an extended hospital will serve us—and all of you—well. Together we can serve two areas, expand our teaching facility, and even add new departments, like your pharmacy. Perhaps even venture into research fields regarding women's and children's health. I know I am looking at a huge picture, but if we do this in smaller pieces, we can bring that picture, that dream, into reality. Both Dr. Bjorklunds left an imprint on our medical school, and it gives me great satisfaction to work further with them both."

Astrid schooled her face to not respond. Both. She wished Elizabeth knew sign language as well as she and Mor did. But Elizabeth had learned only the fundamentals and not practiced like many of the people of Blessing. What if they were able to do research on the ear and different kinds of deafness? Surely there would be progress there, and with the deaf school here, Blessing was a good place to start. She brought her attention back to Dr. Morganstein, who was just sitting down. What had she missed?

Mr. Josephson stood next. "I agree with my colleague that this is a proposal that will impact medicine in many ways. As you all know, the well-respected Alfred Morganstein Hospital for Women and Children is a leader in our field. We desire to continue that leadership. I have here the blueprints we have had drawn up, knowing that you also have designs you feel might work. I suggest that we now lay those plans on the table and begin our discussions." He nodded to Mr. Abramson, who unrolled the prints. Hjelmer laid out the drawings they had compiled. While not fancy, they got the point across. Throughout the morning they talked of where to start and what goals to set for the long range, including the finances, staffing, supplies, support machinery, and community involvement.

Haakan said at one point, "I feel strongly that we need to start simply and add as we go along. When I look at the papers before us, I see today and down the road. If we build with that in mind, we will build in a way that makes expanding easier. We have the ground available, so it makes sense to lock that in now, before someone comes along and buys it out from under us. The section is owned by the railroad, and yes, they are willing to sell."

Thelma served a simple dinner to everyone, and then Astrid insisted that Elizabeth go to the lying-in room to rest. The meeting finally disbanded and the guests returned to the boardinghouse to prepare for the town meeting.

Ingeborg tipped her head from side to side, stretching out her tired muscles. "I'd rather can beans any day." Haakan and Lars left to do chores and would return by six thirty to have supper before the meeting. Mr. Valders stacked his notes together and heaved a sigh.

"I'll see you all at the meeting tonight. Thank you, Thorliff, for leading this. My only concern at this point is how to pay for it. The flour mill is giving a return on our money, as is the elevator. I don't see that happening with the hospital for five years at least." He nodded and left the room, his "if ever," while unsaid, lingering like the aroma of a skunk.

That evening everyone in town, or at least it seemed that way, showed up at the church, since that was the largest building in Blessing. Even with all the windows open, the heat brought out fans and a few grumbles.

Thorliff introduced the visitors and gave a brief summary of the morning's meeting. He called on Mr. Valders to give a financial report on the status of the co-operative ventures of the people of Blessing.

"So the bottom line is this," he said to finish his report. "How long will we be willing to receive no interest on our money?"

"But we are getting a return on the other investments, so shouldn't that money then be used to build a hospital?"

Somebody else asked, "Do we really need a hospital here? What's wrong with the surgery we have?"

"Well, part of the problem," Thorliff answered, "is that the surgery is not owned by the folks of Blessing. It is owned by my wife and me, and yes, it is inadequate. We didn't dream Blessing was going to grow as it has and how it will grow even faster with new folks and new businesses coming to town. You know how far away Grafton and Grand Forks are."

Pastor Solberg stood. "I believe that God is blessing all the people around us and that we are being given a huge mission—to care for the sick and to use our prosperity wisely. As Jesus walked this earth, He healed the sick that came to Him. We have doctors who do what they can with their training and advances in medicine."

The discussion continued until sometime later, when Thorliff asked, "Is there anyone else who has something to say?" When no one answered, he nodded. "Since this is an informational meeting, I call it closed. You have agreed on who will speak for all of us as this project continues. I believe from everything that was said tonight, most of you are in favor of proceeding. We will keep you informed, and if you have any questions, ask me or send your questions to the newspaper." He thanked the Chicago people for coming and dismissed the meeting.

The citizens of Blessing filed out, continuing their discussions as they returned to their homes.

"Thanks for taking Elizabeth home," Thorliff said to Andrew and Joshua as they came back through the door. They had picked her chair up and carried her to the surgery and up the stairs to her bedroom, where Thelma helped her into bed.

"You're welcome." Joshua looked around and smiled at Astrid. "I am amazed at the civility of this meeting. No one got up and yelled; no one left in a huff. Not everyone absolutely agreed, but they listened. You can tell that people here love their town and like working together."

"We've always worked together, from the very beginning. I'll tell you there have been some rather strong debates and a few major disagreements, but Pastor Solberg has always been able to pour oil on troubled waters. I'd like to be listening on the party line later this evening or in the morning." Haakan glanced at his wife, who smiled and shook her head at the same time. He crossed the room to shake the hands of the two men and thank them for coming. Then he turned to Dr. Morganstein.

"You have made our lives richer by the lessons you've taught two of my daughters. I cannot thank you enough. I don't begin to understand all the medical advances, but I do know farming. You plant the seed in the soil, pray for the right amounts of rain and sun, and be there to harvest at the right time. I think our two lines of work have a lot in common. God brings both the healing and the harvest, and we all do our part to the best of our ability."

"You speak very wisely, Mr. Bjorklund," Dr. Morganstein said. "Thank you for giving me and my hospital the privilege of training the two doctors Bjorklund. I am so glad to see you again and in such better circumstances."

"Ja, my Ingeborg recovered well. Thank you that I still have her. I have our buggy outside to take you back to the boardinghouse if you are ready. I know you must be weary after a day like today."

"Weary, yes, but so excited at the prospects." She looked to Mr. Josephson. "We will take you up on the ride, or at least I will."

Astrid walked them out. "I will see you again in the morning. Thank you."

"Good." Dr. Morganstein took her arm. "I can see why you didn't want to leave Blessing." They walked to the buggy, and Haakan assisted the doctor into the seat.

THE NEXT MORNING Mr. Josephson handed Thorliff a packet before they were to leave for the train and an envelope for Astrid. "We look forward to our joint venture, if possible."

After the farewells and the train had left, Astrid opened her envelope and scanned the contents. She handed it to Thorliff. "Does this say what I think it says?"

He read the paper and looked into her eyes. "Perhaps it will be negotiable."

Astrid stared at the words that leaped out at her. *This agreement is contingent upon the proviso that both Dr. Astrid Bjorklund and Dr. Elizabeth Bjorklund are in a position to oversee the hospital.* What was she to do? *Lord, is this your answer?* Her heart cried out to say yes, but she knew that as God did not break His promises, she should not break hers. Here she was, caught in the middle, and she did not know which way to turn.

30

They know that I am committed to two years in Africa. Dr. Morganstein and I talked about that." Astrid felt like tearing the letter into shreds and throwing it into the air for the wind to scatter. "Why wait and hand me a letter? Why not talk this over face-to-face?"

"I don't know." Thorliff opened his packet and pulled out several sheets of paper. Glancing through them, he stopped at one that matched Astrid's. "It is dated this morning, so it must have been a recent decision. There was no time for a discussion."

" 'Contingent upon.' " She humphed and stomped. "It's going to take a year to build this anyway, is it not?"

"Not necessarily. Once they finalize the purchase of the land, we can begin immediately. We would want the initial building set in for the winter, when we would finish it. The real contingency is having enough labor here to do both the hospital and machinery at once, plus houses for future residents. We need to put advertisements in newspapers here in North Dakota and as far away as Chicago and St. Louis, I would imagine. The Twin Cities for sure and others south."

Astrid listened to both her brother and her pounding head. "I'm going to talk with Elizabeth and then go out to see Mor. Or maybe I should telephone for her to come in so I am near the surgery if there is an emergency."

"You go talk with Elizabeth, and I'll call Mor. Then I have to get this edition to bed. I'm going to have Samuel help with the printing tonight."

"All right." Astrid climbed the three steps to the side porch and the surgery entrance. At least there was no one sitting on the bench waiting for her to open. As far as she knew, there were no appointments either. Glancing into the examining rooms to make sure they were ready for patients, she shut the doors and climbed the stairs to where she knew Elizabeth was waiting for any news she had to share. She certainly wasn't expecting what Astrid had to say.

She entered the bedroom, where Elizabeth was half lying on the settee in front of the window. A slight breeze billowed the sheer white curtains, wafting in summer fragrances, redolent with lilac, rich earth, and all manner of things growing.

"I was beginning to think you had stopped off to talk with Sophie or something."

"No. Thorliff and I had a brief discussion about the bombshell we were given." She dropped the letter into Elizabeth's lap. "You better be feeling strong right now, for this is a shock."

Elizabeth pulled the letter out of the envelope and read through it, closing her eyes and heaving a sigh as she leaned against the back of the settee. "Shock is right."

Astrid crossed to the window and stared out toward the

boardinghouse. Ringing hammers and the grate of a saw reminded her that building was indeed going on in Blessing. A man called instructions to someone else. It sounded like Toby. Children laughed and shouted from Sophie's backyard, where Inga had gone to play too. The new swings that Garth had built for the children, along with a sandbox, were popular.

She looked up to find Elizabeth staring at her. She sighed and turned to the door. "I need to talk with Mor. Thorliff said he'd call her and see if she can come in."

"I'd like to be in on the conversation."

"Okay." Astrid heaved another sigh, a sudden attack of tears impending. "I need to go for a walk."

"I wish I could come with you."

"Me too. Have Thorliff take you down to the back porch, and in the meantime, I ask you to pray for this entire mess."

"All right."

"Mor is coming in," Thorliff said when he met her at the bottom of the stairs. "She had to finish something first."

"I wish I could go out and work in the garden for a while. I seem to hear God there."

"We have a garden," he said. "The weeds are coming up after the rain so fast you can watch them grow."

Astrid glanced down at her dress. "I'll go change." Back up the stairs she pulled a faded dress out of the clothespress and swiftly changed, braiding her hair so it would stay out of her way. Down in the kitchen she donned a faded apron and headed outside, where she sat down on the steps and pulled off her shoes. Setting them aside, she took a trowel from the basket and crossed the recently cut grass to the garden plot. A hoe hung on the rail fence. Hoe or dig by hand? Which helped her think better?

Wielding the hoe, she stuck the trowel into her pocket. Thorliff and Thelma had stuck sticks in at the ends of the rows with the name of the plant in charcoal. Astrid started with the potatoes, now well up and fighting for their lives. Thanks to the rain, the rich black soil was soft and pliable. The weeds fell under the slashing hoe as Astrid attacked the enemy.

"If this is a sign from you, heavenly Father, I thank you for answering my prayers. But what about giving my word to Dean Highsmith? Why did I feel so led to go to missionary school? Wasn't that a waste of time and money?" She jerked a handful of stubborn pigweed out and slammed the dirt end against the ground to dislodge the soil. When the roots were bare, she tossed the clump onto a pile she'd started along the fence. A stack of weeds kept the other weeds from sprouting, she'd learned.

The song of a meadowlark caught her attention, and she looked up to find the bird, shading her eyes with her now dirt-crusted hand. Liquid joy, she'd heard a poet describe a meadowlark's song.

The longer she hoed, the more peace seeped in, until she finally stopped and kneaded her back with her fists. Hearing voices, she glanced back at the house to see Mor and Elizabeth visiting on the back porch.

"Lemonade is on," Elizabeth called.

"I'm coming." Astrid picked up and tossed the remaining weeds on the long pile. She stopped to inspect the peas in need of a trellis, as they were beginning to send out tendrils, smiled at the leaf lettuce about ready to pick, then hooked the hoe over the fence and returned to the house, wiping her dirty feet in the grass as she went.

"Here's a pan so you can dip out some rain water to wash in." Ingeborg came down the steps to hand her one.

"Takk." Astrid dipped water from the rain barrel and sat down on the steps with it to wash her hands and feet.

"Feel better?" her mother asked softly.

"I do. There is something about killing weeds that frees the soul. The lettuce is about ready, the carrots are barely up, and some of the beans are pushing up. I know Thorliff won't be stringing the peas tonight, so I think I will."

"Emmy and I were out in the garden this morning too. We strung the peas a few days ago. I dropped her off at Sophie's to play with the others." She handed Astrid a towel kept on a hook for just such instances.

As they sat down, Elizabeth smiled. "I'm glad I'm not a weed."

"Me too." Astrid took a healthy draught from her glass. "Leave it to Thelma to always know just when to provide relief."

"Your face is red."

"No doubt. I was in the sun." She glanced at her mother. "And no, I did not wear a sunbonnet, as you can see."

"When did you ever?"

Astrid nearly choked on her next swallow, laughter bubbling up in spite of herself.

"How did your discussion with God go?" Elizabeth asked.

"I am either writing or telephoning Mr. Josephson this afternoon—most likely I will write to him, since he is on the train and not in his office."

"To say?"

"That I will be here in Blessing and that you are committed to regaining your strength, whatever it takes and however long it takes." She looked at her mother to see her face shining with such love and joy that it brought a lump to her throat.

"Thank you, Father." Ingeborg sniffed and rolled her lips together. "I know my prayers have been selfish, but I thank God for this turn of events."

"Then I will have to write to Dean Highsmith, or call him, and explain the circumstances." She heaved a sigh. "That will be the difficult one."

"So how do you feel about it?" asked Elizabeth.

"I am running over with joy. I get to stay home, at least for now. Perhaps someday I will go to Africa."

"When you are married, and if your husband wants to go?"

The three women laughed at the sally.

"That one really irritated me," Astrid said, picking up a molasses cookie. And if her husband was ever to be Joshua, she couldn't see him willing to go to Africa. She frowned a little. Did she know how he felt about her being a doctor? Had they ever discussed it?

Ingeborg and Elizabeth exchanged smiles. "We understood that part."

"I'm going to change clothes and, if there is no one in the waiting room, go write my letters. That way I can get them in the mail today. Thank you for coming, Mor. I was sure you were going to have to convince me of what to do."

"Convincing always works better when God does it."

Astrid nodded as she opened the kitchen door. "Sure smells good in here."

Thelma turned from the stove. "Dinner will be ready in half an hour." She eyed the dirty apron and dress.

"I know. I'm on my way upstairs to wash and change. Thanks for the lemonade." She realized she was humming as she mounted the stairs. Did this sense of peace bring on the hums? Once clean again, she sat down and quickly wrote the letter to Mr. Josephson. The letter to Dean Highsmith took more time.

After the salutation she wrote:

> It is with deep regret I am writing to ask you to remove my name from the program. Due to a string of events, I realized that I need to be here in Blessing, at least for the next several years. As you know, we are on the verge of building a hospital here, and the foundation in Chicago said the plan was contingent upon the

two Bjorklund doctors being here to run it. This contingency was a shock to all of us.

She stopped and stared at that line. Was it necessary? She almost crossed it out but then continued.

Perhaps sometime in the future I will be able to continue with service in Africa or some other place. Thank you for all that you have done for me, for your encouragement, and for the time I spent at your school.

In the Master's service,
Dr. Astrid Bjorklund

She stared at the final lines. That was indeed appropriate, for she was and would always be.

The others were halfway finished with dinner on the porch when Thorliff strode up the walk from the newspaper office on the other side of the carriage house. "Sorry I am late, but I had to finish the last article." He served himself from the bowls and platters handed to him. "This smells wonderful, Thelma. Thank you." After a few bites he looked to Astrid. "Garden looks great."

"Thank you. Lots more to go."

"There's always work to be done in the garden. It's a good way to work out frustrations."

"Really? I never knew that." Astrid's eyebrows tickled the wisps of hair that fell over her forehead. They all laughed at her arched response, but the look she shared with her brother invited him to join her in her newfound peace.

Later, after tending to a farmer with a swollen jaw and pulling the offending tooth, Astrid picked up her letters and walked over to the post office.

"You are just in time," Mrs. Valders said. "In fact, if you would take the mail pouch over to the train, I would be most grateful. My foot will be grateful too."

"Of course I will, but what is wrong with your foot?"

Mrs. Valders ignored her question when another patron walked in.

Astrid slung the pouch over her shoulder, walked over to the station, and handed it to the stationmaster. He hung it on the hook by the tracks, and they both stood watching the train grow to life-size, smoke trailing from the stack and steam screaming from the locked wheels. Several people stepped off the train while the engineer swung the water spout over the engine and opened the trap for the water to gush into the boiler. Another man swapped the incoming mail for the outgoing and tossed the full bag to the stationmaster.

"You want to take this to Mrs. Valders?" he asked.

"I will. Thanks." Astrid crossed the street again and swung the bag up onto the counter. "All right, now tell me about your foot."

"It will be better soon. I think I just sprained it." She pulled back her skirt to show a swollen right foot. "See? I told you, nothing to worry about."

"How about you sit down and let me make that decision." Astrid pointed to the chair behind the counter. "You can sort mail while I check your foot."

Mrs. Valders grumbled but did as she was instructed. She flinched when Astrid removed the shoe and pressed around the ankle and the arch with gentle fingers.

"Hurts, eh?" She rotated the foot to check the ankle. "Did you put ice on this?"

"No. It's not that bad."

"You need to put ice packs on it three times a day and elevate it for the swelling to go away."

"How am I supposed to elevate my foot when I am running around here like a chicken with my head cut off?"

"What happened?"

"I tripped over Benny's scooter. It wasn't his fault. I just wasn't paying attention."

Astrid nodded, making sure her doctor face was in place. Hildegunn Valders sticking up for Benny? Wait until she told her mother.

"Okay, how about we do this? You put ice packs on the foot in the morning, at noon, and when you close up the post office. When you are here, you do as much as you can sitting down. Use that stool sometimes too, and we'll wrap your foot with strips of an old sheet."

"Thank you. Say, that was a good meeting last night."

"Yes, I thought so too." Astrid got to her feet. "I'll get some bandages and be right back."

When she returned, the mail was in the slots, and Mrs. Valders took the chair without grumbling. Astrid wrapped the ankle, making sure it wasn't too tight, and ripped the end of the strip in half the long way so she could tie the wrap on top of the foot.

"There now, let's put your shoe back on and see if this doesn't make it feel better."

"It does feel better," Hildegunn said when she put her weight back on the foot. "Thank you, Dr. Bjorklund."

Astrid nodded. "Remember, stay off it as much as you can." She picked up the mail from the Bjorklund boxes and headed back to the surgery. Setting the piles on the table, she saw two letters addressed to her, one from Dean Highsmith and the other from Red Hawk. Out on the porch swing, she opened the school one first, setting the swing in motion with her foot as she read.

Dear Dr. Bjorklund,

I am writing this with a heavy heart and after much prayer and discussion. We of the mission board have come to the conclusion that you are not ready to commit one hundred percent to serving as a doctor in Africa. I know you have struggled with the calling, wondering if this is indeed where God was telling you to go. Sometimes the knowing is rock solid and other times not, but I have always recognized a peace that comes with walking in His will. I saw that peace come to you at first, but now it seems He is leading you in another way. Sometimes He uses circumstances to lead us, and that is what we see happening in your situation.

Therefore, it is with regret and yet profound peace on our part that we release you from your commitment to the school and the missionary program. I know God has a plan for you, and He will reveal it, or perhaps He already has. Please keep in touch and let us know how we can be praying for you. At the same time, we ask that you pray for us and our program.

Sincerely yours,
Dean Highsmith

Astrid read the letter again, alternately chuckling and wiping her eyes. Wait until she told the others. Pastor Solberg would shake his head and say one of his favorite sayings, *"God may be slow in answering, but He is never late."*

She tucked that paper back into the envelope and pulled out the other.

Dear Dr. Bjorklund,

I don't know if you are in Blessing or on your way to Africa, but I am writing this in the hope that you are indeed in North Dakota. I also hope you are not going to Africa, but that is my selfish prayer. Remember our discussion when I said that perhaps my people could be your Africa?

Right now the people of Rosebud Reservation are dying from the measles. If I go home at this time, I will lose my place in the rotation, and as Dr. Morganstein fears, I might never make it back here. The needs are so great on the reservation. I know your people in Blessing sent food and supplies earlier this spring, but now a doctor is needed, one who can teach my people how to fight off this dread epidemic. The lack of food and cleanliness is part of the problem, as is the disease itself.

Please can you go? And I beg your people to be generous again to those who are so proud and so needy. I will finish here at the end of the summer and will return as soon as possible. But they need help now.

Your friend,
Dr. Red Hawk

Astrid tipped her head back and stared at the tongue-and-groove ceiling. All these things at once. *What is going on? Lord God, I am overwhelmed. My Africa? Am I to go to South Dakota?*

31

So why did I attend missionary school?"

Pastor Solberg shredded a leaf that had blown onto the porch.

Astrid waited. She had taken the two letters directly to him, before she even spoke with Mor or Elizabeth. Anyone watching her run from the surgery to the Solbergs' might have thought her slightly, or even massively, deranged. He had been sitting on his porch working on his sermon for Sunday and immediately put that away to give her his full attention.

"I don't know."

She dropped her hands into her lap and her chin to her chest. "This just isn't making any sense."

"Oh, I'm sure it does. Only you can't see all the pieces yet. God has a plan for you."

"I know that. I know His thoughts are for good and not for evil. I believe that. But three things happening at once? I know three is a godly number."

"You have listened well through the years. Watching you grow up has been one of my great pleasures."

She looked up at him and had to swallow a lump at the love in his smile and reflected in his eyes. "Now what?"

"What does it look like to you?"

"I am obviously not going back to missionary school."

"I think it very interesting that you sent the letter to Dean Highsmith before you heard from him."

"How so?"

"You made the decision."

"It's not like I wasn't forced into it."

"Really? You could have said, 'No, I am headed for Africa. We can build the hospital when I get back.' "

Astrid thought a long moment. "Never entered my mind."

"You asked God to make this clear to you. Did He?"

"Yes. With a second confirmation."

He picked up his Bible and handed it to her. "Read the story where Abraham is to sacrifice his son."

Astrid flipped through Genesis to chapter twenty-two and read it through.

"What was Abraham told to do?"

"To take his son and a load of wood and the knife to the place God would show him."

"For what purpose?" Pastor Solberg leaned toward her, his gaze intent.

"To sacrifice." Astrid swallowed. "And Abraham did that. He

followed all the instructions, even to laying his son on the altar." She paused. "His only son. His long-awaited son."

"His most precious thing." He kept his look steady on Astrid, as if willing her to go further.

"But then God provided the sacrifice with the ram. So he didn't have to kill his son."

"What is one of your most precious possessions?"

She thought. "My family and my life here in Blessing."

"And?" He waited. Astrid shook her head, fighting to think through where he was leading her.

"What is Abraham's greatest attribute? What did he do all his life?"

She frowned, thinking. "Whatever God said?"

"Yes, that is true, but even more so he trusted God." He let that settle in before he continued. "Do you think that everything made sense to Abraham?"

"No, it couldn't have. Not with being told to sacrifice Isaac."

"Or the journeys or the promises or the instructions. But still, Abraham trusted God. Perhaps He has had you on a journey of trust. Could that fit?"

"And I didn't have to carry through with the sacrifice. I had to be obedient and trust Him?" Astrid ran that sentence through her mind again. *Trust.* She looked at Pastor Solberg through a shimmer of tears. "But what is He providing as a sacrifice in that place then?"

"Good question. I don't know, but eventually, looking back, we will see clearly. Or perhaps there is none visible. Jesus paid for all our sacrifices already."

Astrid nodded slowly. "Now what about Red Hawk's letter?"

"All we can do is ask our people if they are willing to give again. We will lay it before them on Sunday."

"Aren't the women meeting for quilting tomorrow? I thought that was what Mor said."

"You want to go speak to them?"

She shook her head. "About as much as I want to go to Africa. I've seen some of those discussions."

"But you will." He looked steadily at her, encouraging her to do so.

"You think this is part of God's plan for me?"

"I think so, and I also believe this will be the first outreach clinic from the Blessing Hospital. This is what you and Elizabeth dreamed of doing, and God is giving you the opportunity."

"Then I hope He gives the people of Blessing the same dream and the same heart."

"We will make a decision on Sunday, but I think you better begin to collect supplies." He closed his eyes. "Lord God, we praise and thank you for your plan for Astrid and also for the rest of us. And your Word tells us that to whom much is given, much will be required. Your plan for us to go to other nations is part of this family, this church, this community. Lord, you say that with you all things are possible, and we are trusting you to make that happen. Amen."

Astrid wiped her tears, and after blowing her nose, she stood and gathered her letters. "Thank you." She walked home, lifting her face to the westering sun. Stopping first at Elizabeth's, she found her on the back porch, dozing on the cushioned swing.

"You've been gone a long time," Elizabeth said with a smile, stretching her arms over her head. "Lying here listening to the children playing is a new experience for me. I thought you went for the mail."

"I did."

"What happened after that?"

"I took my two letters to Pastor Solberg so he could help me understand what is happening. Here." She handed the two envelopes to Elizabeth. "Read them and tell me what you think. Read the one from Georgia first."

Sitting on the quiet porch, Astrid could hear the pounding thunder of the printing press at work. Usually Thorliff ran it at night. Had he gotten Samuel to help him? What would Thorliff think of her news? Maybe she should stroll by there and take them a plate of cookies and a pitcher of something cold to drink. While the day wasn't overly hot, it was June, and the printing press created a lot of heat.

Elizabeth laid the first letter on her chest. "Talk now or wait until I read the next?"

"Now is fine." Astrid pulled one of the rocking chairs over to face her. "Well?"

"You did mail your letter to the dean, correct?"

"I did. I handed the mail sack to the railroad employee."

"So you think God is answering your prayers for wisdom?"

"Seems that way to me." She thought to tell Elizabeth all that she and Pastor Solberg had discussed but then changed her mind. "Made me feel that He has been listening."

"Good." Elizabeth opened the other letter. "From Red Hawk?" She read swiftly. "Well, I'll be . . ." She couldn't get words out. "Our first distance clinic."

"Oh, I hoped you would see it that way too. But isn't the timing amazing? You know the 'God is never late' comment that Mor and Pastor Solberg say?" Elizabeth nodded. "I guess I better believe it. No doubting. I don't know all the answers yet, but I am grateful."

"Me too. The thought of you clear in Africa always made my stomach tie up in knots." She folded the paper as she talked. "When do you think you'll be leaving?"

"As soon as possible. People are dying, and we might be able to save some of them. Red Hawk is not one to exaggerate. Do you think Mor can help here a little longer?"

"For this, yes. She has been praying for that tribe ever since we first sent the supplies. Let me think on what we have here that could be helpful, along with food, of course. At least we aren't fighting a cold winter on top of it."

"I am going to talk to the quilters tomorrow, and Pastor Solberg will bring it to the congregation on Sunday."

"Have you had the measles?"

"Yes. We all took turns having them in the first or second grade."

"I wish I could go."

"I'm praying you get strong enough to help Mor here if she needs you."

"I will be. Every day is better. After all, I can even dress myself now and walk down the stairs without assistance. If I had to, I could sleep downstairs. I can always give advice from a chair."

"And I won't be gone long enough to cause Chicago any concerns. That contingency thing threw me for a loop for a bit."

"They know the hospital is one of our dreams. We just didn't expect to get to do it so soon. Think when we have interns here what all we will be able to do." Elizabeth rested her head against a cushion. "Lying around has given me plenty of time to think ahead."

"When you weren't sleeping?"

"I haven't been sleeping all the time. Just resting my eyes."

"Right. I'm going to see Mor. Do you want me to spend the night here?"

"No, you go home. Thorliff should be finishing up the paper soon, so he'll be here. Inga and I will read together for a while, and maybe I'll get to know my daughter again. I imagine she has a million questions."

Astrid nodded. "I was going to offer to take her home with me, but this will be better." She stood and took the letters Elizabeth had put back in their proper envelopes.

AFTER ASTRID GOT home, she and her parents talked long into the night about what Hjelmer had said regarding his trip to the reservation with supplies in late winter. He had spent time with the Indian agent and the elders of the tribe. The supplies he brought had been appreciated but were nothing more than a bandage on a festering lesion.

"Right now we can bring medical help that will ease some suffering, but what else can be done? Dr. Red Hawk will be back in September, but the effects of starving will still be there."

"We have to get them planting crops, gardens at least, and raising cattle and horses. That area is okay for crop land, but they have no machinery and no farming knowledge. They were hunters and took what they needed from the land, much like Metiz did. From some things she said, her family was struggling to adapt to our non-traveling way of life." Ingeborg looked up from her knitting. "She taught us so much. I always feel that we need to do more for her people too."

"We will. But Red Hawk's people are the ones we help now."

THE NEXT MORNING Astrid read the letter to the women gathered for the last time in the summer to make quilts. When she finished, she looked to them for answers, only to find several shaking their heads.

"We already cleaned out our closets and household things, including the cellars. How can we find more when our own gardens aren't producing yet and our cellars are low?"

"I can send a crate of chickens," Mrs. Geddick said. "If they keep the hens for the eggs instead of eating them, that can help for a long time."

"Thank you." Astrid looked around the group.

Penny heaved a sigh. "I've had Mr. Sam repairing old gardening tools. I'll send them and a barrel of flour. I have a bag of beans too."

"Anyone have any leftover seed? It's not too late to start a garden."

Several nodded and said they'd bring things to church in the morning.

"Who is going with you?" Mrs. Valders asked. "Mr. Valders cannot take weeks away from work again like he did before. Besides, he wasn't too convinced that the Indian agency would do as they promised. The Indians said that was not unusual, to promise and not deliver. There are some on the reservation who are threatening to run again, so they can hunt like they used to."

Another voice from the back said, "They don't like the white man's ways, so why should the white men, meaning all of us, give them ongoing help?"

"What if it were your son or grandson starving?" Kaaren asked softly.

"I would do anything I had to, to feed my family," one of the newer women said.

"You know, I am thinking something," Mary Martha Solberg said, nodding slowly. "Since the men went last time, I'm sure they were never able to talk with the women. When you go, Astrid, you make sure you talk with the women. I've seen that if you want change, that's usually the best place to start. They were the ones gathering from the land. Maybe they will see the wisdom of planting a garden, raising chickens and pigs, and tending the cattle and the sheep. I read about a tribe down south, the Navajo, that are herders and planters. Their braves don't see that as beneath them."

Astrid nodded. "They are the ones caring for their families. You are right. Mor and I were talking about Metiz last night. If only we had her here to be our go-between."

But the next morning the tone was different after Pastor Solberg read the letter and asked for help.

"We did our share," one of the men said. "If we keep providing, they don't have to work."

"How can they work when they are dying of the measles?" Solberg asked.

"How come the government don't go in and help them? They put them on reservations."

Astrid glanced up to see Joshua nodding. His crossed arms and narrowed eyes didn't look too promising. What did he have against the Indians? Hadn't he said something in one of his letters about the last trip? She tried to remember, but all she could think was that he'd been irate about the support.

Haakan stood up. "I believe God told us to feed the hungry, clothe the naked, and give a cup of water to those in need. We have another chance to do that, and I think we should do the best we can."

"Easy for you," someone grumbled. "You got your dairy herd built back up and both pigs and steers for meat. Some of the rest of us aren't there."

Astrid watched her father nod. "You are right. God has indeed blessed us with much, and we believe we must give back. So we will. I don't think anyone is being coerced here. You give what you feel you can, and if you choose not to, no one is going to hold that against you."

She saw Mr. Jeffers on the far aisle lean forward, as if intent on someone's answer. His hands were clasped almost in prayer.

"I thought Astrid came back here to take care of the surgery while Dr. Bjorklund is recovering."

Pastor Solberg chose to answer that after a glance in Astrid's direction. "You needn't worry. Between Dr. Bjorklund and Mrs. Bjorklund, we will be cared for in case of an emergency."

I'm glad I wasn't here last time, Astrid thought, at the same time making sure her face didn't mirror her thoughts. More grumbles came from the rear of the church. She glanced over to see her mother holding Emmy, her cheek resting on the black hair braided in two braids, like her own daughter's had been. *Maybe we should bring some of the Indian children up here to live with our families and attend school too.* She determined that would be one more thing to look into. Was there a school there? How did Red Hawk get his education?

"If no one else has something to say . . ." Solberg paused and glanced around the room. "Then we will close with the benediction and our final hymn." He closed his eyes and raised his arms like he always did. "The Lord bless thee and keep thee . . ." At the end, Pastor Solberg led the group in singing "Blest be the tie that binds our hearts in Christian love." As the hymn continued, Astrid took a deep breath. She noticed that though he was playing his guitar, Joshua wasn't singing. Right now there seemed to be a lack of that Christian love in some quarters.

"May I walk you home?" Joshua asked after he and the other musicians finished playing.

"I believe so," Astrid answered. *But be prepared for some questions here.* She answered someone else's question and filed out of the church.

"Don't worry," Pastor Solberg said as he shook her hand at the door. "God will bring about healing here too."

"I hope so. I should be ready to leave by Tuesday."

"We may not fill a boxcar this time, but there should be more than a wagonful. Who will be going with you so far?"

"I don't know yet."

"I have had the measles, so I am planning on going. We'll see if we need drovers if it's a wagon. The crate of chickens will take some space."

"Thank you."

He turned to the family behind her, and Astrid walked down the steps.

"Having you home again feels so good," Rebecca said. "I am planning a party for when Grace gets home. A girl party again, even though most of us are married. Guess that makes us girls grown up."

"That will be fun. Give me some time to get back."

"How long do you think you'll be gone?"

"I don't know. Probably no more than two weeks. Depends on if I can help them or not."

"Oh, you'll be helping them. But I have a feeling a certain gentleman here is not happy with your going to the reservation."

"I got that feeling too. I wonder where it comes from."

Joshua, guitar case in hand, stopped beside her. "I'm ready if you are."

"I'll see you later, then." Rebecca turned to go with Gerald, who had Benny on his shoulders.

"You be good, Dr. B." Benny beamed from his high place.

"I have a new name?"

"Yup. Ma says to me, 'Be good,' and I do, so now I say it to you."

"Benny." Rebecca rolled her eyes. "Sorry."

Astrid reached up to shake Benny's hand. "I promise I'll be good."

He stared down at her, eyes and mouth serious for a change. "You always are."

"Thank you, Benny." She patted the stump of one leg. "But I kind of liked My Doc."

"Okay."

"See you later," Gerald said as he took his wife and son toward home.

Astrid looked after them, her smile warming her like the sun. God sure did a good thing when He gave them all Benny.

"Would you rather ride?" Joshua asked.

"No, I need a walk." And a talk. There would be too many people at the house to do much real talking. They started out, moving out of the way of the few remaining buggies. Her mor and far had already left, taking Mr. Jeffers with them. Andrew and Ellie had Thorliff and Inga with them and waved as they passed by.

When the dust settled, the two moved back onto the roadway.

"May I ask you a question?" Joshua asked, breaking the silence. His voice sounded a little strained.

"Of course." She glanced up at him from under the brim of her straw hat. *And then I have questions too.*

"Have you given any thought to our other discussion?"

"You mean about asking Far if you could court me?"

"Yes. You never answered."

"If I remember right, I was rather rudely interrupted."

He nodded. "I wasn't too happy with that."

Astrid felt a chill settle in her heart. "Being a doctor means that kind of thing all the time. I am prepared to go whenever I am needed."

"Yeah, I've noticed." He scuffed at the ground, as if afraid to look at her. Then he sighed and shook his head. "I tried to talk with you again."

"I know, but I was really busy and didn't feel I could leave." She waited for some kind of response, but none came. *Does he not know we were fighting to save Elizabeth and her baby?* "Now I have a question for you." She took a deep breath. Was she ready for his answer? *Remember where your trust lies* whispered into her thoughts.

"Okay."

"What do you have against the Indians?"

"I'd rather not talk about that." He moved a little away from her.

Astrid stopped and looked at him directly. "Why not?"

"It's a long story and not a happy one." He stared down at her. "Just accept that, please."

Astrid narrowed her eyes. More questions bubbled under the surface, but she hesitated. How could he ask to court her and at the same time refuse to share his feelings with her?

Joshua continued, "I don't think you should go to the reservation." They began walking again.

"People are sick and dying there." Her voice came out flat, almost accusing.

Their pace picked up. "Send someone else."

"Who is there to send? My mother? Dr. Bjorklund? Have you noticed any other doctors around here?"

"They have their medicine men. Let them do their job."

"You believe in the power of the medicine men?" Astrid stopped and stared at him.

"Doesn't matter what I think. They have their own beliefs. They don't want us around, and I don't want them either." He glared at her.

"No one asked you to go or take part in any way if you don't want to. I am going, and that is the way it is." She strode ahead of him.

"Tell your mother that I had to leave, will you?"

"No. You tell her yourself. Just because you are angry with me doesn't mean you have to disappoint the ball players." She clamped her fists to her sides to keep from shaking them at him.

He glared at her and, after touching his finger to his hat brim, stalked off in the opposite direction, back toward town.

Astrid stared after him. Well, of all the nerve. She shook her head. He just didn't understand. But the part that saddened her most was he had no intention of trying to. She felt as though spring flowers blossoming inside of her had just blown to dust.

"Where is Mr. Landsverk?" Ingeborg asked when her daughter came through the door. "Oh-oh. You don't look too happy."

"That man can be downright insufferable." She hung her hat on one of the pegs rather than taking it upstairs to her room. "Give me something to do that I can beat on."

"Mash the potatoes."

Astrid was silent as the families discussed what they could send to the reservation. When her father said he was going along, she hugged him. "Thank you. Pastor Solberg said he could too."

The discussion took over the dinner hour but came to a halt when the men and boys headed to the baseball diamond out behind the barn. Yelling for her favorite team did Astrid some good, but when someone asked her where Joshua was, she just shook her head. She saw Mr. Jeffers laughing with Samuel on Thorliff's team. He spotted her and waved, then sprinted over.

"Thank you for your invitation to the family dinner. And I wish I could offer my services to join you, Dr. Bjorklund, on the journey to the reservation. It is a noble errand of mercy."

Astrid nodded. "Thank you." Inside, she could only think what a difference she was seeing between two men in the last two hours.

MONDAY EVENING THEY began loading the car the railroad had pulled off onto the siding for them. Both Samuel and Johnny were going along to herd the donated cattle, while the three young pigs would ride in the same wagon as the crate of chickens. They would have two days of travel after they left the railroad.

When the train left on Tuesday morning, Joshua had still not come to apologize. *Better to know this now than to have agreed to his courting plan,* she told herself. Somehow the facts didn't offer much comfort. What could be so important or such a secret that he couldn't tell her?

Pastor Solberg prayed for their journey and then they said good-bye to those gathered and slammed the door. As the train whistled, Astrid heaved a sigh. She was leaving Blessing again, but this time she knew where she was going and why. Off to her own personal Africa? One dream beginning while the door closed on another. Peace about one and disappointment with the other. *Lord, it looks like Joshua Landsverk is not the man you have planned for me. It seemed so, but I guess this is another one of those cases where I trust you. I do trust you, but . . .* She took a deep breath and sighed. *This hurts. I even wondered if I was falling in love with him. But I guess not. I know, you have a plan for me, a plan for good and not for evil. A plan that is the best for me.* She sniffed and dabbed at her nose with her handkerchief.

At least South Dakota wasn't as far away as Africa, not a distance too far at all. Closer to home even than Chicago. A bubble of excitement bounced in her belly. She glanced over at the men and boys, laughing at something someone had said. Not so long ago they had wondered if Far would recover from his stroke, and now he was on this train heading south. He looked up and smiled at her. God did provide, in ways that no one could plan. Astrid smiled back. She was ready to trust the adventure because she knew her heavenly Father was indeed in charge—and to be trusted.